LIFE #6

LIFE #6

A NOVEL

DIANA WAGMAN

PUBLISHING

BROOKLYN, NEW YORK

Printed in the United States of America
10 9 8 7 6 5 4 3 2 1

Ig Publishing
392 Clinton Avenue
Brooklyn, NY 11238
www.igpub.com

Library of Congress Cataloging-in-Publication Data

Wagman, Diana.
  Life # 6 : a novel / by Diana Wagman.
      pages ; cm
   ISBN 978-1-63246-005-9 (hardcover : alk. paper) -- ISBN
978-1-63246-003-5 (pbk. : alk. paper)
   I. Title. II. Title: Life number 6.
   PS3573.A359L54 2015
   813'.54--dc23

                                        2015006237

For Benjamin and Thea

No longer exalting in the swimming seas
will I toss up my neck, rising from the depths,
nor will I blow around the fine prow of a ship
leaping and enjoying the figurehead.
But the sea's blue wetness threw me up on
dry land
and I lie on this narrow strip of beach.

-- Anyte, 300 BC

It is never quiet on a boat. Riding in a car can be silent as you travel down the highway with the windows up and the night sky outside. Huddled inside a small tent in a spring snowstorm, the snowflakes make no noise as they fall on the blue nylon. Even on a foldout couch in an apartment in New York City the world can be hushed, everything outside so unimportant it seems mute. But boats are never quiet because they are never still. They rock and jiggle and complain. The wood creaks, the lines vibrate and hum, the water licks and laps and swallows. Even at night the small flags, the sails and bits of canvas, fwap and snap. It is incessant, a constant sloshing and sighing of desire, "I want to go. Let me go."

I sat on a bench in front of my favorite statue of Venus. Her marble skin, her empty gaze comforted me. The news from my doctor had been bad. Dr. Carolyn had left a message on my cell phone, which wasn't very professional, but then she'd been my ob/gyn a long time. I had cancer. Cancer. Just the word is ugly, two hard syllables, the hissing "c" in the middle. I was glad I worked as an educator at the Getty Villa. Glad I could turn to ancient, immutable beauty. This statue, the Mazarin Venus, Roman, circa A.D. 100, had not changed for two thousand years. Her pupil-less eyes were in eternal serene contemplation. She was beyond life or death; cancer didn't matter to her. The hands that formed her, the very world she was created into, all gone. Now she stood among humans with cell phones taking digital photos, protected by a laser beam alarm. She didn't weep or protest. She wasn't smiling. She didn't care.

The lights clicked on automatically and I looked out through the door of the gallery. The sky had turned the gray of smudged charcoal, and darker clouds were rolling in. Rain was coming, always a surprise in southern California. Beyond the sycamore trees I could see a black line of ocean. The sea always there—covering most of the planet. I turned my back to it. I'd been in LA for twenty-four years and all that time I pretended it was a desert community. I ignored the beach, the docks, the watery life. Even the occasional rain seemed an affront.

It was October 27, 2009. Almost exactly thirty years since I went to sea in a brand new 52-foot sailboat, sailed into a storm, and should have died. Five of us, the owner and his hired crew, left Newport, Rhode Island on that cloudy November morning bound for Bermuda. The storm became a hurricane and many things went wrong. In the years since, I can say I have capsized, floundered, and run aground, but those are only metaphors for the darker periods in my life. I have never been on another boat.

Why did I go? What possessed me—for I was possessed. I don't know how to swim. I am afraid of water. I have a recurring nightmare about the deep end of a swimming pool. Why did I go? It was a boy, of course. A wild, Greek, ringlet-haired boy named Luc Kazaros. Oh, I was young and crazy mad in love. In an old photo, I am looking up at him and my face is like a slice of just baked bread, soft and white and open. If he was beside me, I had to touch him. I tried to match his breath, inhale and exhale with him, so we would share the very same air. We met in a college modern dance class. I was a freshman dance major. I came in and Luc, a senior and a star in the department, turned around and our eyes met and I was hooked, line and sinker. I was caught and never wanted to be free. I was so young. My own son has never been that young.

I dropped out of school to go with Luc to New York City so we could become famous dancers. When we signed up as crew on that sailboat we were between gigs—non-existent gigs—out of work and money, sleeping on his sister Lola's foldout couch. In a month I would quit dancing and be terribly lost in a different kind of sea, but I didn't know it at the time. In less than a month, he would be a junkie, but we didn't know that either. I had told a friend Luc was "It." Every cliché: he was the love of my life, my knight in shining armor, the man I had been waiting for. For all of my nineteen years, I had been waiting for an olive-skinned party boy with an arabesque higher than mine.

Why did I get on that boat? Why did I, non-swimmer, faint-hearted, so deeply planted in the earth, decide to go with him across the ocean? I had already followed him to New York. I would have followed him anywhere.

We set sail on November 5, 1979 when I was nineteen-years-old and on that boat I killed a man. Back on shore, I left another one to die. Telling this tale is the only cure for history.

1.

Fiona woke up early on the sailboat that last day in port. Luc was already awake. He smoked a cigarette and scratched his arm. The scratching had become a habit.

"Listen," he said. "Io. Listen."

She rolled toward him. Io was his nickname for her, the two middle syllables of her name. Io was a nymph who Zeus seduced and Hera, his wife, jealously turned into a cow. Fiona liked the name, loved that it was Greek, didn't mind the cow business, especially since Io didn't stay a cow, but eventually regained human form and gave birth to Hercules. Luc had given her the name and told her she had a Greek soul, even though she was ash blond, blue-eyed and alabaster-skinned, Anglo-Saxon through and through.

He was looking for a way to open the sealed and bolted porthole. "Listen," he said. "What the hell are we doing?"

Her stomach clenched. "I thought this was what you wanted." This trip had been his idea. She sat up and faced him. "Remember? Three hundred bucks and our plane tickets back to New York?"

They'd met Nathan, the owner of the boat, at their catering job. He was a party guest and Luc had struck up a conversation. Nathan said he needed crew—better than waitering, isn't it?—and Luc immediately said yes. To Fiona sailing sounded terrifying, but okay, okay, if Luc was going, she was too. An adventure. She suppressed the little voice in her head that asked if she was out of her mind. Going across the Atlantic Ocean with a bunch of strangers? She and Luc needed the money. Dance classes were expensive and she was desperate to rent their own apartment and stop sleeping on his sister's couch. And—even though she had told Luc she didn't mind about him and she really, truly didn't—Billy sashayed into her thoughts. Billy, the beautiful gay dancer, and everything he brought with him. She needed to get Luc away. Away.

He scratched his upper arm, scratched and scratched. He sighed and his handsome, classic face sagged. The corners of his full lips drooped, his eyelids grew heavy as if they could no longer support his thick eyelashes. This had been happening lately, a sudden gloom like a shroud would fall over him. His hand with the cigarette trembled. She tried to hold his other hand, but he lifted it out of reach, went back to scratching.

"Io," he said. "Listen. Listen. Listen. Would you still love me if I only had one leg?"

She almost let out a laugh, but caught it before it escaped her lips. Luc, who was never afraid, looked frightened of what she might say. Would she still love him? Ridiculous.

Before she could answer of course, of course, he continued. "What if I couldn't dance anymore because my leg was missing?"

She tried to make him smile. "You'd be an incredible one-legged dancer. Amazing. People would come from all over the world to see you."

"No, no. What if I cut it off—"

"You cut it off?"

"If a piano fell through the ceiling right now and amputated my leg, would you still love me?"

He didn't want her to make a joke, so she couldn't say it would have to be a grand piano, or ask him to sing her a few bars, or offer a peg leg so he could be her pirate king. He looked at her with such agony it made her chest hurt. She wanted to scratch this Luc away, dig down to the old, joyful him, the one who would never ask such a thing.

"I will always love you," she said. "If a piano cuts off your leg and your teeth fall out and you go completely bald, I will still love you. I will. Always."

Fiona repeated the conversation in her mind. Again and again as she walked around town that last day, doing the grocery shopping, buying supplies, outfitting the boat, she thought about what he had said, what she had replied. She had assured him she would love him forever. And he had looked so disappointed at her answer.

She shivered and wished—for the millionth time—she had her winter coat. She and Luc had come to Newport from New York packed for Bermuda, not a New England November. Nathan had said he'd supply foul weather gear if necessary. She'd expected the boat to be heated like an apartment, but the single, small electric heater in the main cabin didn't do much. She couldn't wait for the sultry island air, the clatter of palm fronds, lying on deck under a warm sky. Paradise.

She trudged back to the boat laden down with bags and packages. They banged against her legs, the corded shopping bag handles digging into her cold hands. She wished she had her gloves. It was her job to outfit the kitchen—galley—with everything they needed besides the two pots and frying pan already on board. Nathan said to skip the plastic crap at the boat outfitters and buy the best. He told her which pretty little store to go to and gave her a list of items and a credit card. She had never seen one before. A rectangle of plastic that could buy anything.

She worried over every item. Were these the right wine glasses? The very best china soap dish? She'd grown up without money, much less proper glassware. That's why she didn't know how to swim; lessons had been too expensive for Mom as she drifted from man to man, but Fiona hadn't been able to say that to Lola. We're going to sea! Luc had announced that night after they met Nathan. She had nodded and grinned and kept it to herself that she'd never been on a boat, didn't know how to swim, that water anyplace but a bathtub terrified her. She knew Lola would frown, could hear her disappointed sigh as if the girl her brother loved had let him down—again. Fiona had never been to New York, ridden in a taxi cab, eaten feta cheese or black olives or a gyro until Luc. She had never heard Greek until he and his sister spoke it to each other.

"You couldn't pick a Greek girl?" Lola had poked her brother, then turned and hugged Fiona. "I'm joking, joking. My girlfriend's not Greek either."

Fiona would learn to speak Greek. She would. Luc was a book to be read, a skill to be perfected, an entire country to be explored. He was all she had ever wanted to know or learn or see. And so in the fancy store, with Nathan's plastic money, she shopped for what Luc would like, what she imagined Lola would choose. She did her best and, as her last and favorite thing, bought a ceramic fruit bowl painted with mermaids to sit on the galley counter.

The saleswoman asked if any of it was a gift.

"No," Fiona said. "For our boat."

"But it's all so fragile."

"It's a really beautiful boat." She imagined the sail across the sea like a ride in a large new car along a flat highway. It was the Cadillac of sailboats—the shock absorbers would be fantastic.

"Ask your Captain," the woman was saying. "I'll take them back anytime. If they're still wrapped."

"It's okay." Fiona was getting annoyed. "We're leaving. To-morrow."

"In November?" The woman frowned.

"Newport to Bermuda is a popular route." Nathan had told them so, but everywhere she went people were surprised they were going.

"In the summer. People sail in the summer."

"I never get cold." Fiona had lied, picked up her multiple bags and walked out of the store with her nose in the air.

A man walked past bundled in hat, gloves, a scarf, and an inviting long wool coat. She sighed, then pushed her wishes away. She had nothing to wish for. Luc was waiting at the boat. They were sailing tomorrow. Tonight Nathan was buying everyone pizza. He was nice and smart, a neurosurgeon who had once operated on the brain of the prince of Yemen, and he said he liked the scrambled eggs she'd cooked that morning. The hired captain, Joren, was from Holland. He had an accent and red hair and a bushy red beard and he was handsome despite the scars covering the right side of his face and the two missing fingers on his right hand. "Don't worry," he had said when they met. "Not a sailing accident." His Dutch accent made the words thick and liquid as if they bubbled from his mouth. "Motorcycle. Boats are much safer." He had taken her hand and squeezed it with his three remaining digits. She never would have met anybody like Nathan or Joren without Luc. Luc had warned her that the Rhode Island pizza would be terrible, but she didn't care. She was just grateful she didn't have to cook—that was her job, the hired cook, but her repertoire was limited and she didn't want to use it up on the first day.

Back in New York, the night they met Nathan, Luc had bought her pizza for dinner. Less than a week ago, it felt like ages. It had been cold then too—she remembered wrapping her arms across her chest, pulling her sweater closed as Luc danced ahead of her up Seventh Avenue. He pirouetted and leapt. He had come to pick her up from her temp job, sweaty and stinky from dance class.

When he walked into the office, Stan, her boss, looked up with a grimace. "I knew you were here from the smell."

Luc ran over and lifted an arm, pressing his armpit close to Stan's face. "The smell of a superstar!" He crowed as Stan pushed him away. "Watch, Io. Watch this." He did a fast combination on the narrow strip of floor between the two rows of desks, ending dramatically on one knee in front of Stan. Her co-workers applauded.

"Get out of here," Stan had said with a smile. "Take her with you."

On the street, Luc sang to her. "Oh Fi-o-na, You make me moan-a. With your long blond hair-a, you're mighty fair-a. The way you dance-a, makes me cream in my pants-a." He would not quit dancing. Commuters grinned at him. The guy at the newsstand clapped his hands. Luc was Gene Kelly singing in the wind. She laughed out loud as he ran back to her and lifted her in his arms. He kept singing in his deep, tuneless voice. "Oh Fi-o-na. You make me moan-a. Long blond hair-a, mighty fair-a." He spun her and when he put her down she was dizzy, out of breath.

"I'm so hungry, I could eat... I could eat... this." He ran to a lamppost and pretended to gnaw on it. "I could eat this."

He leapt on top of a mailbox and chewed and chomped. "This too." He jumped up to gobble a street sign, then turned to her. "You!" He nuzzled his warm face into her cold neck and licked and nibbled.

"Class was good, huh?"

"Oh, my Io Io Io. It was amazing. The way I flew across the floor. I think I levitated. Janet said I was magical." He spun away from her. "Pizza! I'll pay for it."

He had a small monthly check from his parents to support his dancing. She had to work. They kept their finances separate, Luc wanted no fussy attachments and she agreed. They were walking past his favorite pizza place, a hole in the wall with three stools at a counter. Fattening, but it sounded great. She tried to stretch and do her sit-ups at night after work, but it was hard sleeping on the couch at Lola's. The apartment was only one room and an alcove. Lola's girlfriend, Stephanie, was usually there.

"Hey, it's Fred Astaire." The pizza guy greeted them. "And Ginger Rogers."

Luc did a couple of quick steps and a spin. "Two of your biggest, best slices," he said. "And a little one for her." He hugged her. "My little ginger snap."

Fiona took the slice and sighed. She had large blue eyes, lovely collarbones, and waist-length white blond hair, but she was not very tall and not the typical, lithe dancer. Bottom heavy. She could feel her thighs and ass spreading already, after just four days of entering invoice numbers into ledgers. "You're killing me," she said to Luc.

"Death by pizza."

"I'll die happy."

The pizza was delicious. The grease dripped down her wrist and she caught it with her tongue just before it stained her sleeve. She vowed to herself that this one slice was absolutely the only thing she was eating that night. She listened to Luc chatter with the pizza man. All the while his feet tapped and moved, he twisted on the stool. She looked at her graceful, beautiful boyfriend, his eyes bright, his wet tongue continually licking his lips. Was he high? He wasn't eating; the pizza slices went untouched on his paper plate. His long fingers fiddled with the shaker of cheese, his napkin, the cuffs of his shirt.

"What did you do before class?" she asked.

"Hung out with Billy."

Then he was definitely high—but not that lazy, loose Luc he became when he did smack. This was an up. Cocaine, she figured, or some kind of amphetamine. He would crash later and she would have to tiptoe around him, ignoring his crabby comments.

"I introduced him to Alison," Luc said. "He really liked her."

"I bet."

Fiona put her slice down. She wasn't hungry anymore. Billy was in love with Luc. Luc hated labels of any kind, but Billy called himself as queer as a three-dollar bill. He joked that Luc was too—he just hadn't met the right guy. And Billy was hot in a Ziggy Stardust meets punk rocker kind of way, eye make-up and sparkles on his freckled skin, too skinny, a wispy and feminine dancer's body more comfortable out of clothes than in. And Alison. She wasn't a dancer, thank God for that. A few years older, tall and thin with great clothes, Alison knew everything, had lived in the city all her life, and adored Luc. Really adored him. Fiona didn't like the way she watched him as he spun around her apartment, or bent over a line, or rubbed a finger over his gums. She didn't like the way

Luc appreciated Alison and her steady and ever ready supply of coke, pot, and hallucinogens. Alison. Billy. Luc's personal groupies.

"Shit!" he said. "What time is it?"

She glanced at the clock. "5:35."

"We gotta go." He threw some money on the counter.

"Too much." The pizza guy began to make change.

"Keep it," Luc said. "Best pizza of my life."

He had taken one bite. The guy put the slices in a box and handed it to Fiona. He looked sorry for her. She smiled and shrugged as if nothing was amiss.

Luc was hopping up and down outside. "C'mon, c'mon, c'mon."

"What?"

"The catering company called. We're on tonight." They both worked when called as waiters for a high end catering company. The money was good, the hours long.

"I'm tired."

"Just think," he said, "our own apartment." He put his arm around her, slid it down to her ass and squeezed. "Our own bed."

She leaned into him, turned her face up for a kiss.

With his lips against hers he said, "Io, I love you. You know that, don't you? I love you you you!"

It hurt how much she loved him back. "Okay," she said. "Okay."

He pulled her down the street toward Lola's.

"Alison leave you anything for me?" She wasn't a big fan, but a line would help her get through the evening.

"Sorry. I couldn't resist."

So instead she would drink coffee, probably snag a couple desserts for the sugar buzz. She felt worse about her sugar addiction than she did about Luc's growing craving for drugs. At least his infatuation kept him thin. He was even more dramatic with his sunken brown eyes and prominent cheekbones. New York was making her fat. She had struggled with her weight all her life, but now it was as if her legs were thickening like tree roots, reaching down, searching desperately for the earth beneath the concrete. She felt more and more grounded as he took flight.

As they headed uptown they saw cops everywhere and traffic was even more crazy than usual. "What's happening?" Luc grumbled.

"It's the Shah," she said. "They were talking about it at work. The ex-Shah of Iran is here. For an operation or something."

"They have to close Broadway for him?"

"It's his ten wives and their camels."

"Very funny." He grabbed her hand and made her hurry.

She tripped over a filthy man sleeping across the sidewalk. "Sorry!" she said to him. She wanted to love New York the way Luc did. But it was so dirty. So full of humans walking, rushing, sloughing off their skin, coughing and expectorating, or lying discarded on the sidewalk with the trash. Luc had assured her New York City was the only place for a dancer to be. Dance capitol of the world, he said. He dove right in. The constant current of people and traffic and sights and sounds and hopes and needs were everything he had ever wanted. Fiona clung to the side. The chaos that nourished him overwhelmed her. Too many people. Each one with a story. Who was that man with no shoes? What was wrong with that old woman's face? Where was that child going alone? Luc was the Silver Surfer slicing through the torrent and she was an old sponge and couldn't absorb it all.

But that was the night they met Nathan and Luc got fired for fraternizing with the guests and she quit in solidarity and Nathan hired them as crew. And here she was. Newport was so pretty. The shops around the wharf were closed for the winter, but she could tell they were upscale places. The sun was shining and a cold breeze blew in from the sea with a fishy tang. Gulls squawked and swooped in the sky, like wishes soaring upward. Just one, she thought, just one wish. She closed her eyes.

"Please, I wish, I wish no one—especially Luc—ever knows how terrified I am."

She would act brave. She would become brave. She'd read an article in a women's magazine about the Secret Door to Success, taken the quiz, and learned that acting flows into being. She could act as if she loved it and she would be a sailor. She would. The smell of diesel, the cramped foam bed, the constant motion and her queasy stomach—it would all be wonderful. It was wonderful. And forever she would have this experience. Forever. That was something, wasn't it?

I wish. She opened her eyes. I wish it were all over.

The wind whipped through her light jacket—the only one she'd brought. It was blue suede, a hand-me-down from a roommate, and she loved it, but it was too small to button over her striped sweater. Her eyes watered. Her nose was running and she knew it was red. She bent her head to the wind and continued toward the boat—home.

At the top of the dock leading down into the marina, there was a metal security gate tied open with a frayed blue and white rope. Blue and white were so ubiquitous they had to be the official nautical colors, like the white gulls against the blue sky, the blue sea and the white froth of the waves. Too bad the sky was gray and the water in this marina was a dark, army green topped with shiny oil slicks and a plastic bread wrapper.

Three men—none of them Luc—stood on the boat's deck. Where was he? She hoisted her packages, put her shoulders back but gasped as she almost lost her balance on the swaying dock. It was like trying to walk on the back of a sea serpent. She hated it—she was cold and her hands hurt and Luc wasn't waiting for her and, truth be told, she hated the boat's unrelenting rocking too. And the smell, saltwater mixed with diesel fuel and bird shit, and how fragile the boat seemed, temporary, as if a year from now it would be gone, just bits of boards and plastic cushions floating out to sea. Nathan said it was brand new, built by the very best Taiwanese boat builder with the finest teak and materials money could buy. But the linoleum was already peeling off the galley's little strip of floor and only one burner on the two-burner stove worked and she knew something was wrong with the engine because Nathan and Joren kept arguing about it.

She tottered down the dock, legs wide. The men watched, Joren with his bright hair and Nathan in his dirty sweater. The third man had to be Doug, the new crewmember. She was surprised when he stepped off the boat and came up to help her.

"Are you Doug? Thanks." He took most of the bags. "I'm Fiona."

His face was as round as a full moon, with broad cheeks, small brown eyes, and a five o'clock shadow although it was still morning. He had to be at least thirty. He wore a navy blue stocking cap pulled down over his ears and all his clothes looked too large for him: a giant green wool coat circling his body, enormous black gloves, flapping khaki pants that were both too wide and too short. Even his bright white sneakers flopped against the boards as he walked.

"Careful. Everything's breakable."

He nodded. She was glad to see he was also unsteady and slow—like her—as they walked down the dock to the boat. It was the newest and nicest boat in the harbor with a bright white hull and a turquoise stripe. She told herself again and again it was the very nicest boat.

Joren gave a little wave and went down into the hold. Nathan waited for them on deck smoking a cigarette. His smoke blew sideways with the wind. Clouds were moving in, turning the sky to dark wool. The temperature had dropped. Rain, Fiona thought, maybe even snow, was coming.

Nathan held up his hand. "Wait. You can't get on. Remember? You have to ask permission to come aboard. Like that: 'Permission to come aboard?' I mean it."

Fiona rolled her eyes. Nathan and his ridiculous protocols.

Obediently, Doug asked. "Pe…pe….pe…permission to c…come aboard?" His eyes slid to her and away. His cheeks went red, more from embarrassment she realized, than the cold. She'd never met a stutterer before. Why had Nathan asked him to say it?

Nathan grinned at Doug and then raised his eyebrows at Fiona. "Permission granted. To both of you." He held out his hands for the bags and Fiona noticed his long and dirty fingernails. Not like a doctor's hands at all. Where was Luc?

She and Doug handed the bags over. Doug gestured for Fiona to hop into the boat first. She hesitated. The distance between moving dock and moving boat was wide. She could see herself falling in between, ending up wet, freezing, most likely crushed against the splintery wood pylons. She had struggled yesterday and today Luc wasn't here to help. She grimaced and leapt. Too far—she banged her knee against the wheel. It hurt enough for tears.

"Want me to look at it?" Nathan's face was all concern.

"It's okay." She rubbed her knee and forced a smile. She turned to Doug and saw him standing on the dock making the same calculations she had. She held out her hand to him and was surprised he took it—the second time he had surprised her.

"Thanks," he said.

She smiled. "Too cold this morning for a swim."

Nathan put his hand on Doug's shoulder. "Doug was my patient," he said.

"Ca...cancer."

"Quite a large tumor. It damaged his left inferior and middle frontal gyrus, plus the head of the candate nucleus. That's why he stutters. Won't last. Probably. Not sure. It'll be interesting to see."

Fiona watched Nathan's hand on Doug's shoulder, the way his fingers prodded and squeezed. There was something in his eyes too when he looked at Doug, like he was looking at a specimen. Nathan yanked off Doug's cap.

"Hey," Doug complained.

A red mountainous scar ran up and over Doug's shaved head from ear to ear, like the strap on a pair of headphones.

"It's quite remarkable, isn't it?" Nathan's eyes shone. "A truly extraordinary job. One for the journals." He clapped an arm around Doug's back. "And here he is, crewing on a sailboat."

Doug grimaced, tried to grin, his moon face even wider, rounder. "Fu...fu...funny thing is, I never st...st...stutter with my Latin." He nodded toward a flock of seagulls in the sky. "Family *Laridae*, sub-order *Lari*." He pointed to a smaller gull with black tipped wings on a dock post. "*Rissa tridactyla*."

"Sounds like a dinosaur," Fiona said.

"Doug's an ornithologist," Nathan said. "Bird expert. Came along to see some special duck that breeds in Bermuda."

Doug nodded. "In the mangroves. The West Indian Wh... Wh...Whistling Duck. I can't believe it. D...d...ducks are my specialty, and it's the la...la...last one on my Life List." He stood taller and looked at Fiona as he almost shouted, "*Dendrocygna aborea.*"

She wanted to clap for him. "Cool," she said. "A Life List."

Doug stepped closer to her. He reached a gloved hand for her hair, then stopped before touching her. "Your hair is b...b...beautiful. Ducks don't come that color."

Nathan looked from Doug to Fiona. "He's from Arizona. Completely landlocked."

"I...did C...Cornell for grad school." Doug looked out toward the horizon. "New York for my surgery. Bu...but I've never seen the s...s...ocean before."

Fiona smiled. She had a comrade, someone else new to boats and ocean life. "Can you swim?" she asked.

"Before the op...operation, like a fish."

"I'm sure he still can," Nathan said. "His brain stem was not involved."

Doug stretched his arms out wide, his hands in the huge knit gloves. The empty fingertips fluttered in the breeze. "It's so v...vast."

"Oh God, thy sea is so great and my boat so small." Nathan threw his cigarette into the water. "Breton Fisherman's Prayer. My wife is from Brittany."

Fiona didn't know where that was, or if it was slang for Great Britain. She would ask Luc about it. Where was he?

"The na...name of the boat," Doug said. "Is that Breton t...t...also?"

"Yes, it's her name for me." Nathan thumped his chest

proudly. "*Bleiz A Mor*, Sea Wolf. Isn't that perfect? I am the Sea Wolf."

He looked more bear-like to Fiona, round and lumbering. She was glad Doug had asked about the boat's name. She had seen it in fancy script across the back—stern—but not wanted to ask in case everybody else knew what it meant.

"*Dendrocygna arborea*," Doug said again. "I'm going t… to write about them…for Au…Audubon." He took off one glove and ran his finger back and forth across his awful scar. Back and forth. Back and forth. Then he saw her watching and put his hand in his pocket. "Sorry," he said. "It's a… ha… habit."

"I get it. I used to wiggle a loose tooth incessantly. Drove my mom crazy. You can't help it."

He smiled at her then and leaned gently toward her. She saw something in that smile and that lean. But he hadn't met Luc yet.

The seagulls squawked. "So you're a bird expert, right?" she asked him. "Why are seagulls so noisy?"

"D…d…demanding. Always hungry. I've seen them… pluck a chicken bone right out of a… man's hand."

"Isn't that cannibalism?"

Nathan piped up. "They're disgusting. Scavengers. Eat anything."

"Let's try it," Fiona said to Doug. "Think they'd take a pretzel out of your hand?" She reached into one of the grocery sacks for a bag of pretzel rods. She ripped it open, handed Doug one, and watched as he broke it into pieces.

"First, let them…kno…know there's food."

His stutter was kind of endearing. It proved how badly he had suffered. He threw a piece of pretzel out toward the birds. It fell into the water and one flew down and scooped it up. Instantly, the entire flock was clustering and cawing over-head. He threw another piece up and two gulls vied for it, one of them snatching it out of the beak of the other.

"It's like telepathy," she said. "One eats, and they all know there's food."

"Bird communication is actually quite complex." Doug paused before each word. "It seems like… telepathy, but birds communicate on a… high level…not always visible to us." The more he spoke, the less he stuttered. "Tiny movements of feathers and wings. They can even transmit and receive information simultaneously."

"Like when you're talking to one person, but actually listening to another conversation?"

He nodded. "Better th…than we can."

"I'll never call anyone a bird brain again—unless he's a genius." Fiona broke up another pretzel and threw the pieces into the air. A breeze blew the pieces back toward her and she squealed and ducked as the gulls came at her. Laughing, she turned to Doug and he put his bare hand on her shoulder.

"Where is… your boyfriend?"

She didn't want to say she didn't know. She stepped out from under his hand, shrugged, leaned over the railing to look at the rainbow stain of oil floating on the water.

Nathan threw his cigarette into the water. "I sent him on an errand. A long time ago."

"Where? To do what?" she asked. "Did he take the car?"

Doug took a pretzel rod from the bag. He held it in the air. "Shhhh," he said to both of them. "Watch." He waved the pretzel a little. A gull investigated and hovered, checking him out, turning its head this way and that. He whispered, "It will be a sign. If it takes the pretzel out of my hand, then we will have a wonderful trip."

"Scientists don't look for signs," Nathan said.

The bird swooped down, plucked the pretzel from between Doug's fingers, and careened away.

"Oh!" Fiona said. "Wow."

"Yes." Doug appeared to swell, his face grew even broader, and at the same time he exhaled and relaxed. His eyes were shining and she couldn't help but smile back at his smile. "Yes," he said again. "This is going to be a very good voyage."

The gull soared, the pretzel in its beak longer than its body. Fiona cheered.

Nathan looked at her. "Put all this stuff away." He gestured to the bags and boxes. "Stop feeding the rats. Then we'll go find your boyfriend."

2.

Approximately two thousand five hundred years ago, Hippocrates wrote that an excess of black bile in the body was what caused cancer. He called it *karkinos*, the Greek word for crab, because the tumors—when they eventually erupted through the skin oozing black fluid—appeared to have many claws. His recommendation was to leave a tumor alone; in his time, surgery killed more than it saved. Cut it out, he said, and it would just reappear somewhere else. He wrote almost nothing about cancer of the breast. His only mention of it is a woman in the town of Abdera having a bloody discharge from one nipple. Did they not have as much breast cancer in ancient Greece? Is it a modern illness brought on by environment, toxics, a stressful lifestyle? As a child, I rode my bicycle behind the DDT trucks that drove through my neighborhood spraying for mosquitoes. I called it flying in the clouds. Now the same company that manufactured that DDT makes the drugs used in chemotherapy. I couldn't help wondering why me, but was there a why? Why me? Why not. I had already lived longer than many people. My child was well on his way to being an adult. My husband and I loved each other and had settled into a comfortable companionship and okay, maybe now it was rocky, the waters turbulent, but if I died tomorrow he would remember mostly good.

I could have sat in front of Venus forever. I didn't want to move, go home, think about what I would do next. I would have happily become a statue: the Los Angeles Fiona, American, circa A.D. 2009, a decent example of post-modern middle-aged life, the spread in the hips and thighs, the rounded perimenopausal belly, unfortunately one breast destroyed, but arms, legs, nose intact. My skin was white enough to be marble, if not as smooth anymore, my pale blonde hair pulled back in a sculpted, sleek bun. If I could just stay on this bench forever. But I would be fifty soon. Too late for anyone to put me on a pedestal.

My high school tour group came noisily into the gallery and I stood up and smiled at them. Twenty or so tenth graders, mostly Latino, looking both bored and happy to be out of the classroom. Their teacher stood in the back, white, rumpled, tired, his brown necktie askew over his beige short-sleeved shirt.

"Hi," I said. "I'm Fiona. Welcome to the Getty Villa." Greek, Etruscan, and Roman art had been my concentration as an art history major in college. This was the perfect job for me, spending three days a week talking about something I loved. And I liked the kids, younger than my son, from public schools all over the city, most of whom had never seen a real marble statue before. I could share the myths, the stories these artworks told, explain how they were the movies and Nintendo of their time.

Two boys in the back whispered to each other in Spanish. They snickered about naked Venus behind me. A girl beside them in tight jeans and a tighter purple top looked over and pretended to be annoyed, but I saw the start of a smile on her glazed lips, the twinkle in her thickly made-up eye. She shushed the boys and then giggled. Would she have cancer one day? Would those fresh fifteen-year-old breasts in her pink push-up bra betray her? I looked at Venus and again envied being made of stone.

The teacher cleared his throat.

"Right," I said, coming back to the waiting group. "Okay. Let's begin. Who is depicted in this statue behind me? Why does she have a dolphin beside her? Why is she naked? Can anybody tell me?"

I walked backwards, I said the words, I even got a few laughs from those who were paying attention, but for the entire tour, my hand kept straying to my left breast or my hair, wondering if I would lose one or the other or both. I'd had a biopsy and the tiny suture stung when I touched it. Which I couldn't stop doing. It was not my best tour. At the end, the students sat down to fill out a questionnaire and I apologized to their teacher.

"What?" His eyes were as empty as a statue's. "They're a pain in my ass." He thought I was talking about their behavior, not mine.

"They were pretty good. That boy in the front is smart."

"One out of seventy-five ain't bad."

I tried to chuckle sympathetically.

I had two more tours and did my best to push my diagnosis out of my mind and concentrate on the art. It wasn't easy. The rain refused to begin and the clouds were pregnant and overdue. I felt the earth's expectancy, the ponderous hesitation before the water broke. I was antsy and so were the students. We all kept looking up to the sky, our limbs trembling like the skinny branches on the olive trees, anticipating the deluge.

On my way to the staff parking lot, I stopped to look at the Lansdowne Herakles, Roman, circa A.D. 125, more than six feet tall, with a lion skin in one hand and his club over his shoulder, the marble so sumptuously carved it looked alive. He was a perfect six-packed specimen I'd seen a thousand times, but in the unusual gloom he was different. The shadows made his head seem to turn more sharply toward me. His curls glittered as if moving in the waning light. His Cupid's bow lips looked on the verge of speaking. The curve of his bicep, the strength of his thigh. I held my breath. He was Luc in marble. Of course he had always been there. I knew in every statue, in every relief and fresco, I could see my lost Greek boy, my vanished Luc—if I allowed it, which I didn't. That day I was caught by surprise, by the impending rain, the gray light, my terrifying diagnosis. I would never see Luc again. I was forty-nine, married, with a son in college, and I had cancer. There was nothing on my horizon but a solitary voyage through ever darkening waters. I leaned my head against the cool wall and closed my eyes. Someone tapped on my shoulder and I jumped. It was another educator, a friend, Eileen.

"You okay?"

"Just tired."

"No kidding," she said. "It's the weather. See you Friday."

"Yup. Thanks. Bye."

In my car, I took out my cell phone and listened again to the message from my doctor, the woman who had delivered my son twenty years earlier. "Hi. It's Carolyn. I'm so sorry. The biopsy came back positive I'm afraid."

She was sorry? She was afraid? What did she know about fear or sorrow? Her husband was also a doctor. Their two girls attended the city's most expensive private school. They lived out here in Malibu, close to this incredible museum. Oh yes, she said when I told her I gave tours, I can see the Getty from my deck. I'm afraid. I'm sorry. Well, me too. I hadn't called

Harry, my husband. I knew he was home in his usual spot on the couch in front of CNN. Two years earlier he'd lost his job after seventeen years as a reporter for the LA Times. He was angry and agitated. He'd taken it very, very personally despite his hundred or more colleagues who had been fired with him. All over the country older, respected, highly paid journalists were out of work. Harry had almost given up looking for a new job. There wasn't much out there and his frustration made him a difficult candidate in an interview. We were broke. My three days a week didn't make a dent in the monthly bills, our refinanced mortgage, our son's college tuition. I felt sick when I thought of how much cancer might cost. Blue Cross could, might, probably would find some reason to cancel our already exorbitantly expensive insurance. Harry would say it didn't matter, I knew he would be willing to sell the house, the cars, whatever it took. But then where would we be? If I died—if I died after all the treatment anyway—there was no point to leaving my family destitute.

I blinked. I'd driven down the Getty's driveway and turned left onto the Pacific Coast Highway on automatic pilot. At this rate, a car accident would kill me before cancer. I still had my cell phone in one hand. I dropped it into my bag. Harry certainly didn't need to hear the bad news over the phone. I would tell him, but at home, when I could look in his gray eyes. I'm sorry, I would say, it's cancer I'm afraid.

The heavens opened—my mother's phrase—and it poured. I crept along, traffic bumper-to-bumper. There was plenty of time to look out at the ocean beside me. The water was choppy, the color of an old file cabinet except for the fleshy froth. Even through my closed windows I could smell the fish and brine. Why anyone found the beach appealing was a mystery to me. A couple jogged along the sand in the rain. Idiots. Harry's favorite word. I smiled. Fucking idiots, his favorite two-word phrase. As crazy as he was these days, he could still make me smile.

In sickness and in health. For richer and poorer. It's too much to ask. Our wedding invitation is framed and hanging in the hallway by the laundry room. It reads, "Join us as we exchange our vows." Perhaps that's all Harry and I should have offered each other: to exchange our vows, our promises, our obligations however small. You do mine and I will do yours. Before the dearly beloved gathered together we should have sworn, "I will write all your thank you notes. I will have dinner with your boring cousin. I will sit through that monotonous meeting at work. Whatever awful thing you have sworn to do will now be my task." Forget rich, poor, healthy, sick, honoring, cherishing and 'til death do us part. Promise something reasonable.

I turned inland and onto the eastbound freeway, relieved to leave the sea.

3.

Fiona climbed up the ladder to the deck before the sun cleared the horizon. Her eyelids were heavy and her face swollen from crying and not sleeping. Overnight she had become Neanderthal.

She and Nathan had spent the night before searching all over Newport for Luc. He had gone on an errand for Nathan—to buy a spool shackle, whatever that was—early in the morning and not come back. She and Nathan had driven the streets of Newport, back and forth, up and down. Nathan had been exhausting, parental, asking about Luc and his habit, how long, how she could stand it. She had answered as ambiguously as possible—he didn't understand, couldn't understand Luc's life—until finally, finally she saw him through the window of an all-night donut shop. He was nodding off in the back booth, a cup of untouched coffee in front of him. He looked up when she said his name and took her hands. He was wobbly, unmoored, his muscles oddly disconnected from his skin, but he was glad to see her. That was all that mattered.

Nathan was upset and Fiona kept urging him to be gentle as they helped Luc to the car. Nathan asked him questions, but Luc had no answers. "A guy." "The park." "No, no, no."

Back at the boat, she put him to bed, smelled that metallic

tang on his skin she recognized from New York. She told him it was fine, it was all right, she was glad he'd had fun. She lied and lied.

"Don't be mad," he whispered. "I can't wait for you to try it. It's wonderful, transcendent, ambrosia, the stuff of legends."

His words slipped and slurred together. She bit her lip but the tears came anyway. In the dark, Luc could not see—as high as he was, he would never notice. He scratched and scratched. She took his hand, put her leg over one of his. She would be his anchor.

"You're the only woman for me." He struggled to sit up. "Io, you know what I realized?" His whispers grew louder. "I saw it, like a sign in the sky. I saw it. I love you. I love you so much. You're not like anyone else. You're the only one I'd ever ask to go across the ocean with me. The only one. Only you can sail my seven seas, be my pirate queen, my mermaid, the maiden of my maiden voyage."

Doug, in the bunk across the cabin, stirred.

"Hush. Go to sleep," she hissed.

"I can't."

"Try."

"Sing to me."

"Everybody's sleeping. That's Doug—the new crew-member—right there."

"Please?"

She breathed a little tune he liked, a lullaby about the things she would give him. A mocking bird. A looking glass. A diamond ring. When she got to the billy goat, she stopped and punched him in the arm. "Billy. This is his fault." It was beautiful Billy who had introduced Luc to heroin, skinny Billy who strangely was strong enough to take it or leave it, dancer Billy who now—in his dreamy, giggly way—told Luc to slow down. "Fucking Billy." She never swore.

"But you love me."

"I—" She didn't want to be conventional. He hated conventional.

"And I love you, Io, Io, Io." He rolled over on his side away from her. He scratched his arm, his thigh, scratching and scratching until he fell asleep.

She stayed awake beside him most of the night. At one point she turned to wipe her tears and saw Doug's eyes open, watching her. She shook her head. Go to sleep, go to sleep. She had turned her back to him.

A bleached winter sun was creeping over the horizon. It was colder than the day before. Fiona wrapped her arms across her chest as she stepped up the final rung onto the deck. The boat rocked and she fell against the open hatch, banging her hip hard. She gritted her teeth so she wouldn't cry, again. Why couldn't this boat stay still? She wanted coffee, but couldn't make it without waking Luc and Doug. She didn't want to be back in Lola's apartment, but she wanted to be somewhere— somewhere else. She felt depression rising with the sun, a dark red feeling in her head and a knot between her eyes, scratching in her chest as if she had swallowed the dish scrubber. She zipped up her new sweatshirt over her ever-present striped sweater. The sweatshirt was a gift from Doug. After dinner, before she and Nathan had left the boat to find Luc, Doug had given her the dark blue sweatshirt. It was a nice thick one that zipped up the front and had a sailboat on the back.

"You're c…c…cold all the t…time," he had said. "That jacket isn't w…warm enough."

"Wow. Thank you. Thank you so much."

"And… I hate your sweater." He grinned as he said it.

"Really? Luc's sister gave it to me. It cost a lot." Lola was the most beautiful and best-dressed woman she had ever met. Lola had chosen this sweater. The horizontal blue and white stripes were nautical, she had said, like cruise wear—whatever that was—and it had something called a boat neck that had made them laugh.

"I r...r...really hate it."

Honestly, she never would have chosen the stripes for herself. She really did like the sweatshirt a lot more, but she didn't like the way Doug looked at her, his open mouthed desire. She had Luc, only Luc. Besides, Doug was too old for her. He said he'd be twenty-nine on his next birthday. He loved birds and he lived in Arizona. Still, he was right about the sweater. The wool was itchy and the stripes made her look fat. The cuffs were already dirty. She felt like Nathan in that stained fisherman's sweater he always wore, but it was the warmest thing she had. She wished again she'd brought her winter coat. She wished she could go home, not Lola's apartment, but a home she could imagine, somewhere with heat and a tree outside the window and a nice rug on the floor. She could pack different clothes, start this whole trip over again.

She heard a breathy whistling and Nathan came up through the hatch already smoking a cigarette. His hair hung in oily strings. He wore the same whale covered pants and filthy sweater he had on the day before and the day they arrived and even the night at that party where they'd met him in New York. Fiona could smell his dirty hair and body odor. As a dancer she was used to bodies smelling, but they hadn't even left yet. How ripe would he be in four days? She sighed. She did not want to talk to him or have to field any more of his questions.

She followed his gaze. A heavy curtain of darker clouds was closing to the northeast. The wind swirled and whipped under her collar, a dry icicle down her back. Her eyes watered. She felt a pressure on her shoulders and the back of her neck, the threat of something needing to explode.

"What's happening?" she asked.

"One hour until departure."

"The weather."

"We'll sail right out of it."

"Everyone is still asleep."

"Not for long."

She nodded. The sooner they left, the sooner Luc would have nowhere else to go. She didn't even care about getting to Bermuda anymore, she just wanted to sail away. Anywhere that was away.

She looked again to the clouds and the ominous sky and thought about the woman in the shop. "In November?" And the Harbormaster's secretary when she'd stopped in for the weather report. "Send in your captain." And the old guy at the grocery store. "You're crazy to go now." Their words rattled in her head.

"Joren should go talk to the Harbormaster. The secretary said it was important."

Nathan gave a humpf. "Too late for that."

"Oh!" She suddenly remembered. "We have to go to the Coast Guard station for the three-day forecast. The Harbormaster didn't have it. I'm so sorry I forgot yesterday. I'll take the car and go right now."

"Doesn't matter." Nathan shrugged. "Que sera sera," he sang. "Whatever will be, will be."

She reached into her back pocket. "I did get this." She handed him a Xeroxed list:

Items Necessary for an Ocean Voyage

1. Fresh water

2. Non-perishable food

3. First-aid kit

4. Flares

5. Life raft—inflated and secured on deck

6. Life jackets—one per person

7. Two-way radio

8. Charts

9. Navigational systems

10. Training in sailing

11. Physical fitness

12. Mental preparedness

Nathan looked the list over. "Thank you," he said. "Thank you very much. This is very important. And I am going to put this somewhere special."

She was pleased until she saw him crumple the paper in his hand and chuck it into the water. Of course he knew all this stuff. She had probably insulted him.

"'My soul is full of longing/ For the secret of the sea/ And the heart of the great ocean/ Sends a thrilling pulse through me.'" He lit a fresh cigarette and exhaled in her direction. "Know any Longfellow?"

"Hiawatha, right? Paul Revere's Ride?"

"Bleh. The Top Forty of poetry."

"That's what they teach us."

"School." He said it with disgust. "I was too smart. Bullied. Teased. Always ate lunch alone. Boo hoo. Boo hoo. But I showed them, didn't I? It feels so good to be a genius." Nathan looked at her sideways and recited another fragment. " 'With the old kindness, the old distinguished grace/ She lies, her lovely piteous head amid dull red hair.' Lovely piteous head."

"Who's that?"

"Yeats. William Butler Yeats. I think he wrote it about you. You are so kind. And graceful. And you have a lovely piteous head, if white instead of red hair." He squinted at her. "Your skin is so pale, almost transparent. I can watch your blood moving in your veins—there in your temples. You're practically an albino."

"No, I'm not. I have normal pigment, blue eyes. I just haven't slept."

"Your hair really is an unusual color. Absolutely your best feature."

She couldn't say thank you, it was more dissection than compliment.

"You could still skip this," he said.

"Skip what?"

"Take the bus back to New York. You're terrified. I can see it. Ha. I can smell it." He picked his nose and flicked something into the sea. "Your boyfriend, Luc. Aren't you worried about what he's been doing? He could go to Bermuda with me, get clean, and fly back to you a new man."

"We've talked about it," she said. "We each do what we want."

"So why don't you do what you want and go home?"

"But Luc is going."

"Don't you have a mind of your own?" He grunted. "If you don't use that lovely piteous brain of yours it will atrophy.

Think for yourself."

"I have to go on this trip." She tried to put conviction in her voice. "I want to."

He gave a toot-toot trying to mimic some kind of boat whistle. "I thought you'd say that. Yes. All right. Go kiss Mother Earth goodbye. Bye-bye. Bye-bye." He handed her a ten-dollar bill. "Get a dozen donuts for all of us. They smelled so good last night when we found your drugged boyfriend, didn't they?"

She almost fell jumping from the boat to the dock, teetering on the wooden boards. She was glad she wouldn't have to do that again until the water was warm. She clumped up to the sidewalk, stamped her feet to get her land legs. They were sailing. She took a deep breath. They were sailing today. Nathan was crazy to think she would miss it. Of course she was nervous—not terrified—anybody would be. She was sick to her stomach, but she was sure that would stop once they were underway. She felt claustrophobic on the boat, but soon she would have the whole ocean to look at.

Donuts and coffee. She didn't want to go back to last night's donut shop. There had to be someplace closer, different. Sure enough, Bob's Donuts, just off the main street. It was bright and crowded and warm inside. The two waitresses were in shirtsleeves. Fiona sat down at the counter, shed her jacket and the sweatshirt and her shoulders relaxed, her palms opened.

The TV was going with the sound loud. Every customer was watching intently. It took her a minute to figure out what she was seeing on the screen. A crowd of dark haired young men holding signs, shaking fists, burning an American flag.

"What happened?"

"Hostages," a fisherman answered. "Yesterday they took American hostages."

"Who did?"

"Iran. A bunch of Islam militants, fundamentalists, goddamn hoodlums broke into the embassy and took over. Americans are prisoners to these nut jobs!"

Iran was far away. She couldn't even imagine what it looked like. Were there cities? Cars? She pictured a flat expanse of sand, a camel, and a man in a white billowy robe. Like Lawrence of Arabia.

"Damn rag heads."

No one on the TV was wearing a turban. The hostage-takers were in khaki pants and short-sleeved button down shirts. They had dark hair and prominent noses and looked Italian or Greek. They could be Luc's cousins.

The fishermen were drinking coffee and eating glazed crullers and they were furious.

"We got to go in there and get our guys," one of them said.

"Carter should just drop the bomb," another said. "Blow 'em all to kingdom come."

"Here, here." The others agreed.

Fiona asked for hot chocolate and an old-fashioned do-nut. She deserved a final treat. They were sailing today. Out-side a tree spread its bare black branches like a witch's fingers reaching for the overcast sky. A piece of newspaper skittered down the street and the color had drained out of everything, the whole world a fuzzy gray. When the counter girl brought her donut and cocoa, Fiona ordered a dozen assorted to go.

"Big group at home?" The girl was just being polite.

"We're sailing."

"When?"

"This morning. We're sailing to Bermuda."

Everyone stopped and looked at her. Fiona would always remember the moment like a scene from a movie. The counter girl froze with the coffee pot in one hand. The fishermen turned around in their booth. The TV blared, unwatched.

"The weather isn't good," one of the fishermen said.

"Should have left yesterday," another one said. "You'd have missed this."

"Missed what?"

"She's going to blow."

It sounded like a joke, a phrase borrowed from Popeye. But the fishermen weren't smiling.

"I guess our captain knows what he's doing." Fiona nodded at the girl loading the box of donuts, trying to hurry her along.

One of the fishermen called out, "Who's in charge?"

"Joren—something." She didn't know his last name. "He's Dutch."

"What kind of boat?" Another asked.

"A sailboat."

"What kind?"

"I don't know. It's called the *Bleiz A Mor*." She tried to smile. "It means Sea Wolf."

"It means See You Later." The fishermen laughed. One of them caught her eye and shook his head as if saying, don't go. He had graying blond hair and watery blue eyes. He could have been her father, except her father was not a sailor and her father never told her what to do. She hadn't grown up with him in the house, hadn't even seen him in almost two years. When she spoke to him last she said she was living in New York, going to be a dancer, and had dropped out of school. He told her great, have fun.

She took the box of donuts and left her hot cocoa and half-eaten donut behind. She didn't even use the bathroom. The last real bathroom she would see for days and days.

Back at the boat, she felt better. She remembered to ask permission to come aboard and Nathan was pleased with her donut choices. Everyone was up and busy—even Luc. He was working down in the hold, stowing the gallon jugs of scotch, gin, and vodka behind the lattice work doors of the cupboards under Doug's bunk.

"We're leaving," she said to him. "We're really doing it."

He said nothing. His face was closed up tight.

"Luc. Luc," she whispered. "Everyone says we shouldn't go. The fishermen, the saleswoman, the secretary in the Harbormaster's office."

"We're going to have a wonderful time," he said. His voice was flat. Automatic. "We'll swim and lie in the sun." Finally he gave her a sideways smile. "Maybe we'll never come back."

Her worry lifted. Her heart grew, pushed at the wall of her chest, reached toward him. She put her arms around him. Never come back. Never.

"I'm working here," he said, but then he turned and hugged her. His hair was damp. He had showered in the boat's tiny bathroom—head—the shower the size of her high school locker, and he smelled almost like himself again, the awful chemical scent had faded. Her head fit just like always in the hollow of his shoulder. She lifted her face and he kissed her. A real kiss. His hands tried to find her body under all the layers.

"Bermuda. Bermuda. Bermuda," he breathed. "It's about fucking time."

She opened her eyes and saw Doug staring down at them through the hatch. He blushed and turned away as Joren pushed past him down the ladder and into the cabin.

"Break it over you two. We have much work."

"What can I do?" Fiona asked.

"A real breakfast. Donuts are not enough."

"Fried egg and bacon sandwiches." She knew they were Luc's favorite and she knew how to cook them. "Easy."

"Yes. Easy as the cake. Right?"

Luc caught her eye and they laughed.

"We leave at nine!" Nathan bellowed from above.

"Aye, aye, Captain." Luc called back. "Oh wait." He turned to Joren. "You're the captain. Our Flying Dutchman."

"No, no. You know this story?" Joren shook his head. "Not so good."

Fiona nodded. "Doomed to sail the seas for eternity."

"I get off in Bermuda." Joren found the box of stuff he was looking for and headed back up. "Come, Luc. We can use you."

Luc followed and Fiona turned to the little stove. Her little stove. She was in charge. This galley was hers. They were going. She was sailing. She got out the eggs and bacon from the tiny fridge under the counter. This is my ship, she thought, I live here now. She spread her legs to absorb the sway. Her stomach was not great, but she was sure it would get better, she would get used to it—the roll, heave, pitch—all those other sailor words. She caught the new potholder on fire, but put it out before anyone saw. She burned her thumb, but not badly. Cooking on the little stove would get easier. She could do it. Grilled cheese sandwiches, cans of soup, maybe even hamburgers. She cracked the eggs into the bacon grease and put slices of bread on the blue and white china plates she had bought.

Doug came down. He tried not to look at her, but she saw his eyes sliding in her direction. "N...nothing like...b... bacon." He sighed.

"Almost done," she said. "Are you excited?"

"Y…y… yes." He turned to her and tried to smile, but his cheeks wouldn't move. His muddy brown eyes were frightened and his hands were shaking.

"We'll be fine." It felt good to be the brave one. "After what you've been through, this is nothing."

"635 miles." He didn't stutter. "With unpredictable weather. A week or more."

"A week?" She shook her head. She didn't think they had enough food for a whole week. "Nathan said three or four days."

"Have you read *Moby Dick*?" To keep from stuttering, he spoke so slowly it made her a little crazy. "I've been… thinking of Captain Ahab."

"Will we see whales?"

"No… not that." He rubbed his fingers over his scar, back and forth, back and forth.

"I haven't read much. Not the important things. But I want to. I do. I will read it."

He stopped rubbing his scar. With his other hand he pushed a strand of hair off her face. "You're so young," he said.

"Hey. I've been taking care of myself for a long time."

"I know, I know. That's… not wh…wh…what I meant. Lots of t…time to read."

He lowered his voice. "I saw Na…Na…Nathan throw something overboard. Black p…p…plastic."

His eyes were so small, his forehead so wrinkled. She patted his arm. "He throws everything overboard. It's gross."

"It's just, that that p…p…. N…never mind." He got his stocking cap from his bag.

"Are you cold?"

"Wind irritates my scar." He shrugged. "So d…does the hat."

"Think how good the sun will feel in Bermuda."

"Fiona," he said. "You don't have to go."

Why was everyone saying that?

The boat lurched and Doug fell against the counter. She put out a hand to catch him and awkwardly grabbed his neck. His skin was rough, sandpaper under her fingertips, grown up and foreign.

She said, "Maybe you're the one who should stay home."

"Eggs."

She turned just in time to pull the pan off the burner. "Thank you," she said. "Thank you."

4.

All five of us were on deck when we motored out of the harbor. It was after eleven but the two-hour delay had given the clouds a chance to lift. The November sun was shining the best it could. Nathan sang and Luc joined in, "Sailing, sailing, over the bounding main!" I waved goodbye to the wharf. Ours was the only sailboat going out. The others were tied up at the docks, their sails rolled and stored, their cushions taken home, everything battened down and tightened up for winter. I waved to the Harbormaster who had come out on the widow's walk to watch us go. He didn't wave back. Everyone in town thought we were crazy for going, but I looked at Joren calmly rolling a cigarette as he sat behind the helm and Luc talking happily with Nathan and I thought, this is it—my adventurous life is beginning. Luc and I would stay with the boat in Bermuda, be island sailors and live in our bathing suits. My thighs would not embarrass me, my too white skin would turn brown. Did you hear about Fiona? I could hear my high school friends ask each other. We thought she was a loser, but she lives on a sailboat in the South Seas. I wasn't sure Bermuda was in the South Seas, but it sounded good.

I felt a drop of rain. Then another. And another. Dark clouds rolled across the sky. Joren turned the engine off. The mainsail flapped and shook as he steered us directly into the wind.

"This is no-go," Nathan said. "Come on, Captain."

Joren looked confused.

"We'll end up in irons!" Someplace Nathan obviously didn't want to be. He pushed Joren out of the way and turned the wheel right—starboard. The boat creaked as it slowly made the turn, but then the wind caught the sail and suddenly we were going.

"This is it!" Nathan hollered. "Reaching. Yes!" He turned to Joren. "Even an imbecile can sail a boat with wind like this."

We hurtled through the water. The rain came down. The boat leaned away from the wind. I grabbed the cockpit railing. The speed was okay, the leaning was not. Doug's teeth were clamped together. The knuckles of Joren's remaining fingers were white around a metal cleat. Only Luc, and Nathan—of course—were having fun.

I wanted to say wait. Slow down. I managed, "Why are we leaning?"

Nathan yelled over his shoulder. "Heeling. The wind. This is how we move."

"Why don't we fall over?" This could not go on for the whole trip. My strong thighs were already tired and my feet hurt from my toes gripping inside my sneakers.

Nathan just shook his head. Too much to explain.

I closed my eyes and sent two wishes aloft: one, to be brave and two, to get there quickly. I opened my eyes and saw that Joren's eyes were closed. His lips moved and it worried me that he was also wishing, maybe even praying. But Nathan was calm and Luc was smiling and it was raining but not hard and the open ocean stretched out in front of us in grays and frothy creamy lace and I could see how sailors thought it beautiful.

The wind and rain in my face were cold. I turned back to look at Newport. And I gasped. Newport was gone. The shore had disappeared. There was nothing but water in every direction. No land, no other boats. No place to get off. The sea was not beautiful, only endless, eternal, and alien. I gulped, sucked at the air. I could not breathe. I opened my mouth wide, pushed against my chest with both hands. I was drowning in the open air. The boat was very small and very full. There was nowhere I could go, no place to be alone, no room to walk without stepping on someone. I wanted off, right away. I turned to Luc, but he was talking to Nathan. I looked at Doug, but his face was tucked into his enormous coat. Stop, I wanted to say. Turn around and take me back. Nathan was doing something with a rope. He pulled the sail tighter. The boat heeled more sharply. I crouched in the cockpit, holding on with both hands. Luc hollered in joy. Then, over the sound of the waves and wind, I heard a crash. Thirty minutes into our voyage and the fruit bowl with the mermaids—my favorite purchase—was the first thing to break.

From: Fionartlvr@hotmail.com
To: Luckyman@kazaroswellness.org
Sent: October 27, 2009

Dear Luc:

Well. It's raining here—very unusual for southern California. The only rain boots I own are hand me downs from my twenty-year-old son. Yes, I have an almost grown up son. He is older than I was when we went to sea on the *Bleiz A Mor*.

Thirty years since we were in Newport. I wonder what it's like now. I wish I could stand on that dock and look out at the Atlantic Ocean.

Do you remember the boat? The trip? Nathan Carmichael? Do you ever think about it?

10

I had driven home in the rain, and sat in my driveway watching the rivulets and puddles forming in my front yard. Eventually I got out of the car. Looking up at the spitting sky, my wet face reminded me of being on that boat. Of sitting next to Luc on deck as we went out to sea, his arm around me, huddled into his chest, trying to be brave and happy before everything went so horribly wrong. Twenty-six years had passed since I had seen Luc or even heard about him. Last time, half a lifetime ago, he was strung out, an incoherent junkie. Right after that, Lola told me never to call or contact either of them again. I wasn't helping and he was on his own path, she said. I could see only one direction that path was going, only one place it would end. That's why I had never looked him up before. Twenty-six years and the Internet, I could have done a search for him on my phone for chrissakes, and I never did. The last time I saw him he was fading away, more ephemeral and more beautiful and more fucked up than ever before. Maybe I thought by not knowing I could keep him alive.

On the front porch, watching the rain drip from the eaves, I took out my phone and listened again to the message from Dr. Carolyn. It hadn't changed. I went inside the house where I'd lived for more than fifteen years. It didn't look the same. I didn't recognize the furnishings. Was that chair always so green? When did I buy a throw pillow with a bird on it. A bird? Really? And everything was so dirty. The gray drizzly light through the dining room window revealed dust bunnies in the corners, dog hair on the rug, crumbs on the table, and a layer of grime over everything. I sat down on the couch and Lulu, our old black and white mutt, trotted over to me. She was antsy, anxious to go out, but I held her sides and buried my face in her ruff. She wagged her tail and whined, confused by me and the unfamiliar weather.

I wanted a puppy. Harry would get a job soon, Jack was across town at school, and a little cuddly pup would be just what the doctor ordered. I went to the door and picked up my car keys. I thought I'd go to the pound that minute. I couldn't wait another second. I opened the front door and then I put my keys down. I was going to die. Who would take care of a puppy?

I went to the kitchen. Harry had left a dirty mug on the counter, dregs of milky tea in the bottom. A banana peel splayed next to it—empty, abandoned. I turned away and opened my computer. I intended to look up cancer information. I found myself thinking of Luc instead. My fingers trembled as I typed "Luc Kazaros" into Google. I tried to push away the memories of his hands on my body and his tongue on my skin, his grin, his quick steps and light touch, the boy he had been and the girl I was.

"Dance with me," he said the day we met. He grabbed me around the waist before I could answer and pulled me into a polka. "C'mon, c'mon, c'mon." I didn't know then it would become his constant refrain with me.

A long list came up, filling my computer screen. I held

my breath, preparing for an obituary or a news article ending with him going to jail. But he'd gone to graduate school. He was a psychologist with his own Kazaros Wellness Clinic in Orlando, Florida. Body therapy. Dream work. Reiki. Same old non-traditional guy, but with a PhD after his name. Hard to believe he wasn't choreographing or at least teaching dance. And Orlando was where his parents lived. He had loved New York. All those years ago when I left the city and wanted him to come with me, he was adamant he would never live anywhere else.

I wrote my email to him—upbeat, noncommittal—and hit "send" before I lost my nerve.

The dog ran to the front door. Harry was coming up the walk. I put the computer to sleep. I didn't know where Harry had been. He was dressed up in khaki pants and a button down. The pants were a little tight after all his time on the couch. His strong, stocky body had always pleased me, made me feel lighter and more graceful. In our early days he often picked me up and carried me. His face was kind and intelligent. He was such a nice guy, a good guy, a sweetheart. It didn't seem fair to tell him I had just emailed my old boyfriend. Or to tell him I had cancer.

"Where've you been?" I said.

"I had an interview." He smiled a little. He was standing straighter, his chest forward, chin up.

"Where?"

"A trade journal. The Hemp Growers Association."

"Seriously? You never even got high."

His smile disappeared. His eyes went small. "Aren't you happy for me?"

I felt like a jerk. "Sorry. I know hemp isn't just pot. It's fantastic. Really."

He gave a small, tired sigh. So many interviews, so many rejections. Harry had a graduate degree in International Studies from Yale. He'd written stories on the President, members of Congress, the environmental impact of plastics in Mumbai. He had spent three months embedded with the Marines in Iraq. Boys, he said, no older than our son, Jack. There'd been some awful fight, an explosion, and most of the boys had died. Harry had pulled two of them from the burning Humvee. President Bush sent him a letter of commendation, but he threw it away. And here he was, excited about hemp.

"You know," he was saying, "these smaller, targeted journals are really the way of the future. Pretty soon no one will read a general newspaper, only articles—online probably—about their specific interests."

"Is it full time?"

"You're not even listening to me."

"I am. I am."

"All you care about is the money. Isn't that what you were going to ask me next? How much does it pay?" He shook his head. "Jesus. I haven't even got the job yet."

"I didn't ask."

"Money, money, money. That's all it is with you." His face was red. His belly jiggled as he shouted at me. "Fucking money isn't everything."

I fled to the bedroom. He wasn't making any sense. I didn't care about money. Not like he did. I'd grown up with my mother counting pennies to make the rent. We had spent more than one night in the dark because there was no money for the electric bill, eating pancakes for dinner made with one egg instead of two. Then some new man would come along and we'd be fine. We were always fine. Harry and I would be fine too. We were educated people. We had gone to college and done everything right. Of course we'd be okay. Yes, next month we would have to cash out our 401k, but I was looking for full time work and had asked my boss at the Getty for more days. I pushed the thought of cancer away. Plenty of people with cancer worked full time.

The telephone rang and Harry answered it. Through the bedroom door, I could hear his voice, but not what he was saying. I crossed my fingers, hoping it was the hemp journal offering him the job. I turned on the TV to my favorite, The Weather Channel.

A stalled front over the Midwest set the stage for severe thunderstorm complexes from Nebraska to the Ohio Valley.

Shots of Iowans scurrying along the Des Moines streets under their umbrellas, frowning up at the sky as if it had betrayed them. I pulled a pillow into my lap, ran my fingernails along the seams, back and forth, back and forth.

Some of these storms were significant with damaging wind gusts the main threat. Heavy rainfall is also an ongoing concern. Downpours of one to three inches or more in a very short time caused dangerous flash flooding. Two people were found dead in a ravine where they were apparently fishing, while Marilyn Hobart was trapped on top of her car for almost five hours.

I watched the footage of Marilyn Hobart being lifted to safety by helicopter. Harry opened the bedroom door. I could see on his face he was sorry. I was too.

"Look at this," I said. "Flash flood. This woman was stuck on top of her car for five hours."

"Jack's coming over."

"That's a nice surprise."

Harry sat down beside me on the bed. I leaned against my husband of twenty-two years and put my hand on his back. It had been more than a year since we had made love.

At first, I admit I didn't miss it. But eventually I began to crave his touch, his full weight on me. I would snuggle against him in bed and he would turn over and tell me to go to sleep. Once he yelled at me to leave him alone, stop pawing at him. Since Jack had gone back to school, Harry had been sleeping in his room.

I opened my mouth to tell Harry my bad news. He stood up. "Harry." I reached for him. He stepped away from me and opened the closet door to change out of his interview clothes.

"I'll make dinner." I slipped past him to the kitchen.

I made fresh pesto, Jack's favorite. Harry opened a bottle of wine and clinked my glass in a toast to hemp. The rain was coming down even harder, and I was relieved when I heard Jack pull up.

I went out on the front porch to greet him. He jogged up the driveway carrying a bag of laundry over his head. Inside, he gave his one-sided grin, dropped his bag and hugged me. I could smell the rain on him and his boy scent of French fries and minty deodorant. It was impossible to tell him I had cancer. I didn't want him to be one of those brave kids with a sick parent and a haunted look, coping and grown up before his time. He pushed his dark blond hair off his smooth forehead. Handsome as the day is long. Another of my mother's phrases. And this day had been long and I was so glad to see him I almost cried.

He wiped his wet hands on his jeans. "Has it ever rained this much before?"

"Global climate change," Harry said from the couch. "People need to take it seriously."

I nodded. "After dinner we're building an ark."

Jack followed me into the kitchen and I poured him a

glass of wine. He was such a good kid, so much better than his mother. By the time I was his age I had snorted plenty of coke, dropped many tabs of acid, spent whole days stoned. Wake and bake had been my high school motto. Jack grimaced after his first sip, so I poured the rest of his glass into mine. I made a salad and we talked about school and his music.

"It is really a big storm," he said. For a moment he looked six-years-old, frightened by the wind and rumbling thunder.

"Maybe you should spend the night."

"Yeah right, Mom."

The chimes on the front porch clanged. I smelled the rain, felt the tremble of our old house, and remembered the screech of the fiberglass boat straining in the storm. Once again I was at sea.

Harry started shouting from the living room. He was obsessed with the Najibullah Zazi arrest. The press said Zazi was another Islamic terrorist who wanted to blow up America. Harry didn't believe it. He thought the government was framing him, making Zazi a scapegoat so Homeland Security would look good. Harry thought our country had gone to hell.

"Listen to this!" he yelled to me, to us. "They're calling him the Beauty Parlor Bomber. Catchy, don't you think?"

Jack went in to watch with him.

I drank the rest of my wine. I put the big pasta pot in the sink and turned on the faucet. The water came out, clear and clean and exquisite, as if I'd never seen water before. The pot filled and I watched the water run over the sides, fascinated by the waterfalls and eddies in the sink. I plunged my hands in and shivered from the cold.

What was I doing? I emptied the pot and dried my

hands. Filled the pot again, put it on the stove and turned on the flame. Concentrate, I told myself. Stay with the program.

My computer dinged from the corner where I'd stuck it. I opened it and everything—water, pasta, cancer, even Jack— fell away:

Io (you still use that name?) Io, Io—

Jesus, I've missed you. I can't help it, but your name falls from my lips at all hours. At work, at home, with my kids. I married Beth. Remember her? She helped me when I needed it. I have three kids: two girls, Lily, from my first marriage, and Sophie, and a boy, Jack. He is spoiled rotten by his sister, just like me. Are you really thinking about Newport? Can you meet me there? When, when, when? Tell me you can go to Newport on Thursday, November 5th and go back Sunday. Tell me you can do that. Can you? Please. Can I see you?

I wrote back immediately, before I could think:

My son's name is also Jack. Okay. Thursday to Sunday. I'll be there.

Jack shouted from the other room, "You have no idea what I'm doing!" Harry yelled back. They were fighting. Again. I had left them alone too long. Since Harry had lost his job he was angry with Jack all the time. Jack wasn't working hard enough. Music was a ludicrous major. He needed to think about his future.

"That's the way things are done!" Harry roared.

"Not for me!" Jack banged the coffee table in frustration. I came into the living room. "Dinner's ready."

"Fiona, please."

"I'm not hungry," Jack said. "I have to go."

"I saw on TV," I began, "about a flash flood. A woman who needed to be rescued from the roof of her car."

"Mom."

Harry rolled his eyes. "We're talking about something else."

"You're shouting."

"I AM NOT!"

Jack gave some excuse and escaped. I ran after him through the drizzle to his car with a Tupperware container of pasta and pesto.

"Sorry, Mom."

"Your dad just needs a job." I leaned in his open window to give him a kiss. I kept my hand on the door. I didn't want him to go. I didn't want to go back inside. Take me, I almost whispered. "Drive carefully," I said. "Are your tires okay? Do your wipers work?"

"Bye, Mom. Tell Dad I love him."

"Even if he is an asshole."

He laughed and drove away and before he was out of sight I missed him. I missed the smaller him, the lap-sitter snuggly boy he had been. I missed the ten-year-old; I missed the pimply pre-teen; the new driver; the high school senior. I missed them all. They were gone. And this Jack, this young man, was going, going.

We experience so many deaths in our lifetime. Not just the actual demise of people or animals. Not just the end of a job or relationship or the departure of our children into their own lives. We suffer personal deaths, little bits of ourselves that pass away. Our hair and our memory. Our quick step. Our joints betray us. Our eyes give out. Our libido fades. But humans, we mourn, but we don't stop. We get facelifts and take exercise classes and eat kale and buy all kinds of products to keep us going, even if we're not exactly whole anymore. *Brewer's Dictionary of Phrase and Fable* says a cat has nine lives because a cat is "more tenacious of life than any other animal." Really? I think humans win. Humans hang on. Humans take the pills, do the tests, have the twelve-hour surgery, and finally demand to subsist for years attached to tubes and machines, unable to walk or wave or even swallow. Talk about tenacity.

On the boat, Doug told me he knew people who should have died and didn't. He used himself as an example and said he believed each of us is given many lives to live. How many? I asked him. His wool hat glittered with raindrops every time the strobe light flashed. The sea moved up and down behind him, up and down. If cats have nine lives, I asked him, how many do I have? How many have I used up?

LIFE # 1

When I was five-years-old, I sailed through the windshield of my father's car. Not his fault; we were hit from behind. I wasn't wearing a seatbelt, but I don't think there was one to wear. I launched from the red vinyl seat of his classic white Camaro and my pig-tailed head hit the glass and shattered it. I ended up sprawled half in, half out, my chest and stomach on the hood of the car, my legs and feet in pink socks dangling over the dashboard. My patent leather Mary Janes had flown off my feet into the back seat. I lay perfectly still watching the broken glass sparkle in the streetlight. My father's nose was bleeding as he crawled over the hood to my upper half.

"Are you all right? Oh no. Oh no."

"What happened to your nose?" I asked. To this day I remember flying and crashing and landing on the warm metal. My head hurt and the streetlight was too bright in my eyes, but I said, "I'm fine, Daddy."

My father smiled and I was glad I'd made him happy. When the sirens and emergency vehicles arrived, he was energetic and trembling, joking with the cops and the guy in the other car. He was giddy until he had to call his ex-wife, my mother, and tell her he had almost killed me. His voice got low and scratchy the way it did whenever he had to talk to her. When he brought me home, she said he could never see me again, and that's when I cried. His upper lip was swollen and bloody from hitting the steering wheel. No airbags in those days. No seatbelt laws. He walked back down the steps to his car with no windshield. There was a rip in the shoulder of his jacket, the white lining flapping farewell.

"Daddy!" I screamed.

He raised a hand. "Call you tomorrow, Button."

Later, as my mother undressed me for my bath, she found splinters of glass in my thick hair and ground into the shoulder of my yellow sweater. It hurt too much to brush my hair so I went to bed without and in the morning my pillow had scratched my cheek from all the glass. Daddy called to see how I was and my mother cried and then she heard another woman in the background and got angry and hung up before I could talk to him. My headaches did not go away and when, three weeks later, I finally saw the doctor, he said I had a fractured skull and I should have died.

5.

Fiona was sick. Seasick, sick of the sea, and they'd only been sailing for a few hours. She huddled in the cockpit beside Luc, doing her best not to throw up. Nathan was giving them some sailing tips—too late, she thought. She wasn't listening anyway. She would just do whatever she was told. She leaned her head against Luc's shoulder, but that made her feel worse. She had to keep her neck straight and her eyes on the horizon, barely visible in the gloom. Rain threatened, a few constipated drops fell. She knew a downpour was coming.

Doug squeezed in beside her. He wasn't listening to Nathan either. He whispered in her ear, "Three is my lucky number. Remember. Threes are good." Last night at dinner, before she and Nathan went to look for Luc, Doug had told her the story of his cancer. The luck he'd had and the signs. Three times the department secretary suggested he see a doctor for his headaches and the third time he went. Two doctors had told him it was inoperable; the third was Nathan. Three black crows on the telephone line outside his house in Arizona the morning he left. Three white seagulls on the dock before they set sail. She was the third girl he'd met since cancer. The first a nurse, the second a grad student, and now Fiona. She would be lucky for him. But there were five people on board this boat. This was her first voyage. And she had almost puked a zillion times.

The wind was picking up, the waves—constant and un-countable—growing larger.

Nathan said the mainsail was flogging. No one moved. He ordered Joren to reef the mainsail. Joren looked up at the sail and pushed the hair from his eyes.

Nathan frowned. "Don't you understand 'the English'? Think, Captain. What to do?"

The boat had become a demented seesaw, tilting one way and then banging down the other. At the same time the bow rose and came down hard, slapping the water and covering them in freezing spray. Fiona braced with her feet and held the bottom of the bench with both numb hands and gritted her teeth so she wouldn't bite her tongue. Her stomach roiled, her eyes watered, her blue suede jacket was soaked. She watched Luc trying to light a cigarette and laughing—actually laughing—at the struggle. She almost hated him for feeling so good.

"Captain!" Nathan yelled. "Come on! Tighten her up!" He made a cranking motion with his arm. Joren headed for the winch on the left—port—side of the boat.

"Not that! The halyard!"

Joren shook his head.

"On the mast!" Nathan gestured. Joren turned to front of the boat. Nathan nudged Luc with his foot. "Help him."

Luc grinned and jumped up to give Joren a hand. Fiona had worried yesterday's heroin would be debilitating, but he was completely fine. His balance was perfect, he wasn't sea-sick at all. Maybe she should have gotten high with him. She would try anything at this point to calm her stomach and her fears. Luc kept the lit cigarette in his mouth as he scrambled along the side deck to the main mast—as if he'd done it a thousand times. But then he and Joren didn't appear to know what to do. She saw them talking and the sail kept flapping and the boat kept slamming against the waves.

"Oh Lordy." Nathan looked out at the sea. "Wind's probably at twenty-five knots. Blow!" He shouted at the clouds. "Blow me down!" He scampered over the deck to Luc and Joren.

She couldn't hear what he was telling them, but she saw them nodding in reply. They folded part of the sail down and looped a line through a hole and around the boom. The wind caught the tightened sail and the boat heeled over so far Fiona was afraid it would tip. She almost screamed, but Joren turned a crank—the winch—and the boat held steady and moved more smoothly through the water. Joren and Luc stayed out by the mast, sitting on the deck with their feet over the high edge. They looped their arms over the steel cable—the lifeline—that circled the boat.

Nathan scrambled back and motioned for her and Doug to come out of the cockpit and climb up beside him, on the high side. "This is the windward side! Like this!" He had to shout to be heard even though he was right beside them. He shifted his weight and straightened his legs while leaning against the boat. If the boat had been flat he would have been parallel to the water. Doug couldn't quite get his balance and Fiona worried he'd fall overboard backwards. She straightened out, doing it—hiking out—just fine, but the strain made her sicker. She closed her eyes, but that was worse.

Nathan leaned close and spoke in her ear. "I should have sailed alone. I've always been alone. That's what I was made for. Solo sail. The real test of a man."

She turned toward him, close enough for them to kiss.

"Wouldn't you be lonely?"

He tapped his head. "'That man is happiest who thinks the most interesting thoughts.' William Lyon Phelps. I was a fool to bring all of you along on this, my voyage of the soul."

She wanted to ask him what he meant, but it was too hard to talk and his breath was rank. The boat flew over the water, but it straightened out and they could return to the cockpit. Fiona relaxed for a moment. Then the boat crashed over a big wave and the spray filled her open mouth and that was all it took. Her stomach lurched. She turned just in time and vomited over the side.

"Egg and bacon sandwich overboard!" Nathan cock-a-doodled like a rooster.

She curled up on the bench and pulled her knees close. Doug patted her back. Unlike the stomach flu, she didn't feel any better after heaving. She came up as green as she was before. Now there were real tears on her cheeks. She looked again at the empty sea all around them. Nothing in any direction. She craved that moment on a long car trip after driving for many miles when she pulled into a gas station and turned off the car. The wonderful thick silence, everything perfectly at rest. But there were no gas stations at sea. No place to pull over and fix a flat or get a greasy grilled cheese. That would be a business, she thought; ocean islands like rest stops on the freeway, the Howard Johnsons of the deep. The boat lifted and fell hard. She looked up at Nathan. Turn back, she begged him silently. Turn back and drop me off. You were right, she thought. I shouldn't have come. He could be right forever if he would just take her back to shore. He knew what she was asking, she could see it on his face, but he slid his gaze away, out to the east where the clouds were black and swollen and coming toward them.

"What are we going to do?" she asked.

"Enjoy it!"

Doug retreated to the other side as Luc sat down beside her. "Popeye the sailor man." He sang into her ear. "Yak yak yak."

She could barely smile.

"Tell me about pirates." Luc turned to Nathan. "Did they really make people walk the plank? Cat o' nine tails? Keel-hauling?" He gave her a squeeze. "Isn't it bad luck to have a woman on board?"

"I am bad luck," Fiona said. "Look at the weather. Take me back to shore, drop me off and you'll have blue skies."

Luc laughed as if she were joking.

Nathan ignored her. "It's just common sense. Think of sailors at sea for months at a time. A woman on board would drive them completely mad." Of course he had a quote. "On land, it's women and rum. At sea, it's brandy and bum."

Luc laughed again.

"A woman can drive a man mad even if they've been at sea for less than one day. Completely out of his mind." Nathan looked at Fiona and then toward Doug.

She started to protest, but turned and threw up again. Luc pushed the damp strands of hair off her cheek.

"It's going to be a long afternoon," Nathan said to her. "Go to your bunk. Sleep will help."

Gratefully, she went to the hatch. She slipped on the first rung of the ladder, but caught herself. She looked at Luc and he grinned. He blew her a kiss. She pretended to catch it and swallow it—an old joke of theirs. It was only the first day. It would all be fine. It would. It would. In the meantime, she'd lose some weight. She smiled at him. That wasn't a bad thing.

She continued down the ladder into the main cabin and

lay down on the bench. She didn't bother to fold the table and make the bed, but simply pulled a pillow from the cabinet—locker—underneath and buried her nose in it. She smelled Luc instead of salt water and diesel fumes. Nathan was right: it was better lying down.

Joren clattered down the ladder and went into his cabin for something. When he came out, he stopped by her bunk. "Look there. It will be calmer now. The farther we get from the land, the better. Wind is…" He struggled for the English word. "…Stirred around, crazy, from the land."

She sort of smiled and he went back up the ladder. The boat did seem straighter in the water. She could hear Luc laughing. The wind moaned through the sails, the lines screeched against the winches, and the waves banged against the hull. She had not expected sailing to be so loud. She had imagined it more like the Greyhound bus ride from Manhattan to Newport. Quiet, temperature controlled. On the bus she and Luc had chatted and giggled and eaten the turkey sandwiches Lola had sent. They almost made love in the tiny bathroom, but the smell was disgusting, diesel fumes blended with a tincture of shit, and she had pushed him away. Luc had slept against her shoulder while she stared out the window and whispered each thing she saw. House. Girl. Tree. Fence. Black car. White car. Truck. She had made a song of it, no idea then that those simple things on solid earth would be so special three days later. She could sing it now, lying in the bunk, trying to think of anything other than her sick stomach. House. Girl. Tree. Fence. Black car. White car. Truck. And then they'd been almost to Newport. The road became busier, too many things out the window for her to name. Gray shingled houses with upstairs dormers. Low cinderblock buildings that sold auto parts and aluminum siding. A used car dealership. Forgotten, drooping Halloween decorations. The trees had mostly lost their leaves and children played outside in cheap shiny jackets. There'd been a ratty little dog peeing on the sidewalk and an old woman in purple pants holding his leash. It looked like her home in Delaware until the bus had turned a corner onto America's Cup Way and everything was shiny clean and brilliant. As if they'd entered Oz and left the black and white land of reality behind. There were white mansions in the distance with green lawns rolling down to the dark brown bluff. There was the magnificent ocean, a deep ultramarine with white-capped waves. A picture postcard world. Arriving in Newport she was so dazzled she forgot to notice that the sea went on and on forever. She'd been taken with the town, the boats, the life she'd never known. She had ignored the warning signs, the breath that caught in her throat when she first saw the tiny *Bleiz A Mor*. She had paid no attention to her queasiness. She had refused to remember that the ocean was for creatures that could swim, not for her.

There was a clinking in rhythm with the rocking. Her wine glasses were knocking together. She thought about getting up to wrap them in something, move them some place safer, but she didn't know where that would be and getting up was impossible. She heard the crack as the first one broke. Her beautiful long-stemmed wine glasses. She opened her eyes when she heard Doug come down the ladder. He fell into his bunk.

"Seasickness makes you sl...sl...sleepy," he said. "I read all about it."

"The wine glasses," she said. "They're breaking."

"N...N...Nathan's problem."

"I'll get in trouble."

He shook his head, no.

"I bought them."

"Nathan's fault. He's to b...blame," Doug said. "Not t... too late. T...te...te...Demand to go home."

Impossible. Fiona curled on her side and slept.

6.

Who is that girl? I barely recognize her, that sweet and untarnished face. Her platinum hair is the same as mine, her blue eyes water in the cold as mine do. I remember that ugly sweater so well I could be wearing it now. But she is so passive, so quiet. I wish I could reach back and shake that girl, tell her to speak up and say what she thinks. She is smarter than she knows. I see her trepidation, her need, her desperation to keep Luc loving her. Stop it, I want to say. You're strong. I wish I could remind her how tough she'd been to leave home and travel 2000 miles alone to college. She had packed her suitcase and asked a friend to drive her to the airport. She had found a place to live, a part time job, paid her tuition and her rent all by herself. And there, on her own, she had met Luc and everything went to hell because nothing else mattered, not her school or his drugs or their monogamy, because he said he loved her and that was enough.

Who is that girl?

Thirty years later, here I was buying a ticket to fly across the country, using money we did not have, to see Luc—just because he had asked.

Who was I kidding? I am that girl.

I stood in front of the open refrigerator. I could not stop eating, could not get enough to fill me. All the food in the world would not satisfy the hole in my gut. The phone rang.

"I'll get it." I called down the basement stairs to Harry. It was Dr. Carolyn.

"I'm sorry," she said again.

"Why? Is this your fault?"

She didn't laugh. I took the phone into the bedroom. I still hadn't told Harry my news. Hadn't told him I was going to Newport either. I had said nothing about everything. Dr. Carolyn gave me the name of her favorite oncologist—it bothered me she had a favorite—and said he could tell me more. What stage cancer I had. What to expect next. I should make an appointment very soon. Right away. I pretended to write it all down, uh huh, uh huh, thanked her very much and hung up.

I went back to the refrigerator. I ate the last dry heel of bread. I scraped the mold off a tiny block of cheese, and then ate the moldy part too. I dug a finger into leftover guacamole turned brown, took two bites from a container of yogurt past expiration. In the cupboard I found stale crackers, potato chips so old I could fold them in half. I squeezed the chocolate syrup out of the bottle right into my mouth.

Outside the rain continued. Our basement had flooded, and Harry was down there sloshing around. The hemp journal had not called and between that and the flooded basement and the mice he was more angry than usual. We had families, communities, whole continents of mice living in our basement. They nibbled into our winter clothes and old sleeping bags. They chewed through the box of earthquake supplies into the plastic ketchup bottle and left bloody red footprints across the shelves. Their shriveled black droppings were everywhere. And when it rained they came up into the house. In the middle of the night before, when I turned on the kitchen light to get a glass of water, I caught a mouse scurrying to hide, its long, gray-pink tail sliding under the stove. Back in bed, I heard it scratching, skittering, laughing at me inside the wall.

Something fell in the basement and Harry shouted, "Fucking idiots!"

I felt my breast, fingered the lump I had grown well aware of, fingertips walking gingerly around the stitch from the biopsy. I liked my breasts. I didn't want them to change. Either of them. They didn't look bad for a woman almost fifty. Fifty. It loomed on the horizon, three short months away. It was no longer possible to pretend I wasn't middle-aged even if my stomach was mostly flat, my breasts still a little perky. Why couldn't I have cancer of the thigh? If they were going to take something off, couldn't it be a saddlebag or a little inner wiggle?

The Weather Channel buzzed from the bedroom, CNN from the living room. I threw the now empty bag of chips into the trash. I put the crackers away. I didn't want to be bloated and fat when I saw Luc. I needed to feel as good as a middle-aged, adulterous, cancerous, mother could. I would get on the exercise bike right after dinner. I decided to make Harry his favorite Swiss cheese omelet. I put the frying pan on the stove. I got out the butter and the eggs. I pulled open the potholder drawer and a mouse jumped out at me. I screamed. The mouse ran toward me. I leapt onto the counter, knocking the eggs to the floor, breaking every one.

Harry came running up the stairs with a shovel, the dog barking at his heels. He backed the mouse into a corner and swung at her. He caught only her tail, maybe part of a leg; she shrieked, a horrible high-pitched noise. Lulu barked and growled.

"Stop! Harry!"

He stamped his feet and the mouse tried to claw under the

baseboard. He let the shovel fly. It scraped the wall, a long dark scratch in the yellow paint, but he hit her. He lifted the shovel and hit her again and again. Blood spattered the floor and the wall.

"Enough," I shouted at him. "It's a mouse. Not the U.S. Government."

I was horrified, but I tried to make it okay. He turned to me and his eyes were dead. The shine was gone. They were flat and small. I saw dots of blood on the toe of his wet sneaker, more on the leg of his faded blue jeans. He dropped the shovel and backed away from the smashed body.

"Take your shoes off," I said. "The blood."

His hands balled into fists. "Where was it?" he asked. "Where did it come from?"

I pointed at the still open drawer. We looked inside. The mouse had chewed up my potholders making a nest, and four pink and hairless babies were curled in the fluff. Harry scooped up the potholders and strode to the bathroom. I followed and watched as he dumped the baby mice into the toilet. Their eyes weren't even open. I worried about our plumbing. I was careful not to flush a tampon, I could only imagine the blockage their thumb-sized flesh and guts and bones would create.

"Harry," I said.

"They don't deserve to live."

I didn't recognize the man I'd married. Each infant mouse opened in the water like a flower. The paws stretched, the mouths went wide looking for air. They drowned before he flushed. I turned away, unable to watch them sucked into the pipes. Harry went to pick up their crushed mother. I closed the bathroom door. I could smell their death, worse than an old man's shit in the toilet.

"I'm going to Newport, Rhode Island." I said it softly, trying it out.

I walked into the kitchen. I held the paper bag open for Harry to drop the mouse remains inside. "I'm going to Rhode Island."

"What?"

"A conference. Art History. Teaching jobs. People will be there from all over the country."

"We can't afford it."

"A thousand bucks. I need to do this."

"You won't get a job."

"How the hell do you know?" I was angry with him and he was right—this weekend was not going to get me a job. I swallowed. "Sorry. I have to try."

He took the bag and rolled it up. A little spot of blood bloomed on the brown paper. We both stared at it.

"I'll put this in the trash." He started for the door. "I'm sorry. You're right. You'd be a great teacher."

He walked out and something went with him. A little bit of our marriage, our life together, was scraped off like the paint from the wall.

I went to bed early that night and dreamed I was back in college in the group house I had shared. I'd had three housemates: short Raymond, tall Norris, and the giant woman they both slept with named Beatrice. Beatrice didn't like me. It was okay. It was like living alone with people around. My cat died there, killed in the yard by a raccoon. In my dream, I stepped over my poor cat's vivisected body and went to the bathroom and the toilet was overflowing. Floating among the turds and used tampons was a yellow boat filled with tiny pink mice in pants and sailor hats. They waved to me. The babies had become sailors of the sewers. In my dream I was glad they were alive.

LIFE # 2

I was eight, it was late autumn and the trees were bare. Becky, the girl next door, was thirteen, a magical age to me, a teen age, and she had allowed me to play hide and seek with her and her friends that day after school. Bonnie and Ginny and Joan—beautiful eighth graders—and I ran off to hide. Becky was It. There were bubbles of joy in my chest because I was playing with the big kids.

I found the best hiding place: a pile of leaves at the curb. No one would ever suspect I had covered myself in the dry dead leaves. I couldn't wait for the big girls to be impressed, tell me what a good hider I was. I smelled dirt and dog shit, but no one would ever find me.

And no one did. I hid for a long time. I heard Becky find the others one by one. Then they all started calling for me. They would never find me. Finally I heard a car coming down the street and I picked up my head to see. Ginny's mother was at the wheel and I saw her mouth open and heard her scream at the same time the brakes did. She stopped an inch from my face. She was about to drive through the pile to park in front of her house. That was what everybody did, the leaves would scatter and then someone would have to rake them up again. She got out of her car, grabbed me and smacked my behind.

"Of all the stupid thoughtless things to do!"

The big girls stared at me, hands on their budding

hips, eyes narrowed to unfriendly black lines in their faces. "Stupid," they repeated. "Stupid."

Ginny's mother made her quit playing and go inside and Becky said it was my fault, now no one could play. She and her friends walked away from me.

"You could have been killed!" Ginny's mother shouted. She stood on her front porch trembling with anger. I saw her start to cry.

"It wasn't your fault." I meant it as an apology, but only made her more furious.

"Little smartass!" She stamped her foot, went inside, and slammed her front door.

I thought I would get in trouble when she phoned my mother to tell her she had almost run me over. But she never called.

7.

Aloud crash woke Fiona. Something big had broken. A lot of little things were already gone; the fruit bowl, a coffee cup she'd left in the sink that morning, and, of course, the wine glasses. Luc had joined her in bed and rolled into her, pressing her against the cold side of the boat. She struggled to sit up, her stomach arguing, her head spinning. The boat was tipped over so far her shoulder was against the porthole. She saw Doug as if he were up a hill from her, wide awake and holding on so he didn't tumble out of his bunk. In the dim overhead cabin light she could see his white face and his hands gripping the railing. Now she knew why the bunks had sides like a baby's crib. The boat slammed down and rocked way over in the other direction with another enormous crash.

She forced herself up to look over Luc and down to the floor. The gallon jugs of alcohol had broken through the teak latticework locker doors under Doug's bunk. The doors were ruined. Every time the boat rocked one way, the bottles slid across the floor and slammed into the lockers on the down side. The boat rolled the other way and they slid back and broke into the other side. She was afraid they would go right through the locker and knock a hole through the wall—the hull—into the ocean. She scooted down to the end of the bench and tried to get her feet on the floor to stand. A piece of her beautiful mermaid covered fruit bowl slid toward her. The fruit had rolled away. She bent and grabbed the gallon of vodka by the handle just as the boat rose again and tilted in the other direction. She fell forward off the bench, the weight of the bottle pulling her over. Her shout woke Luc, but Doug was already on his feet. He caught her before she fell.

"Are you okay?"

"Fine."

Only not. She was sick again the moment she stood up. She ran to the head just in time. Let someone else deal with the liquor bottles. She closed the door and threw up into the miniature toilet. When she was finished, she pumped the handle, but the vomit kept coming back up.

Doug opened the door. "Don't pump!" he said. "In seas this rough, it won't work." He was sick then too and she got out of the way in time for his vomit to follow hers.

Luc opened his arms to her. "This isn't much fun, is it?" Her tears spilled. "It'll get better," he said. "This can't last. Storms never last long."

She wondered how he knew. He said something else, but she couldn't hear him with the clatter and banging of everything sliding around. "I didn't think it would be so noisy."

"What?" Luc asked, "What did you say?" Kidding her until she smiled.

Doug was putting on his rain gear. There was a set of yellow rubber-coated pants and jacket for each of them. He looked like a cartoon character in the baggy bright yellow with his tiny bald head.

"Captain's Courageous," she said. Luc guffawed and her chest lightened.

"You mi...mi...might feel better on deck. F...f... air." Doug headed up.

"It feels calmer up there too," Luc said. "C'mon, baby." He helped her into her slicker and pants. They were enormous, the pants a foot too long and the sleeves hanging way past her hands. The drawstring waist, tight as it would go, hung on her hips. Luc snickered at her, said they'd have to use the gear in a dance. "For our company, Apples and Oranges," he said. "It will be part of our first show. Flapping around the stage. You on my back. I'll be the boat." He found the scissors in a galley drawer and cut her pants legs shorter and put the pieces in her pockets. "In case you grow," he said.

She giggled. She liked thinking about them starting a company and dancing together. He rolled her sleeves. She was a toddler getting dressed for a snowstorm. He started to kiss her and she stopped him and covered her mouth. She knew her breath was rancid. He hugged her instead, the stiff suit crunching against him, and then reached for his gear.

"Wait," she said. "The liquor."

They used the embroidered throw pillows and a lovely hand knit blanket to make a bed for the gallon jugs. They seemed secure. The damp might damage the pillows, but it was better than more glass breaking. Fiona worried that Luc would be held responsible for the broken cupboard doors. He'd put the liquor there. Then again, he was Luc and Nathan liked him. She held his hand as they staggered up the ladder onto deck.

It was dark and cold and raining, but the boat was not leaning so much and in the fresh air she felt better. She looked up. There. No, there. Was that a peek of sky showing through? The twinkle of a star? The clouds were clearing. She was sure of it.

"What time is it?" she asked Nathan.

He sat behind the wheel with a fifth of scotch between his thighs and a cigarette going. He handed his pack of Marlboros to Luc as he said, "7:30."

That was all? She knew what it meant to have a sinking feeling; her stomach had truly sunk below her knees. Only 7:30. Day one.

Luc put his arm around her and she breathed in his familiar cigarette smell. "What's the weather report?" he asked. "Anybody check the radio?"

"Don't make no never mind, honey child," Nathan said. "We're in for it now."

8.

Just after midnight, the phone rang, cold and blue. Jack was my first thought. I knew disaster was always possible. The turn taken too quickly, the wet shoe on the staircase, I knew we lived each day barely avoiding catastrophe. And I was right.

"Mom?" he asked in a high, thin voice. I said his name. "Mom," he said again, more normally. Not a question, but a release. "I was robbed. Two guys robbed me. With a gun."

I sat up. "Where are you?"

"I'm home. I'm safe. We ran in a restaurant and called the cops right away. They took my watch." An old-fashioned boy who still wore a watch. He said the robbers took his wallet, but not his phone—too old or too easily traced. I could hear him breathing. He told me about the gun, "A handgun, I think it was a Glock." His only knowledge of weapons from video games. He said the two guys were young, maybe teenagers. He asked me why anyone would rob him, a college student with nothing. Because he looked so privileged, I told him. White. Well-dressed. He was silent. I was afraid, angry that those robbers had taken his confidence, the belief that he was and always would be safe from harm. I wanted to get in the car and rush across town to him. I told him I could be there in twenty minutes.

"No, it's okay. Natasha is here."

"Natasha?"

"We were out. We were just walking back to the car. She was great, Mom. Didn't even cry."

I heard a female voice in the background.

"Is that her?"

"She's talking to her folks."

"Where are they?"

"San Francisco. We're going to visit them for spring break."

He was leaving me, little by little, one foot after another. We talked some more, and I could tell he was anxious to get off the phone. He had checked in, now he was fine. I was too upset to sleep, but he was already over it. I told him I'd like to meet Natasha and he said he thought that'd be great. Great. Oh Mom, he told me, she is fantastic. Soon I wouldn't be the person he called with his news, bad or good. I told him he could bring her to dinner any time and I said I love you and I meant it. I meant it more than to any other person in the world, without any other ingredient mixed in, no need or want or fear or conditions.

"Bye," I whispered and hung up.

He was fine, but I was antsy, uncomfortable. I felt the tight yarn of time strapped around my chest, the moments of my past suffocating me in blue and white stripes. My flat chest and thick thighs were the first tight rows knit around my collarbones. My lackluster performance in school another inch or so. Not pretty, not special, my dad saying, at least you have nice hair. At least. That refrain was three rows across my chest. Dance, dance, dance, my lack of talent and ability were row after row after row after row. I had started dancing because my father was sleeping with the dance teacher. He said if I couldn't be beautiful, at least I could be graceful. At least. I kept at it for him when I didn't like it, wasn't good at it. It was all I had to share with him, the car rides there and back and his approval when I didn't quit. Rows and rows. Sex with strangers, nights I could not remember I was so high, my mother telling me not to come home, each row was more rigid than the last.

And then there was Doug and the boat. And Luc. The tightest yarn of all, rows knit from steel wool. Doug watched me from across the room, leaning against my unused exercise bike, his head tilted to one side, his wool stocking cap covering his scar. He didn't look angry, only resigned and concerned about me. You see? Maybe I said it out loud. I have cancer too.

Harry stumbled into the bedroom, chasing Doug away. "What?" he said. "What is it?"

"It was Jack. He's fine. He was robbed, but the police came and he's home and safe."

Harry ran to the large window that looked out on the back patio. He grabbed the curtains and tried to pull them closed. No one lived behind our house, it was just a steep hill leading up to another street. He knew the curtains were for show. He yanked and tugged saying, "Shut. Shut. We have to shut these windows," and then the rod came loose and the whole thing tumbled down on his head. He scrambled and waved his arms and shouted as if attacked.

"Harry!"

He sat down on the floor with his legs out in front of him like a bear. He shook his head.

"Harry."

He looked up at me and his eyes were dull, blank. He was still sleeping. He hadn't walked in his sleep since our first nights together. Back then it had been funny, endearing. I scooted to the end of the bed. My flannel nightgown twisted around my legs and I tugged on it to straighten it.

"Who are those people?" he asked. "Where are my boys? Where? Where?"

"Wake up, Harry, it's me. You're home."

He shook his head again. The end of one curtain lay across his lap and he fingered it as if he didn't know what it was.

"It's okay. Wake up." I crouched beside him, stroked his forehead. He closed his eyes and lifted his face to me. He even smiled. "Wake up."

Finally he pushed himself to his feet. He shook his head at the bare window behind him, then turned around to me. "It's too quiet. I don't like it. I'm afraid something is going to happen."

"Something did happen. To Jack. But he's fine."

He rubbed his face and started for the door. "Sorry. Didn't mean to scare you."

"You were sleepwalking."

"I dreamed Jack was dead. I dreamed he was fighting in the war. In Iraq. Sand, so much sand. There was a boy in the paper. Jackson. A boy named Jackson, PFC, twenty years-old, dead from an IED. What if it was our Jackson?"

"Were you reading the casualty list again? Don't."

"Boys are dying and I'm doing nothing." He was so sad. "Nothing. I can't even get a job writing puff pieces about hemp." He sniffed, rubbed his eyes. "My wife has to leave me to get a teaching job."

"I want to. Teaching sounds like fun."

"Don't try to make me feel better. Just don't." He went on from my job to the government's role in Iraq, to 9/11, to food safety and air pollution and public education, cataloguing his own failures to do anything about any of it. I lay down and pulled the covers up. I knew he felt sad and overwhelmed, but I'd been hearing it for two years. I thought about Newport, went over the things in my suitcase. I dozed, only responding when Harry asked me a question, "What do you think?" or "Right? Am I right?" I always agreed, assured him he was strong and kind and that he knew best.

When he was quiet, I asked, "Can you sleep now?" I moved over for him, pulled the sheet and blanket back. He hesitated, but went back to Jack's bed.

Alone, I opened my mind and let the thoughts of Luc come. For thirty years he had hidden in my memory, poised to jump out like a stripper from a birthday cake. For thirty years if I overheard a Greek word, or saw a dance program on TV, or a man with curly hair, or graceful fingers, even that handsome junkie sleeping outside the Post Office, my guilt about Luc threatened to overwhelm me. Now I knew he was alive and well, but I was puzzled why he would want to see me. At the end, I had watched him run down that alley, into that abandoned building, up to a high he loved more than me. I hadn't stopped him. Didn't even try. My fault. That's the way it had felt for thirty years. It was my fault. I was grateful he was still alive, but it was no thanks to me.

"My she was yar," Katherine Hepburn says to Cary Grant in The Philadelphia Story. She says she's talking about their sailboat, the True Love, but she's really talking about the two of them. We all have one that was yar: responsive, nimble, quick to the helm. For the rare and very fortunate few, yar is forever. But quick also implies impermanence. Nothing that good lasts for long. The seas get rough and the tides turn.

9.

The boat cut through the choppy sea, leaning hard, but rocking less. The rain had backed off to a drizzle and Fiona was mostly dry in her yellow outfit. Her seasickness had lifted with the clouds. She was trying to understand why the boat had to lean over so far—that was what scared her most of all. Nathan explained that heeling actually slowed them down as more wind hit the sail, and the weight of the keel would always keep the boat upright. She wasn't sure she believed him. Her father had rolled his brand new Jeep the year before. He'd taken a turn too fast and the car had tipped. Certainly the boat could do the same.

She looked at the others. Luc sat behind the wheel grinning. Some of the color had returned to Doug's face. He was calm, holding on with only one hand and scratching his scar under his wet wool cap with the other. The call of the sea, the sailing life, the freedom of the open ocean, all those clichés— she could admit there had been some allure docked in Newport. She had felt a kind of snotty pride when someone saw them on deck in the early morning after having obviously slept on the boat. She had loved telling her boss back in Manhattan and her mother in Delaware she was sailing to Bermuda. She and Luc had been special, adventurous, about to do something remarkable. There were plenty of adventures to have on dry land. Adventures that didn't make her sick to her stomach.

"Hey, Cook!" Nathan called to her. "Dinnertime."

He had to be kidding. "I'm not hungry," she said. "Nobody is."

"I am." Nathan gestured toward the hold. "You're the cook. At least make me a sandwich."

She wanted to tell him to make his own damn sandwich, but she never would. She staggered to the ladder. The brackish smell of saltwater and vomit wafted up from below and threatened to make her puke again.

In the hold, she found that one of the whiskey bottles had gotten loose from its shelter amongst the pillows and blankets and had slammed into the wall and broken into a million pieces. She cleaned up the glass as best she could. She looked for a trashcan, but couldn't find one, so she dumped the glass in the bread drawer, first taking out the bag of Wonder Bread. The white and polka dotted wrapper belonged in some bright suburban kitchen, not this damp and disgusting gloom.

Luc followed her down the ladder. "Some food might help you," he said, but she shook her head. "A slice of bread anyway. Soak it up. Doug too."

"Yes," Joren said. He was over at the tall desk—the navigation station—looking at the map—the chart. For what reason, Fiona couldn't be sure. How could he tell one patch of ocean from the next? Turn left at the second wave, no that wave, no that one. "You should all eat." He looked at his watch. "It is almost at nine. It will be a long night."

"Only nine?" Fiona groaned. How much longer could this day last?

She bent to open the small fridge. Just then the boat rocked and the milk and orange juice, the cheese, the jar of martini olives, the plastic package of bacon, all slid toward her. She slammed the door shut.

"Peanut butter and jelly?" she asked.

"Great," said Luc. "Delicious."

She loved him then—again—always. She had to smile at his concerned face. He cupped her chin and kissed her nose. She held his arm, leaned into his chest. His yellow raincoat smelled better than anything else.

Nathan thundered down the ladder. Suddenly the hold was very full. Warmer, but smellier. Fiona had to close her eyes, keep one hand on Luc.

"Captain." The word from Nathan was a rebuke. "Captain De Groot, once we set a course, you need to assign watches. We're not all going to sit on deck all night. Two people at a time." He gave a little grunt. "And no kissy kissy. Put Luc with Doug. You and Fiona. I will be alone. Done. Four hour shifts."

"I already had the plan," Joren said.

He and Nathan began to argue about the course and the sails. Fiona didn't understand what they were talking about. They continued quarreling as they went up on deck. She spread peanut butter on the bread, breathing through her mouth. Luc made a funny face on his sandwich with the strawberry jelly. He gave it a voice and had it talk to Fiona. "Love those hands, oh and when you lick your finger. Come on, put it in my peanut butter again." She had to smile.

Together they finished the sandwiches and went up on deck to hand them out. Joren shook his head no. He said he was tired, maybe coming down with "the influenza," not seasickness. Of course he couldn't be seasick because this was his job, and he had so much experience.

Nathan looked at his peanut butter and jelly. "Dinner?"

"C'mon," Luc said. "Give her a break." He put his arm around Fiona. "She'll be better tomorrow."

"Fine, fine."

Fiona offered Doug a sandwich, but he declined. Luc and Nathan each took an extra one. She nibbled on a slice of bread. It tasted of saltwater and fish. After one bite, she tossed it overboard.

"You'll bring the sharks," Nathan said.

"I'm sorry. Oh my god, I'm so sorry."

Everyone started laughing and she realized he'd been joking. Even Doug chuckled at her. She laughed at herself. Ridiculous. The water was too cold for sharks—of course it was.

Nathan finished his second sandwich and started in on a bag of cookies, taking big swigs of scotch throughout. He wiped his mouth and belched loudly. "I'm going to bed," he said with the bottle in his hand. "Doug. Luc. You guys too. Bedtime." He turned to Fiona. "You and Joren have the first watch. Wake Luc and Doug in four hours." He turned his face up and opened his mouth, filling it with rainwater. He gargled and spit over the side. Then he spread his legs wide and shouted into the wind, "'For he commandeth, and raiseth the stormy wind, which lifteth up the waves therof. They mount up to the heaven, they go down again to the depths.'"

Right on cue the boat banged down into a trough between two swells.

"Thank you oh Lord our God." Nathan tripped as he went toward the hatch. Fiona put out a hand to catch him— as if she could. "Psalm 107," he said to her. "Aren't you a good Christian girl?"

"No religion," she said. "Mom wasn't interested."

"No one to ask for help. Too bad. Too bad." He turned to Luc. "C'mon, boy, I know you're Greek Orthodox. Time to say your prayers."

"I pray the toilets keep working." Luc gave Fiona a squeeze as he passed her. "I'll make the bed," he said. "Warm it up for you."

She watched him leap gracefully down the steps after Nathan. He patted Nathan on the back and took the bottle from him for a drink. She couldn't hear what he said, but Nathan smiled and ruffled Luc's hair.

She jumped when Doug grabbed her leg to get past her.

"Glad we're here?" he asked. "Y…y…you were so ready to leave. And now this."

"I'll be fine when the sun comes up." She had to reassure him. "So will you. It'll be great tomorrow."

In the sickly yellow glow from the running lights she could see the open pores on his jaw, each individual facial hair sprouting. She saw the look in his eyes too, the way they opened to her, inviting her. But where, she thought. Where did he want her to go? We have fifty-two feet for five of us. He's dreaming. And while it wouldn't be terrible to give Luc a taste of his own medicine, the boat was too small and her stomach too upset. She couldn't be interested in him anyway. He was older. He'd had a brain tumor.

He touched her hand as he went down into the hold. His finger was an icicle on her skin, and a tiny flame in her heart. Thank you, she wanted to say. At the very least, thank you.

10.

I carried my suitcase to the car while Harry got dressed. He had filled the basement with poison and the mice had crawled into the walls to die. The whole house stunk. I sniffed my sleeve. Was it in my clothes? My hair? The bitter, pungent odor of death. I could taste it in the back of my throat. The rain had stopped, but the California sunshine was still missing. I had spent money we didn't have to see a man I'd never stopped thinking about. The love of my life, the man of my dreams—all the ridiculous ways I thought of Luc—all the labels Harry never was. Harry had never taken my breath away. I had never felt drunk from his kiss; my heart didn't thump when he came to my front door. Harry had never been a cliché. Well-meaning friends introduced us. My heart was tired. Luc had been a marathon and after him I was only interested in short sprints. A couple of hours with someone. No spending the night. No when will I see you again. I wasn't up to any exertion, but Harry did all the work. He convinced me I could not be a sprinter forever. I finally fell in love with him when Jack was born. I loved how his hands trembled the first time he held his son, loved how warm his eyes got when he watched Jack sleep. I loved how protected and secure I felt. We had good times, good sex, we laughed a lot, but that was years ago. That morning we'd had a big fight about the stink, his cruelty, the blueberries I bought that we couldn't afford.

"It reeks in here."

"The sweet smell of success." He thrust his fist in the air.

This was what we had come to: his manhood pumped up by poisoning a few mice and then sitting proudly in the stench. "Big white hunter," I said. "How about I just fry up some of that mouse meat?"

"Cheaper than blueberries. I can't believe you bought blueberries. In November."

I didn't tell him the antioxidants were good for fighting cancer. "You can just get off your ass and go to the store yourself."

My fingers touched the lump under the lace of my nicest black bra. What would I do with my bras if I only had one breast? I had not called the oncologist and I had not told Harry I had cancer. If the plane crashed, if my rental car tumbled off a cliff, cancer wouldn't matter, but Harry would find out I hadn't gone to any conference.

The night before, I'd unearthed an old photo of Luc sitting on the deck of the *Bleiz A Mor* just before we set sail. Rather than put it back in the basement, I'd hidden it underneath my underwear. If I died and Harry had to clean out my things, he would find the photo. He would see how handsome Luc was, his head turned to someone just out of view, the sun shining on his curls, his jaw strong, his nose classic in profile. Harry, nonsmoker, would see Luc holding a burning cigarette in his long, lovely fingers as he made some gesture, the open ocean behind him. That photo—and the fact that I still had it—would break Harry's heart. I thought about going back inside to hide it better, but if I died on this trip, he would see everything anyway.

A drop of rain spattered on the driveway in front of me.

Another drop on my shoulder. I looked up at the clouds. So weird for Los Angeles. Otherworldly for it to rain for days and days. There is no Greek god of rain, but the Hyades are five sisters who were put in the sky as stars by Zeus because they would not stop crying after their only brother, Hyas, was killed. Their constellation appears in Greece in November, signifying the start of the rainy season. It was November and it was raining in Los Angeles and it was a "damp, drizzly November in my soul." I wanted to tell Doug I had finally read *Moby Dick*.

I shifted my coat in my arms. It would be cold in Newport. This time I would have the proper coat and a scarf and gloves. I was wearing black jeans, expensive boots, a blue sweater that brought out my eyes. I was almost the exact same weight, but the pounds had shifted post-childbirth. At least I was smarter now. Luc didn't know I'd studied Art History when I went back to school. He didn't know I was good at it, had won a scholarship, published articles in important journals while in graduate school. He only knew me as young and agreeable. Harry would roll his eyes at that—me, agreeable. I hoped Luc wouldn't be disappointed in who I had become.

My mother used to say, "Nostalgia is like a grammar lesson: it makes the past perfect, and the present tense." Then she would give a high and frightened laugh. She couldn't take her own advice, she died while napping under a 100-year-old quilt, her heart stopped from the weight of her memories. The regrets of her past were her constant refrain, like waves on the beach. "I made mistakes, it's too late now, I made mistakes, it's too late now." She only ever wanted to go back. Not me, I told myself. Not me. But here I went.

In my memory, the seventies are the cream color of a ribbed polyester turtleneck. Some accents of rust and brown, that popular avocado green. The younger women wore their hair layered and feathered back; the older matrons curled it under shoulder-length. I remember women laughing with lifted heads and exposed throats, like a tribal ritual offering their jugulars to the chiefs. The men had moustaches, thick sideburns, and jacket lapels wide enough to match their anxious smiles. I had been a baby and a small child in the sixties—the years of love. By the time I was nineteen, America had passed through love and then disappointment and into disillusion. On our way to despair.

It was very hot in New York the summer of 1979. The country was in the middle of an energy crisis; the papers were filled with pictures of long lines at gas stations and ads that said, "Don't be fuelish." We weren't supposed to use our air conditioners and people were sticky and annoyed. OPEC meant nothing to me. Oil from the Middle East could just as easily have been dragon teeth from middle earth. On television, President Carter admonished the American people. He said we were self-indulgent and greedy: "Human identity is no longer defined by what one does, but by what one owns."

"Whose fault is that?" Lola's girlfriend asked. "After Kent State and Vietnam and Watergate."

"Yeah," agreed Luc. "And John Wayne died." John Wayne died on June 11, 1979, from cancer. He got it shooting *The Conqueror* in Utah amidst the radioactive fallout from tests of the atom bomb. Ninety-one of the 220 persons who worked on *The Conqueror* came down with cancer. Luc didn't want to listen to the President. We changed the channel, got high, and watched *Mork and Mindy*.

Almost at the end of the decade, November 4, 1979, the day before we set sail, fifty-two American hostages were taken in Iran. Two days later, I lay in my bunk on that boat and wished with all my heart to be one of them, a hostage in a hot, dry land. I was so sure they would be home before me. I was wrong. They were captives for 444 days. Harry said that was the beginning of the end for America, that the hostage taking proved we were both vulnerable and myopic. Harry thought if we had acted differently then, denied entry to the Shah, recognized an Islamic state, seen them for who they really are, we wouldn't be where we are now. 9/11 might never have happened. Our son, Jack, had a classmate whose grandmother was on one of the 9/11 planes. She was on her way to LA from New York to see her grandchildren. We kept Jack home from school that day. Harry didn't go to work. We kept the television off because Jack was young, but I kept looking to the sky for planes. Harry had reassured me, been silly, and gotten Jack and me to dance with him.

Harry. Cuckold. Fiona. Adulteress. Cheater. Bitch. The words thumped against my forehead. I would make it up to him by taking a job—any job—and working as many hours as I could and not complaining. I would never tell him I had cancer; I would do whatever was necessary without bothering him with that or anything ever again. I closed my eyes. Just give me this weekend, I asked. One weekend.

When the hostages were finally released and returned to America, they were greeted as heroes. "Heroes? We're not heroes," Charles Jones, a communications specialist, said. "We're survivors. That's all. Just survivors."

I think the word survive is wrong. It implies that we are done, that we have succeeded and therefore can return to normal—better than normal. In the newspapers and on television survival always implies victory. Cancer survivors say they have beaten their disease. Hurricane survivors say they faced the storm and won. As if survival is a thing of the past. But in fact it's inexhaustible. We don't "get over" or "beat" our disasters—they just come with us. We accumulate our illnesses, mistakes, and defeats until by middle age we can barely stand up under the weight. The Iranian hostages, thirty years later, continue to suffer from depression, nightmares, and flashbacks. Harry's forced retirement is like a pair of cement overshoes. The rejections fill his pockets with rocks, until a trip to the gas station takes all the energy he has.

It has been so many years since I had my ocean adventure. My survival hangs around my neck, my twisted version of bling, a rapper's diamond encrusted necklace so heavy it keeps me bent. I have not been on a boat since. Harry and Jack took the ferry to Catalina Island and I stayed behind. I never learned to swim. I took nothing but fear away from my experience. My predicament—both then and now—was and is my own fault. I ignored the experienced sailors in Newport. I trusted Nathan, a stranger, for no reason. I made no preparations, didn't follow the list provided, and I never said a word. I should have died. And now? I hadn't had a mammogram in six years. Obviously I hadn't learned a thing.

Ten Traits of Survivors

1. Adaptability

2. Resilience

3. Faith

4. Instinct

5. Purpose

6. Tenacity

7. Ingenuity

8. Hope

9. Intelligence

10. Love

Love was what got me into that mess.

Harry came out of the house and stopped to pat the dog. He'd been asked to come in for a second interview at the hemp journal. He was almost optimistic.

"You look nice," he said. "Pretty."

"Thanks."

I started to get into the car, but he put his hand on my arm. He never touched me. I jumped a little, then blushed. "Sorry."

He looked at the ground. "I'm sorry I was negative. Maybe this conference is just what you need. Maybe you'll get a job at the University of Nebraska or Iowa and we'll move and you can teach and I can grow corn or squash or something."

The picture of farmer Harry was too absurd, his apology too sad. "We'd better go." I had hours before my flight, but I couldn't stay home any longer.

In the car Harry reached for my thigh, then rested his hand on the seat beside me instead. "The woman at the journal said I should come in tomorrow."

"Oh, terrific. You'll get this job. I know it. You will."

"Don't jinx it." Seriously. "Don't say anything. Bad luck. Bad luck."

He was so desperate he had turned to luck. Whistle on deck, leave port on Friday, kill the albatross, I knew none of it made any difference. Except maybe having a woman on board. Maybe that really was unlucky. "Sorry," I whispered. Sorry for everything.

The rain began again as we drove. Harry was aggressive on the freeway, changing lanes, tailgating and suddenly braking, and my stomach lurched. I closed my eyes. I felt the waves rocking under my feet, the salt and spray in my nostrils. Newport was on the horizon. I wanted to be excited to see

Luc, but I had not felt so sad in a long, long time. The rain turned into a downpour. Traffic slowed and finally stopped. Doug floated to the surface. I saw his hand move over his scar and heard the faint brush of his fingers against his stubbly head. Doug, born in Texas, ornithology professor in Arizona, who had never seen the sea. If I had married Doug I would be living in a house in the desert, keeping the birdfeeders full, sweeping the sand from the front step. Everything would be different. Wouldn't it?

The windshield smeared under the wipers, the dust and dirt from the dry days and the streaks from the last rain combining to make visibility poor. We nudged forward. The Hollywood hills to our right were invisible behind the clouds. The houses and buildings surrounding the freeway were as muted and insubstantial as if I had dreamed them. I could be in the center of some great, wide plain. Nothing as far as my eyes could see in any direction. Never a good feeling for me. Panic started in my chest, my feet wanted to run. Get out. Get out. Stop it, I told myself.

I put my hand on Harry's shoulder. He smiled at me.

"Don't worry," he said. "You won't miss your flight. You'll have fun. This will be good for you. You'll hang out in the bar with other art historians and tell art jokes—like, I don't know, Picasso and a parrot. Right? "

"It's Picasso and a donkey. That's the joke."

He laughed. My fingers went back to my lump. I thought about the cancer cells under my skin growing, multiplying. The spot on my chest was a vast expanse and I couldn't see the end. There was no place to get off, no way to stop for just a moment and rest.

LIFE # 3

It was the summer I was thirteen. My mother had a new boyfriend, Paul, who she hadn't been seeing long, a couple of months at most. He was okay. He was gray—the hair on his head, his skin, his pants and Polo shirts. Even his lips were just another shade, a kind of purplish gray.

"I don't know how much longer I can take it," my mother said one day.

It was hot outside, but the window air conditioner in the TV room was humming. We were watching the Watergate trials. Or my mom was watching. I was lying on my stomach on the shag carpet playing with the long fibers, thinking about a boy I knew.

"Take what?" I roused myself to ask.

"Paul." Her voice dropped to a whisper. "He's not very nice. And he's a Republican."

"A gray Republican," I said. "Imagine."

"What?"

"Nothing."

"He's an angry, angry man." Mom went to her bedroom to use the phone.

That evening he came over. He didn't ring the doorbell, just walked in as if he owned the place. I was sprawled on the living room couch with a book. "Nice shoes," I said, hiding a smirk. Suede Chukka boots—gray of course. "Didn't know they came in that color."

"Shut up," he said.

That was new. I sat up as he strode into the kitchen where my mother was making dinner. "What are you doing here?" I heard that familiar tone in her voice, knew she was looking at him from under her eyebrows, probably with her hands on her hips. "You broke up with me." I heard him whine and my mother answered in her imperious tone, "Yes, I did."

And then she screamed as he shouted, "Bitch!" and there was a thud.

I ran into the room. The meatloaf was on the floor. He had his hands around her throat; her skin was bright red between his cadaverous fingers.

I leapt onto his back and pounded him with my fist. I hit him hard in the right temple.

"Cunt!"

I had never heard that word before. I thought it was something in a foreign language. He let go of Mom and backed up hard into the refrigerator, knocking the wind out of me. With a woof I slid off his back to the floor. He didn't even look at me as he went for Mom again. She tried to climb up on the counter crying, "No, no, no."

My hand closed on the leg of a kitchen chair and I flung it toward him. It hit him in the side, not hard, but he bellowed like an ox and spun to me. In a moment he was over me, in another moment he had me in his arms. I wiggled, I writhed, I tried to get away. At thirteen I was slight, my heavy ass and thighs yet to come. He was big. He turned me upside down and held me by my ankles, shaking me. He thumped my head on the linoleum floor.

"Mom!"

"I can't breathe!" she croaked. She staggered away from him—from me.

He swung me by my feet. "Just like you." His voice was quiet, terrifying. "She'll grow up to be just like you."

My head banged against the underside of the kitchen table. I put my hands up to protect my face. Swing and bang. Against the cupboard in the other direction.

"Just like you! Another useless bitch."

He swung harder. I could hear him grunting with the effort.

My mother gave a little whimper and collapsed. "My neck, oh, my neck. I can't get a breath. You've killed me."

He stopped swinging. I tried to pull my legs from his grasp.

"Mom, help me."

"I can't," she said. She looked at Paul and beseeched him, "I'm dying."

"Asshole!" I said. Him or my mother or both. I twisted and bit him in the calf.

With a guttural shout he threw me hard across the room. I crashed through the screen door and tumbled down the cement back steps into the grass. I was lucky it was a summer night and it was only the screen door. I would find out the next day I had broken my elbow. I struggled to get up, get back into the kitchen. The blood on my face, the odd angle of my arm, the red ring around my mother's neck, were enough for him. He ran back through the house and out, never to return. My mother had to go to bed. I washed her face, tucked her in. Forever after in family lore that was the night my mother saved my life.

11.

Fiona heard a steady banging. It was loud and in rhythm with the rocking of the boat. One way. Bang. The other way. Bang. She sighed, something else breaking. So many of her luxury purchases had been destroyed; she had listened to the cracking and tinkling in every cupboard and now knew why the boating supply stores carried plastic. Why hadn't Nathan told her? His money, in shards and pieces.

Bang. One side. Bang. Then the other. It sounded like someone trying to break in. A battering ram. Whatever it was could not be good. She could feel it through the bench and her foam rubber mattress. She sat with a book on her lap, but it had been too rough to read, her stomach too sick. She must have dozed. No light through the porthole. Was it still the same night? Where was the sun? The wind cried, the rain came down. Had she been asleep for hours or minutes? If Luc was not beside her, that meant it was still his turn at the wheel. Not much time had passed. Her head knocked against the wall with every rock of the boat, every bang of whatever it was. She fell back on the mattress, hiding her face, her tears.

Joren opened the door to his room—the aft cabin—and the banging got louder. He closed the door and rushed up on deck. She heard his voice, high pitched and scared, but couldn't make out what he was saying, couldn't hear Luc or

Doug's reply. Joren came back down. He looked back at his cabin. The banging continued. He looked forward to Nathan's stateroom—the fore cabin. Luc came down the ladder, jumping the last two steps.

"We have to tell him," he said.

"But we can do something."

"It's not your fault."

Doug screamed from deck. Fiona gasped as the boat tilted up and up and up and then tipped to one side and smashed down. She fell out of bed and landed against the broken cupboards on the other side of the cabin. The boat righted itself and she rolled on the floor amongst the fruit and broken bits of everything.

Nathan came roaring from his cabin, "What the fuck is going on? Who's on deck?"

"The rudder!" Joren hid his face in his hands.

"It's broken," Luc said calmly as he helped Fiona to her feet. "Hear that?" They all listened to the steady knock. "It's not connected to the wheel anymore. It separated somehow. We can't steer."

"Take the sails down." Nathan threw up his hands. "Joren! Did you at least do that?"

Obviously not, because Joren scurried back up the ladder and Luc followed. Doug came down into the hold. He moved stiffly with his eyes half-closed. She reached out to help him. He wasn't looking well, besides being scared and seasick she saw something else going on. Nathan turned on every light in the hold and Doug groaned and hid his eyes.

"Headache?" Nathan said to him. "Now?"

Doug ran to the head to throw up, but forgot it was out of commission. When he opened the door, the overused toilet had flooded. Puke and seawater and urine gushed into the hold. The smell was overpowering. Doug gagged, covered his mouth and ran up the ladder. Fiona heard him retch.

Nathan turned to her. "Help me. Now."

There weren't any rain boots, so she had to put her canvas sneakers into the muck. Her feet would be wet for the rest of the journey. She followed Nathan into Joren's cabin. At least the floor was dry in there. Nathan lifted the foam mattress, and they managed to fold it and push it to one side. There was a trap door in the platform underneath. He opened it and she saw a series of poles and levers, some plastic pipes, possibly from the head. He reached in and grabbed the center post. The banging stopped. "Get me a line," he said. "Quickly."

She knew where she had stowed the clothesline, planning on drying her bathing suit in the fresh Caribbean air. She hoped that was what he meant. She sloshed into the hold and stood up on the bench in her disgusting feet to grab the rope from the locker above her bunk. It didn't matter—a little vomit and piss was nothing anymore. She ran back to Nathan. His face was red from holding the rudder steady, but the boat was calming; Luc and Joren must've gotten the sails down. She handed Nathan the line and watched him tie a series of complicated knots from the center pole to a wooden piece of the bed. The rudder was secured.

She nodded. "Wow. You really know how to do that."

He sucked a tooth and his cheeks flushed. She wasn't sure she'd pleased him. As he stood and brushed past her he said, "Be sure to tell the others I tied an excellent knot."

He went up on deck and she followed. Doug was curled in a corner of the cockpit, his hood up and his eyes closed, vomit in a dribble down his front and across the deck behind him. She sat beside him and took his cold white hand between both of hers. He didn't respond. The wind was blowing hard, rattling the metal winches and thrumming through the halyards, sending foamy spindrift across the bow. Without sails or rudder, the boat tossed without stopping.

"What do we do?" Luc asked Nathan.

"Call for help." She tried to turn it into a joke. "Ocean Triple A. They can send a tow boat."

"No. We need no help," Joren said. "No one comes."

She ignored his angry tone. "Are there tow boats? There should be."

Nathan spat messily into the sea and wiped his mouth. "I told you to stay home," he said. "I gave you your chance."

"Hey, hey, hey," Luc said. "She's kidding. We just want to know what to do."

"I will fix this," Joren said. "When the water is warm, the weather okay, I can go over the side, I can repair."

Nathan looked at Joren. "Oh Captain," he said. "My Captain." He paused, thinking, then smiled. "Very good. Until then we will set up a relay. The rudder is still attached to the boat and working, it's just broken from the wheel."

"Easy as the cake," Joren said.

This time Fiona didn't laugh.

"Outstanding," Nathan said. "When the weather breaks. Soon. It's almost dawn."

So it was finally Day Two. The weather hadn't changed. The sky no less oppressive. She felt the clouds in her throat.

They set up a fireman's brigade: one person sitting at the helm watching the waves, another at the top of the ladder, another at the bottom of the ladder, and one in the aft cabin with the rudder. The person "steering" would shout directions to the top of the ladder, who would shout it down to the bottom of the ladder, who would shout it into the cabin, and the person manning the rudder would push it one way or the other. Doug wasn't well enough to push the rudder, so he was on the ladder at the bottom. Nathan sat at the wheel, Joren on the rudder, Luc at the top of the ladder. She was supposed to make coffee and find Nathan something to goddamn eat. She stood at the tiny stove with her shoulders and belly tensed, her legs shaking. She couldn't imagine it could get any worse. Poor thing. She didn't yet know there was a whole other level of fear, one where she would be unable to speak or move, an immobility that meant all hope was lost. At that moment she still had hope.

She looked up at Luc at the top of the ladder. "I think we should turn around." They were not twenty-four hours into their voyage. They couldn't have gotten that far. It would be a good time to turn around, go back to the dock, get the boat fixed and set out again. Luc shrugged, he didn't know.

She went to the back—aft—cabin door and shouted to Joren. "We should go back to Newport."

Joren jumped out of the cabin, his red hair standing up in all directions, his face bright red. "No! I can fix this. Soon as it clears. We will be fine."

"Why not get some help?"

"Never. Nathan agrees with me on this." He went back into the cabin.

Fiona couldn't understand. The boat was falling apart. Maybe Joren could fix this, but the water was so cold and rough, it had to be easier in Newport. She thought longingly of the swaying dock, the gentle bob of the boat as they sat around the table the very first night. Even if she had been queasy, they had talked about nothing and they had opened champagne. Her first bottle. Luc said it was good, promised to buy her the same kind in New York. They had all toasted the boat and each other in English and Dutch.

"Cheers. *Proost*," she whispered. "To your health. *Gezondheid*."

"Hard to port!" Nathan shouted, then Luc shouted, then Doug shouted and she shouted with him.

The boat swung around. It crested a big wave, but didn't tip, only slid down the other side. Luc cheered. She got the burner lit and the smell of fresh coffee almost masked the odor of the repulsive backwash three inches deep in the bottom of the boat.

She looked up the ladder at Luc's face. He was propped between the handles, perched like Puck in a tree branch. Her Puck. He pushed one sleeve back on his yellow slicker and in the gleam of the running lights she saw the tiny scabs on the inside of his arm. He had leapt off an edge without her. She would have to follow him, go with him next time. It was the only way she could keep him safe, to be there with him, share every moment. She would try to be enough for him.

12.

How To Survive An Ocean Voyage

1. Be prepared

2. Know who you're traveling with

3. Check the weather

4. Have the right equipment

5. Make sure all parts are in good working order

6. Drink plenty of water

7. Have plenty of food

8. Stay calm

9. Believe you will survive

10. Never give up

Know who you're traveling with. Drink plenty of water. Make sure all parts are in good working order. A good list for any endeavor—certainly for an adulterous weekend.

Harry dropped me off at the airport. He didn't get out of the car. We didn't kiss goodbye.

"Thanks for taking me. See you Sunday." I was already stepping toward the glass doors.

"Call me when you get there." What he always said when

I traveled, what I always said when he traveled.

I was glad I hadn't told him I was sick. I would go see Luc and when I returned I would call the oncologist. Tests. Surgery. Chemotherapy. Radiation. The entire kit and kaboodle (a British Navy term), the whole nine yards (a typical square-rigger had three masts with three yards of sail each), from stem to stern (obvious). Many phrases we use every day come from sailing, some you might never expect. To "let the cat out of the bag" is to show a sailor the cat o' nine tails too soon before his punishment. To "turn a blind eye" is from one-eyed Admiral Nelson because he deliberately held his telescope to his blind eye, refusing to see the signal to retreat. (Sure enough, he fought on and he won.) The longest seam around a wooden ship, from stem to stern and back to stem, is called the devil. Sailors have to hang over the side to repair it, caulk it, with a nasty mixture called pay. Hence the phrases, "between the devil and the deep blue sea" and "having the devil to pay." To be "pissed off" comes from sailors who were assigned to ships full of urine—used in dying fabric and making gunpowder. Footloose, bamboozle, hard and fast, hodgepodge, loophole, scuttlebutt, allow a little leeway would you please, all had their start as nautical terms. Whichever way you said it, I was in for every treatment the doctors had to offer, right to the bitter end (the loose, unsecured end of a ship's line).

"Believe you will survive."

There are so many little ways we survive every day, so many little things we do almost unconsciously that keep us out of harm's way. Not only for safety, like locking the doors at night or driving carefully in the rain or staying on the trail when we go hiking. Even smaller things. We take out the garbage before the bag gets so full it splits. We put the second piece of pie back in the fridge. We bite our tongues to avoid a fight with our spouse. We say "thank you" and "no problem" when we don't mean it. All are survival of a kind, things that make our lives secure.

I could survive. I could put the cancer out of my mind. I could believe all would be well, clear sailing ahead. At least for one weekend, I could coast. Three days were not going to sink me.

I sat in my seat on the plane by the window. Outside I saw a baggage handler's jacket billow as he turned his back to the wind. A man and his wife stopped at my row and discussed who would sit in the middle. I will, the wife offered. But you get up so often, the husband complained. She sat beside me. He sat on the aisle. I turned my back to both of them. To be aloof is one of my favorite nautical words. It comes from the Dutch, te loef, and means to luff, a natural consequence of heading up into the wind. It will slow you down, but any control you think you have is an illusion.

"Sorry." The woman bumped me as she tried to get her enormous purse under the seat in front of her. "Sorry," again. And a smile.

Now I didn't want to chew the fat, if you catch my drift. Couldn't she see I was overboard and overwhelmed, hard up, high and dry? I had reached a dead reckoning. Luc had always had me over a barrel. I was listless, in the doldrums.

"No problem," I said. "These planes get smaller and smaller."

"And I get larger and larger," the woman replied.

I nodded. "I know what you mean."

I pulled the in-flight magazine from the seat pocket and it opened right to an article about lying and liars. I closed the magazine—even talking to the woman next to me would be better than reading that. The ancient Greeks were keen on retribution. They had three winged, fanged, serpent entwined deities they invoked for vengeance. The Erinyes—the Furies we call them—were especially hard on liars. They made the dissembler mad and diseased. They could provoke him to pull out all his hair or use his fingers to dig festering sores into his own skin. The Furies sprang from the blood of the sky god, Uranus, the three drops that fell when his son attacked and castrated him, and they have been searching for any lying dick ever since. In the Iliad, Homer writes, "they punish whosoever has sworn a false oath." Harry's unhappy face as I got out of the car was a condemnation. My suitcase packed with my favorite underwear was a curse. I didn't believe, I had no faith, but still I heard the Furies' chthonic cries coming for me.

I had lied to Harry only once before, and it wasn't a real lie, because if he'd asked, I would have told him the truth. He knew about Luc, knew what he had meant, did mean to me. So I didn't tell Harry the last time I flew to New York to see Luc twenty-seven years ago. I just said I was going for a special show at the Met. I assumed he knew what I was really doing. Harry was about to ask me to marry him. We had joked about white dresses, rings, and happily ever after. We'd been to two other weddings and discussed what we would and wouldn't do. But it wasn't official. Soon he was going to get down on one knee and ask me in some lovely, romantic way. So I called Luc. I couldn't marry Harry until I'd seen Luc one more time. It had been three years. I'd been in touch, more with Lola than with him. She said he was struggling to get clean, said he was still dancing. Of course he was dancing. I held on to that, sure that if drugs got in the way of dance, he would stop the drugs. He was dedicated to his art. I didn't know he was just as devoted to the high.

I called him and said I wanted to see him.

"Come," Luc said. "Come right away."

"Promise me you'll really be there."

"Oh God. Io. Just come."

I arrived in the city as snow began to fall. It was February 12th and the airport shops were decorated for Valentine's Day. Cupids and kisses and shiny heart-shaped boxes of chocolates. Lovers were arriving to be together. I almost bought Luc a tiny Teddy bear wearing a tutu with red velvet hearts, but he was not my boyfriend anymore. I took the subway from JFK feeling brave and confident. I was more than halfway through graduate school. I'd had successes and Harry—brilliant, star reporter Harry—was in love with me. I was a different, stronger person.

As I emerged from underground, the city once again took my breath away. I felt the familiar rush, my breath tight and short, my heart quickening. So fast, it went so fast. People walked urgently, the cars sped down Broadway, and I stood immobile. I had expected to be over it. That was what I'd told myself on the plane. I'm over it. Instead I couldn't swallow. I could feel Luc, knew he was somewhere in the city. I could hear his blood and his heart and feel his arms reaching for me. No, no, no. C'mon, c'mon, c'mon. I had to shake my head. I had to think of Harry and the "A" on my last research paper to make my feet move. I shouldered my over-packed bag and headed uptown. I had thought I missed New York—but New York had nothing to do with what I missed.

The snow fell harder as night began to fall. The lights went on in the stores and restaurants and spilled onto the sidewalks, turning the snow golden. The flakes seemed to fall in slow motion, each one specific and enormous, sparkling on my new red gloves before melting. I remember I was worried about what I was wearing. I know I must've dieted like mad before I went. I have an image of me covering my nose as I walked so it wouldn't be red from the cold. I stopped in a coffee shop and brushed my teeth in the cramped dirty bathroom with a waitress snorting a line of coke in the stall beside me.

I had chosen a bar as our meeting place. Luc had suggested his apartment, his first apartment without Alison or his sister. I was surprised how much that hurt, of all things, that he had finally gotten his own place. I wanted some place neutral, so I picked the Shamrock, a neighborhood pub a few blocks from Lola's. We'd been there many times before the boat, before Billy and the rest.

I reached for the door and looked up the street and saw him coming toward me through the snow. He hadn't seen me yet and I was struck again, as always, with how beautiful he was as he strode toward me, long wool coat open and flowing behind him in the snow and cold. He was thinner than I remembered, his cheekbones so sharp they cast shadows. He wore jeans and a gray pullover sweater. He was smoking a cigarette and his purple scarf—a scarf I had given him so long ago—was a sail behind him.

"You," he said and pulled me into his arms.

He felt the same. He didn't feel the same at all. I couldn't help it, I measured his size against Harry's. There was so much less of Luc, so little substance. He was like a bird in my arms, a seagull that could not stay still. Flapping, pushing me away, pulling me close. I smelled him, he hadn't showered and I didn't mind. His sweat was something I had missed. But beneath it there was that taint of metal I knew too well.

I turned to the bar's door, but he stopped me.

"I just have to do a thing." He looked up at the falling snow, catching snowflakes on his tongue.

"Can we stop at the apartment so I can leave my bag?"

"No time. One thing. And then we'll go. We'll eat. We'll talk. I'm so glad you're here. Isn't the snow great? Let's go. Just have to do this one thing."

I was pulled along in his wake. There was no fighting it. He put his hand up for a cab, his other arm around me. We hopped in a bright yellow Checker, another kind of foul-weather gear. The cab smelled of hanging pine tree air freshener and cold vinyl. We sailed downtown. Luc was talkative, funny. I touched his face, his hands, his chest, my fingers trailing along his jumpy thighs. The usual. The same. The years fell away. I had never left. We had never been apart. I was where I was supposed to be. I kept watching the angle of his jaw as he talked, the way his neck moved when he swallowed. I was there with him. It was everything I remembered and more. "Just this one thing," he kept saying. "And then I go there and there and I'm done."

The back end of the taxi fishtailed in the deepening snow. It was turning into a blizzard. The traffic slowed. "C'mon, c'mon, c'mon," Luc said to the cabbie, who shrugged, nothing he could do. "C'mon."

"The guy you're meeting will understand." I tried to mollify him. "It's a snowstorm." I smiled. Tried to get him to look at me. Me.

Luc shook his head, fluttered his foot against the floor. It was dark outside and in. He stared out the window, cursing the snow, reading the street signs. "We can run," he said.

He pulled me from the cab and we ran downtown, my weekend bag thumping against my back. It never occurred to him to take it, never occurred to me to ask. I was wearing heels and my feet were wet. Luc was in leather boots, leaping through the wet snow as if it was nothing. I stopped to rest once, but I saw the impatience, the anger glittering behind his smile and I kept on.

We got to a black door down in Soho somewhere. A street of warehouses, pre-upscale lofts, the industrial squatting lifestyle Luc found so gritty and romantic. This was the true living art of New York, he'd said to me more than once. He knocked on the door. He rang the bell. He was smiling, happy now that we'd made it. No one answered. He kept trying, knocking and pounding. Eventually, he was kicking it, his wet boot splashing against the metal door.

"C'mon," he said to me. "I know where to go."

I wanted to tell him to stop. I wanted to tell him to take me someplace where we could sit and have a drink and look at each other, but I could never tell Luc anything. I never disagreed or fought or said I wanted anything other than what he offered. A small new part of me was aware of this. The larger part of me was still Luc's good old girl and I nodded and went along. The rest of the night was more of the same. The storm raged. Cabs were non-existent. We took subways and ran, then walked, then trudged this way and that across the city. We found a guy. Luc gave him money. We found another guy. I waited outside in the dingy hallway, dripping snow on the cracked and dirty beige floor tiles the shape of oyster crackers, the grout as black as tar. At the next place, I went in with him and sat with two guys and a girl and static on the television while he went into a bedroom and shut the door. At three in the morning, the city quiet and empty and blanketed in snow, Luc went out into the middle of Fifth Avenue and screamed at the top of his lungs, frustrated, scared, and strung out.

"It's beautiful," I said to him. "Look at the city. Look at it."

He couldn't see anything. I tried to hold on to him, but he twirled away. We finally, finally ended up at his place and the dieting and the outfit didn't matter at all. Not one bit. I fell asleep on his sofa in my coat. I don't know what he did.

When I woke, he was gone. He'd made coffee in a percolator. I wrote him a note, "Please take care of yourself," and left. The sun was shining and the city was celebrating the snow; everywhere, people were making snowmen and throwing snowballs and having fun as they slid on their hard-soled city shoes.

I took the subway back to the airport and changed my ticket for an earlier flight, then called Harry and told him to expect me home in time for Valentine's Day. I got off the plane bedraggled and sad, my shoes ruined, to find Harry waiting for me at the gate. A complete surprise. He hugged me hard and I breathed in his clean, soapy smell. He took my bag. His gray eyes saw nothing but me.

13.

The wind roared. The boat slammed from side to side. The dark was endless, the night permanent. It had been a very long time since Fiona had seen the sun. The rain had stopped for about an hour and she had thought the weather was changing. She was wrong. The clouds were just preparing, filling for a deluge. The heavens opened—as her mother used to say—and it poured. Icy rain pummeled her shoulders, the top of her head. A thousand tiny needles pricked whatever bare skin she couldn't help but reveal. With the wind and the tossing of the boat her foul-weather gear was almost useless. The water went inside the hood and down her neck, up her sleeves and through the fasteners until she was soaked inside and out. The only good thing about the rain gear was its yellow color, a bright spot in the relentless murk.

Her arms ached from holding her position at the top of the ladder, waiting for instructions from Doug at the helm. Her shoulders were bruised from banging into the open hatch with each rock of the boat.

"What time is it?" She called down to Nathan.

"Stop asking."

She felt like a child in the back of the car, miserable, carsick, desperate to get out.

Nathan turned back to Joren and banged the tall desk.

The charts were spread out in front of them and they were once again arguing. Luc was in the aft cabin manning the rudder. She looked out the hatch at Doug, strapped in and holding on. He was watching her—always watching her—and he stared into her eyes before giving her a thumbs-up. His headache was better. Nathan had given him a pill from his doctor's bag and it had helped. She had asked for one too, but Nathan said he had nothing for her. He told her to eat, but that was impossible.

"We're on course," Nathan was insisting.

"Obviously not." Joren pointed at the compass.

"That thing? It's a piece of shit. How can that be north?"

"You knew this? Why not make the replacement at port?"

"We're on course now."

"The wind it is against us."

"It was. Now we're headed in the right direction."

What direction was that? She hoped it was back to Newport or whatever was the closest shore. They must have traveled some miles—nautical miles—but south or east or north or west, she had no idea. Bermuda was way below them. Somewhere.

"We need the engine," Joren said. "We can motor through the waves."

"Fine," Nathan answered,, obviously disagreeing. He pushed his hair back and belched.

Joren went to the controls and turned the engine on. The motor sputtered to life. Chug, chug, chug. A comforting grumble of civilization. Now they would get somewhere, she thought. Now they would drive like a car flat and straight through the rain with the windshield wipers going. If it got too bad, they could wait it out under an overpass, watch the rain plummet in curtains around them, turn on the radio and sing along to old songs.

"Starboard," Doug shouted from up on deck. Fiona shouted to Nathan and Joren. Joren shouted to Luc. The boat moved more gently than usual. They were going forward. They were under power. Now if the sun would rise all would be well.

"What time is it?" Fiona asked Joren. Nathan threw up his hands.

"Almost eight-thirty."

"It's morning?" It couldn't be. The sky seemed no lighter than it had four hours before. She looked up and got a face full of rain. She had to see something else. She crawled into the cockpit. Doug reached out a hand to help her; his face was pale, his open mouth a black rectangle, his eyes like holes in his head. The face of a skull.

"Where is the sun? Where?" She begged him. "Have you seen it?"

What if it never rose? What if they were in some kind of Twilight Zone where the sun would never shine again? She was beginning to panic, panting, sweating inside her awful rubber suit. Doug squeezed her hand. He pointed the other way. She looked, right into the rain and wind, and there, very far away, was a small patch of lighter sky and pale gray clouds. There it was. The storm was not everywhere.

She stepped around the wheel and hugged him. She wiped the rain from his face. He leaned in and tried to kiss her. She pushed him away.

"It doesn't matter," he said. "We're going to die on this boat. I know it."

She shook her head. She wasn't listening to this. He pulled her down beside him and whispered in her ear.

"Down, down to Davy Jones' Locker. We're all going down."

"The engine is on. Hear it?" She couldn't hear anything over the wind and rain. "Joren turned it on. We're going." Where she didn't know, but not down.

Doug pressed his hands on either side of his head as if trying to keep it from coming apart. "Nathan lied. I feel the tumor gr…gr…growing."

Maybe the pill was making him hallucinate. Why else would he think these terrible things? She put the back of her hand on his forehead as if to check his temperature.

He held it there, closed his eyes. "Your little hand. Mother."

"Stop worrying," she said. "When the rain stops we'll be fine."

"We're sinking." Doug opened his eyes. "Even he will be dead. I'm only sorry for you. You don't deserve this." He put his arms around her and tried to kiss her again.

"Cut it out," she said. But she wanted to be nice. It wasn't his fault the medicine was making him crazy. She patted his back, tried to be comforting.

"Don't," he said. "Don't pat me like that. That's not what I want."

"I have to get back to my post."

"Luc ran off and got drugs. You can do whatever you want." He paused. "You can kiss me. You know I'm right."

Now she was angry. She pushed him away. It was none of his business. He grabbed her hands again, kept her close. She shook her head but couldn't get free.

"Fiona," he said. "Do you know about the nevers? All the nevers? The nevers are passing before me. Never, never, never."

"What are you talking about?"

He spoke plainly, without stuttering. "All the things I will never do. I'm never going to spend the day in bed with a girl. I'm never going to have sex in the shower. I'm never going to get married. Never show my wife the house where I grew up. Never be a father. Never see a West Indian Whistling Duck. I've never been in love—until now."

Her wet hair whipped into her mouth. He pulled it away with his fingers. She put her hand on his. "No. No." But she leaned toward him. His love—delusion that it might be—was warm and dry.

"Starboard!" he screamed.

A wave, ten or fifteen feet high, rolled straight toward them.

"Starboard!" She wailed as she crawled to the top of the ladder. "Starboard!" she shouted down into the hold.

The boat seemed to lurch and the wave came under the tail and lifted it, pushing the front down. The sea exploded over the bow. Doug was strapped in, but she was not. Somehow he slid toward her and grabbed her as the wave surged upward and over them. She felt the ocean try to tug her away, its liquid fingers grabbing at her hair and clothes, but he held on. The water receded and she gasped for breath. She was still in his arms, both of them coughing, choking, drenched, but still there.

"You okay?"

She began to shiver. She was freezing suddenly. He pulled her close and she surrendered, ducking her wet head into his chest.

"Do you hear that?" he said. "That is my heart beating for you."

She couldn't hear his heartbeat over her chattering teeth.

"I will always keep you safe," he said. "I give you this never: you will never have to wonder where I am. Never go looking for me."

He held her tight, but he was as cold as she was.

"Go down," he said. "Find something dry to put on." He let her go and she stumbled to the hatch.

Joren came up just as she got there.

"Remember," he said to both of them. "It is good to steer us into the wave, not go away from it. At an angle."

"Sorry," she said. She wanted to tell him to shut the fuck up. Fuck you that I was almost washed overboard, that I hate this boat, that I hate this whole thing. Silently she went below.

Down in the hold, Nathan wouldn't stop singing, "Sailing, sailing over the bounding main. Where many a stormy wind shall blow, 'ere I come home again." The only words of the song he knew. He stretched his arms wide taking up more room—all the room. "Sailing, sailing."

She squeezed around him to her bunk. She peeled off the slimy yellow rain jacket. The sleeves clung to her soaking horrible striped sweater. She took it off and her T-shirt underneath was just as wet. Her bag, tucked in the compartment under the bench, was wet on the bottom—the muck on the floor was creeping into the lockers. She pulled the bag out, looked around for somewhere dry to set it down. Nothing was dry. She dug in the bag for a shirt, a clean bra. She turned her back to Nathan to change. Her hair hung cold and damp against her naked back. Her hair band had broken and she needed a new one of those too, but couldn't find one in the bottom of her bag. She refused to cry. If only the sun would come out. If only the boat would stay still for one goddamn minute.

"Over the bounding main. Where many a stormy wind shall—"

"Will you just stop?" She snapped. She turned to face

Nathan, spreading her legs to keep her balance, but staggered, stumbled, and grabbed the counter to hold on. "Damn it."

"Weather's getting worse," he said. "I can feel it in my bones. A real Nor'easter." He hooted. "Could be a hurricane. Waves are already seven to eight feet. Argh." He tried to sound like a pirate. "Blow me down!"

She tried not to cry. Her sweatshirt, Doug's sweatshirt, was the driest thing she had. She reached for it on the hook in the kitchen—galley—and the boat rocked and she fell on her hands and knees in the muck. Nathan bent to help her, his big hand on her thin arm. He squeezed too hard.

"We should turn around," she said.

"Many things we should do. We should run out the sea anchor, steer in an 'S' pattern, bear away from the waves, but it's the Captain's call. He's in charge."

"You're enjoying this."

"I find the whole inexperienced thing exhilarating."

And she saw he did. The worse it got, the happier he seemed. Every time the boat lifted and fell, every time a wave crashed over the bow and set them rolling, he would whoop like a cowboy.

"Yee ha!" He yelled. "We'll see what you're made of! Sugar and spice and everything nice. Snips and snails and puppy dog tails." He shook her arm. "I'm hungry," he said.

"No."

"Me too." Luc peeked through the door from where he was manning the rudder. In the shadows, in the wet, in the constant rocking, he still looked handsome. His lips were swollen from the salt, as were hers, as were everybody's, but she still wanted to kiss him. She wanted him to want to kiss her.

"See? Nathan leaned toward her and his breath was gross

and a piece of his awful hair brushed her face. "Luc is hungry. We're sailors, he and I. Cut from the same cloth. I will be Blackbeard and he can be my first mate, Israel Hands. Aye wench—we need to eat." He looked at Luc with admiration. "Amazing center of gravity, boy. I'd like to see you climb the rigging, dance on a plank, swim in the sea like a mermaid. Merman. Whatever."

She pulled her arm free and put on her sweatshirt.

"No more peanut butter," Nathan said.

But the burner wouldn't light and the milk and eggs slid out of the fridge into the muck before she could catch them. The tomatoes that had been in the fruit bowl were now somewhere smashed under foot. So she made cold cheese sandwiches with soggy bread.

"Sorry," she said as she handed a sandwich to Luc.

"Delish," he said. He leaned his forehead against hers. The diesel smell in Joren's aft cabin made her stomach complain. She tried not to breathe but didn't want to pull away.

"Put on your rain jacket." Nathan tapped her. "We will do our watch together. I'm sure Doug has a headache. A head-astonishing-roaring-ache. His head might possibly explode." He grinned and his teeth were yellow. "All our heads will be aching before this is over."

Joren was slumped on the bench. Nathan thumped on his head. When he looked up his face was green, his red hair wet and dark against his skull.

"Top of the ladder," Nathan said.

Joren got up. He had argued enough.

"I'm supposed to be on deck with Joren," Fiona said.

"Not this time. C'mon," he said. "Now."

She sighed, fastened up her jacket, put up the hood. Luc leaned around the cabin door and blew her a kiss. She caught it. He would remain on the rudder. Doug would move to the bottom.

She followed Nathan up the ladder. Doug looked terrible, obviously relieved they were taking over. He gave her a squeeze as he went past her. She and Nathan strapped themselves into the cockpit. The harness was too big for her, the webbing loose around her waist and falling off her shoulders. Right away, a ten-foot wave came rolling toward them. Nathan did nothing. She waited. She waited. Finally she screamed, "What should I do? What?"

"Port," he said calmly.

"Port," she shouted.

Joren was sitting at the top of the ladder, facing away. He didn't hear her.

"Port!" she tried again. Her voice wasn't loud enough.

Nathan threw his lit cigarette at the back of Joren's head. It hit his shoulder and he spun around. "Port," Nathan said. "Oh. Too late."

The wave hit them. The boat swung wildly at the same time as it rolled up and down—broaching. Fiona thought she would fly out into the sea. She clutched at the wheel, grabbed it with both hands, but—stupid girl—it spun and slammed her, head first, into the deck. She came up and vomited over the side—nothing but salt water. The boat straightened and she huddled down into the cockpit, seeking any shelter she could find.

"I'd like to see your amygdala at this moment, the synapses in the lateral nuclei," Nathan said. "I'd like to know what they're doing right now."

What was he talking about? He just went on and on.

"The problem with studying the brain is that my samples are always dead. A living subject. Now that would be wonderful.

That would get me the Nobel." He slid his hand under her hood, palmed her head like a ball. "If I disconnected your central nuclei, or just jammed it, pushed a scalpel into your amygdala, literally cutting off the power, you would be fearless. Wouldn't you like that? No fear at all." He pushed her hood back. The downpour plastered her hair to her head. "Your perfect round head." He palpated, probed with his fingers. "Your parietal and occipital bones are completely smooth. A phrenologist would have nothing to study."

The rain poured down her neck. She was afraid to move, afraid to tell him to stop. She had no idea what he might do.

14.

To "bring her up" means to face the boat into the wind. "Take her down" means to turn away. The sails will tell you if what you're doing is wrong. They will billow from too much wind or shake and luff from not enough. A telltale is a strip of fabric tied to the sail that conveys both the direction and the power of the wind. The wind is invisible, so Nathan told us to watch the telltale, watch the ripples on the water, watch which way his cigarette smoke blew. Birds take off into the wind. An animal generally faces downwind. You need to know where the wind is coming from. Windward and lee-ward, port and starboard, bow and stern, it is important to know the right words so you can scream them during a storm. It is important to know which wind is your friend, which will help you, and which will kill you. The prevailing winds, the trade winds, the gentle westerlies, and the horse latitudes in between.

Aeolus, the Greek god of wind, gave Odysseus a bag containing three of the four winds: North, East, South. Aeolus sent the West wind to help speed Odysseus and his men on their journey home. All went well and the West wind was happy to comply until Odysseus fell asleep and his sailors opened the bag. The crew thought there was treasure inside. Instead, the other winds escaped and blew in all directions, squabbling with each other and pushing, tossing the boat thousands of miles off course.

I should have noticed which direction Nathan was facing. I should have listened to the wind in his breath, the way he exhaled and sighed. He had a bag of sorrow he couldn't help but open. We were ignorant, trusting, and he was the darkest cloud passing in front of us. His dirty cable knit sweater and preppie pants hid the view. We couldn't see. I couldn't see.

There was a clatter from somewhere below me, then a strange whirring I'd never heard on a plane. I stretched up in my seat to look for the flight attendants. Were they worried? They were nowhere to be found. I was sure they were strapped into their jump seats making final cell phone calls to home. I was convinced bad things were happening to the plane. Disasters do occur. On Christmas Eve, 1971, a plane from Lima, Peru was struck by lightning and blew apart. Ninety-one passengers and crew died, but a seventeen-year-old girl was thrown from the plane, still strapped into her seat. She later told about the silence as she whirled through the air, the view of the lush, green jungle below, and the oddly warm feeling of falling. She fell more than two miles. She should have spattered when she hit the ground, but the jungle canopy slowed her down. She landed hard—still in her chair—but she didn't die. She had a broken collarbone, many cuts and bruises, and her right eye was swollen shut. She was in the middle of nowhere and no one had seen her fall. Fortunately, her father was a scientist in the Amazon and he had taught her things. She found a stream and knew to follow it. She walked downstream, avoiding the crocodiles and watching her cuts become infested with maggots. She had a few pieces of candy in her pocket that she ate. Finally, she found a little hut. She waited there, cleaning her wounds, until the Peruvian workers returned. They brought her to civilization and she was reunited with her father.

The girl, now a woman, said she never wonders why she survived. It was just luck that the tree branches cushioned her fall. Just a coincidence that she had some knowledge about what to do and that she was young and strong. These are the intelligent explanations. But why her? Why did her mother sitting right beside her die? Why was she the only one to live? She has said the why doesn't bother her. It bothers me.

I clutched the armrests, sure that the plane was about to spiral out of the sky, and vowed if I lived I would make amends to Luc. I would do whatever it took to convince him I was sorry. I'd left him and I shouldn't have.

After we returned from the boat and after I went back to school, I slept with a woman, Katy. My first. My only. I wasn't really interested, but she was a kind of offering to Luc. See how brave I am, how adventuresome. Katy was an environmental lawyer with a long, brown braid and tow truck chains in her trunk so she could padlock herself to trees and backhoes. I admired her. The sex was okay, she was industrious in all areas and I liked that there was no comparison between her soft openings and Luc's firmness. I didn't like the yeasty way she smelled. Sometimes a special beer Harry orders at a bar will have that same fermented smell of hops and grain. Too many sprouts, not enough washing.

I called Luc to tell him about Katy. He didn't know who I was at first. Then he wouldn't listen to what I was trying to tell him. So I called Lola. I thought my lesbian affair would please them both, would prove I was one of them. Of course I hoped Katy would make Luc jealous. But Luc seemed too high to care and Lola was angry with me. She was not impressed that I had slept with a woman. It didn't seem courageous or cool to her. To her, it only proved my guilt. I had left him for greener pastures. No, no, no. But the truth is, she was right. I had deserted Luc and gone to bed with a stranger. He told me to go, I said to Lola. So? she asked. So? It had killed me to look at him gray and nodding off in the diner where we'd gone to talk. It had been hard enough to weather his need for people other than me—to watch him flirt and fondle the girls and boys in dance class. When he began to disappear for days with Billy, it wasn't just the sex that bothered me, I didn't know how to compete with the high. When he mumbled, then yelled at me to go back to school, I complied. I always—almost always—did what he told me to do. Of course I begged him to come with me. "We were so happy there." He answered he would never leave New York.

Katy was furious when I said I wouldn't sleep with her again. She yelled at me and told me I was a fool. When would I ever meet another lawyer? She went to work and I took all her carefully organized recycling and threw it jumbled together in the trashcan. Take that. To hell with saving the planet. To hell with you. I called Luc to tell him I'd broken up with Katy and he sounded glad. He made me laugh. When I told him I missed him, I loved him, I had to come back, he said he didn't want to see me. He had moved in with Alison.

Thirty years ago Nathan explained to me that the brain can't tell the difference between physical and emotional pain. The ache of a broken arm is the same—to the brain—as the pain of a broken heart. I could tell Nathan from firsthand experience the heart takes longer to heal. And like a broken bone, it is never quite as strong, never completely whole.

The whirring stopped. The woman beside me snored. Two flight attendants began down the aisle with the drink trolley. I let go of the armrests and thought about the girl who landed in the jungle, now fifty-five-years-old. I suspected she was a nervous traveler too. Lightning actually does strike twice. Her scientist's brain would tell her that. The Weather Channel had a special show on lightning and said it happens all the time. The Empire State Building is struck about twenty-five times a year.

LIFE # 4

"Here, take this." Scott handed me a pill. "Here, drink this." He handed me a bottle of tequila. "Now, smoke this." He handed me a pipe. It tasted funny but I took a deep toke.

I was sixteen, but I looked thirteen until I did myself up in makeup and halter-top and hip huggers that hung so low they nearly showed my pubic hair. My hair was long enough to touch my butt and like every other girl at that time I parted it in the middle and brushed it perfectly straight. I knew the ash blond was unusual. My best feature.

I had driven myself to the party anticipating romance. Scott was so cute. And he seemed glad to see me when I got there. He was a good guy, everybody liked him. He was someone I trusted. He said Angel Dust was the best drug he'd ever done—especially when you cut it with a Quaalude and a cocktail.

I had never been so high. I couldn't judge distances and dropped my drink on the floor instead of putting it on the table. He opened the front door so I could look outside and in one step I was at the mailbox, up the street, on the highway, and back on the couch in the living room. I wanted to say something to him. I could not remember what it was. I wanted to tell him I couldn't remember, but I forgot how to say it. The carpet had a pattern of worms and fishes or tadpoles and rocket ships or roses and kitty cats. I held up my hand, but it wasn't mine. What had happened to my hands? They were both missing and these things on the ends of my arms were too big and heavy to be real. I flopped the mystery hand against my face. I felt nothing. I hit myself harder. My friend laughed. "Isn't this great?" he gurgled. He was swimming through the other partiers. I was mired in the couch. I hit myself again. My face, my legs, my chest. I flailed my arms in all directions. I knocked over the lamp. It fell four hundred feet to the floor. I pressed my finger-not-my-finger into the broken light bulb. I licked the blood and tasted pancakes, or toast, or chicken cacciatore. I chewed the grit, thinking it was meat, and swallowed shards of glass.

"Drink more," Scott said. "You're too high."

I drank a lot. He told me to follow him. I couldn't walk, so I crawled down a hallway to an empty bedroom. There were pink sheets on a little bed, and a doll with such a beautiful face I wanted to cry. I tried to cry. I tried so hard it hurt.

I woke up in the hospital having my stomach pumped. I was still high. My father was there and he kept saying, "This is going to cost a fortune." He pulled gold coins out of his mouth and from behind my ears. "You're a magician," I marveled. "When did you learn to do that?" He shook his head. I didn't see him again until the week before I left for college.

The next day the doctor recommended counseling. "You almost died," he said.

"But I didn't."

15.

The day continued with each of them taking a turn at the helm and yelling directions down the chain to the man at the rudder. Fiona's voice was too soft in the storm, so she was permanently at the top of the ladder, permanently wet. The rain was unceasing and the wind continued to roar, but it didn't get any worse. The engine kept chugging, and Joren kept smiling. "She is working! Still going!"

Fiona didn't want him to jinx it. Each time he said it she knocked on the wooden ladder. She had nothing left in her to vomit, and the dry heaves left her shaky and her throat sore. She concentrated on the least dark patch of sky. There was no sun in any direction, but here and there and now and then she would see a lightening of the clouds, an optimistic glow that helped her breathe.

Joren was at the helm. Luc was taking his turn to sleep. Doug was at her feet. Nathan was sitting on the floor in the aft cabin next to the broken rudder, his ever-present bottle of scotch beside him, waiting for Joren's, then her's, then Doug's commands. Fiona wedged herself between two rungs of the ladder and dozed, her head dropping forward on her chest. Uncomfortable as it was, it felt so good to escape into sleep. In her half-dreams there were trees and solid land and a checkered tablecloth.

Her head thumped against the wood. She opened her eyes. The back of the boat—the stern—was sliding around as if it wanted to be in front, as if they were turning in a circle. The bow was sinking lower and lower. She stood up. Joren had fallen over on the bench, his hood over his face, sound asleep. A wave caught the boat sideways and it heeled over severely. The bow tipped even lower. She was afraid they would go end over end.

"Starboard!" She shouted down the ladder as loudly as she could. "Starboard!" Doug had disappeared. "Starboard!"

"Aye, aye," came faintly from Nathan.

The boat turned abruptly, and she fell against the metal hatch lock and cried out. Joren was startled awake and jumped to his feet. He looked at her, then turned and threw up over the side.

"I have to go to bed," he said.

"You don't have a bed." It had been folded in half to get to the rudder.

"*O mijn god.*" He collapsed into a corner of the cockpit and closed his eyes.

Fiona looked out at the roiling sea. The waves were higher than before. It was raining harder and the wind caught her hood and pushed it back. The enormous sleeves of her slicker flapped. The weather was worse again. Again and again.

"No, Joren." She was afraid to take her eyes from the rising hills of water. "Wake up."

And then there was a high, piercing whine like a motorcycle in the wrong gear. Louder and louder, higher and harder, going up and up and up, straining, screaming. Joren's eyes opened wide. Then two harsh, loud pops like gunshots and the engine quit. The boat stalled. The bow tipped up and the whole thing contorted, the fiberglass wailing. Rain and wind and the screech of the rigging and the flapping of the sails against the mast—even louder without the rumble of the engine—as if the boat was fighting with the sky. Fiona knew the boat would lose. She put her hands over her ears, but it didn't help.

"No. No," Joren said.

The rudder started knocking again in time with the roll. Knock. Knock. Knock. Nathan appeared at the top of the ladder. He spoke to Joren. "Come on. We'll fix it." He sunk below, returning to the rudder. Joren unclipped his safety harness, tried to stand, and immediately turned and threw up overboard again. His eyes were bleary, his face an awful color under his ruddy beard.

The boat was rotating, letting the waves roll it more than ever. Joren went below after Nathan. Fiona didn't know what to do, so she took Joren's place, clipped in alone on deck for the first time. She braced herself as they slipped sideways up a wave, balanced uncertainly for one breath at the top and then fell down the other side, leaning the other way. She knew she should shout some direction, but she didn't know what and there was no one to shout it to—her voice would never carry down below. She was sick again but there was nothing left to come up so she closed her eyes and held on. The strong smell of diesel fumes wafted up through the open hatch. First Doug, then Luc emerged.

"It's dead," Doug said. "They can't fix it."

"It stinks down there," Luc added.

The rudder banged and knocked. Nathan and Joren came up on deck and everyone looked at the darkening sky, the sea the color of iron, the waves rising and growing, the white caps coming faster and faster. Surely it was time to call for help. With a dead engine it had to be time. But Fiona didn't want to be the one to say it. Two days out to sea in a storm that was getting worse, without a rudder or an engine, but she didn't want to look bad, to be the scaredy-cat. She had lived her life without speaking up. She had once failed an assignment because she wouldn't remind the teacher she had turned it in on time. She rode silent and terrified as her mother's boyfriend drove too fast on icy roads while eating a meatball sub and swearing at the tomato sauce spilled on his pants. She took the pill someone handed her, snorted the line, had another drink, because she was more afraid of saying no than of car crashes, bad grades, or tainted drugs. She had none of the traits of a survivor. She was only tenacious because she stayed until everyone else had left, paralyzed by her indecision, stymied by wanting to do what everybody else wanted. She squashed her instinct at every opportunity, ignored her intellect. She always waited for someone else to go first. She knew she should speak up and tell Nathan to call for help. She knew nothing good was ahead of them. In the rain, in the storm, on that boat, she knew it was time to get help. She said nothing.

"Look," Luc said. "There."

In the distance, Fiona saw a large black shape coming toward them, like a rectangular wall rising from the water. For a moment her heart lifted—it was land, a cliff. Then she realized it was a boat, a great big boat, an ocean liner getting closer and closer. Could it be salvation?

"Lights on!" Nathan shouted.

Doug jumped below and the running lights all went on.

"Let's get 'em on the horn," Nathan said. "Tell them we're here."

"Will they run us over?" Fiona's voice was high. She held out a hand to stop the ocean liner.

"They're further away than they look." Nathan rushed below.

She followed him. She wanted to hear another voice, a person who might tell him what she couldn't. Turn around, that other captain would say. Go back. Or maybe the ship would offer to pick them up, throw down a ladder and tell them to leave the broken *Bleiz A Mor* behind. The captain of an ocean liner had to be someone even Nathan would listen to.

"This is the *Bleiz A Mor*. Come in." Nathan spoke into the radio microphone. There was static, then nothing. "This is the Bleiz A Mor. Sailboat on your starboard side. On route to Bermuda. Come in?" No response. He handed the microphone to her. "Maybe they'll respond to your little girly voice."

"Hello," she said. "This is the Bleiz A Mor. Anybody there? Hello?"

She tried over and over, eventually begging them to respond. There was static, then not even that. Through the porthole above the radio she watched the liner pass them, massive and black, the windows high up in a yellow row along the side. A wall she couldn't scale. Their little sailboat was in another dimension, a chasm of invisibility. Maybe their boat had been destroyed in the storm, sunk to the bottom. They were already dead and this was hell. The Flying Dutchman times five.

Diesel fumes or no, she took off her foul weather gear, went to her bunk and lay down. She pushed her face into the pillow. She heard Doug begin to scream at Nathan, why didn't he check the radio, why didn't he fix the engine, what was that piece of black plastic he threw overboard? She heard Nathan's rumbling reply, and Doug's voice louder, shriller, demanding. Luc bent down beside her. He put his hand on her back. She heard him speaking to her. She didn't answer.

16.

In October 2005, four Mexican fishermen set off to catch shark in their panga, a small fiberglass fishing boat. They were experienced and the bad weather that came up was not unusual. Nine months later, three were found adrift five thousand miles from home. The captain was gone. The sailors said they prayed over him when he was sick, then prayed more over his dead body and threw him overboard. Some people say the fishermen killed and ate their captain as punishment for their predicament. Other people say that Captain Juan never existed. It is impossible to say for sure, no record was made when the boat left San Blas for a standard three day fishing trip; no evidence of the Captain was found when the small boat was spotted and the others were rescued. They had no reason to lie and pretend another man was there who wasn't. Unless they needed someone to blame. The engine gave out. No one had a radio or a cell phone. The weather was bad. But they had been fishing in these same waters for years. They drank rainwater collected in a bait bucket. They ate raw sea turtles, fish, and birds. And they made deals with God their savior, "I'll quit drinking," and "I'll treat my wife better," and "I'll do something more important with my life."

One month after their return, two of the men were drinking again. One marriage had ended. Only one of the men had given up fishing, but he could find no other work. Did they still feel blessed? Did they regret the promises they'd made? Did they berate themselves for the changes they hadn't made?

The night before I left, I tried to tell this story to Harry. "Harry," I said. "I have a story for you."

"Weather channel?" he said. "I'm not interested."

"I read it in *The New Yorker*. Four men were lost at sea. Fishermen."

"I don't know why you're so interested in this stuff."

"Three survived. One didn't. Why did that one not make it? Now the other three are home and safe, but life isn't what it was."

"Stop. Don't say anything else. I've heard enough."

I was quiet. I looked out the kitchen window.

"All right," he said. "Go ahead."

"Never mind."

"Please."

So I told him about the men and fishing and being lost and the deals they made with God. I thought it would help him. I told him there is no better thing a man can do with his life than survive.

17.

Without an engine and with everybody exhausted and yelling directions too slowly, the boat rocked and tipped sharply from side to side. Doug said they were leaning at eighty-five degrees, steeper than a roller coaster's first drop. Slam! They rocked one way. Bam! They rocked the other.

The constant cacophony of wind and rain and flapping sails and pots and pans and silverware and food and equipment crashing together and breaking against the wood was almost more than Fiona could stand. It was her turn to sleep and she lay in the bunk holding on as best she could. "Port!" would come the shout. Or "Starboard!" It hardly seemed to make any difference. The thrashing didn't let up. She felt the ocean pressing against the hull, making the wood and fiberglass whine and vibrate, as if the angry water would twist them open like a can of Pop N Fresh biscuits. Nathan was on the radio, trying to get anyone to tell them where they were. His charts, the compass, the navigational instruments were making him angry. He pounded his fists on the desk. She watched as he broke a pencil and threw the pieces in the slop at his feet.

A wave hit them hard and ice cold seawater poured through the open hatch. It was almost her watch. She was so tired and at the same time she couldn't sleep; she was tingling as if electricity ran through her veins instead of blood. Once more she put on her slick, wet gear, her trembling fingers fumbling with the clasps, too worn out to roll the sleeves, and slowly climbed the ladder. She looked out on deck and gasped. The sea had become a world of endless black mountains, each tall enough to obscure all but the ceiling of the stormy sky. The wind blew the white caps right off, sending the spray and foam splashing down on deck. Luc was huddled in the corner. He looked at her and grinned. She loved him for that.

"It'll be morning soon," she yelled. Maybe even a morning with sun. "Right?"

"Soon," he agreed. "Better."

She prodded him. "Go down. Rest. It's my watch."

"I'll stay with you."

"You should sleep."

He unclipped his harness and stood up to kiss her and their wet faces slid against each other. They tried again. Bang! A massive wave crashed against the side. Luc stumbled. Fiona reached for him, but slipped on the wet deck, fell and hit her head hard on the edge of the cockpit. The boat rocked back and Luc helped her to her feet. His eyes widened.

"Oh God."

She touched her forehead and her fingers came away covered in blood, the red mixing with the rain and seawater, dripping down her palms. She swayed, woozy in a new way. Her eyes wanted to close. She wanted to lie down.

"Don't faint." Luc said. "Stay with me." He had both hands on her shoulders. "Nathan!" He shouted. "Nathan! Help me."

Nathan came half way up the ladder. He reached out and grabbed Fiona under one shoulder and yanked her to him. He half carried her down the ladder into the cabin and stood her up to face him. He shook her. Harder. Then he slapped her. Her eyes fluttered open. "Jesus Christ," he said. The blood was running down her face. "Don't worry. Head wounds bleed a lot." He grabbed a pillow floating in the sludge and pressed the drier side to her cut. "Sit down."

Doug helped her onto the bunk.

"A sailor's life for me!" Nathan sang. He splashed his feet in the water and muck. "Man the bilge!"

Doug seemed to know what that meant. He went to a covered switch Fiona hadn't noticed before, opened it and turned it on. She heard a sucking sound. A pump. Why hadn't they turned it on before? What day was it? What time? It could have been the middle of the night. Every light was blazing, as if being able to see the broken cabinets and all their ghostly faces would be a comfort.

"Hey," Luc shouted from deck. "Starboard."

Nathan shouted to Joren. She heard him curse. The boat tilted back, the bow going up and up, climbing what had to be a wave as large as a mountain. Doug sat down hard beside her. The boat stalled and hovered at the top as if deciding which direction to fall, back or forward. Her head throbbed. She grabbed Doug's leg. He smiled, but she couldn't help that. She held her breath, sure the boat would flip over like a bug onto its back. Her head. Her head. Then, slowly, creaking and moaning, the boat wobbled forward and slid down, down, down the other side of the wave.

Doug sighed in relief. She let go of his leg, but he took her hand.

"I'll go," she said. "It's my watch."

"You're hurt."

"I'm okay now."

She got up, took the pillow away to see if she was still

bleeding and at that exact moment the bilge pump stopped and all the lights went out. She put the pillow back—absurdly thinking maybe the lights would return. Of course not. The boat rocked sideways and she fell. She heard Joren's high-pitched voice, "*Heilig schijt!*". She was wedged between the table leg and the bench with her yellow rubber-covered ass in the muck. Not a bad place to be so she stayed there, waiting, listening as the others flailed around in the dark. Something else shattered. She hadn't thought there was anything left to break—then she smelled the alcohol. Another of the giant jugs of booze. More glass under their feet. In the dark.

"We have to have light." It was Nathan. "A ship will run us over."

There were no flashlights, or if they existed, no one knew where they were. Fiona found herself making a list in her head for her next ocean voyage: plastic cups and dishes, flash-lights, tall rubber boots, a working radio. As if she'd ever sail again. Cups, dishes, lights, boots, radio. Cups, dishes, lights, boots, radio. She made it a chant, a song, a desperate prayer to have done it all differently.

The boat continued to rock. Luc was still on deck. Alone. She heard him shout, "What's going on?" and he sounded shrill but upbeat, a kid at the amusement park. She struggled to her feet, bracing herself against the constant pitching. She would feel better beside him.

A light flashed on—blue and chilling.

"See?" Nathan said. "See? Preparations were made."

It was amazing he had, and could, find an emergency lantern. Thank God, she thought. Then it blinked. And continued blinking.

"Make it stop." Doug reached for the lantern. "There must be a switch."

"It's a strobe light. It's all we've got." Nathan held the lantern out of Doug's reach like a mean father holding a toy away from a toddler.

Joren struggled to the electric panel and opened it. He fiddled with the switches, looked at the wires, stopping and starting with the flashing light. Her head hurt worse and the nausea began to bubble up again. He would either fix it or he wouldn't, but she couldn't stay down below to watch. She pushed her way to the ladder and went up.

Luc opened his arms for her. She clipped herself in beside him. "No lights," she said.

"No kidding," he replied. "We are naught but flotsam in the sea."

She had read about flotsam in the Harbormaster's office. There had been a display—a wooden barrel, some other stuff mounted on the wall. Her trip to get the weather report seemed a hundred years ago, not two days.

"Flotsam and jetsam are different." She put her mouth against Luc's ear so he could hear her. "Flotsam means the broken bits of a boat floating in the water. Jetsam is stuff thrown overboard to lighten the load during a storm."

"Who would we throw?" Luc asked. "You're too small to be jetsam. Wouldn't help much."

"Let's go home," she said as she rocked against him and rocked away. "I want to go home." Against and away—with every wave. Not home to Lola's apartment. And not to the damp basement rooms they had shared at college. She wanted home. Home sweet home. Home on the range. A place to hang her hat, to rest by the hearth, to lay her weary head. She didn't know where that was, but she remembered a fairytale illustration of a room with a roaring fire, gently curving furniture, little blond heads on white pillows under a quilt of hearts and birds. A picture from a book she had loved as a child. She had put it under her blanket and slept beside it. She had pretended it was her house, her fire, her head on the pillow. Everything a home should be.

Joren came up carrying the strobe light. Immediately Luc performed, making faces and silly poses in the blinking light, like a character from a silent movie. Fiona applauded.

"We must tie this to the mast," Joren shouted over the wind. "So others will see us. Luc. Help."

There were only two harnesses, so she took hers off and gave it to Joren. She wrapped her arm through the railing, holding on tight. Joren and Luc clipped onto the lifeline that ran around the deck. They moved sideways on their hands and knees toward the main mast. Unbelievable, she thought. The boat tipped and they were head down. It teetered the other way and they dug in with their toes. The surface was sandpaper rough to give them traction, but she saw— intermittently, in the winking light—first Joren and then Luc slip and grab for anything. She gasped as Luc fell, one foot coming close to the sea. Joren yanked him back. They reached the mast. It took both of them to arrange the ropes and tie the light on and pull it up to the top. Somehow the strobe stayed up there. Like raising a flag, she thought, their true colors were beckoning, flashing for help. Luc and Joren waited for a calmer moment and scrambled slowly back to her.

"I go to rest." Joren went back down.

Fiona put her harness on again even though she knew if she went in the water—with a lifeline or not—she would never get back into the boat. She would drown. The sea was too cold, too deep, and she was too tired to fight.

"We should have made an offering to Poseidon," Luc said. "God of the sea. I think he's pissed off."

"We've given him our sanity," she said. "What else does he want?"

Luc pulled her close. "To hell with Poseidon."

"Right." She pressed against him. His arm was warm around her. Every wave that curled over the side was like a hand reaching for her, trying to pull her in. She had no illusions that Luc could save her—not against this ocean. She just wanted as much time with him as she could get.

"No rudder, no engine, no lights. Big storm." Luc hummed it. "That's your kind of chant. No rudder, no engine, no lights. Big storm."

She added, "Cups, dishes, lights, boots, radio. Cups, dishes, lights, boots, radio."

He touched the cut on her forehead, kissed it like a mother would. She kissed his salty cheek, licked her lips, kissed him again. "What else can possibly happen?" she asked. "What else?"

"Nothing. Smooth sailing from here on out."

LIFE # 5

The summer before I left for college, I got a job in an art gallery framing pictures. The money was much better than waitressing and I loved the job, cutting mats and glass, seeing the treasures the clients brought in. We framed wedding pictures and kids' drawings and artwork done by Grandpa. I didn't know then I would end up framing my way through school majoring in Art History—then I thought I was a dancer—but it makes sense now.

On this particular day, I was working in the shop alone—as usual—and I was out front measuring a large antique batik. I had it stretched on the floor in the gallery because it was too big for the counter in the back. I was on my knees and I looked up as a man walked in wearing sunglasses. His white painter's pants had filthy brown smudges around the pockets as if his hands were never clean. His hair stuck out in clumps on one side. My first instinct was to run past him to the front door. But I didn't want to be impolite. I knew I could get by him, but I might hurt his feelings. I might be wrong about him so I stayed where I was. He came toward me. He kept coming and walked right over the fabric. There was plenty of room to go around, but he came up to me and pulled out a gun.

"Get up," he said. "Get in back."

Irrationally, I was worried about the artwork. I didn't want him to step on it again. I started to pull it aside. "Now," he shouted. I jumped to my feet and put my hands up like I'd seen on TV.

"Put your hands down," he said. Anybody walking by could have seen us through the storefront windows. "In back."

I walked around the front counter and into the back room where we did most of the framing. There were glass cutters and mat knives. Two by fours. Sheets of glass in various sizes. There were weapons, but I didn't think of using any of them. He had a gun. I'd never seen one before. I reached to turn on the light over the worktable.

"No," he said. "Don't. Lie down on your front." I still had my back to him. "Wait. First, undo your pants." The floor was dirty with scraps of wood and paper, and bits of glass. I didn't want to lie down. I hesitated. "Do it," he said. "You have a nice ass. Don't worry. This will be fun." He poked me in the back with his gun.

My bladder released. Pee spilled down my pants leg and soaked my socks. A strong scent of urine blossomed.

"Oh man," he said. "Oh fuck."

"I'm sorry." I knew I would die. He would shoot me for this. He couldn't rape me now.

"Bitch," he said. "Turn around. We'll do this."

I turned to face him, but kept my head lowered. I watched his hands, the nails dirty, the knuckles dry and covered in scabs, as he unzipped his pants. He reached in and pulled out his penis. At first I thought it was deformed, wrong somehow, but it was uncircumcised. It looked like a mushroom gone bad, wrinkled and brown.

"On your knees," he said. "Do it."

I sank to my knees. I heard cars going by out front, people

on their way to work or lunch or the movies. Just another day.

"Do it," he breathed. He grabbed my head with one hand and pulled me toward his weird dick, now standing up and pointing at me. "Open your mouth or I will kill you." I closed my eyes. I touched my lips to the tip. "Open!"

Just then the bell on the front door chimed and Lydia, the boss, entered. "Hello?" She called my name. "I forgot something," she said as she headed toward the back.

I looked up at the man's face for the first time. His brown eyes were wide, and I could see the whites all the way around. He had a rash on the sides of his nose, dry flaky skin like on his hands. He looked over my head for another way out. He pushed me back and zipped up. Lydia kept coming. I saw her frowning as she saw me on my knees and the back of the man. Her nose wrinkled at the smell. "What the..." she began.

The man turned and ran past her and out the front door. Lydia said she never saw the gun, but she saw me and the damp leg of my green corduroy pants. He left and I was so scared I couldn't cry. I couldn't speak. She helped me to my feet and called the police. They were there in moments. They knew the guy. He'd been doing this around town, and in every place a woman had been working alone. It wasn't about money, the detective said. He always raped and killed the woman.

In another month I left to go to school. Fifteen months later I was at sea.

18.

"Captain's log, star date 11-7-79. To boldly go where no man has gone before." Nathan chuckled as he held on to the high wooden navigation station with his logbook open. He had a pen in his hand, but Fiona wondered how he could write with the boat tossing and bucking.

A sloshing noise had joined the banging and breaking. Water and sewage were more than a foot deep in the bottom of the boat. With the hatch open and the bilge pump not working, the sludge was getting deeper and deeper. The boat stank to high heaven—another of her mother's favorite phrases.

Nathan took a deep and theatrical snort in and exhaled noisily. "Do you know what fear smells like?" he asked. "I can smell it on my patients—that sweet and salty tang. I smell it now on all of you." His voice got mincing, a falsetto. "Doc, am I going to die? Please, Doc, tell me." He tittered.

She tried to ignore him. Joren came down the ladder from up on deck, muttering angrily to himself in Dutch. He banged the wall. He banged again.

"Easy," Nathan said. "The blood is rushing to your frontal lobe. If you don't relax, you'll stop punching the wall and hit a person." He gestured at Doug. "If you're going to hit someone, just make sure it's Doug."

Doug was sitting at the table, his face as cloudy as the sky outside. He had been adamant that they keep trying to reach someone on the radio. Nathan had shrugged and told him to go ahead, but twenty minutes of Doug's incessant, "This is the Bleiz A Mor, come in?" had driven everybody insane, until Nathan finally shouted "shut up" and grabbed the mic. The radio was obviously not working—another ocean liner had passed with no response.

"Starboard," Luc shouted from deck.

Doug and Joren both rushed to the rudder, bumping into each other, neither getting through the door. Joren pushed Doug away. Nathan laughed out loud. The boat tipped up— Joren got to the rudder too late—and through the open hatch Fiona could see the sky was a tiny bit lighter. Day Three. Sunshine ahead.

"Look," she said. "The sun."

Nathan sighed. "How disappointing. We will cross the Gulf Stream and all will be well. Warm. Mild. Our Captain will fix the rudder. So depressing. Where's the battle in that?"

"We have no engine, no lights, no power," Doug said. "The radio doesn't work. The compass is out of whack. That's enough of a battle."

"Small skirmishes," Nathan said. "Salvos over the bow! All part of the plan. I knew the engine would go some time during the trip. Makes things exciting!"

"What plan?" Fiona asked quietly. "What plan?"

Nathan turned to her. "Fridge full of food about to spoil with no electricity. Better wrassle me up something to eat."

She stood cautiously. Her head hurt now as much as her stomach. She hadn't eaten in three days. Worse, she'd had no water. Her brain was functioning almost as badly as the boat. They were all going a little crazy. She fingered her cut. Years from now, she would still be fingering the scar.

"What plan?" she asked Nathan again. He'd been charming in New York and in Newport before they left, but she was beginning to think he had reeled them all in. Part of his plan.

"Now, now. Let me see your forehead." Nathan pulled her to him as the boat rocked up and landed hard. "Boom! 'I swam/ In the blackness of night, hunting monsters/ Out of the ocean, and killing them one/ By one; death was my errand and the fate/They had earned.' Ha! Beowulf. Bet you didn't know that one." She tried to shrug out of his grasp, but he had her tight. "You're not bleeding anymore," he said. "You won't have much of a scar. Just something to remember me by. Get me something to eat. A tuna fish sandwich."

She didn't move.

"I pay you to fucking feed me," he said. "I can leave you in Bermuda." He leered at her. "Or before."

She bowed her head and staggered to the galley, splashing through the vomit and alcohol and smashed fruit filled water.

Doug stared at Nathan.

"What?" Nathan asked as he leaned on the table with both hands. "I forgot to ask you, Birdman: do you believe in God?"

"If the devil proves the existence of God, then yes, I do."

"And you have seen the devil?" Nathan goaded him.

"I'm looking right at him."

Nathan laughed and turned back to his logbook. Fiona spoke to Doug. "Are you okay?"

"I must be vigilant," he said. "Look at him. Look."

She walked over and put her hand on his forehead. He grabbed it and held it there.

"Don't move." He squeezed his eyes shut. "When I stayed home from school my mother would stroke my forehead. She would put a cold cloth over my eyes."

"Do you want another pill?" Nathan asked.

"Take one," she said. "It'll make you feel better."

"I can't. I have to remain alert. I have to keep you safe."

"Feeling a little disoriented?" Nathan chattered. "Paranoid, perhaps? Poor Birdman, do you think the world is against you?"

"I should have spoken to the Harbormaster before we left. I should have told him about you. You want us to sink."

He wasn't making sense. If Nathan wanted to destroy the ship, it meant Nathan would die too. Doug turned his face up to the rectangle of sky visible through the open hatch. The rain continued, but more softly. He opened his mouth for the drops.

"I am a little bird."

She leaned closer to hear what he was saying.

"A black-headed grosbeak."

Nathan chuckled. Doug grabbed Fiona and pointed. The strobe light flashed and cut Nathan's face in half, obscuring his eyes but illuminating his teeth. In the strange, intermittent light, they looked pointed.

"D…D…Devil." Doug hissed.

"Hard to starboard," came Luc's shout from above.

Nathan jumped to the back cabin to yell at Joren. "Hard to starboard." The boat listed heavily, then slowly turned. It rode the big wave gently.

"Did I do it right, Birdman?" Nathan asked as he came back into the room. "Were you watching?" He stretched a hand out. His fingernails were long and filthy.

"Don't touch me." Doug scooted back as far as he could.

Fiona found the tuna and the can opener. She opened the can and and gagged. The smell was overpowering. She dumped it into the last remaining bowl and offered it to Nathan. " I forgot to buy mayonnaise."

"Where's the bread?"

"Wet."

"Crackers?"

"Gone."

"What am I going to do with you?" Nathan's voice was tight and nasty. He took the bowl from her hands and buried his face in it, eating like a dog. He made disgusting gobbling noises.

"Oh God." She groaned and held her stomach.

Doug stood, grabbed the bowl from Nathan's hands and, in one movement, threw it through the open hatch and overboard.

She heard Luc. "What the hell?" and then his high, whooping laugh. "Bowl overboard!"

"He's not allowed to hurt you," Doug said to her.

"Fine." Nathan wiped his face with his hands. "Bunch of babies. I have my own food." He stomped into his cabin and shut the door.

"I knew he had food in there," she said. "He comes out licking his lips."

"He cannot upset you. I will not allow it."

Joren came from his cabin holding a long broken board. He stared at it as if he could not believe he held it in his hands.

"What is it?"

"The rudder. She has broken more. Off. Broken badly. There is no way to control it."

She couldn't understand him; she didn't know what he meant.

"The handle. The tiller we made." He held up the piece of wood. "She is gone, broken off forever." Joren looked up to the ceiling and prayed. "*O God ons helpen.*"

The rudder had cracked and broken free of the makeshift tiller. There was no way to hold on and steer, everything but a tiny bit of pipe was gone.

Nathan came out of his cabin. He and Joren didn't even argue. The only thing to do was tie the remaining piece immobile so it didn't knock a hole in the hull. Steering was impossible. There was no reason to shout anymore, no port or starboard. Nothing to do but wait for the weather to break.

"A wave will tip us over," Fiona said.

"The boat is made to stay upright." But Joren didn't sound convinced. "We will float."

The strobe blinked on and off incessantly. Doug picked up the radio mic to call for help again, then put it down. Luc stayed on deck for no reason except it smelled better. Joren put his bed back together and closed his door to sleep. Nathan retreated to his cabin and Doug told Fiona he would watch over her. She was so tired. She knew she should go up and sit with Luc, but her head ached and her stomach lurched and gurgled. They were like dolls in a bathtub toy and she was sure they were heading for the drain.

"Lie down," Doug said to her. "Conserve your strength."

She nodded and curled onto her bunk.

She woke and knew she had slept for a while. Doug was asleep too, sitting up, wedged in the opposite corner. Between flashes from the strobe, it was even darker than it had been before. She hoped the night had almost passed. She hoped it was another day and they were almost there—somewhere. She reached for Luc, but he wasn't beside her. The hammering of the rain, the screech of the boat, the steady smash of gear and broken equipment had become a drone. Beyond it, she could hear Luc talking. Laughing even. She scooted to the very edge of the bunk and looked up the ladder through the open hatch and saw him strapped in his harness behind the wheel.

Who was he talking to? Someone sat beside him. Doug was asleep across from her, his face white and then black in the flashing light. The person was too slender to be Nathan and protruding from the yellow hood she could see a smooth jaw, no beard, so it couldn't be Joren. But then who? Luc looked at this person with such love, such utter sad and wonderful love. She saw a strong straight nose—just like Luc's. Then the person turned toward her, and she gasped. It was Luc's younger brother, Leander. He had died in a motorcycle accident before she met Luc, but she'd seen his picture many times—Luc carried one in his wallet, Lola had two in her apartment. Here he was, talking to Luc and she watched Luc reach for him, touch him, grab his shoulder and squeeze. If there was one person Luc would want to be with him at his darkest moment, it was Leander. That was when she knew they were going to die. She called to Luc and he didn't answer. Maybe they were dead already.

"Luc!" She screamed. "Luc!"

She had to be with him. She started up the stairs. Her foot slipped off a rung and she fell, banging her knee hard on the step. When she looked up again, Leander was gone and Luc was slumped with his head hanging forward. Her knee throbbed, proving she wasn't dead, but Luc was. She was sure he had died. She ran up the ladder and leapt at him. Her hands slipped over his wet suit and she cupped his face. His eyes opened.

"What? What is it?"

She was sobbing. She held on as tightly as she could.

"I was sleeping," he said. "What happened?"

"I saw your brother. I saw Leander sitting here. He was sitting here with you. Right here."

He gave a wistful smile. "You were dreaming. Oh God, I wish you weren't. Really? Oh, sweet Io."

"I knew we were dead. I knew it."

"Still here. Still on this fucking boat."

They tried to kiss in the storm but it was almost impossible to keep their lips joined as the boat thrashed. They knocked heads and shoulders. It was dangerous to be so close. She heard the wind calling to them, "Noooo mooore, noooo moooore." From the corner of her eye, she saw Leander leap behind the mast.

19.

I woke up on the plane choking and coughing. I was drowning, sure that my lungs were full of water. I had to touch the seats, the window, to reassure myself I was someplace dry. The drowning dream used to happen a lot. Harry would roll over—when he slept beside me—and tell me to breathe. Take the next breath. And the next.

When I remember the boat, it's in black and white, the color drained away. There was never enough light, the constant gloom made the orange plaid benches into squares of gray, Joren's red sweater an old, dried bloodstain, the whitewashed ceiling disappear into dim clouds. The cabin had no definition, no angles or depth. Everything muted, coated in flannel and Cimmerian. Homer wrote about the Cimmerians in the *Odyssey*. They live at the opening to Hades in perpetual murky darkness. My trip to sea had been Cimmerian, both dark and a doorway to Hell. It should have been no surprise when Luc's brother appeared. When I saw monsters swimming outside the portholes. When Doug turned to me and his eyes were gone and he had no bones, just a glowing disc of face. Anything could happen. No food, nothing to drink for four days. I'd been seasick since we left port and thrown up countless times. It is no wonder I hallucinated. Sailors saw mermaids and sea serpents after being too long at sea. They spoke of ghost ships passing in the night. My boyfriend's dead brother was a rather reasonable response to dehydration and fear. That girl on the boat, my younger self, was afraid of the water, afraid to die panicking and unable to breathe. She would thrash and scream and the sharks would come. Biting, tearing at her. One rip into the soft flesh of her stomach and her blood would cloud the water. There would be a frenzy. She wondered at what point it would stop hurting.

I wonder that still. I am still afraid of drowning. On the plane, somewhere over Kansas or Missouri, I took a deep breath. I told myself to breathe, to take the next breath and the next. On that plane, just as on that boat, I could hear Odysseus' vicious, seductive sirens singing their promises. They would give me peace and wisdom, answers to all my questions, if I would just surrender.

According to myth, the sirens were Persephone's companions. When Hades abducted her and made her his wife in the Underworld, her mother, Demeter, cursed the sirens for failing to protect poor Persephone. I imagine they sang the usual excuse—"not our job." They are an indolent bunch, often depicted as lolling about amongst the bones and skulls of their prey or sitting on rocks singing and playing the lute while young men drown at their feet. Now, I was cancerous and filled with regret and primed to give in. Ready for the answer to how I ended up here.

We never travel far from our younger selves. The bullied boy who becomes the successful CEO, or the fat girl without a date to the prom who starts a vegan yoga studio—they're just continuing to compensate. He is still that kid hiding in the washroom and she that girl with candy bars under the bed. I was a good educator at the Getty, but I wasn't firm with the students. I never spoke up to my boss about shifts or breaks or even parking. Inside I was the same girl who went along, never said no, was afraid to rock the boat. That is who I am. Who I will always be.

To land in Providence we had to circle out over the ocean. When I saw the water below me, I started to cry. The sharks were nibbling on my body. The sirens had no solutions. I did not want to die of cancer. I had spent my life wanting to be someone I wasn't, wanting to be different than I am. I wanted to be the girl, the woman that had saved Luc. The girl that never left but stood by him, helped him, was strong and brave. I wasn't that girl, but maybe this time I could be. And then Luc would love me.

20.

Fiona's thoughts went round and round, trying to understand the separate pieces of the storm. Rain wasn't this noisy at home. Even when there wasn't any thunder and lightning, this storm was deafening. She couldn't hear herself think; she couldn't talk to Luc lying in the bunk beside her. The boat shrieked, the wooden boards squealed as they twisted against the screws or whatever held them in place. The wind seemed to come from all directions, howling, "Go. Go. Go. Go awaaaaaay."

Luc was asleep and she should have been. She rolled over in the bunk and pressed her face to the porthole. There was nothing to see, the porthole was either underwater or barely above it depending on which way the boat was leaning. Then she saw a flicker of movement. A glimmer of lighter color. She wiped the glass. It was a man. He was swimming toward her, wearing a suit and tie. Another boat must be nearby! He would save them. She shook Luc.

"There's a man in the water. He's come for us."

The strobe light flashed and she saw Luc's face gray and solid, more marble statue than living boy. She rolled back to the window.

"Everybody." She thought she was shouting. "There's a man out there."

The man was looking at her. His striped tie floated up over his shoulder like a businessman avoiding soup stains at lunch. She nodded at him. I'm coming, she mouthed. I'll come to you. She climbed over Luc to get out of the bunk to go up on deck. She would jump into the water with the man. He would take her to his boat. She started pulling on her yellow pants.

Luc put out a hand. "Where are you going?"

"I have to go. He's waiting," she said. "He's come to save us."

"You're hallucinating again."

"He's right there."

She had her yellow pants on. Her striped sweater—that goddamn sweater—was fused to her body, damp and horribly smelly. Everything was damp. The man's boat would be dry.

"Look outside," she said to Luc. She turned to the porthole, knocked on it. "We're here," she said, "I'm so glad you've come." But she couldn't see the man anymore and instead an enormous fish with spiky teeth and four gelatinous eyes stared in at her, and she saw giant luminescent worms wiggling through the water, and slimy blobs with long floating tentacles. They were all right outside the boat. She pushed herself away.

She had dropped acid more than once and hallucinated spiders in the sugar bowl, an undulating carpet. She had seen her best friend's tongue stretch to five feet long and her apartment window open by itself. She had seen the sounds from outside as if they were colors. A red stripe of siren. Green diamonds of dog barking. Those were hallucinations. But she knew Leander had visited and she knew the creatures in the water were waiting for the boat to go down. She knew the businessman really had come to save them. She had to get to him before he disappeared for good. "I'm coming," she said.

"I'm coming."

There was a terrible commotion in the water outside the porthole. The horrible fish were eating something. Please not her businessman. How could he save her without hands or arms? She had to get on deck. It took all her strength to put her pants on and slog the few steps to the ladder. She put her hands on the railings. Lifting her legs and climbing the five rungs to the deck seemed impossible.

"Come back to bed." Luc sat up. "Where are you going?"

She turned, but it was Doug's eyes she saw, Doug watching her, his face white and swollen in the flash of the strobe light. She saw him. Then she didn't. Then she did. Then he was gone and she was alone. Then he was back. Doug had seen the same things she had. He shook his head. "Too late," he whispered. "Too late. The man is dead."

She sat down on the bunk. Nowhere to go.

21.

Standing at the car rental counter, I kept looking over my shoulder. It was after five and quickly growing dark under cloudy skies. I didn't know if Luc was flying into this airport or Boston. I was supposed to meet him at nine at the hotel. If he showed up.

My rental car was small and smelled like industrial cleaner and air freshener. It was easy to drive. I wound my way out of the airport. I-95 was well marked, the merge onto the interstate easy. I leaned forward in my seat with anticipation. I turned on the radio. NPR was talking about the Beauty Parlor Bomber. I switched to Top 40 and sang along. My stomach flipped and flopped; my hands wouldn't stay still on the steering wheel. Now that I was so close, I was almost frantic to be there. On the list of Ten Traits of Survivors this was number five: Purpose. I had a purpose. With Luc I would find some glimpse of the girl I was before I survived.

My phone rang. Harry. I had meant to call him when I landed, but I'd left him far behind on the couch in Los Angeles. "Sorry," was the first thing I said.

"When were you going to tell me?" His voice was quiet.

I couldn't speak. I pulled over to the side of the road. I was afraid to drive. "I…" There was nothing I could say. I resorted to cliché. "It doesn't mean what you think it means."

"What does cancer mean?"

He was talking about cancer. Relief ran through me. I exhaled. I let go of the steering wheel. "I guess Carolyn called."

"She thought I knew. I felt like a fucking idiot. Thanks a lot."

"I'm sorry."

"Were you ever going to tell me?"

"Of course."

Was I? Yes, of course I was, in due course—another nautical phrase. It wasn't that I thought the cancer would go away by itself. I knew doing nothing meant I would eventually be scuttled (sunk intentionally) so I was going to call the oncologist, I was, but I just wanted to put it off for a while, turn a blind eye (thank you, Admiral) for the weekend at least.

Harry was still talking. Ranting at me. "Are you listening? Oh for fuck's sake. She said you haven't even called the oncologist yet."

I heard him sniff. I thought maybe, horribly, he was crying, but I felt an odd sort of glee. I was so glad he hadn't found out about Luc. Cancer was nothing. I apologized again and again.

"Jesus Christ."

"I'll call the doctor. I was worried about our insurance." I thought that would appease him, me being practical, careful with our money.

"Fuck the insurance. You'll get the best doctor in Los Angeles. I don't care what it costs."

"We'll see—you know our insurance."

"You will have the best. Oh, Fiona. What about Jack? Huh? Were you just going to give up and leave our son?"

"Of course not." Jack was a low blow. "I just didn't want to worry you."

"That's my job. I'm your husband. I love you."

The words lay between us. I told him I loved him too. I did. He did. But our love was like barnacles, crusty and erosive, nothing edible inside our impermeable shells. We hung on our dark wet pilings, the rotting wood of our lives. Too stuck to let go.

"I'm sorry," I said again.

"You should have told me."

"You were waiting to hear from the journal."

"Don't blame this on me." He got angry and I relaxed, his yelling familiar and reassuring. "Don't make this about me. Don't turn this around. This is your bad. Your mistake. All you."

"I'm driving. Harry. We'll talk about it when I get back."

"I want to talk about it now."

"It's against the law here to drive and talk on the phone."

"You're from California."

"It's illegal there too."

I promised to call him from the hotel. I dropped the phone on the passenger seat, then pushed it to the floor where I couldn't reach it.

I exited on Route 4 just as I was supposed to and all was well for a while. But I got lost. The sun went down, the two lane road was dark, the streetlamps at first far apart and then nonexistent. The road was winding with nothing on either side except trees, black and bare and scratching against the navy sky. For a long, long time there were no other cars and no route signs, no posted miles to the nearest town. No town. It had been twenty minutes, twenty-five, more. I was sure I had missed my next turn onto 138.

A smaller road went off to the left, and I took it thinking it would lead to a gas station or something. Nothing. More darkness. And then through the trees I saw water to my right. It didn't seem possible I had reached Narragansett Bay already, but if I had and it was over there then I was heading north, away from Newport.

I was panting. My heart drummed and my nose got hot and my eyes filled. I had plenty of gas. I had a cell phone. My fear was irrational, some small part of me knew that and then forgot it. I could turn around, go back the way I came all the way to the airport. But I was lost. I was in the middle of nowhere in a small flimsy capsule and no one knew where I was. I hadn't seen headlights coming toward me since I left the highway. I leaned dangerously sideways and dipped below the dashboard, left hand on the wheel, right hand reaching for my phone. I got it and sat up. The car was only slightly straddling the center yellow line. No other cars around anyway. I looked at my phone. No service. No service! I told myself to calm down, I could turn around, go back the way I came until I got to the interstate, but I was afraid to pull over. Anything could be in those woods, some backwoods Rhode Island psycho who would mangle and murder me, or worse: a terrible nothing that would swallow me whole. I saw a light up ahead. One light. I sped up. It was a yard light on the top of a tall metal pole and the light was blue and vibrating. The yard belonged to a rundown clapboard house and as I slowed past the driveway I could tell no one was home. The house was sealed. Every blind was drawn. Fallen leaves covered the driveway and there were no car tracks. No one had been there for a long time. Where was I? How could I get out of there? My teeth began to chatter. There was nothing I could do. Helpless, powerless, I was lost and I would never be found, doomed to wander these roads like Sisyphus, driving and driving, only to find myself back where I started.

I kept going. I knew turning around was a better idea, but I didn't. I checked my cell phone again. I had service. I dialed home. Harry would tell me what to do. I got lost a lot and I always called Harry. He would check his computer to find the right route or talk to me until I figured out where I was. He always assured me I would not stay lost forever. Harry sitting on the couch 3000 miles away. But it went right to voice mail and I hung up. I didn't want him to call me back. If I was lost, this time it was my problem. I didn't want him to tell me how to find the hotel where I would meet the man of my dreams. I deserved to be lost. I deserved to never make it to Newport. Conniving, lying self-centered bitch. And just as the tears began, the road curved through the trees and I came to a crossroads with a gas station and a convenience store, both open with lights like beacons signaling safe harbor. I parked in front of the store and got out. I could see a group of teenagers inside, one of them working behind the counter, his friends hanging around. I walked over to the gas station instead, shivering in my coat and wiping under my eyes. The office smelled of oil and gas and was cluttered with windshield wiper blades and chewing tobacco, cartons of cigarettes, cans of motor oil next to cans of Vienna sausages, the requisite candy and chips, and a glass refrigerator case with submarine sandwiches for the microwave. It was like any gas station anywhere and I took a deep breath and let it out. I found a tissue in my purse and wiped my eyes and nose.

A black man in coveralls and a wool stocking cap came out of the garage wiping his hands on a red towel. So handsome he took my breath away. He had high cheekbones and perfectly smooth skin, a long but masculine neck, and eyes the color of the plastic grass in an Easter basket.

"Hi." I blushed.

His mouth opened and his jaw struggled before he said, "Lost?" A stutterer.

"Yes," I said. "On my way to Newport. Did I miss 138?"

He pulled off his stocking cap revealing his closely buzzed hair. My fingers itched to run over his scalp, to rub back and forth. I put my hands in my pockets. He walked over to a dirty map, torn on the corners, pen marks and circles here and there from other adrift travelers. He pointed to a place touched so often it had been rubbed white.

"That's where we are," I said, helping him. He nodded. Ran his long, dark finger across and down to Newport. "That's where I'm going." He nodded again.

I peered at the map. I had gotten off Route 4 too soon. I wasn't lost, just impatient, distrusting my own directions and too quick to accept defeat. It didn't surprise me. I had been down that road before.

"Do I have to go back to Route 4?"

"No." He ripped a receipt out of his book, turned it over and wrote directions on the back. "Don't worry," he said. "Y…y….you're close."

He handed me the paper and his head blocked the single overhead light. For a moment he was in silhouette. The stuttering, that round, naked head, the way he leaned toward me. I saw his wedding ring. I heard the kids outside the store next door, their voices high and fresh as the evening air, and wondered if any were his. I imagined his wife waiting for him with dinner ready. I knew she would wrap her arms around his bare head and hold him. Nothing to be frightened of, she would whisper against his skin. Nothing at all.

"Thank you."

He shrugged. Happened all the time.

22.

"Where are we?" Doug's voice was shrill, tight behind his teeth.

Fiona could see the effort it cost him to speak. His eyes were closed against the blinking light, his hands over his ears as if everything was too loud. She was grateful to him. He was asking out loud what they all wanted to know. Three days, almost four, now they were drifting and where would they end up? Because drift was all they could do. There was no reason for anyone to be on deck. They had given up the watch and now slumped in the dirty, stinking cabin waiting for whatever would happen next.

"We should begin calling for the mayday," Joren said.

"The radio doesn't work." Doug said. "We know that."

"This *kuthoer* boat." Joren flopped down on the bench.

The rocking continued, the pounding continued, the driving wind crooned incessantly. Fiona could almost hum along in the wind's pitch. She ran her hands over her legs, definitely not sea legs. She had always hated them, been embarrassed by her fleshy thighs, sorry for her muscular calves. How silly, how useless to hate her legs. She would mourn them when they were gone, when the fanged fish she continued to see out the porthole chewed them up and swallowed them away. They had done what they were made for, getting her from place to place, keeping her firmly on the ground. Where she should have stayed. "On the ground."

"Exactly," Doug agreed.

She hadn't realized she'd spoken. Luc looked at her quizzically. She was glad she had seen his brother. She smiled and put her hand on his wet face.

"So what's the answer? Where are we?" He moved her hand away.

"Nowhere. Weren't you listening? Nowhere and no one knows we're here."

She was worried about Doug. He spoke too loudly, his voice dry and squeaky, his cheeks pink and his eyes shiny as if he had a fever. He needed a glass of water. She would find him one. She started to get up, then remembered all the glasses were broken.

"We're not nowhere." Luc chided Doug. "We've been moving. If the wind is blowing from the west, then we're moving east, right?"

"But Bermuda is to the south." She was glad to have something to contribute. "Something has to be to the east."

"England," Joren said. "Only three thousand nautical miles."

"Don't you guys have a sextant or whatever it's called?"

Joren's laugh was the bark of a dog. Woof. "This boat very modern," he said. Woof. Woof. "The latest thing. The navigation it is electric. Do we have any electricity on this boat?" Woof woof woof.

"We can't use a manual sextant if we can't see the stars or the horizon." Doug said. "We haven't seen them once. Have we, Captain? We have not seen a single star."

"Only me." Luc tried to make them laugh. "C'mon, there has to be another way." Ever the optimist. Nice but useless, she thought. Not just him, all of them, they were all useless.

Nathan had been silent. Fiona saw his hands opening and closing against his thighs, how he shook his head as if going over something in his mind. He was figuring out a solution, a way to get them home. He had to be.

"What?" She smiled trying to encourage him. "What have you come up with?"

"It shouldn't have been a surprise." He didn't look at her, at any of them. He spoke to himself. "I should have realized it months ago. That damn Smith-Johnson Prize going to Harris instead of me. The work I did was too advanced. Too difficult, complicated, avant garde, for the dim-witted committee to understand."

"You told me you were winning the SJP." Doug squinted at Nathan.

"What?" He struggled to focus on Doug, to come back to where he was. "Oh I deserve it, my work is exceptional, but the judging is completely political."

Then he shook all over, like a dog after a bath, and gave a forced chortle. He looked at each of them, one after the other. "This is when it gets interesting. I'm keeping copious notes. Stress and brain function. I'll win it next time."

"That's all this is? A brain study?" Luc threw his cigarette into the muck.

"Won't matter if we're at the bottom of the ocean." Doug smiled. "Fat lot of good your notes will be then."

"I have my ways."

Joren stood up. "I will fix the rudder. When the weather clears."

"That's your answer for everything," Doug said. "What if it doesn't?"

"Of course it must," Joren said.

"We'll see," Nathan said. "We shall see." He took the Captain's Log Book and went in his cabin and shut the door.

In response, the weather quickly worsened. The relentless rocking got stronger, they tipped farther and faster back and forth. The crashing and creaking grew louder. Joren disappeared into his cabin. Fiona pulled up the damp hood of her sweatshirt and put her fingers in her ears. The wind was like a Halloween record, 'Oooweeooo,' like a child's concept of howling wind. She would trade one of her toes, she would gain five pounds, for one minute of calm. She offered up to God or gods a deal: if we get home safely, I will be the person I should be. I will stand on my own two feet. I will not hide anymore. I promise I will speak up.

She ran her fingernails around the bottom seam of the sweatshirt Doug had given her. Back and forth. Luc was trying to light another soggy cigarette with a damp match.

"So, Luc," Doug began.

Luc looked at him. His wet hair framed his face in glossy ringlets. His lips were swollen from the salt water and she wanted to kiss them. Sick as she was, tired and scared, she wanted to kiss him. He finally got his cigarette lit and exhaled gratefully. The smoke went up. At that moment, 'up' was at about 45 degrees. Fascinating. On this boat, up was always other than where she expected.

"Luc," Doug said again.

"What?" Luc asked.

"You and Fiona. You planning on getting married?"

Such a strange question in this vomit-filled boat. Marriage was white dresses and kitchen appliances. A house with a yard. Not this.

Luc shrugged. "Why do you care?"

"You could ask Joren to marry you. He's the ship's captain."
She took a deep breath. Now? Now?

Doug looked at her. "You should get married before we all sink."

"No," Luc said, "Not in this mess." He laughed. "We'll do it in the islands, man. The warm ocean air. On the beach." He turned to her. "You can wear a grass skirt and a bikini top made of coconut shells."

Yes, she thought. Yes.

But Doug clenched his fists. "That's Hawaii, man," he said without smiling. "They don't wear grass skirts in Bermuda. I don't even think they have coconuts."

"We'll be the first," Luc said. "We'll start an island fashion trend."

"Don't believe him." Doug waved a hand. "Guys like him never get married."

She wanted to tell him to shut up. She wanted to say he was out of his mind. The boat leaned sharply and he fell forward. She and Luc helped him back onto the bunk.

"Are you all right?" she asked.

Doug grabbed her arms. "I'll marry you. Right now and forever. In the sight of heaven and earth, ocean and sky, man and beast and all the birds of the world, I thee wed."

"Congratulations," Luc said. "Hope you're very happy." He closed his eyes and leaned back against the one remaining pillow.

Doug kissed her on the cheek. "My watch," he said.

"We're not doing that anymore."

"I am watching. Always." He stumbled up the ladder.

She turned to Luc. "He's crazy," she said. He barely nodded, his cigarette still burning and stuck to his bottom lip. "He's nuts," she said again. He sighed. He wasn't jealous, he didn't believe in jealousy. She admired his enlightenment, but she wished—one more wish—that just once she could make him worry. She nudged him. He had fallen asleep. She took the cigarette from his mouth and stubbed it out on the beautiful teak.

23.

I fingered the scar on my forehead, almost invisible now, but still palpable. Usually I forgot all about it, but that evening as I drove toward Newport, I rubbed it back and forth, back and forth. Our third day at sea was the roughest we had. All through the day and night the weather got worse. There was lightning and Nathan said the boat could be struck at any time. He said it was hurricane. He said it with relish. "Bam! This is a hurricane, boy!" He clapped Luc on the back \\\. "Most people never see this!" Lucky us.

Twenty-five minutes after the *Bleiz A Mor* set sail, the rain began and the wind picked up. A 'moderate breeze' Force 4 on the Beaufort Scale, named for its inventor, Royal Navy officer Francis Beaufort, in 1805. Force 4 is great sailing—if you like sailing.

Day One—when there was still time to turn around—the wind swelled to Force 5, a 'fresh breeze,' winds gusting at 24 miles per hour, waves 6-9 feet.

Steadily through the night and all the next day, Day Two, the wind grew more intense: Force 7, 'moderate gale.' By evening it was Force 8, 'fresh gale,' winds 39 to 46 miles per hour, waves 18, 19, 20 feet high. "Use motor or seek shelter," the chart reads. The motor was gone by that time. There was no shelter.

Day Three winds were sixty miles per hour, the waves were forty feet tall, and what started at only Force 10 passed quickly through Force 11 and by noon was a hurricane. The boat was pummeled mercilessly, heeling severely until the masts were parallel to the sea. The churning foam and spray made it terrifying to be on deck. The waves were dark and high on either side as if we were squished between a freight train's solid gray boxcars, the wind the whistle, the constant rumbling and screeching the wheels on the track. My hips and ribs were badly bruised from sliding into things every time I tried to walk. The galley cabinet on one side. The nav station on the other. Those bruises would still be there after Thanksgiving when I finally got back to New York. The skin had begun to peel off my palms. From the salt and never being dry. I had forced myself to drink some water, everybody had, but I had a raging headache and my eyelids were so swollen I could barely open them. Like all of us. The good thing about being dehydrated was nobody was peeing. The toilets had completely failed and we were forced to go up on deck and piss off the side, an almost impossible task for me.

The crew, if we could call ourselves that, agreed with Nathan when he recommended we just ride it out. We closed the hatch, sealing it as best we could—although the rubber stripping had come off on the second day—and huddled together in the cabin to wait. For what I wasn't sure.

The sewage and seawater was up to my knees and made its own waves as the boat rocked. Slosh. Splash. Every single bottle of scotch, whiskey and vodka had finally slipped and smashed, adding glass and alcohol to the brew. Fruit floated by and broken bits of boards and equipment. The book I had planned to read on deck in the warm afternoons while getting a suntan had fallen in and banged against the side with every tilt, a small, persistent thump. And the big chart, the main chart, not laminated, but plain paper, had been wet more than once. It was beginning to disintegrate under Joren's hands. Not that it mattered. We had no idea where we were.

I wondered about Nathan's brain and stress study. It seemed pretty obvious we were all coping the best we could. I wasn't sure then or now what he planned to study. Fear. Anxiety. We each reacted in our own way. I could have predicted that without going to sea.

Thirty years later, almost to the day, I drove through the dark, dry night. The handsome, bald, stuttering man's directions, written in large block letters, were easy to follow. The black words on white paper my telltale. He was right. I was close. It was an easy trip to Newport. Even in the darkest miles, I did not waver. I believed him and he didn't let me down.

24.

Six hundred thirty-five nautical miles from Newport to Bermuda. Fiona wondered how far they had gone, in which direction and if nautical miles longer than regular miles. She had no idea. Everyone else was asleep, but she was too sick and too afraid and the strobe light kept her awake.

She thought Doug was sleeping until she saw him kneel down in the disgusting water. He whispered, praying, begging God for something. She heard him say her name and then "amen." He crawled across the cabin and whispered into her ear. "Hear me," he began, "I love you. From the morning we met. When we fed the seagulls. If you'll have me, I will take care of you forever. I will never let you down. I will put you before all others and cleave only to you. Everything you want that is in my power to give, I will give to you."

She slipped away from Luc, took Doug by the hand and led him back to his bunk. No one had ever said these things to her. No father or stepfather or boyfriend—not Luc—had ever offered to take care of her. She sat down beside him, her shoulder pressing against his and wondered what his chest would feel like against hers, his skin against her skin.

"Do this," he said. "I'll die happy."

"You're not going to die," she whispered. "None of us

are. You have to see your duck. Your precious whistling duck. Remember?"

"All I want is you. You are beautiful, your eyes are like the morning sky over the desert. Please let me show you Arizona, the rocks and hills and cactus, the way it all goes purple in the evening."

She closed her eyes. For a moment, she was in his desert. The boat was gone. The world was still. His thigh against hers like a solid rock.

"I want to show you everything." He went on, listing the places they would go, the birds she would see, the things they would do. He hardly stuttered at all. She dropped her head onto his shoulder. He stroked her hair. She was so tired. His scratchy coat could have been her father's as he carried her into the house after she'd fallen asleep in the car. He would put her safely in her soft bed with the clean sheets and the tree outside her window. She could smell his aftershave and feel his dry fingers around her cold hand.

"I will give you everything you want," he said.

She nodded—yes, please—and heard his sigh.

"Thank you, my love."

Nathan threw open his door and splashed loudly through the cabin. He had the log book in one arm and he thumped on it with his other hand. "Damn, I slept well. The weather is better. A fine, sailing day."

He threw back the hatch, and Fiona saw he was right, the sky was lighter, more like a dirty gym sock than lead. The rain just a drizzle. It was morning. Day Four. The day she had thought they would arrive in Bermuda. Nathan put the log book on the table and stroked it gently. He had a little smile on his bloated face. He'd even put his hair back in a ponytail. Still dirty, but they were all dirty, no one had washed for days and days.

"Rise and shine!" Nathan started up the ladder. "Time's a' wasting!"

Luc groaned and sat up. "Is this necessary?" he began.

Suddenly there was static on the radio and a recognizable word or two. Nathan jumped back down into the cabin. Fiona looked out the porthole, then scrambled up on deck, Luc right behind her. An ocean liner was passing very close, so close they could see the crew waving from four stories above.

"Stop!" Fiona waved. "Stop!"

She heard Nathan below, trying to reach the ship on the radio. She hurried back down.

"Come in! Come in!" Static in return, then nothing. The ship was going away. "Stop them," she said. "Talk to them. We need them."

"Baloney. We don't need them." He reached over and palmed her head like a basketball. "Fascinating." She stepped out from under.

Luc came down. "Did you reach them?".

"We could hear them. That's all that matters. The radio is fine—it just has a little distance problem. And the weather is breaking. Joren will go over the side and fix the rudder. All will be well." He closed his eyes, put a hand on his log book. "One way or the other."

Joren came out of his cabin and Doug stood up by his bunk. Fiona could still feel Nathan's fingers on her skull, his nails digging in her skin. She stepped behind Luc.

"See? What did I tell you?" Nathan looked at them all.

"Nothing," Luc said. "You told us nothing."

Nathan's face went hard, mean. "How is it, Greek boy, that after four days at sea, you still look like Adonis?"

"Stop it. Someone should be on the radio."

"Send up the flare," Joren said. "We are in the mess."

Fiona was surprised to hear Joren wanting to ask for help. Finally, finally.

"Here's what I'd like to know." Nathan continued to Luc. "What would you look like after four days in the sea? On a trolling line behind the boat, the hooks through that beautiful, olive skin." He laughed. "Joking. Joking. But think of the fish we'd catch."

"That's disgusting," Fiona said. "There's something wrong with you."

"I told you." Doug swayed on his feet. "I told you."

A wave came and tossed them sideways. Everybody stumbled. Joren fell.

"It is still the storm," His eyes were red from seawater and possibly, she thought, tears.

"Oh my God." Nathan pulled himself straight. "You are all so cranky. Isn't this exactly what you signed up for? Sailing, sailing. You are all my children, and I am your wise and educated leader who has gotten you through the worst."

"Shut up." Doug sat on his bunk, put his hands over his ears. "Stop, Devil. Be gone!"

"I know what we should do." Nathan was jovial. "Let's have breakfast."

Fiona groaned.

"Eggs and bacon. And start a watch. Next time another ship gets close, I want to hear about it. One person on deck, just two hours at a time. I'll take the first watch myself. I am the Sea Wolf."

Luc laughed at something Joren whispered.

"What's so funny?" Nathan asked. "Tell me."

Fiona heard his schoolboy whine, the voice of the child who had been bullied and teased and always ate lunch alone.

"Tell me."

"I was just wondering what fancy tourist is going to rent this boat in Bermuda," Luc replied. "And Joren said someone who likes the shit."

Nathan tried to laugh. "It's not so bad," he said, looking around. "We'll clean it up in no time." His eyes fell on Doug, sitting there with his arms crossed, a frown on his face.

Doug nodded toward the hatch. The sky had grown dark. The rain and wind had increased. The boat heeled steeply in a rising wave. The bad weather wasn't over. It had become timeless, permanent.

Nathan grinned. His incisors seemed longer, sharper than the rest. "Joren," he commanded. "We're putting up the mizzen sail."

"But you say we always put up the mainsail first."

"Not this time."

"But no rudder. The weather—"

"Fuck the weather. We have to get moving. C'mon. Right now! You and me." He fastened his yellow slicker and climbed up the ladder, leaving them with a fart.

Fiona made a list in her head:

Things That Had Gone Wrong Up To This Point

1. No one checked the weather report

2. The rudder broke—and then broke again

3. The engine died

4. The electricity failed

5. The radio was iffy

6. None of them knew what they were doing.

She thought that was it. That was enough.

25.

In the dark, through my foggy windshield, Newport was like a ghost town. A light drizzle had begun—it seemed I couldn't get away from the rain—and every shop and restaurant I drove past was closed. It was only eight, but shades were drawn and the main street by the water was empty. Nothing looked particularly familiar. The cobblestones were still there, shiny in the rain. The buildings were still brick and colonial with historical markers on posts and brass plates by the front doors. Somebody slept here. Somebody had slept there as well. After thirty years it could have been any New England tourist town.

My hotel was half a block up a cobblestone street, around the corner from the wharf. I parked in the small lot behind the hotel and hurried around to the front door pulling my suitcase.

There was an envelope with my name on it taped behind the glass storm door. I knew it was from Luc. He wasn't coming. I wondered why it was taped to the door and not left with the desk. I huddled under the awning and opened the envelope. Inside was an old fashioned key with a green plastic tag. And a note, not from Luc, but from the hotel:

Hi –

This is your room key. Please come in and make

yourself at home. We'll see you tomorrow.

Have fun,

Holly and Rick

P.S. Your friend is here. He's gone to dinner just around the corner at Drake's.

I pushed the front door open and went in, yanking my rolling suitcase over the threshold. The lobby was fussy and overdone like somebody's grandmother's house. Colonial furniture in flowered fabrics, cliché vintage sailing prints, cute little embroidered sayings: "Anyone can hold the helm when the sea is calm" and "When you get to the end of your rope, tie a knot and hold on." There was a sign in old English-style lettering pointing to the tearoom, but that door was closed.

"Hello?" I called. No one answered. It seemed I was the only person in the whole place. Too many scenarios went through my head—front door open, a note expecting me, plus the key. Anybody could be waiting in my room. But Luc had made it after all. He was around the corner. He was early. I needed to comb my hair, brush my teeth, fix my smeared mascara.

The tag on my key said 311. I didn't see an elevator and wouldn't have taken it if I had. The narrow, carpeted stairs creaked. I passed the second floor landing. No evidence of human inhabitation. Dragged my rolling bag—thump, thump, thump—up another floor. One of the fake candle wall sconces was out and the hallway was dim. I took a deep breath and tiptoed down to 311. I tried the door. Locked, thank god. I opened it and peeked inside. My bed was turned down and there was a chocolate on my pillow, a single Hershey's Kiss. I left the door open as I looked in the bathroom, behind the shower curtain, under the bed, and inside the closet. I shut the door and locked it; I was alone.

I washed my face and redid my makeup. I changed my sweater, then changed it back. I brushed my teeth and combed my hair. I usually wore it up, but left it long. It was not as long as it had been, but still well below my shoulders. The rain had given it more weight than usual—or maybe that was my head, heavy with guilt.

My cell phone rang. Couldn't be Luc, I hadn't given him my number. It was Harry. I almost didn't answer it, but I had to.

"Hi," I said. "Just got here."

"I went to the library," he said. "Did some research."

"The library?"

"I can't use the paper's search engine anymore. I wanted the latest on breast cancer. The librarian snuck me onto her Nexus."

"Really?"

"She's a friend."

I felt a nip of indignation. A tiny, sharp, child's fingernail-sized poke of jealousy. "You told the librarian your wife has cancer?" I could imagine her smile as she sat at her library desk waiting for my demise—as if out of work, neurotic Harry was such a great catch.

"She's a researcher. It's her job."

"Okay. Okay." I could not complain. "I'm… just on my way to dinner."

"There's a specialist you should see. In Boston. Not far. At Dana-Farber, one of the best cancer hospitals in the world. This guy is good. He's the best. I've done the research. Take another day or two. Keep your rental car and drive down to Boston."

"Up," I said. "It's up to Boston."

"Whatever. Google says it's less than two hours."

"The conference."

"Fuck the conference. This is more important than a job fair. You can't work if you're dead."

I heard him suck in air, wishing he could swallow the "d" word. Too late.

"I didn't mean that," he said quietly. "You're not going to die."

"I have to go."

"Okay. Go to your stupid conference. I'll text you the doctor's name and number. I'll call tomorrow and make you an appointment for Monday afternoon."

"It'll cost 100 bucks or more to change my flight."

"Who cares? Jesus Christ, Fiona, who the fuck cares?"

"How will we pay for this doctor?" I asked. "Will insurance pay for a second opinion in another state?"

"I'll make them pay. It'll be my greatest pleasure. This country gave you cancer. Pesticides. Monsanto. Contamination. The colossal insurance industrial complex conglomerate will pay for you to get well. Fuck Blue Cross. Fuck COBRA. Whatever the fuck you need. Whatever. It will happen, I promise."

I was a cause, something for Harry to fight for. He sounded energized—like the old Harry, the one I knew best. I was about to ruin his life, and he was trying to save mine.

"I'll talk to you tomorrow," I said.

"Go to dinner. Have fun. Don't worry." He paused. His voice got low, soft, like he was talking about sex. I hadn't heard this voice in over a year. "I'm not angry you didn't tell me. I'm really not. I know you're frightened. We're going to beat this. We'll fight and we'll win." He spouted more militaristic phrases—the things people usually say.

"Thanks. Uh huh. Talk tomorrow. Love you. Bye."

I checked the clock radio, cheap plastic made appropriately colonial by a crocheted doily. Fourteen after eight. I was supposed to meet Luc in the lobby at nine. I redid my lipstick, brushed my hair again—too long for a woman my age, but still my best feature.

Eight twenty-three. I decided to walk around the corner to Drake's. If he wasn't there, I'd have a drink and come back. If he was—then he was.

My phone buzzed. A text from Harry: "FUCK IN-SURANCE COMPANIES SUCK ASS COCKSUCKING FUCK FUCK ASSWIPES!!!!" I turned my phone off.

26.

At least Fiona could tell it was daytime. It was possible to look around inside the boat and see the mess. For a brief stint they did a bucket brigade to bail out the main cabin while Nathan sat on watch, but no one had much energy and in the rain it didn't seem to make a difference.

Nathan's watch passed, and Joren's, and Luc's. When it was Doug's turn, he kissed her cheek before climbing the ladder. She thought of the things he had said to her, that he would always take care of her. Doug was familiar, like a pair of old jeans, loose and worn-in, comfortable, but something she would never wear to go out anywhere. Luc was a fine leather jacket. She was careful with him. He still made her nervous—made her toes and her fingers clench. He was sitting with Joren, trying to teach him English. It was sweet. Luc was sweet. She watched him push Joren's hair off his forehead and run his finger down a scar on Joren's cheek. She felt a familiar twist in her stomach, saw the warning sign, "danger ahead." He would do whatever he wanted to do. She didn't want to stop him. She did not want to want to stop him. It was absolutely what she loved about him: he had all the confidence she lacked.

They had met Billy together in an advanced dance class right after they got to New York. They had trooped up the stairs to the room with the high arched windows, already filled with beautiful bodies stretching and warming up. Billy had immediately grinned appreciatively at Luc, thrown his arm around him as he introduced him to the other dancers. And he had leaned down and whispered in her ear, "This is a hard class. Do the best you can." She had kept up, but Luc had surpassed them all, out turned, out jumped, out danced the very best. Afterwards, she was red-faced and sopping. Luc said Billy had invited him out. "You don't mind?" She couldn't mind. She had gone home to Lola's alone. And when Luc had come home at three in the morning, high and loose and smelling of Billy's vanilla aftershave, she had not shown him her tears.

She closed her eyes and heard Leander whispering he had been there, really been there. It's possible, she thought. Anything is possible. Poor dead Leander. A Greek boy bound by that name to die. The Leander in the myth had died in the sea. He angered Aphrodite by making love to her priestess, Hero. Each night, Hero put out a lantern to guide Leander as he swam through the ocean to her. When Aphrodite found out, she blew out the lantern and whipped up the water. Leander lost his way and drowned. Luc's brother had spun out on a motorcycle in the Everglades, flown through the air into a tree. He'd been drinking. But she could tell from the photos that he, like his namesake, had been beautiful, lovelier and more ethereal even than Luc.

She lay down on the bench. She hadn't said anything to Doug. She had to talk to him, had to tell him there was no way, no chance, no how. When they got to Bermuda they would go their separate ways. The sun would shine, the breeze would be warm, and all this would be forgotten. She would be strong. She would tell him that Luc was her man and only Luc. She rubbed her cheek where Doug had kissed her, where she had seen Luc touching Joren. She rubbed and the damp skin came off under her fingers. The skin on her arms was shedding too. She was peeling away, layer by layer. By the time they reached shore, she would be down to bone.

"Io," Luc said. "Your watch."

The time had gone by so quickly. She put on the horrid yellow raincoat, pulled up her hood and tightened the string. Slowly she began to climb the ladder. One rung. Two. It hurt to lift her legs. Three. The boat lurched and her bruised hip slammed against the railing. She looked up. Doug was there at the top, waiting for her. He had unclipped his harness to come help her. His smile was wide in his round moon face. Behind him, the sky was a little less gray, the rain a little less insistent. Things were going to be fine. And if they were going to live through this, end up on that warm beach, she had to tell Doug the truth.

"Here," he said. "Take my hand."

She looked up at him, at his small brown eyes so filled with love. It made her want to cry. She saw his neck, raw from rubbing against the wet slicker, rough with three day-old beard. She did not want to kiss that neck. "No."

The boat rocked and he stumbled and grabbed on to the railing above the hatch with both hands. He spread his legs and braced himself.

"Come on," he said. "I can hold you. I will hold you forever."

She had to tell him. "Doug," she began. "You have to stop. I'm going to stay with Luc. Really, I am. I love him. Only him."

"Don't say that."

"It's true. I don't love you. I never will."

His mouth fell open. He threw his head back and wailed,

an unearthly cry to the rain.

She was sorry. She was. She looked down, anywhere but his face.

Abruptly, the world went dark. The light turned off as if a blanket had been thrown over their heads. Had she done that with her cruelty? Had he with his misery? She raised her head. A giant wall, no, a massive wall-sized wave of black water was rising over the boat. It hid the sky. It blocked the rain and the wind and for one brief second everything was calm and silent. She heard her own sigh of relief. Doug gave an almost imperceptible nod. Okay, he mouthed. Okay. The wave curled over the boat. He looked up, let go of the railing and stretched his arms wide. "I surrender."

The wave broke and hit directly into the small mizzen sail. It filled the cloth and pushed the boat over and over, all the way over until it was upside down. Fiona fell back down the ladder, tumbling onto the table, banging into the high cupboard face first. The boat groaned and shuddered. The wood whined. Joren's leg hit her chest. She flailed her arms, banging into Luc, Joren, the cupboard doors. She tried to keep her head out of the water but it was everywhere, no direction was up. A sudden wrenching jolt. A terrible snapping and then cracking and creaking. Slowly, slowly, the boat righted.

Fiona scrambled back up the ladder and onto the deck. "Doug!" She screamed. "Doug!"

Luc and Joren were right behind her. "There!" Joren pointed to a speck of something far behind them, bobbing up and down in the sea. There, and then hidden by another wave.

Luc ran from one side to the other. "Is that him? Or a bird?"

"It's yellow!" She wanted it to be him, it had to him. She ripped the life preserver from the railing and flung it in his direction as far as she could. Nowhere near far enough. He knew how to swim. Like a fish. He'd said so. She turned to Joren. "We have to go back!"

"But how?" he asked. "How?"

Doug's harness flapped against the bench. He had undone it for her. She couldn't stand it. She howled as loud as she could, not his name, not any recognizable word, a piercing keen for him.

Luc grabbed her. "Jesus, baby, your face." Her forehead had opened up again, and she had new cuts on her cheek, above her lip and on her chin. There was a lot of blood. She couldn't answer him. She stared out at the rotten sea, the color of a trashcan, the color of death. The life preserver was far behind them. Then it too was gone.

"Oh my *Gott*," said Joren.

She and Luc spun around. The main mast had splintered in two. The top half was hanging in the rigging. She looked at Joren and he shook his head. Even if the weather cleared, even if he got the rudder fixed, they were going nowhere. No engine. No sail. They were done. They were finally done.

She grabbed the railing and rocked and shouted for Doug as she scanned the empty sea. She opened her arms as he had. Let it take me too. She lifted her face to the rain and felt her blood washing away.

Nathan came up on deck holding a towel against his elbow. "Knock down." His voice was unusually subdued.

"A rogue wave," Joren said. "The main mast is gone."

Nathan looked at Fiona. "Where's Doug?"

She didn't cry. There was enough water in the world. It was Joren who began to sob.

Luc said, "He's gone. We can't find him."

Nathan inspected his bleeding elbow. "Overboard?

Really? Did you look carefully? Around the boat? He could be hanging off the side, tangled up. That can happen. He could still be there. Strangled and right beside us."

"He didn't have his harness on," she said. "I was coming to relieve him."

Nathan started to make some remark—she could see it in his eyes—but he took a breath. "We're in a pickle now." He threw his bloody towel into the sea.

Luc's voice was strong. "We should all put on life jackets. We should blow up the life raft and have it ready. We should get on the radio and say mayday." Everyone looked at him. "I read it on the inside of the closet door. Emergency procedures."

"The radio doesn't work. Remember?" Fiona closed her eyes.

The sea was getting rougher, the sky darkening, the wind picking up. Again.

"We should go down," Joren said, "Before…" There was no reason for him to finish his sentence.

They filed down into the hold. Fiona stared at Doug's bunk. She saw his warm wool coat lying half in the muck. Why wasn't he wearing it?

Luc got the life jackets from storage under Nathan's berth. He handed them out. There weren't enough to go around.

"We only have three life jackets?" Luc asked Nathan.

He shrugged. "They came with the boat. We're not going to survive if we fall in this water anyway. Too cold. Doug was probably dead in three minutes. Actually, in his condition, instantly."

Fiona didn't believe he was dead. Nathan had been wrong about everything else. Doug could swim. He could tread water. She hoped he was angry, furious with her. His rage would keep him going.

"Life raft," Joren said. "Where is that?"

"You're the captain." Joren didn't answer, so Nathan continued. "Should be under the bunk over there."

Luc pulled it out. It looked used, or at least opened. It hadn't been folded properly when it was put away, just wadded up and pushed back into the locker. There was a foot pump, but when Luc and Joren tried to connect it a part was missing, the black plastic tube that connected to the pump. Fiona remembered Doug telling her about the bit of black plastic he saw Nathan toss overboard. She turned to him.

"You did this."

He pulled a can of beer from the pocket of his yellow raincoat and opened it. He took a drink and ignored her.

"You did this. You knew we didn't have enough life jackets. You made the raft useless. You wouldn't fix the engine. You wouldn't listen to anybody. You killed him."

Luc put his hand on her arm. "Fiona, stop it."

"He did this to Doug." For once she knew more than Luc. Doug had told her about the black plastic. She was the one who had seen the way Nathan looked at Doug, at Joren, at all of them, like science experiments.

She said to Nathan, "You killed him."

"Actually, babe," Nathan said quietly, "I think you killed him. Didn't you? Why were the two of you up there? What did you say to him?"

Fiona fell back as if he had punched her. He was right. Of course he was. He had made the boat unsafe, but the rest of them were still alive. If Doug was dead, it was her fault.

"What do we do?" Joren asked in a small, high voice.

Nathan squinted at him. "A little Whitman is called for. 'Oh Captain, my Captain! Our fearful trip is done/The ship has weather'd every rack/ the prize we sought is won/ Here

Captain! Dear father! This arm beneath your head/ It is some dream that on the deck you've fallen cold and dead.'"

He finished his beer and dropped the can into the swill at their feet . He sat down on Doug's bunk. Fiona wanted to tell him to get up, not to touch Doug's things, but she knew he wouldn't move. He wouldn't do anything she asked. Luc took her hand. His face was worried, his skin smooth. After three days, only a few whiskers sprouted on his chin. His eyes were brown, but not like Doug's.

"We'll be fine." He whispered in his melodic voice. "Someone will find us."

"And Doug," she said, but Luc just sighed.

Someone would find him. She imagined children on the beach in Florida stumbling over his body washed up on shore. She heard their screams when they saw him, bloated, green, and partially disintegrated. No, that was too awful. He had to be alive, treading water and waiting for them. Waiting for her.

Joren got up and went to the radio. "Mayday," he said into the mic, his voice hoarse from crying. "Mayday." He looked at the compass and almost started to cry again. "Mayday. Mayday."

A wave sent them up and up. She grabbed the counter and held her breath. Would they go over again? Bam! The boat slammed down the other side.

Joren was knocked off his feet, but he came up yelling. "Look! Look! This here!" Strapped underneath the navigation station was an orange cylinder. He unattached it and held it up like the Olympic torch.

"What's that?" Luc asked.

"EPIRB." Joren breathed the word and grinned.

"Let me see." Nathan held out his hand.

Joren cradled the cylinder like a child. "Emergency

Position Indicator Radio Beacon. It sends a high frequency signal. Beep. Beep. To say distress."

Nathan kicked his feet in the water like a child. "Came with the boat. I didn't know it was there." The implication was that of course it didn't work.

Joren flicked it on and a small green light began to blink. Luc cheered. Fiona felt a tiny teardrop of hope.

"Give it to me," Nathan said.

No, Fiona thought. No.

Joren ignored his boss and looked right past him to Luc. "We will tie it on up there," he said. "It is a chance. Help, please."

Luc and Joren hurried up the ladder. She climbed halfway up and watched as they strapped in, clipped their harnesses to the lifeline and crabbed over to the broken mast. Joren used his knife to saw through the lines holding the pieces together. The top fell away into the sea. Good, she thought. Doug might find it and hold on. He's dead, Leander said in her head. "Shut up," she said aloud and banged her temple. He's dead, was the reply.

Joren called to her. "The weather is better."

She looked up at the sky and a tiny patch of blue. The rain seemed to be easing off and she realized she was standing on the ladder without holding on, only her legs braced. She hoped Doug—wherever he was—could see the clearing sky.

What had it been like for Leander? Not Luc's brother, but the boy long ago, leaping into the sea to visit his lover as he had done so many times before, and this time losing his way. He must have been surprised. Maybe he got angry. He probably imagined he saw the light ahead of him. There. No, there. It had always been there. There were no other landmarks, no signposts in the sea. A boat coming to save him would be hidden by the rough waves. How long until his arms got tired? How long until the first drops of water went into his mouth, into his lungs? Did he ever think his lover had forsaken him, that it was she who put out the light? Did he die calling her name?

27.

I could smell the ocean as I stepped out of my hotel. The air had a tang as if something had spoiled. It reminded me of the dead mice at home and I thought of Harry. I could not think of Harry. I put up my hood against the drizzle—remembering another hood in much more rain— and concentrated on walking on the picturesque but silly, slippery cobblestones in my high-heeled boots. The saltwater smell and the memories were making me queasy. I turned the corner onto Thames Street and a regular cement sidewalk, thank god. The harbor full of sailboats was just across the way. In the dark, the masts looked like toothpicks, too thin and delicate to fly a sail. A couple splashed past me in their Topsiders. Both blond, both in khaki pants and navy blue rain jackets. I had never seen a pair of Sperry Topsiders before I came to Newport thirty years ago, but back then— maybe now too—everybody wore them. The gas station attendant. The checker at the grocery store. The secretary in the Harbormaster's office. And, of course, every sailor. A Topsider makes a distinctive cwap on the wooden planks of the dock, a scuffing sound on the rough coated deck, and a quiet skid and thwuck on the cobblestones. Joren and Nathan both wore them. I don't know where he got them, but when we showed up at the boat Luc pulled a pair from his bag. Of course he did.

Nothing on this street looked familiar. I didn't remember the shops or the restaurants and thirty years ago there had not been a Starbucks. I looked around for the Harbormaster's office, but couldn't see it. A lot had changed. Had I? Yes, damn it, yes. I stood straighter. I was an accomplished woman, a mother, slim and healthy—except for one small thing. I would sit down, have a drink with Luc, apologize to him for leaving all those years ago, tell him how glad I was it had all worked out for the best, and go back to my room an even better woman. Yes, I told myself, I'll do exactly that.

Drake's had to be the brick and clapboard building with the American and British flags flying in the rain, and it was. Big glass windows faced the sea, it was new, built in faux-Colonial style. It was surprisingly pretty inside, lots of wood and brass, with a subtle pirate theme and an oversized copy of the famous sixteenth century portrait of Sir Francis Drake hanging on the far wall. I pushed back my hood and shook out my hair, hoping the rain hadn't made it too limp and stringy. I started for the women's room to check my hair and blow my nose. But then I saw him. Luc. Sitting at a high table in the window. He must have seen me walk by and not recognized me with my hood up. His hair was still full of loose curls, shorter and now streaked with gray. He looked the same but thicker; he had widened a little and appeared more solid. He wore a businessman's blue button down shirt with the sleeves rolled and dark, new jeans. His shoes were brown and sensible, the most surprising thing about him. He looked down at his drink—clear with a lime wedge—and I saw the slump of his shoulders, how his jaw had softened over his bones.

I paused. Maybe this was a bad idea. Maybe it was better for him to remember me as I had been—for me to remember him that way too. I almost turned away, but he reached for his glass and I saw his long, graceful fingers, and the way that one curl of hair tucked into his collar. He was Luc. My Luc. Alive and well. I began to tremble. Every part of me was impatient to be near him, but I held back, enjoying the want, the pull, the mystery of what would happen. See me, I sent the thought to him. Look over here and see me. If he did, then I would know it was going to be all right.

"Here for dinner?" A young girl in black startled me.

"I'm meeting someone." I smiled. "Him."

At that moment he turned his head and saw me. He grinned, that same grin. The years fell away and I was nineteen again, anxious to see him and wondering why I'd been away so long. It was as if I'd never gotten married, never had a child, but been suspended someplace, waiting, as I had always been waiting, for Luc to come and get me. C'mon. C'mon. C'mon.

He stood. I walked to him, but kept the table between us. We didn't hug. Had it been a girlfriend I was meeting, I would have easily hugged her hello. I was afraid, and it seemed he was too.

"Io," he said.

My chest opened. I caught my breath. "You know." My voice quavered. "The moon of Jupiter is pronounced Eye-oh."

"But in Greek, it's Ee-oh. Io." He said it again. "It suits you even more now than it did then." His voice was exactly the same. "A nymph emerging from the woods."

I couldn't speak. It was as if my younger self stood in front of me. In front of him. The old nickname, Luc's gift. He had been the only one to use it, and that identity came forward. The nymph. The cow. The girl who wanted so badly to be whatever he wanted her to be. I put out a hand to push her away and he took it. It was her hand, and it belonged in his.

"Sit down," he said. "Please."

"Luc." And when I said his name I decided if he wanted to sleep with me, I would. I wouldn't try to make it happen, but I would not say no. I never had.

I took off my coat and sat down across from him. We traded inanities. When did you get here? How was your flight? Did you drive from Providence? I wasn't listening to his answers. If there'd been a quiz I would have failed. We both avoided looking at the other.

"Something to eat?" he asked.

"A drink."

"French fries," he said. "With vinegar. They have them here. I remember how much you loved French fries."

I hadn't loved them, but I had watched him eat plate after plate. "Okay." And I did it again. I ordered them because he wanted me to.

I surprised him with my drink order: a single malt scotch, water back. He reminded me that thirty years earlier I didn't drink at all.

"Well," I said. "I don't like wine as much. At home, when I'm cooking, okay, but I prefer scotch. The color. The idea of it. Short glass. Ice. Detective stories. Movies from the forties." I was babbling and he smiled.

"You're even more beautiful," he said.

"In the dark."

"I watched you walk by the window." He smiled bashfully in a way that surprised me. "Didn't want to seem overanxious."

I nodded, not sure what to say. He seemed embarrassed and turned to the window. I studied him, the width of his chest, his bottom lip, the pattern of hair in his eyebrows. I had been sure I'd never forget, but now I wondered, had his nose always been that long? Had the lobes of his ears always curved that way? Yes. Maybe. I looked for him, for the Luc I knew, and I found him. His hands were the same, the bone of his wrist round and visible exactly as I remembered. He was there. Not entirely the same, but still there. His younger self blended more with him than mine with me. I didn't want her around, but I wanted him.

"Newport has changed," he said.

"I don't recognize anything."

"We were only here for two days."

"Two and a half."

We laughed for no reason. I told him about my room key taped to the front door of the hotel, how that would never happen in LA. He agreed, said it would never happen in Orlando either. We laughed about the hotel's silly décor. We avoided talking about our families. We commented on the rain, how fitting it seemed. He asked me if I wanted to go on a sailboat ride the next day and I almost shouted no. I told him I hadn't been on a boat since, not even the ferry to Catalina. I tried to laugh. "Crazy, huh? And I still can't swim."

He frowned. "Really? My folks bought a cabin cruiser. The kids love it." He shrugged. "So do I."

Of course he did. I caught him taking quick glimpses at my breasts, my mouth, before returning to my eyes. I looked him over too. I saw no evidence of the addiction. He wasn't skinny anymore or dissipated in any way. He was the picture of health. How had he gotten clean? Why had I ever left him? I took a deep sniff to see if he had the same scent I remembered, but there was only the odor of spilled beer and fried food, restaurant smells. The French fries were gone. I'd only eaten one. Had he noticed? I poked in the bottom of my empty glass with my stir stick. He cleared his throat. I shifted in my chair, aware of my clothing against my skin. I was suddenly horny, filled with a teenager's readiness. Maybe there were other ways to apologize to him—more intimate but less revealing.

"So?" he said. His eyebrows lifted. Now was not the time to ask the hard questions, to say what I'd been waiting thirty years to say. He was looking for something else, and despite my decision to say yes, I was happy sitting there, the table between us. Still faithful, still pure. For twenty-two years I had been with Harry and Harry alone. Other than the very occasional lunch with someone at work, I had not shared a drink with a man other than Harry. I had given up flirtation, given up the interest even. I'd used up that part of me. Post Luc, pre Harry, I'd been a slut. It only took a turn in my direction, a glance from under half-lowered eyelids, a particular tilt of the head, and my breath would come faster, my heart beat a little quicker. Me? You want me? A square male hand sliding toward my thigh, or feminine slim fingers handing me a glass. Male or female, a hand, someplace, anyplace, and I was on my back or on my knees.

That had been a long time ago. I hadn't wanted anyone else in years. I thought of the bald black man at the gas station. How I'd wanted to touch his head. I looked at Luc's hands, one on the tabletop, his chin resting on the other. Still long and lovely. No wedding ring. I put my left hand in my lap.

"Another drink?" I asked. He was drinking club soda.

"We could take a walk," he said.

I looked out the window at the rain. "Okay."

He paid the bill and helped me with my coat. He had learned to do proper man things, grown up things.

"I love your hair," he said. "Always. I'm so glad you didn't cut it off." He pulled it free of my collar. It didn't count as a real touch, but my whole body leaned toward him. "Women always cut their hair. Lola. Beth."

I remembered Beth, long dark hair, tall and thin, but with wide shoulders and a proud chest, like the bow of a schooner cutting through calm water. She was a high school student when I met her in New York—the daughter of Lola's boss. Sixteen and a ballerina. I had seen then Luc's attraction to her. I wondered how Beth felt about this trip to Newport, if now, with three kids and a mortgage and a business to run, he still believed in an open relationship. Somehow I doubted it, but then again, Luc could get away with anything.

We stepped out into the night. The rain had slowed until it was just a mist.

"I remember these streetlamps," I said. "How they looked like dandelion puffs in the rain."

"That's a funny thing to remember," he said. "When were you out at night?"

Looking for you, I wanted to say—but didn't. Instead I followed him across the street. The water was right there, past the sidewalk and the strip of grass and the slim metal railing. I heard it lapping and smacking against the pilings. Saw boats bobbing in their berths. Through the harbor, out there, was the Atlantic Ocean. In the dark I couldn't tell where the sea ended and the sky began. I closed my eyes.

"You okay?" Luc came up close to me.

"I hate the ocean."

"I'm sorry."

"It's not your fault."

"Isn't it?"

No. "Shall we try to find the Harbormaster's office?"

He walked beside me. "Isn't our hotel the other way?" He took my hand. I jumped and he felt it. He let go, stepped away, shook his head as if talking to himself. I moved closer and took his hand, leaned against him. He was tall, taller than Harry, but I remembered how I fit under his chin.

It was happening and I wanted it to happen. I did. It wasn't my husband in my mind holding me back, only the twenty-two years of marriage, the long time that had passed without transgression. This line once crossed could never be erased. I wanted to be faithful. I wanted to have faith. I rationalized it couldn't be adultery when you slept with someone you'd slept with before. When it was simply a return to that skin, the same parts, those cells and molecules that had blended with yours so many times before. It was something akin to masturbation when you had sex with a body you had known so well, you never stopped thinking about, you had imagined all this time. I turned to face him. He turned to me. We hesitated, mouths ready, and slowly leaned toward each other and kissed. I thought it would be strange, but our lips were like campers finding the trail after being lost for a long time.

"Oh," I said when I finally could.

"Still here."

I wasn't sure what he meant. The feeling was still here? Or that the world was still here?

I put my hand on his arm and felt him quiver. When I looked in his deep brown eyes they were wet. I couldn't believe it was because of me. It was the passage of time. How old we had gotten. He was fifty-two. Thirty years could be ignored when you lived them each day, but looking right at each other we could not avoid all the days that had passed. I could see it on his face and he on mine. No way to pretend they hadn't happened.

"Io," he finally said. "Has anyone else ever called you that?"

"You are the only one." I saw his satisfaction. "A friend calls me Fee."

"Awful."

"I work at the Getty Villa—ancient Greek and Etruscan art. We have a frieze of Io, but she's a cow."

"The price she paid for being Zeus' lover."

"You mean his victim."

"That's not the way I read it."

"Read it again. It's basically rape."

He took two steps away from me. I recognized his dismissal, the curve of his shoulder separating us. I felt the familiar ache, the desperation to take back what I said, to make him happy. That younger girl was still here. She was me. I was still caught on his hook. I assumed this was nothing special for him, his open marriage, plenty of other lovers, Beth happily at home with the kids. Unlike Harry. I pushed Harry out of my mind. Then Jack swam into view. He made me hesitate; his boy face and his puzzled eyes stopped me.

"Where is Beth tonight?" I almost whispered.

His back straightened. "She doesn't know I'm here."

"Would she mind?"

"Maybe. No. Doesn't matter. We split up over a year ago."

"Oh, I'm sorry." Then, truthfully, "Not really."

He chuckled, a middle-aged man's laugh I didn't recognize, and came back beside me. He put an arm around me. I forced myself to relax into his chest. I smelled his chemical deodorant and something else unfamiliar, like damp wool.

"You were married before?" I asked. "To Lily's mom?"

He hesitated. "It was Alison. I didn't actually marry her, but we had Lily. She has issues."

"Alison or Lily?"

"Both."

I opened my mouth to ask about the past, about the

drugs, about what happened after I left.

"The hotel gave me a bottle of champagne." He changed the subject and I was relieved.

The disparity didn't surprise me. Luc was still Luc. "But did you get a chocolate on your pillow?"

"Let's go check."

Once again, I wasn't ready. I had been sailing toward this moment since I got on the plane that morning, no, since I'd sent that very first email. The wind picked up and in it I smelled boat and salt and that damn diesel fuel.

"Wait," I said. "Wait." But for what? For more time to go by, for some other chance, for me to run away again? I was tired of waiting. We could talk later—tomorrow we could talk and talk and talk. I would show him how sorry I had been, how happy I was that he was okay. I would make it up to him however I could. He pulled me to him and the tiny suture on my breast, now just a red mark, gave a twinge from the pressure of his chest. No more waiting.

"Keep walking?" he asked.

"Kiss me again." I pulled him to me.

The rain came down harder. I put up my hood and led him back to the hotel. He was here. He had come. He was still Luc. There was no reason to remember how bad it had been.

LIFE # 7

After the boat, I left New York and went back to college. I lived in that group house with the ménage a trois, Beatrice and her boys. I called Luc almost every day. He didn't answer, or he was on his way out, or he didn't make any sense.

"Soon as the semester is over I'm coming back," I said.

"What color is the sky where you are?"

"You lived here too."

"Are there clouds and birds where you are?"

I called Lola.

"He's staying with Alison now," she told me. "You know, she's not with Jerry anymore. How's the lady lawyer?"

A day later, I spoke to Luc. "Are you with Alison?"

"Don't call me," he said. "Don't call me again. I'm not interested in any of that, in any of you. Ever again."

"Tell me to come and I will."

"Never. Never, never, never." He hung up. Two nights later, he called me. He was crying, whispering. "Please come, Io, please. Come right away."

I borrowed money, told my part time job I was sick, missed class, and flew to New York. I went right to Alison's. He was expecting me. The key was where he said it would be under the mat. I knocked, no one answered, so I let myself in. The apartment was disgusting—dirty, cockroach infested, half-eaten food and piles of clothes. I did some dishes while I waited. I saw evidence of his new attachments in the stained sheets, the darkened spoons, the filth. Two hours later I called Lola.

"Alison kicked him out," she said. "He's probably with Billy." Then, "What are you doing here?"

"He asked me to come. He called me and practically begged me to come."

"He's a mess," she said. "Since you left—"

"I didn't want to go."

"But you did." Her disgust came in little wet puffs through her teeth.

"I'm here now. I'm back. I won't leave again."

"I'm working on it. With our parents. We'll get him well."

"I can help."

"You hurt him."

I wanted to protest, wanted to make her understand I'd only left because he told me to. But she had her own ideas.

"I wonder if you realize how much of this is your fault," she said.

No. No.

"Luc thinks so too." Her final weapon. "I don't want him to see you. Or talk to you. You've already done too much damage. You left him. You're gone. Stay that way."

I took the train to Delaware to my mother. The wheels chanted, "Doug and Luc, Doug and Luc, Doug and Luc." I had killed one, was killing the other.

Mom was in the process of unloading her boyfriend, Roger. "Mommy," I cried, "my heart is broken."

"Mine too," she said, and introduced me to Tigger. A grown man called Tigger.

Alison's phone was disconnected. I didn't know where Luc

was. I called Lola again and again and until she screamed, "He's on his own path" and hung up on me.

I went back to school. Mom had no place for me, Roger's house was on the market and she was moving to a one-bedroom apartment with Tigger. On the plane my ears wouldn't pop—all I heard was Doug and Luc, Doug and Luc, Doug and Luc.

When I got back to the group house where I was not a member of the group, my cat was dead in the front yard. Torn open by raccoons. No one had moved its decimated body; they had left that for me. I put the stiff and maggot ridden corpse in a black plastic bag and threw it away. Then I stole my housemates' liquor, drank too much, and slit my wrists with a kitchen knife. I didn't know how it should be done and went across instead of lengthwise, but I went deep. I wanted to cut through the sinew and vein, gristle, even bone. I put an apple in my mouth to stop the screams. I expected my flesh to surrender like a prostitute. Doug and Luc. Doug and Luc. Doug and Luc. But nothing I ever did was good enough. The knife wasn't good enough, the apple not good enough to keep me quiet. Beatrice found me and called 9-1-1. When I got home from the hospital, she and Raymond and the other guy asked me to move out. I couldn't blame them—even I didn't want to live with me.

28.

Fiona sat on Doug's bunk, writing a letter. It was quiet in the cabin. No one was saying "mayday" into the radio. The wind and rain and rocking boat were barely noticeable to her anymore. She was writing to her mother and father. She wrote to them together, thinking her funeral would be their final act of togetherness. She did not address the letter to the step-mother she barely knew. I love you Mom and Dad, she wrote. I always knew you loved me. She started to say she would miss them, but she didn't think she would. She'd be dead. Instead she wrote, don't be sad. I deserved to die. She had to write the truth. I killed a man, she told them. I am responsible for his death as surely as if I'd pulled the trigger. He had held onto her in that other big wave. He had been strong enough to get both of them through that. If this wave washed him overboard it was because of her, because she had rejected him. He let go. She saw him let go. She should have waited until they were on the warm sands of Bermuda, until the sun was shining and the sky was clear. Why did she think she had to break his heart on this boat? She had lied so much in her life, she should have lied a little longer.

I'm scared and tired and seasick, she wrote, but I chose this. I followed Luc even though I didn't want to go. I never even told him I was scared. And when things started to go wrong, I should have demanded we turn around, but I said nothing. When I finally did speak up, it was about the wrong thing, for the wrong reason. I was thoughtless and cruel and I hurt him and so he died. I love you, she wrote again. I'm sorry if I was a disappointment to you.

She signed the letter and ripped the page carefully from the back of Nathan's log book. It was the only paper she could find. She folded it small and wrote her mother's address on the outside—she wasn't sure where her father was living. She put the letter in a plastic sandwich bag, squeezed the air out of it, and taped it shut. Water tight, she hoped. Then she stood up carefully and pulled down her yellow rain pants and her jeans underneath. She taped the sealed letter to her upper leg, laughing to herself that her sizeable thigh was finally good for something. The tape caught her hairs and pulled, but she welcomed the pain. She hoped that when her body washed up on shore, whoever found her—perhaps those same children who found Doug—would send the letter to her parents.

The boat tossed and creaked. The muck sloshed against their feet. It couldn't last; another knockdown or a ramming from a passing ocean liner and they'd end up in the drink. Luc said she should wear a life jacket since she couldn't swim, but she refused. They each did things to prepare. Luc opened a can of soup and ate it cold, knowing he would need his strength. They untied their shoes so they would fall off and not fill with water and pull them under. Joren sat at the table using a rope to connect the three life jackets. "For us like a raft to hold on to," he explained. She drank some water, although it made her stomach worse, and washed her face gently around all the cuts. Luc braced himself in the bunk and somehow fell asleep. She sat beside him, her hand in his. And Nathan? He opened another can of tuna fish and ate it with his fingers. He announced they were all too gloomy and he would cheer them up. He sang, "If you want my body and you think I'm sexy, come on baby let me know." He swung his hips back and forth. No one laughed or clapped.

"The brain stores such interesting data, doesn't it?" he asked. "I would have liked to see Doug's brain when he died. The fear. The tumor."

She glared at him.

"Oh yes." Nathan said. "His tumor wasn't gone. Inoperable I'm afraid. I gave him a little time is all."

"He thought you cured him," she said.

"I didn't want him to be unhappy. I thought he'd last longer than this. But he had six months at most—even if he hadn't fallen overboard."

"You lied to him."

"I'm not the only one." Nathan winked at her and danced through the disgusting water. "If you really need me, just reach out and touch me. Come on, honey, tell me so."

She had not lied. She had told Doug the truth—and killed him. But it was Nathan's fault. Doug should never have been on the boat.

"He was right," she said. "You are the devil."

Nathan turned to her to reply as a wave picked up the stern and sent the bow sinking. He slipped, and grabbed the galley counter. "Whoopee!"

The bow pointed down and the stern went up and continued to rise until they were almost perpendicular to the water. Nathan looked as if he was doing a push up against the fore cabin door. Joren was wedged between counter and table. Fiona held the railing above her with one hand, held onto Luc with the other. She was sure this was it. Luc clutched the sides of the bunk. I love you, she mouthed. I love you.

"Pitch poling!" Nathan yelled. "Never before!"

They stayed suspended in this horrible position long enough for the boat's screeching to end. Fiona had time to wonder if a sailboat really could go forward end over end. Then slam! The stern fell back down and banged hard into the sea. She bit her tongue and tasted blood.

"Next knock down," Nathan said with a huge smile, "only I will be saved. They'll find me spread eagle on the upturned hull, arms clasped around the centerboard."

"No one will find you," Luc said. "No one knows we're here."

"Oh, how I'll cry and carry on." Nathan ignored Luc. "I tried to save them. I watched them go, one by one. I held on as long as I could." He grinned at Joren. "Perhaps a tear or two."

"No one will save you." Luc sat up. "Any of us."

It was the first time she'd heard him be pessimistic. She touched the letter in the plastic bag underneath her clothing. She had told her parents how much she loved Luc. She couldn't have said it enough.

"At least we'll die together." She said it out loud and he put his arm around her.

"When I die," Nathan said, "my wife will be devastated. Just like Mary Shelley, pulling her hair, rending her clothing, after her husband, Percy Bysshe Shelley, died in his sailboat in a storm." He took a deep breath and recited, 'My cheeks grow cold, and hear the sea/ Breathe o'er my dying brain its last monotony.'" He laughed. "I have a remarkable brain. I remember everything. My death will be an incredible loss for my wife and my colleagues. Even my patients will despair. Then they will appreciate me. They'll put up a plaque at my hospital in New York."

"A plaque?"

"*Si, certamente*. Like the one in Italy for Shelley."

"Oh shut up, shut up." Joren faced Nathan. His hands were curled into fists. "If we die, it is sitting on your head. Your head."

"Tell us the truth," Nathan said. "Have you ever captained a sailboat before?" He waited. Luc and Fiona waited too. "Fess up. Don't you want to die with a clear conscience? You told me you had been a captain of a large sailboat."

"Okay. I have not been the captain. No." Joren held on to the tabletop. "I was second in charge."

"On a sailboat?"

"Yes."

"In the open ocean?"

Another long pause. The boat rose and rocked in the waves. She heard the wind moaning, low and guttural. She thought she saw tears on Joren's cheeks. With everything wet, it was hard to tell.

"I have sailed the canals. Mast up!" he said. "Real sailing."

"In the canals. Never in the open ocean." Nathan put a hand on his shoulder. "You lied to me—and now you blame me. But you have no idea what you're doing, do you? I knew it. I knew it on the phone when I hired you." He laughed. "I knew you were an impostor."

"The boat is bad. Everything breaks."

"You knew," Fiona said. "And you hired him anyway."

"She's got a point there," Luc said. "And it's not Joren's fault this boat is crap and there's a hurricane."

"Poor little piece of crap boat," Nathan caressed the railing around the shelf above the stove. "Nobody likes you." Snap. He broke the railing in two, yanked off a piece and dropped it in the guck. "Poor little boat." He punched a cupboard door and put his fist right through it.

Doug had been right—Nathan was crazy. Quietly, she opened the log book still wedged beside her. She found his latest entry and began to read aloud.

"'Thanatos,'" she read, "'the drive to die, to see our deaths before us. It is impossible to be happy, impossible to have the life force satiated. Why rage against the dying of the light. Death is the only answer. The only true and complete state. To meet death we must take it into our own hands. That is our only power, our only choice. The only true question is why we continue to fight. My poor hired crew—I have not educated or transformed them. My failures. If I had a gun I could help them escape what is to come. Their lives. So ordinary. So mundane. They would thank me if they knew. Return to the primal state. The beginning. Lifelessness. This force, this living essence, is like trying to hold onto a handful of water, I cannot keep it from dripping through my fingers. Why bother. When no one else understands, why go on?'"

Nathan had dropped his head. As she'd read, she expected him to stop her, but when he looked up, she saw he was grinning.

"There's more, there's more. All of it as exceptional as that. My notes. My observations. As long as that book and I survive—well, the Coast Guard says they always find the boat."

"What is he talking about?"

She turned to Luc. "He wants us all to die. He wants to be famous. The hero. The only one left who watched us all lose our shit while he kept notes."

She saw Luc didn't believe it. It was incomprehensible to him. His life had been so good and easy. He didn't understand how failure made someone feel. Luc had never loathed himself for a moment, never hated being in his own skin, never watched others and felt he was a different species. In a way, her heart went out to Nathan.

"The EPIRB," Joren said quietly. "It is working. Someone will hear it." He stood up. His eyes were bloodshot and he was trembling. He pointed to Nathan's cabin. "Go," he said to him. "Go in there and do not come out. Stay away from us."

"What's done is done." Nathan plucked the log book from Fiona's hands.

"We're not dying," she said. "Unless we all die."

"Go," Joren insisted.

To her surprise, Nathan went. The door closed behind him. Joren collapsed back onto the bench and shut his eyes. Luc's laugh sunk into the bottom of the boat with the sewage. She felt the ocean right outside, wrapping around and pushing on the boat, waiting for her. She was already gasping for air. Drowning was going to be awful. Luc was strong and a good swimmer. He would last so much longer. She closed her eyes, willed a happy memory to come, but it was Doug's face she saw leaning into her, telling her he would love her always. She was glad it was all over for him. She prayed he would not be waiting for her at the end of the tunnel or whatever. She hoped when she died there was only nothing. Any afterlife where she ended up would be hell.

The boat plunged forward. The hold had grown dark. Without the strobe light—it had broken with the mast—there was no light at all. There was nothing to keep an ocean liner from running into them. Nathan had said it happened all the time. Through the flimsy cabin door, she heard him reciting.

"'They cried to the Lord in their distress. From their straits he rescued them. He hushed the storm to a gentle breeze and the billows of the sea were stilled.'" Then he sang. "If you want my body and you think I'm sexy, come on, baby, let me know."

She couldn't listen. She pulled the hideous striped sweater off over her head. Her cruise wear. She put on her yellow jacket, told Luc she'd be right back, and struggled up the ladder into the rain. She had no idea what time it was. There was no way to tell. The clouds and the sky were black. It could be noon or it could be midnight. The boat rocked violently, the foam and spray slapped her eyes, the floor of the cockpit was wet and slippery as she climbed up on the bench and got as close to the edge of the boat as she could get. It rocked, she held on. She should clip in, but there was no point. Nathan expected them all to die. She didn't think they would be saved.

She threw the sweater, bloodstained and filthy, into the sea. It floated on the waves, the arms outstretched like a body in the water. It drifted closer to the boat. Closer. No. It had to go. Go under. Go away. She hissed at it. That sweater was a curse. It would not sink. So much more buoyant than a man. She finally forced herself to turn her back on it.

The boat threw her forward and back. She found a harness and put it on. She clipped herself in. She prayed to whatever was out there to at least save Luc, the man of her dreams, the love of her life. She deserved to drown but it wasn't fair that Luc, so much beauty, so much life ahead of him, would die and never dance again. Icy rain attacked her damaged face. The cuts stung and opened and bled. She fought her interminable seasickness and swallowed the bile. She took the torn strips of yellow rain gear from her pocket and tied them to the railing. They were the brightest things she had. They were the only things she had. It was all she could do. She didn't believe anyone would see them. She knew Doug was waiting for her in the water. She heard him whispering to her, felt the tug of his desire. The sirens, Poseidon, all the monsters of the deep were waiting, singing to her in the wind, calling her to let go, let go.

29.

One afternoon when Jack was in elementary school, I sat in my sunny, dry kitchen and looked up drowning on my laptop. I thought it would help alleviate my nightmares to know what drowning really felt like. I don't know why I thought that. In 1892, Dr. James Lowson described in the *Edinburgh Medical Journal* what happened when his boat sank. He was rescued at the last minute, chest pumped to bring him back to life, but he experienced drowning right up to and including blacking out. He described being desperate for air, "in a vice which was gradually being screwed up tight until it felt as if the sternum and spinal column must break." Then the pain went away and he thought of friends and family, and in this "pleasant dream" passed out.

I thought of Dr. Lowson as I led Luc up the stairs at the hotel. I was drowning in love, a vice around my heart so tight I worried it would explode. I hoped I would crawl into his bed and the pain would go away and in that pleasant dream I would pass into his arms and out of my life.

What I should have known as I climbed those stairs was that Harry was pacing the floor at home, frustrated and furious. I should have known he would call our insurance agent and demand they pay for my second opinion in Massachusetts. If I'd thought about it for a minute, I would have known he started calmly, but got angrier and more abusive until the agent hung up on him. I would have known that the office was now closed and because Harry couldn't get anyone on the phone, he had left rude messages and sent a volley of angry emails threatening exposure at every major newspaper. And if I'd known he sped off in the car with the tires squealing to spend twenty-eight dollars at the hardware store and then driven downtown to a fabric shop—my husband—to spend another nineteen dollars—my husband who wouldn't buy blueberries—I would have paid attention. I should have looked at my phone when I got to the hotel. If I'd read his last confused and enraged text about breast cancer and the President's responsibility to American women, I would have worried, called him back. But I was underwater, immersed in who I had been, all the wrong decisions I had made, and Harry didn't exist in that sea. My phone stayed in my purse.

At the second floor landing, Luc's hands reached under my coat to graze my ass. I was weak, about to understand the definition of swoon.

"Here?" I asked.

"Up again. And again."

His room was on the top floor. He fumbled with the key and in that moment we both grew shy. I noticed his bed was not turned down and he didn't have a chocolate.

"You didn't get a Hershey's Kiss," I said.

He nodded at the champagne chilling in an ice bucket. "Just a poor substitution."

"I'd complain if I were you."

He opened the bottle and poured me a glass in one of the plastic flutes. He had told me he didn't drink and it seemed he meant it. I hadn't had anything to eat since the peanuts on the plane and then a few French fries, but the glass of scotch had not touched me. I was sober. I wanted to stay that way, to do this deed while I knew exactly what I was doing. I put my champagne on the bedside table. I took off my coat and dropped it on a chair.

"Luc," I said.

He was standing by the desk, one hand clutching the neck of the champagne bottle, the other balled in his pocket. I had never known him to be nervous. Not about anything, certainly not about this. He looked down at the floral carpeting.

"Okay," I said, "Okay." I was going back to my room. I had misread the signs. Kisses were one thing, this bed between us a trip of another kind. I picked up my jacket. He lifted his head. In one step he came to me. He took my jacket out of my hand. This was the Luc I remembered. Finally, finally, I could smell him. The same Luc he'd always been, salty, starchy, like a warm New York pretzel. I leaned forward, he bent and ran his lips up my neck. I shivered like the muscles on a horse's flank.

"Cold?"

"No."

And then he walked away from me. The room was small, there wasn't far for him to go, but he leaned back against the desk and crossed his arms. His face was shadowed, his eyes in the dark. I didn't know what he wanted. I thought of my empty room two floors below, the Weather Channel on the room's TV, a quick phone call to Jack.

"You," he said. "It's really you."

And then he surrounded me. Arms, lips, his body against mine. We kissed. A lot. He fingered the bottom of my sweater, anxious to pull it off over my head. I felt the flesh around his middle, not the lean light Luc I remembered, but still the same. The smooth, dark skin. The length of him. The narrow hips and long neck. My sweater came off. My jeans unbuttoned and opened. He pushed me down on the bed and I watched him undress.

"A few pounds," he said.

"The same. You're just the same."

He lay beside me and we kissed and I closed my eyes. "Don't," he said. "Keep your eyes open. I will too."

As I arched and stretched and sighed and smiled, I saw Luc in front of me, beneath me, above me, behind me. We took our time. We both hesitated more than once. I was surprised. I was ecstatic. But sometimes the guilt dripped in through the spaces between us, got in my way, like a sudden chilly breeze giving me goose bumps. Not just my lifelong guilt about Luc, but my current guilt as well. He felt so unlike Harry and he responded differently. Then he would make me laugh—at both the awkwardness and the familiarity. He reminded me who I was, who I had been, all those things that used to be ahead of me. He was Luc and I finally, finally surrendered. I said his name out loud as I had silently so often over the years.

Later he opened a window and smoked a cigarette sitting naked on the sill.

"Still?" I asked.

"Still wonderful." He took a deep drag and blew out the smoke as he looked over at me. "Still delish."

I reached my arms to him. He tossed his cigarette in the toilet and came back to bed. "Why did you write to me?" He asked with his arms around me. "Why now?"

I spoke into his neck. "I've missed you my whole life. I think I see you in every crowd. Just ahead. Just out of reach."

"Yes. Oh god, yes, me too. But why now? Why did you wait so long?"

It was the perfect time to tell him I had cancer and couldn't stop thinking about him. I had cancer—I reminded myself—and this might be my last chance for reparations. But it wasn't that. I didn't want him to think it was cancer that made me email him. Not anymore. I shook my head against his shoulder.

"I'm glad you did," he said. "So many years, but I'm just glad you're here."

He could have called me. The phone went in both directions. Email too. I wanted to tell him Lola had forbidden me to call. I wanted to tell him I'd convinced myself he was dead. Later. I would say all that later.

He rolled on his back, stared at the ceiling. "I've missed you. I guess I shouldn't say this. It's not cool, maybe I'm coming on too strong, but I crave you. I do. At night, I wake up wanting you. I dream I'm in New York. Remember how the light came through the window onto that awful sofa bed? I used to watch you sleep. You were so pale, like a ghost sleeping beside me. The most beautiful woman I'd ever seen."

I had never known he watched me sleep—or that he thought I was beautiful.

"I want you. I always have. It went away for a while after you left and I was so high, again when I first got clean and married Beth. But it always came back. Wanting you. You. You. You."

It was what I wanted to hear.

"You're really here." He hugged me hard, laughed. "I have so many ideas." He sounded like a kid. "It's going to be great. We're going to have so much fun."

I had to tell him about the small red mark on my breast. I had to ask him if he blamed me for his lost years. Wasn't one of the Twelve Steps to make amends, to at least apologize? I needed a program to get over my life of guilt. Guilty Culprits Anonymous. *Mea culpa.* I whispered it. The French fries and scotch threatened to return. How appropriate it would be if I started puking. "Let's talk about it in the morning," I said. I threw back the covers.

"Don't." He held my arm. "Stay. I want to sleep beside you. I want to wake up next to you. I've dreamed you were in my bed for all these years."

"We finally have a real bed."

"I should have given you that. Found us an apartment."

"I was always waiting for you to give me something, instead of just doing it myself."

"No," he said. "It was my choice."

I opened my mouth to retort, but he was right. Back then everything was his choice.

"Oh Fi-o-na," he sang as he pulled me closer. "You make me moan-a. With your long blond hair-a, you're mighty fair-a. The way you dance-a, makes me cream in my pants-a."

He remembered—he knew me. Tomorrow. Tomorrow. We would have tomorrow. I would tell him I was sick and needed treatment. I would tell him some choices were all mine. I would make him understand how sorry I was. I laughed out loud.

"I remember that laugh of yours. You laugh with your whole body."

"Like a horse."

"Or a cow." He squeezed me tight. "Newport is a lot nicer this time around, but I kind of miss the rocking boat, the smell of upchuck and diesel fuel."

"I almost puked a while ago," I said. "Would that help?"

"You were that nervous?"

"Not at all. It's just what I do when I'm near the ocean."

"Here," he said. "Hold onto me. The only rocking this bed is doing is from us."

I curled against him. I didn't really know where to fit; we shifted, twisted, couldn't get comfortable. Our bodies had changed and we weren't used to each other anymore. I pushed Harry's broad chest from my mind. It would come, I decided. Luc and I had fit together perfectly once; we would again.

His voice was quiet. "You loved me. Back then. You really did, didn't you?"

"I loved you more than anything. Luc. I've always loved you. I never stopped."

He closed his eyes as if in pain. Without seeing he ran a finger down my neck, between my breasts, down my stomach to my crotch. My hips lifted to him. Could I ever say no? He looked up at the ceiling and I saw that small spot he always missed shaving. Those hairs I had loved still there.

"Don't leave me," he whispered.

"Don't say that unless you mean it."

"Don't leave me. I should have said it then. I should have screamed it at you."

"I'm sorry," I said. "I never should have gone. I'm sorry. I was so sure you were dead. That's why I didn't call you years ago. I thought you had died."

"I did my best," he said. "I tried my damnedest to follow my brother into oblivion." He sat up. "Io—I still love you. And not because you're pretty or sexy or sweet or funny, which you are, I love you because I have to. I don't have any choice."

If he had said it then, where would we be now? Where would I be? Would I have helped him come back to life? Or would he have found oblivion with me? The sheets were stiff, the pillows made of spongy foam, growing soggy under my tears.

"I'm so sorry," I said.

Luc whispered into my hair. "It's okay," he said. "Everything will be okay. You'll see. I love you."

This time I would not leave. I would go wherever Luc's current took me.

30.

Incredibly, Fiona had fallen asleep huddled in the cockpit. The boat rocked, the cold was numbing, but she was exhausted. Something woke her. Her hands were frozen; she could not open her fingers.

"Luc?"

Someone was on deck. Whoever it was, scrambled toward the broken mast. She peered through the spray and foam. The wind caught the person's hood and pushed it back. It was Nathan. Crawling across the deck. She got to her feet, stepped forward and the harness snapped her back. She'd forgotten she was wearing it.

"Nathan!"

He looked at her and continued on his way. Hand over hand. He was going for the EPIRB. She knew it. She unclipped the harness. "Nathan!" She started toward him. "Luc! Joren!"

Her words whipped away in the wind. Nathan reached the broken stub of mast. She could see the EPIRB's green light blinking. He looked over his shoulder at her. The devil. She was afraid to go to him. She wasn't strong enough. If she fell she would slip into the water and die.

"Luc! Luc!" No one came up the ladder.

She had to stop him. Nathan was pulling at the EPIRB,

trying to get it free, struggling with his cold fingers against
Joren's good knot.

"Stop it!" She climbed on top of the hatch, clipped herself
onto the wires running here and there. They were so flimsy
she knew they wouldn't save her. She scooted forward on her
butt. "Nathan. You stop that, right now." Her mother's voice.
She almost laughed. What do you think you're doing? That
was next.

He turned to her. "Go away."

"Come back inside."

"I don't want to go home." He crossed his arms over his
chest. "I should have won that prize. It was mine. I deserved it.
The committee hated me. I'm too smart for them."

If she was the mother, he was the recalcitrant child, unhappy, scorned, not invited to the popular kid's birthday party.
"There will be other prizes and awards." She slid a little closer,
clutching the insubstantial wires, sliding her feet along the
slippery deck. "You'll win next time," she said to him. "When
we get back you'll write an article, about fear—this trip."

He shook his head, ran his hands through his wet hair.
"I watched Doug. Every day I saw evidence of his tumor
growing, twisting in his brain, changing him. His speech,
his paranoia—fascinating. But he was gone before I could
operate."

He took something from his pocket and held it up. It
glinted. Metallic. A knife? A scalpel.

"Come closer," he said. "Your beautiful head. I will open
all your secrets now before you die. You will be immortalized
in my work."

She scurried away. The boat rocked violently and she fell
onto her side. Her feet slipped around her and she skidded
down and kept sliding toward the sea. "LUC!" Her harness

finally caught and she hung there until the boat rocked the other way and she slid and crawled back to the hatch.

Luc came up the ladder. "What are you doing?" Then he saw Nathan at the mast. The scalpel. The EPIRB blinking. "Nathan. Stop."

Joren came up then too. "What happens here?"

Nathan screamed. He kept screaming and, as if his voice could frighten the heavens, the rain lessened, the wind subsided, and behind him the sky was almost blue.

"No," Nathan said. "No!"

The boat shuddered and stalled. Nathan wasn't wearing a harness. His hair hung wet and stringy, his face and hands glowed a soggy white. A blotch of something, oil or food, stained his yellow slicker.

Luc stretched his hand to Nathan, gesturing for him to come back. The EPIRB blinked. The clouds were lifting, the sea growing calmer.

"The weather is changing," Luc said. "We will be saved."

Nathan smiled pointedly. He gave a formal bow and when he came up he put two fingers on his neck as if feeling for his pulse. He smiled again, shook his head, and jammed the scalpel into his neck. His smile became a grimace. Luc shouted his name, climbed toward him, but Nathan, blood gushing from his artery, pushed himself backwards over the edge like a scuba diver going into the sea.

They ran to that side of the boat and saw nothing. Not even a bubble. He had disappeared.

"He's gone." Joren snapped his fingers. "It is like that."

No, she thought. It took so long. It took his whole lifetime for him to go.

"No," Luc said. "Three minutes. He said a healthy person could live three minutes. He might come up."

Fiona stared at the smears of blood on the deck. She stretched her hands to the sky. She thought of how Nathan's raincoat pockets always bulged, the beers and bottle of scotch he always carried. He wasn't coming up.

"Look." Luc was pointing. "Look."

A single Topsider floated to the surface, upside down, its beige sole a footprint on the sea. The sun broke through the gray flannel clouds. Fiona knew the morning had finally come.

31.

Oh god, it felt great to be bad. The early morning sun came through the hotel's windows and I felt wicked and young and desired—feelings I hadn't had in years. My legs were longer, my hair shinier, the wrinkles gone from my eyes. I was my old self, the girl I'd been missing. I'd been responsible for so long, a wife, a mother, a good girl. I hadn't even realized how dull I had become. My shoulders relaxed, my hips twisted, I rolled closer to Luc. He pressed up against me in his sleep. I was in bed with Luc.

But my aging body intruded, I had to pee. I extricated myself and tiptoed into the small bathroom and shut the door. On the wall was a faded photo of a racing sailboat. There were whitecaps and the boat heeled way over. I stared at the sailors, perched over the upside of the boat, almost parallel to the sea—hiking out. A label underneath read, "The Min-O-Din, Winner of the Fastnet Race, 1991."

A British yachtsman, Weston Martyr, set up the first Fastnet Race in 1925. The race begins at the Isle of Wight, goes through the Irish Sea and back to Plymouth, England. Six hundred and eight nautical miles—only twenty-seven miles shorter than Newport to Bermuda. In August 1979, three months before we set sail, the Fastnet Race met with disaster. Calm and clear weather the first two days, a moderate to fresh breeze, Force 4 or 5. Those who were there talk about the stunning red sunset on the second afternoon, the exquisite conflagration of winds meeting from the Bristol Channel and the Irish Sea. But "red sky at night, sailor's delight" did not prove to be true. A Force 10 storm came up rapidly. The wind went from 20 to 60 knots—almost 70 mph—in minutes. These were experienced sailors, the best of the best. Harnesses were broken, ships capsized and sunk. Fifteen lives were lost.

I flushed and washed my hands. I found Luc's toothpaste and rubbed a finger full over my teeth. I cleaned up my smeared mascara, and pulled my fingers through my hair. Luc and I were together. My stomach growled. I wanted a real breakfast, eggs and toast. I was ravenous for so many things. More sex. Laughing out loud. Butter, jam, toast. I never allowed myself to eat toast at home.

Home. Harry's face came up as suddenly as that Fastnet storm. It made me seasick. I imagined walking through my front door and telling him I was leaving him. Would I move to Luc's town? There was no reason for him to come to mine. He had a business to run. His kids were younger. I imagined us starting over somewhere new. New Mexico. A place without an ocean. All our children would come for Christmas. Jack would see how happy we were and he'd understand. The desert, the cactus, I would be brown and strong. Long mornings in bed. And lots of toast.

I hurried back to him. I touched a curl of his hair and saw the scar on his cheek. I remembered the way the corners of his mouth turned down as he slept. What if I never told him I had cancer? If I pretended—lied—that it didn't exist. The cancer would grow, but I wasn't sure how fast. A when it got bad, at the end, would Luc change my sheets, brush my hair, help me in the bathroom? How far did loving a memory go?

The sun crawled through the window into his eyes and woke him. His smile was like a welcome home banner for a returning soldier. He wrapped his arms around me. He told me he had stayed awake and watched me sleep. I looked the same, he said, and I felt better in his arms than I ever had. We laughed about our morning breath and kissed anyway. We made love again. Less energetically, but easier, without inhibition, moving each other for maximum effect. There were things Luc did to me that no one else ever could. There was a place he reached I only visited with him.

"I'm starving," I said. "I want to see Newport. I want to go to the dock."

"It's raining."

"Of course it is." I laughed and he did too.

"Look at you," he said. "Look at your hand on my arm. That hand. Your hand." He put his hand over mine. "If I died right now, I'd be happy."

"Oh no, not yet. I have plans for you." I kissed him. I felt loved. I felt beautiful.

We didn't make any plans other than meeting in the lobby in fifteen minutes. "Ten. No, five," he said. "Sooner. I can't stand it."

I put on my clothes from the night before and went down to my room to take a shower.

But alone was not a good place to be. My unused room held too much evidence of my other life. I had bought my suitcase when Jack and I went to look at colleges. Harry had given me my silly polka-dot toiletries bag. He had been with me when I bought the shirt I was going to wear. The room was a reproach. My bed was still pristine. My nightgown still packed. I ate the chocolate kiss knowing it would not sit well on my empty stomach. I messed up the bed so the maid wouldn't know I was an adulteress, a slut, easy as the cake. I showered and brushed my teeth and got dressed and when I sprayed my wrists and neck with perfume I remembered how much Harry loved my scent. I'd been wearing it for years, since before I met him. Not as far back as Luc, but close. It's mine, I thought, only mine. Surprised at how aggressive I sounded.

I forced myself to look at my two-timing face in the mirror. My eyes went to my left breast, completely normal looking in bra and blouse. Damn it—that belligerent tone again—I could be dead soon. I deserved this. And then I grimaced. Bad luck to use cancer to justify my bad behavior. Bad karma, just bad. I would tell Luc, but not yet. Not yet.

We walked along the Newport streets in the rain arm in arm. He looked at me often and I at him. We found the Harbormaster's office. It was the same, but everything around it had changed. We went to the docks, but the gates at the top were locked and we couldn't walk down to the boats. It was cold, rainy November—not a sailor in sight.

"What an adventure," Luc said.

"We were fools."

"We were kids. It sounded like fun. It should've been."

"Nathan was crazy. He really was."

"I thought sailing would be a vacation. A get away."

"Not from dance. You wanted to get away from New York—" I stopped. He'd found heroin here in Newport too. "What happened to Billy?" I don't know why I asked; I didn't really want to know.

"He died." Luc turned to me. "A long time ago."

"Overdose?" Of course it was.

"AIDS." He rubbed his face with his hands, a gesture that had become a habit. "Jesus, I was young and stupid. And very fortunate."

"You thought you were immortal."

He gave a sad laugh. "And now, feet of clay. I need to eat." "Me too."

He got quiet and I was sorry I'd brought up Billy. He stopped to tie the lace on his sensible, brown shoe. He tried to stand on one leg and lift his foot to his hands, then leaned against a mailbox, then gave up and crouched. He gave a little "oof" as he bent. I remembered him leaping and spinning in New York, balancing on one foot, pretending to be the Greek statue he always was to me.

"Remember how you danced on top of mailboxes?" I asked.

He took my hands. "I remember everything. Do you?"

I had tried so hard to forget. "Do you still dance?"

"I remember dancing with you. I remember how good you were, how flexible and light. You moved like a gazelle, a bird, a swan."

I didn't share those memories. I laughed. "I remember watching you."

"Oh!" He looked up to the sky and his eyes were the happiest I'd seen them. "New York was incredible, wasn't it?" He went on about the classes we took—he took—how he met Paul Taylor and Erick Hawkins, other famous dancers. How fun everything was. He talked about eating hot dogs from the street vendors and pizza on every corner and the way the wind whistled between the buildings. "It almost blew itty bitty you away." He twirled in front of me. I watched his body trying to return again to the dancer he'd been. The food, the weather, the foldout couch in Lola's apartment, he said all of it was perfect. "Those days, those days in New York, were the best of my entire life. The absolute best."

I cringed. "Before the boat," I said. "Even before that, you mean, when we first got to New York."

A cloud settled in his eyes. "Drugs. A scourge—a plague that feels so good before it kills you. Ring around the rosy, pocket full of posy. Just like that. Dancing myself to death." He looked at me. "You were lucky."

I saw on his face the same envy and anger I'd seen then. Quickly I said, "It wasn't luck. I was just scared. Remember? Terrified."

"Lucky, lucky you."

"Do you blame me, Luc? I blame myself. Lola blames me. Do you?"

"I can't. Of course I can't. I'd like to." He almost smiled. "I thought I'd die after you left, but I was glad you were gone."

"I didn't want to go."

"I was glad not to have you staring at me when I got back to the apartment. I'd sit at Alison's and hear your little voice telling me you loved me, asking me to go back to school with you." He shuddered. "It didn't help."

He took a few steps away and it was as if he was leaving me again. My heart tightened in my chest, my hands reached for him. I wanted to bring him back. I scanned the past. "Do you remember the rats in the alley behind Lola's apartment?"

"You threw bread to them out the window."

"Lola was so mad. And now I'm cursed. My house is plagued with mice. Gross. And when they're dead—"

He interrupted. "Do you remember the pirouette competition I had with that girl in class?" I didn't. "And we went to dinner at that funky place in Chinatown and the Chinese waiter touched your hair? 'Pletty, so pletty.'" I didn't remember that either. "And the park where we played on the swings?" I had a faint image of Luc climbing a jungle gym. "We used to go all the time after class or after you worked and I would push you so high and you weren't frightened at all."

I didn't remember not being frightened.

Luc took a run at the mailbox. I held my breath. I saw the emergency room, having to call Beth or worse, Lola. He stopped right before he jumped, banged both hands on the blue arch. "Ha!" he said. "I was the mailbox king." He turned to me. "Wasn't New York the most wonderful place on earth? Oh, I've missed you. I've missed you so much."

He opened his arms and I held him. I was used to Harry's height, my forehead above his shoulder. With Luc I felt like a child. New York had been amazing, but it hadn't been wonderful. Not like my semester abroad in Greece, my discovery of ancient art, the ouzo and friends, the assistantship I was awarded so I could spend the entire summer there. Not like the first time I made Harry dinner and we let the food get cold as we danced in the kitchen. Not like having Jack, those milky baby nights when he slept against me after nursing. Laughing at the toddler, so proud of the first grader reading. All of that was wonderful. And amazing.

"What about your kids?" I asked. "Funny we both have sons named Jack."

"I never thought I'd have kids. The first, Lily, was a complete surprise. Alison was too high to remember birth control."

Of course it was Alison's fault.

"And Beth had to talk me into having Sarah. I was so angry when a couple years later she got pregnant with Jack. I had said one, only one."

His choice, not hers—again. Harry would have had a baseball team of kids, but it just hadn't happened for us. "But now you must be so happy to have them."

He spoke quietly over my head. "I was crazy when we got

back to New York after the boat. I couldn't wait to get high. I wanted to forget the whole thing. What I'd done to you. You quit dance. You were a mess. Remember how you stopped and stared at that man in the green coat?"

I had a flash of cold New York wind and a man in a big green coat and stocking cap staring back at me and opening his hands like "what did I do?"

"I was thinking of Doug."

"I almost killed you by going on that boat."

"I wanted to go."

"Only because I did. You always did whatever I wanted."

"Isn't that why you liked me?" I tried to make a joke.

He threw his hands in the air, a gesture I knew too well. "You were right to leave, even if you broke my heart," he said. "But when you told me you'd slept with that lady lawyer, I thought I'd kill myself."

No, no, no. He was already with Alison. He had it backwards. Not his broken heart, mine. All these years I was miserable because I was the one who had been dumped, left, thrown over for a city and a drug he couldn't resist. I remembered his face clearly, his nostrils flared and his lips in a sneer. "Go," he had said, "I don't want you here. Go back to school or whatever. Go now." I didn't remember the pirouettes or the swing or the Chinese waiter, but I clearly remembered his disgust. For thirty years I had wiggled the loose tooth of his disdain. For thirty years I had berated myself for not staying and putting up with it—trying to help him even though he was done with me. And for thirty years I knew I was the one whose heart was broken. I had only that miniscule speck of comfort. I had loved him more than he had loved me. It was my only talent. What would it mean if all these years I'd gotten it wrong?

"You broke my heart," he said. "But whatever you did, I

brought it on myself. I know that. I'm the one responsible for what happened to me."

He sat down on a bench and dropped his head. His hair had more gray than I had seen at first. His curls fell forward and I saw the back of his neck creased and dry. He had absolved me. I felt worse than ever.

"Luc," I said. "Those days in New York were—without question—the best days of my life."

He looked up, eyes shining as if I'd given him a gift. "They were, weren't they? They really were."

No, not exactly, but those days had been filled with possibilities I never felt again. "I'm starving," was what I said. "Can we please have breakfast?"

He stood up. "You always were a good eater." He nuzzled in and pretended to nibble on my neck. He sent a shudder down my spine. "I'm hungry too," he said. "I'd like to eat you up."

That I remembered.

32.

Day five. Fiona thought the sky was a shade—maybe two shades—less dark. Everything else, waves and wind and drizzle, was the same, the same, the same. She and Luc stayed on deck in the cockpit, buckled in their harnesses. Joren had gone below, saying it was too cold on deck.

Luc slept against her shoulder. The boat rocked like a cradle. She had stopped crying, stopped watching for Doug in every swell, afraid it would be Nathan who floated to the top. She looked out to the horizon. Like a cartoon character, she rubbed her eyes and looked again. Something was out there. It was white, not black like the ocean liner or cargo ship that had passed them. "Look," she said. She nudged Luc awake. "What's that?"

Bright, searching lights swept the ocean. Back and forth, back and forth. She could hear the ship—it really was a ship—rumbling and chugging toward them .

She stood and shouted. "Here! We're here!"

Luc roused himself. Stood up with her. "What?"

"Look."

The ship's hull caught the only ray of sun and shone through the rain like a gull's white breast. They could just make out the red stripe of the insignia on the side.

"The Coast Guard!" Luc hugged her, removed his harness, and ran to the hatch. "Joren!" He yelled below. "We're saved."

Joren came up, shouting, hollering, and waving his arms. "It was the EPIRB," he said. "They heard it."

If Doug had only held on, Fiona thought. And then she was glad Nathan was dead. The ship chugged closer, close enough so she could see the men on deck with their serious, concerned expressions.

"What do we tell them?" Joren asked.

"About what?" Luc said.

"About Nathan. And Doug."

"We tell them the truth. We were in a storm. They went overboard."

A male voice came through some kind of megaphone. "This is the United States Coast Guard. Prepare to be boarded."

A red rescue raft with six men in red jumpsuits dropped slowly down the side of the ship into the sea. It struggled at first in the rolling waves, not making much headway. The ocean was still rough, the rain coming down harder again, the wind picking up. A young guardsman in the back was holding on and gritting his teeth. Fiona could see he was scared and his fear made her feel stronger. If he was frightened, then it made sense so was she.

When the raft got close enough, Joren threw the men a line—the first competent sailing thing she had seen him do. The men began to shout; the raft and the *Bleiz A Mor* were about to collide. The raft backed away. They tried again, getting close and moving apart. The Coast Guard men weren't happy. Let them ram this stupid sailboat, she thought. Knock a hole in it and sink it. But they knew what they were doing and eventually, they pulled perfectly alongside.

Four men climbed aboard the sailboat. They had their guns drawn and ready--unsure what kind of desperadoes would be out in a hurricane—but they took one look at her banged up face, saw how grateful and happy the three pale, weak sailors were to see them, and put their guns away.

"Oh man," Luc said. "Thank you, thank you for coming."

"Only three of you?" The man in front had incredible turquoise eyes. He scanned the boat and then each of them up and down. "Sailing this boat?"

"Did you find anyone?" Fiona asked. "He said he was a good swimmer. A very good swimmer."

"You lost someone? How long ago?"

"Yesterday. Or the day before. I don't know." The trip was one continuous storm in her mind, one long, eternal night.

"Water this cold—" The man didn't need to finish.

"In the storm," Joren said. "We have no steering. Rudder—it is broken. No power, the boat is dead. We couldn't go back."

"We had a knockdown," Luc said. "He—they—weren't strapped in. There was nothing we could do."

"Two people went overboard?" The guardsman frowned. "That's rough."

Fiona, Luc and Joren nodded, silent and complicit.

He had a walkie-talkie and he spoke to his ship. Then he said, "Time to evacuate."

She didn't want to cry, but tears of relief slipped down her cheeks. She'd been afraid the Coast Guard would fix the boat and send them on their merry way to Bermuda.

"Are you the captain?" He asked Luc.

"No. The owner—the guy who hired all of us—he was." Luc turned to the ocean. Fiona saw his hands clench and how he bit his lower lip. He must've liked Nathan, seen something in him that she had missed. Of course Nathan had been half in love with Luc. "This has really been crazy."

"Horrific," Fiona said.

The man put his hand on her shoulder and squeezed. His aquamarine eyes were exactly the color she had imagined the ocean would be. Maybe somewhere, she thought, somewhere the ocean is as beautiful as his eyes.

"Where were you headed?" he asked.

"Bermuda," Joren replied. Luc had not ratted him out as the captain. She could tell he was thankful. "We come from Newport, Rhode Island."

"Do you know where you are? Three hundred nautical miles straight off the coast of Virginia. Heading east."

"Where would we have ended up?" Luc asked.

"Morocco or Africa someplace, but you wouldn't have made it. Not on this boat." The man sighed, impressed with what idiots they were. "Time to board the cutter."

They were told to grab a toothbrush, any dry clothes. They could pick up the rest of their stuff when they got to shore. The Coast Guard planned to tow the *Bleiz A Mor* all the way back—for what reason she could not imagine.

Down below, she stopped at Doug's bunk. Some part of him should be saved. She saw his little travel kit and grabbed it. Then she saw Nathan's log book. All the notes that would make him famous. She picked it up.

"Io? Come on." Luc called. "We're leaving."

She handed the waiting guardsman Doug's travel kit with her few things. She didn't have any clean or dry clothing. "I'll hold this," she said about the book.

They helped her over the edge and just before she jumped into the raft, she pretended to fumble and dropped the book into the sea. "Oh no." She tried to sound sorry. "That's too bad. No, don't bother fishing for it. Let it go."

In the boat, a sailor wrapped a blanket around her. She

hadn't realized she was shivering.

As they banged across the waves and through the rain back to the big ship, she did not look back. There was nothing to see.

33.

Luc and I left the main street and the tourist restaurants and walked up the hill away from the water. We found a little coffee shop. Inside, it smelled of toast and coffee. There was a table of fishermen, just as there had been in the donut shop thirty years ago, but instead of wool, they wore Goretex and fleece. One of them was texting on his phone.

We sat and ordered and Luc reached across the table and took my hand, my left hand with my thin, gold wedding band. He played with the ring with his thumb. "How old is your Jack?"

"Twenty," I said. "A junior."

And that started it, the exchange of all the news and information. Lola still lived and worked in New York. She had a long time partner, a successful artist. Our parents: mine gone, his still around. Our kids. His youngest daughter was a dancer. His Jack's obsession with baseball, my Jack's obsession with music. My career—such as it was—in art history. We skittered across the surface, never going very deep. Luc sat across from me and his face was lined, but his eyes were clear and he was looking at me.

I asked, "Do you like being a therapist?"

"It's fantastic," he said. "And our space is very alternative. We help people in many different ways. Traditional medicine is just part of it." He kept holding my hand.

The time had come. "Do you see sick people? You know, really sick, like with cancer?"

"Sure. All the time. Sometimes we help."

"Only sometimes?"

"People bring cancer on themselves. When their cells mutate, it's their own fault. Every cancer patient I've met has been filled with negativity."

"Well, sure. That makes sense: they have cancer."

"No. From before the diagnosis. They're unhappy people. They say we are what we eat. Actually, we are what we think. Think dark, troubled, jealous, or vengeful thoughts and—" He shrugged. "Look what happens."

Before I left, I'd done some research, seen the websites that said people get cancer for a reason. We do it with our pessimism, our frustration and anger and fear actually cause our cells to revolt. According to those websites—according to Luc—I had made myself sick by feeling bad all those years about him and the boat and Doug. How else would he explain it? I didn't drink much. I had never smoked cigarettes. I ate organic vegetables. And I thought good thoughts most of the time about my coworkers, my high school tour groups, even Harry. It was worrying about what I'd done to Luc that kept me up at night. Luc and Doug. How would he explain Doug's cancer? Harry would say Luc was an idiot. A fucking idiot. I smiled.

"What?"

"Nothing." I gestured to the waitress for more coffee.

"It makes sense, you and art history," Luc said. "You loved the museum. The Met. I remember. You spent day after day there. I bet you're good at it."

"Wish I could find a full time job."

"I have an idea." He looked down at this plate. "What about art therapy—you know, with me?"

"At your place?"

"I'll change the name. We can call it Apples and Oranges Wellness Center."

My stomach turned. Apples and oranges. "This is hard."

"But wonderful. Wonderful. Right?"

So anxious for my agreement.

Breakfast arrived. I looked across at his brown hair streaked with gray, the way he pushed his eggs around with his fingers. I was going to give up everything so I could see him every morning for the rest of my life. I was finally going to learn to make Greek food. I grinned.

"Now what?"

"My heart is so full. And my stomach so empty."

He leaned across the table to kiss me.

I dug into my cheese omelet, spread butter and jam on my toast, poured catsup on my hash browns. The waitress came by with more coffee and I asked for a side order of fruit. Luc said he'd never seen me eat so much.

"So much you don't know."

"Can't wait to learn."

"Can we live in Greece? On an island? You speak the language." I thought of Doug and all his nevers, the things he'd never do. The things I thought I would never do—I would never live in Europe, I would never see Luc again. I would never leave my husband.

Luc frowned. "Greece. Awful. The first time I got clean, my parents sent me to my uncle in Kallithea."

"The first time?"

"People do heroin everywhere."

"We could live in Paris or Madrid."

"I need to be near my parents. My kids. The business—in this economy."

The real world seeped in, but then he reached his hand across the table and ran his fingers down my arm. My breath stopped. My toes clenched. I'd thought that part of me was over. That morning I felt wanted and it made me insatiable. Like a teenager, I had the same youthful optimism—so much ahead of us.

The waitress brought our check and I said I'd pay for breakfast. I put a twenty-dollar bill on the table.

"Do you remember playing poker on the Coast Guard ship?" Luc asked.

I wanted to talk about now, about tomorrow, about two weeks from now. "Apples and oranges? You can't change the name of your clinic."

"C'mon," he said. "You must remember. You won twenty dollars."

"Do you remember the last time we saw each other?"

He nodded.

"In New York? Didn't seem like you missed me then."

He didn't disagree. "It was snowing," he said. "You came from California. You were so...fresh, so wholesome and healthy, even more than I remembered. Your skin looked like it was full of juice. That's what I kept thinking, you looked so juicy."

"You wouldn't touch me."

"How could I? I was embarrassed. I was strung out. The baby had come. Alison had dumped me. I was using, a lot. Even Billy was tired of me. Not long after you were there, I ended up on the street. Lola put me on a plane, flew down to Orlando with me. She and my parents tried to save me. I was in detox, then rehab for ninety days. When I came out, I was clean, but I was numb. I couldn't dance. They sent me to my uncle in Greece and I got high again as quickly as I could."

"You should have called me from Florida."

"Why? So you could say I told you so?"

"That is the last thing I would have said. For a smart guy," I said, "You're an idiot." Harry's favorite word. I couldn't help it.

"Hey. Hey. I was a heroin addict." He thought heroin, like dance, made him special. So damn special. He was frowning. He crossed his arms over his chest.

I didn't care if I made him angry. "How can you say I broke your heart? All I wanted was to be with you. I would've stayed forever if you'd asked me."

"Two junkies. That's what we would have been." He was shouting. "Two dead junkies." People in the restaurant were turning to look. "Do you think I could live with that? I took you on that boat trip and you almost died. Then I wanted to get you high. Do it with me, remember? That's what I wanted. All I wanted. I was going to kill you, if not on the sea, then in your veins, in your blood. That was my goal. Damn Billy, damn New York. Damn boat."

"Damn boat," I echoed.

I looked at Luc's tired, handsome face. He thought he'd pushed me away to save me and I thought I'd left him to die—and we had missed each other for thirty years. Was death from an overdose preferable to a life badly lived, a life that Luc would say gave me cancer? I thought of all that Luc and I would have shared—the high, the dark, the blame— and it scared me as if I was nineteen again.

The waitress came by. Neither of us wanted any more coffee. Before we left the restaurant, I had to tell Luc about Doug. I had to. I thought it would help him to know he wasn't the only one who'd made mistakes. I knew it would help me. I'd never told anyone how Doug died. Not Harry. Not even the therapist I saw briefly when I was pregnant with Jack and all the terrors of the deep had come back. I always stuck to the watered-down version of my adventure at sea, the one where nothing was my fault, where Doug and Nathan died together.

"Let's get out of here," Luc said. He tried to smile.

"I killed Doug."

"What are you talking about?"

"He let go because of me."

"It was a hurricane."

"I killed him," I said. "He told me he loved me more than you ever could. He said he would marry me and take care of me forever and I said yes."

"You what?"

"I didn't mean to. I only nodded. I just wanted him to stop talking. And the next day or night or whenever it was, he undid his harness and went to the ladder to keep me from falling. I wouldn't take his hand and I told him I didn't want him. I told him I loved you and only you." I took a deep breath. "When the knockdown happened, the big wave, he let go. He looked right at me and let himself be swept away. He died because of me."

"It wasn't your fault. It wasn't. No one could hold on in a knockdown. Truly, Fiona." It was jarring to hear him use my whole name. "As a therapist, as a human being, I can tell you unequivocally you didn't do anything wrong."

"I've felt guilty for thirty years."

"Ridiculous. Just give that up. You couldn't have saved him. Same with Nathan. I've gone over it and over it. He was out of reach in an instant. His pockets were full of heavy things. The water was freezing. To say nothing of the scalpel in his neck. He wanted to die. That's the whole reason he took that trip— to kill himself. We're just lucky he didn't take us all with him."

"But Doug."

"Doug was dying. He knew Nathan hadn't fixed him. He knew what the headaches meant. He let go because it was better to be washed overboard than die slowly in a hospital bed."

Luc looked at me as if I were a child and touched my cheek. He was absolutely sure of himself. I had held the truth of Doug's death alone for so long, it was hard to give it up. Doug was the only other person who truly knew and he was at the bottom of the sea. They never did find his body. I had thought I'd feel better confessing to Luc—but he was looking out at the weather, putting on his jacket. Speak up. I had spoken up. It didn't seem to matter. My guilt had gnawed and picked at me for thirty years. According to some, that had given me cancer, but now Luc had forgiven me for leaving him and told me I had no reason to feel guilty about Doug. Maybe my cancer would shrink away as easily.

"Where did you go?" I asked. "That night in the snow-storm in New York when you left me at your place. Where did you go?"

"To Billy's. I needed him. I knew you were leaving again."

"You asshole." I hissed the words. It wasn't Billy—it was all the years between us. I wanted to slap Luc, scream at him, but his shoulders sagged, he was pale under his olive skin, his eyes were huge and dark and weary. The wind went out of my sails.

"I'm sorry," he said. "Stupid. I was stupid."

"We all drowned on that boat. None of us survived."

We stood and gathered our things. We left and walked toward the water.

Luc asked me, "Do you remember when you saw Leander sitting beside me? I said you were dreaming, but actually I believed he was there. I could swear he was. I've looked for him ever since. In every spoon. In every flame. Thought I found him once in an alley on the Lower East Side. Saw a glimpse of him in the train station when I visited Lola last year in New York. I'm still looking."

"You don't want to find him," I said. "Not yet."

He caught my hand and turned me to him. He stared into my eyes, a question on his lips.

Yes, I nodded, anything, yes, yes, of course. Whatever you need. Yes. I could make it up to him for all the years. I could. I would.

He put his arms around me and hugged me hard. He had become so measured, so careful. That's what I realized. That's what his sensible brown crepe-soled shoes told me. He was no longer joyful and adventurous. I could see the albatross of regret hanging around his neck.

34.

It took five days for the Coast Guard cutter to tow the *Bleiz
A Mor* to Norfolk. The weather continued to be bad and
the seas continued to be rough, so towing was difficult and
slow. Fiona wondered why they even bothered. She and Luc
stood on the deck watching the tossing sailboat, so small, so
fragile, so hideous. "Cut it loose," she said. Luc agreed.

Those five days on the cutter were not good, even though
the Coast Guard did its best to entertain them, showing
movies and bringing out special food. Whenever Fiona
walked into the mess hall, every sailor stood up. It was 1979
after all, there were no women in the Coast Guard, and the
boys had been at sea for two and a half months. The bruised,
blond, shipwrecked girl was the first woman they'd seen in
a long time. The cook made her pasta primavera. The purser
found her an old romance novel to read. The doctor cleaned
and re-bandaged her cuts every day and reassured her that
only the one on her forehead would leave a scar. She was
less queasy, but she had a hard time lifting her feet, getting
up from a chair, moving. Her sadness about Doug was like
a two-ton anchor. Luc acted silly and kidded around with
the officers. He made them laugh. But Fiona, despite the
continuing rain and wind, spent most of her time on deck
staring out at the sea. How long did Hero, the priestess, watch

for her Leander? Did she take a boat and go to sea herself? Did she curse Aphrodite? She was lucky to have someone else to blame.

"We're playing poker." Luc came out to get her one afternoon. "Aren't you cold?"

She shook her head. One of the Coasties had given her his thick waterproof coat with a hood so deep it was like wearing blinders. She didn't look at Luc as she held onto the rail with both hands.

He sighed. "They didn't find him. Either of them."

"I know."

"Come in and play with me." He put his arm around her. "Please."

She couldn't say no and perversely, she hated him for her weakness. She went inside silently, darkly, loving him a little bit less than before.

On the last day, she met the scientist on board, an older guy in corduroy and tweed. She'd seen him occasionally at dinner, and he was obviously not a guardsman, so when she ran into him by the coffee machine that final morning, she asked him who he was.

"I'm a marine biologist," he said. "I'm studying the way dolphins communicate, verbal and nonverbal."

"Like birds?" she asked. "Do they use their flippers and their tails?"

"Exactly." The scientist smiled and nodded. "They have individual and unique voices, but I think they also use movement patterns and signals." He paused. "Why were you on that boat?"

"Good question." She shrugged as if it was nothing, no big deal. The scientist frowned. She didn't want to disappoint him. "Actually," she said, "my boyfriend thought it would be fun."

"Shouldn't you be in school? Not high school, right?"

"College. I dropped out."

"To go on a sailboat? Couldn't wait 'til summer vacation?" He quickly backed off. "Sorry, none of my business."

"That's okay."

"Do you want to listen to the dolphins? I have microphones in the water."

She followed him to a room filled with equipment and lights, like an alien spaceship in a science fiction movie. There were guardsmen working with headphones on, checking and writing things down. The scientist held his finger to his lips, but she already knew to be quiet. At a small desk off to one side he had a radar screen and headphones. He pointed to the screen: many small dots behind a larger dot. "Dolphins," he whispered, pointing at the small dots. "Us." He pointed at the big dot. "They follow us because we throw our food waste overboard."

He shortened the strap on the headphones and fitted them over her ears. They were tight and she liked the feeling, as if they were holding her aching and too full head together. She didn't hear anything except a muted fuzzy silence. It was the first time in days and days she hadn't heard the ocean and the rain and the wind. She closed her eyes. Quiet. That would have been enough. For the scientist to have given her this minute of peace would have been enough. Then she heard a coo. Another longer coo, sliding from high to low. Oh, it was saying. Oh. Is it you? In answer came more ghostly, plaintive calls. The dolphins sang to each other. The songs pierced her chest like hot sticks, each call sharper than the last. She hoped Doug could hear them. She began to cry.

"I'm sorry," she whispered to the scientist. "I'm sorry."

"It does that to me too."

That night she told Luc she wasn't going to dance anymore. He was stunned and almost angry. "You have to," he said. "You're a dancer."

"I don't like it," she said and knew that was true. "I'm not good at it. It makes me sick to even think about going back."

"What are you talking about? What about me? We're a team."

"You're so much better." She insisted he was amazing, fantastic, and going to be a star. She reminded him she could never keep up. It didn't hurt her to say it—in fact quitting dance was the first moment since Doug had gone overboard when she the clouds in her head began to clear. Luc fought with her, demanded she continue, but she was adamant. It wasn't until she said, "I will only hold you back," that he gave up trying to convince her. They were together in his bunk in his tiny cabin and she kissed him and wrapped a leg over his. He said she should go back to her cabin. The Coast Guard had made it clear they had to sleep apart. "Don't want to piss off the Coast Guard."

As she walked back to her room along the cold, metal passageway, she felt so much better. Pounds lighter, as if she had dumped everyone—her father, her mother, Luc—and all their expectations off her back. She was a failure as a dancer, but she had always been a failure and she could admit she hated it. It was like going on the boat, she realized. She never wanted to in the first place. She did it for someone else.

35.

Luc was just a man. We went back to the hotel so he could use the bathroom. I said I'd meet him in the hotel tearoom and I had to wait a while. Eventually, he came down with the newspaper, some article to show me. A man who reads the paper on the toilet. A man.

I had always loved his hands, long and graceful, but now I noticed he chewed his cuticles and didn't take great care of his nails. He still didn't like to answer questions. I pressed him to leave the past and he told me stories about his clients and his clinic. All the New Age stuff sounded questionable—being from southern California didn't make me a believer. Reiki? Biofeedback? Aromatherapy? He described his condo and the swimming pool, the health club he went to before work in the morning, how often he had dinner with his parents, and which weekends he had his kids. He held my hands and said I'd fit right in. He didn't ask what my days were like, what I'd be giving up to move in with him.

He had to make some work calls, so I sat with him in the nautical, colonial, laughable lobby with a book open, sneaking peeks at him as he talked and gestured and made notes on a tiny pad of paper he carried in his pocket. It was strange to see him work, a glimpse of a Luc I didn't yet know. A youngish woman walked in with her suitcase and I saw her look him up and down. I noticed how she stood straighter, flirtatiously circled one foot behind her as she waited at the front desk to check in. He hadn't changed that much. He still had something everybody wanted.

At least he seemed oblivious. He chuckled into the phone—the grown up laugh I didn't know. His head was up, his neck long and grazed by his curls, and he looked like my Hercules in the small gallery at the Villa, like that Greek boy I remembered—ageless, eternal, perfect. Then his hand went to his nose to scratch and he shifted in his chair and the reality of him confronted me. He shook his hair back, the young woman clumped her suitcase up the stairs, he watched her for a moment, then turned to me and smiled. Sorry, he mouthed. Then sucked a tooth. I laughed. Real or not, I was ready to give up everything for him.

Alcyone was the daughter of the wind god, Aeolus. She fell in love with King Ceyx of Trachis, and he with her. They married and their lives were filled with bliss. Even the gods took note of their idyllic love for one another. But Alcyone and Ceyx were too happy, and they took to calling each other Hera and Zeus. This angered Zeus—only he had that name and only he and his wife were allowed to be that happy despite his many peccadilloes.

One day, Ceyx decided to travel by ship to visit the oracle of Apollo at Carlos. Alcyone begged him not to go, reminded him that even her father could not completely control the impetuous winds. Ceyx assured her he'd be fine. But he was wrong. Zeus took advantage of the opportunity and sent a hurricane. The ship broke apart and Ceyx was thrown into the sea. He knew he was about to die and he prayed to Aphrodite, goddess of love, to make sure his body was washed ashore to be reunited with his beloved Alcyone. For days Alcyone waited for word. Where was he? She knew something was wrong. Finally his ghost appeared to her and said he was waiting for her on shore. She ran to the beach, found his lifeless body, and threw herself into the sea and drowned. She could not live without him.

Zeus felt terrible remorse once he realized how much Ceyx and Alcyone had loved each other, so he turned the couple into Halcyon birds—what we call kingfishers—and for seven days when the female lays her eggs, Zeus commands the winds to be still. Hence the phrase, halcyon days.

Those halcyon days are dangerous. Too much joy still tempts the gods.

36.

When the Coast Guard cutter docked in Norfolk, Virginia, Fiona was on deck and the sun was shining. No rain, not a cloud in the sky, the sea calm and gentle. She and Luc and Joren said their goodbyes and thank yous and Fiona hugged the man with turquoise eyes who had rescued her. For the rest of her life, every Christmas, she would make a donation to the U.S. Coast Guard.

Luc and Joren walked the long gangplank to the pier, while Fiona ran all the way to solid ground. She didn't bend down and kiss the earth, but she did close her eyes in gratitude. More Coast Guard officials were waiting for them; there were papers to sign, and then they were free. The *Bleiz A Mor* had been towed in and was tied up at a dock nearby. Fiona stayed on shore as Luc and Joren climbed back aboard. She didn't want to get on that boat again—ever.

"Do you want your stuff?" Luc called to her from the deck. "Then you have to come get it."

She sighed. "Okay, okay." She hopped on board like a pro. She ignored how instantly queasy she was and went down into the hold. Three guardsmen had ridden on the boat as it was being towed. They had done a remarkable job fixing the engine, pumping out the muck, and getting rid of the broken bits and trash. To her surprise, Joren had decided to stay with the boat while Nathan's wife had it repaired and took it to Florida to sell.

"Who knows?" he said. "Perhaps I will learn to sail."

"Or you'll ride in the tow truck," she said.

Joren nodded. That was possible too. He and Luc were going out for dinner, but Fiona didn't want to spend another night on the boat. She got her bag, damp and smelling of seawater and diesel fuel, and hesitated by Doug's coat, hung up and dry. "What will we do with," she began and stopped. It didn't matter. Doug didn't need it anymore.

At the pay phone at the top of the dock she called a cab to take her to the Greyhound bus station. She wasn't far from home; it was only four hours by bus to Delaware and her mom had bought the ticket. Luc would get on a plane to Florida the next morning. Thanksgiving was coming up. It made perfect sense they both wanted to be with their families. Her farewell to Joren was brief. He told her to come visit him in Amsterdam, but she knew she never would. A never that was just fine with her.

She hugged Luc. She couldn't look at him.

"Wild, huh?" he breathed into her hair. "The earth feels good."

They were standing by the road where the taxi would pick her up. The docks and the sailboat were behind her. She heard Joren singing in Dutch. She stamped her feet and was satisfied when nothing gave or moved or swayed.

Luc laughed, but when she looked up at him she saw his eyes go small. He couldn't help her; she saw his frustration that he didn't know how. She would be sad for a long, long time and that wasn't his style. He shuddered as if—her mother would say—a crow had walked over his grave. "We have a story to tell, don't we?"

"I'll see you in New York," she said.

He grinned. "Back to the madness."

If that was madness, then what had just happened? She stepped out of his arms. She slumped. She sat down on the ground. She couldn't stand up any longer.

"Jesus, babe. Jesus."

She was crying again. He stood above her and looked out to the water. She saw his hands open and close, his feet shuffle impatiently. Something. She could see he wanted to do something. She was sorry she couldn't help him.

The taxi arrived. Luc reached out a hand, but she got up on her own. She could almost see the space between them, a wall of viscous liquid, seawater and blood and heroin and guilt, combined and stronger than them both.

"Bye."

"Call me at my parents," he said. "I'll be there tomorrow afternoon."

She nodded and closed the door. The cab was warm and quiet and she was alone. She had gotten away. Away. She didn't look out the window as they drove along the sea. In her pocket were Doug's fingernail clippers. A tiny thing that had touched his hands, provided his most intimate droppings. She held on tight.

37.

Luc had to make another call, so I left him on a bench and went into the Seamen's Church, a three story brick building on the wharf. It was the only building I recognized from long ago. It smelled of tea and books and musty carpets, like an old folks' home. A library was upstairs, and next to it, the Chapel of the Sea. That's where I wanted to go. A giant ceramic clamshell held the holy water. A beautiful fresco showed saints and holy figures hovering behind and around sailors in boats. The floor was marble and inset were an anchor and a knotted rope and a sun bordered by the words, "Courage Charity Duty Faith Honor Obedience Love Hope."

I sat in the little chapel, hoping to feel something about Doug, some release or relief, but without Luc beside me, I just felt tired. The next few days were going to be so difficult. I would go home and there would be tears and shouting. I thought how easy this would be if Harry had died during those three months in Iraq. If he had died a hero. I imagined the funeral, Jack's tears, Harry's father in a dark suit. I would be free. I wouldn't have to hurt him. Then I stopped myself. Oh my god. Harry didn't deserve to die. I was about to ruin his life—that was bad enough.

It was only Friday. Luc and I had two more days to figure things out. Two more days before I had to confront Harry.

I got up and took out my cell phone to check the time and remembered I had turned it off last night. It felt so foreign in my hand, like a relic from a lost civilization where a different blond woman carried it as she went to work and the grocery store and the bank. I didn't turn it on.

I came out of the building expecting to see Luc where I'd left him. He wasn't there. I walked around to the right—toward the docks. I couldn't find him. I walked quickly around the left side and then ran around all the way around the building and I even went back inside and he wasn't anywhere. He should have been right there. Right there. He was gone. My breath stopped. I was dizzy and for a quick second thought I had imagined the whole thing, the emails, the talks, the sex. Too good to be true. He had left. I was too much for him, he was sorry for all the things he'd said. I'd frightened him, or he'd been playing me. He was gone. I knew it. I knew it. There was something about him I didn't trust. All this new information. His condo in Florida with the leather couch. Luc? Absurd. I couldn't believe him.

My chest hurt, a sharp pain in my left breast—not cancer, but my heart. My heart would break again. I groaned. I would crawl back to the hotel, pack my bag, and go home. I wanted to be home. My home. I wanted my kitchen table, my coffee mug, Harry on the couch yelling at the TV.

I trudged around the far end of the building and found Luc staring up at the seagulls. There he was. I walked to him. He opened his arms for me and I pressed against him, but some part of me held back.

"Look," he said. "Look what I can still do."

He took two steps back onto the cement sidewalk, then did a single pirouette. Once around, beautifully. I clapped my hands.

"More," he said. "Watch me."

He did a double. And another one. I saw how he consciously placed his feet and his arms. He had disappeared somewhere to practice for me. I was supposed to be impressed. And I was.

"Luc," I said. I have cancer was next. If he would stop spinning I would tell him.

"Pretty good, huh?" He was out of breath. "For an old guy. I still have it."

"You do." I was having a hard time breathing too. "I thought you'd left."

"What?"

"I came out to tell you something, to find you, and I couldn't."

"I was just over there." He sucked in his stomach and patted his chest. "I could still teach a class or two. Maybe we'll offer it. Look at this." He lifted his leg high, higher.

"Okay. Wow."

He took my shoulders. His face was serious and more lined and softer than it used to be, but his breath was the same, sweetened coffee and cigarettes. "Listen," he said. "Listen."

I listened.

"All these years I've wished I could go back and start over. I've wanted to be that young, strong, beautiful kid graduating, heading to New York for the first time. I was a star. I should have been a star."

I nodded. I agreed.

"But it all got derailed. There were roadblocks. Accidents. I know, I know." He waved a hand as if I had started to say something. "I know I'm mostly responsible. But now, now with you, I can start again. With you I can go back. I can have the life I was meant to have."

I knew he didn't mean as a dancer.

"It'll be as if the rest never happened. Only the good memories. We'll be happy. That old couple that love each other so much. People will smile to see us. We were always meant to be together. We are Io and Luc. It's written in the stars. We just were too young to see it."

He wanted thirty years to disappear. But I had a son. A marriage. A life. Was I ready to pretend they had never happened? In his arms, yes. Standing beside him, I wasn't so sure. Five minutes earlier, I had been positive he'd left, gone back to Florida without a word. That hadn't surprised me at all. Every night I would wait to hear his key in our front door, be relieved when he showed up, worry when he was fifteen minutes late.

"C'mon," he said. "I can see you've had enough sightseeing."

He was right. I didn't want to see anything else.

We went back to the hotel. His room again and before we made love I took his face in my hands and looked into his eyes. I saw my distorted reflection in his dark pupils and my eyes filled with tears. He kissed me and continued and this time was more tenuous than the first or the second. I kept touching him, making sure he was there.

"Remember how cold the studio was?" he asked drowsily, almost asleep. "I had to jump to stay warm. You wore a scarf."

"I remember," I said. "I remember."

I watched him sleep, a middle-aged man. I closed my eyes and he was perfect, my Greek statue, unchanging, timeless. I curled up beside him with my hand on his back. I breathed in his exhales, holding his breath in my lungs as long as I could. Be real, I whispered to him. Be you for real.

38.

Fiona stayed with her mom and her mom's boyfriend, Roger, a week longer than she planned. She might have stayed even longer except it wasn't home, it was Roger's house and she slept on a cot in his den on new sheets. Her mother wasn't interested in her ordeal at sea—she had her own problems to worry about. Her toenail was ingrown, the doctor was an idiot, Roger was a pain in her ass. Fiona tried to care. She wasn't sleeping or eating. The Thanksgiving turkey rocked on the table, the pumpkin pie tasted like diesel fuel. She couldn't get the smell of salt water out of her nose, the back of her throat. When she woke screaming her mother complained, "Roger has to work tomorrow." When she left to go back to New York, no one was sorry.

She knocked on Lola's door. Nobody home. She took the key from its hiding place and let herself in. She expected the apartment to look different, bigger or smaller or brighter or darker, but the only change was a vase of flowers on the counter in the kitchen. She bent to smell them and saw a note. "Welcome home'" and hearts and exclamation marks. Lola's handiwork.

It would be okay. Okay, okay was the chant in her head as she had come back into the city, once more on a Greyhound bus, the diesel smell making her stomach churn and pitch.

New York was an ocean, never ceasing, never still. But she would get her bearings; once she was with Luc she'd be steady as she goes.

The door opened and Luc came in wearing his jacket over his dance clothes. From across the room, she breathed in his smile and his stink, ignored the metallic tang and grinned. She should have come back sooner.

"Hey, hey, hey." He ran to her. "You got here early."

"It was a fast bus."

"I missed you."

"Me too."

They held each other. She would never let him go. It was ridiculous they'd spent Thanksgiving apart.

"Have you been to class?" she asked. He was clammy, but not sweating.

"I'll go later. I was just out."

"Thank you for the flowers." He must've had something to do with them.

"Did you hear about Lola?" he asked. "She got a big promotion."

"You told me. Remember? You called me and told me."

She pushed his coat off. He had his hands under her shirt. Pressed together they walked, laughing, to Lola's bed.

"She won't mind?"

"I don't care."

"We'll change the sheets."

"Worry, worry, worry-wort."

The sex was bad; he took forever to get off. She had to pretend. He wanted her to be her sweet self, the girl she had been, but afterwards she cried. He smoked a cigarette. She made his chest wet with her tears.

"Aren't you glad to be here?"

"Tears of joy." She watched the smoke from his cigarette unfurl, heading for the door. Watch the smoke, Nathan had said, it always tells you which way the wind blows.

He was scratching the spot on his arm. Scratching and scratching. He would draw blood. She put her hand over his to stop him and he rolled over to her.

"What are you going to do now?"

"You mean this?" She held his penis and laughed.

"No, no, no. I mean not dancing." He ignored her hand. "What's next?"

She shrugged.

"You'll get fat."

"So what." She pretended she didn't care. "Warmth in the winter, shade in the summer."

In response he grabbed her ass and squeezed until she yelped. She was as thin as she had ever been.

"Did you look at any apartment listings?" she asked. Checks had come—much larger than expected—from Nathan's wife.

"We're fine here."

"We're not."

He sat up. "Alison invited us over. Jerry left her."

She put her head in his lap. She saw the spot under his chin he had missed shaving. She loved the little hairs, was sorry he might cut them away tomorrow. They were hers, only she knew about them. "You said it would be great to have our own place. Our own bed."

He stood. "C'mon, c'mon, c'mon. Let's get out of here."

Obediently, she got up and dressed. She hurried to the bathroom to wash her face, run her fingers through her hair. In the medicine chest mirror she saw big circles under her eyes and the blue veins in her temples that had fascinated

Nathan. The scabbed over cuts on her cheek and forehead, upper lip and chin were harsh black marks against her skim milk skin. She had been through something, that was obvious. Since she'd given up dance, she had stopped putting her hair up. It fell across her shoulders, down her back to her waist, the color of ash and bones, and she didn't care. She was not a dancer anymore. She said it. She meant it. She didn't have to do that ever again. Thank you, she whispered to herself, to whomever. Thank you.

Luc knocked on the door. "Alison's waiting."

He was just the other side of the door. He was right there and her heart yearned for him. She was back where she belonged. She was crazy to have stayed away so long. They had survived together. They would tell Alison the story and they would be together doing it. It was their story.

She came out of the bathroom and hugged him. He patted her back once, twice—the same way she had patted Doug. She stepped away.

"I want to go to the art museums," she said. "I want to wander through all that art. Old art. So still. Immobile. A painting on the wall. I want to go someplace where nothing moves and hasn't for hundreds of years. Come with me, okay?"

He was already out the door. "I just want you to be happy." He sounded angry. "Right? That's all I want." Below her on the stairs he stopped to light a cigarette. "I'll go with you." He looked up at her. "You do something for me." He had a look on his face she'd never seen before, a kind of desperation in his pursed lips and wide eyes. She took a step down and put her hand on his chest. His heart was thumping against her palm, trying to break free. Give it to me, she thought, I can keep it safe.

"Anything. Anything you want."

"Really?" he asked.

"I sailed across the ocean for you."

He shrugged her hand away and walked on. He was scratching again, through his jacket. "Hurry," was all he said.

Fiona had only been to Alison's apartment a couple of times before. It was different without her boyfriend, Jerry. He had taken the television, the rug, the lamps, all pretense of a normal life. The cupboard doors hung open with almost nothing inside. A single coffee cup. A can of tomato soup. A chipped plate dirty in the sink. The fridge was empty except for two cans of diet soda. As if Alison needed to diet. She was wasting away, heroin light and otherworldly.

"C'mon, c'mon, c'mon."

Luc stretched out his hand. He sat on the stained couch. He kept looking at the battered coffee table that held the works. That was all he wanted. She took his hand. It was cool and moist, but still the hand she loved. She would do what he wanted. She always had. She tried to be brave, but it must have been obvious she was frightened because he smiled and touched his forehead to hers.

"You'll love it."

"It's so expensive." She wasn't really worried about the money, she just needed to say something. She couldn't say it was the addiction that scared her. Luc swore he wasn't addicted. He had days when he was clean—whole days, he said—when he slept for hours and went to dance class and showered and shaved. Whole days. But she wasn't as strong as he was. She had no willpower when it came to chocolate. How could she resist heroin? She heard Nathan in her head: "Don't you have a mind of your own?"

Luc's eyes were so big in his drawn face, his eyelashes like a mascara ad. She said, "Are you going to dance class today?"

He frowned, curled his shoulders away from her. "Of course. Don't I always?"

She didn't think so, not lately. She closed her eyes and swayed with the rocking of the boat. She smelled the salt water. She was shaking and Luc took her hand. She opened her eyes. The spoon, the hypodermic, the dirty rubber tube, the foil packet were all she could see.

Alison came in. "Let's get this show on the road. Or launch this boat. Whatever you sailors say."

"You know our story?"

"Heard all about it from Luc." Alison didn't smile. She was businesslike, professional, if there was such a thing for what they were doing. She opened the packet and tapped the powder into the spoon. She added a little water and held the spoon over the lighter. Fiona looked at Luc. He was watching the spoon. The hand not holding hers opened and closed in anticipation. He had a twitch under one eye she could see jumping under his skin. She shook her head. Nathan tossed his cigarette into the sea and she heard the hiss. She stood.

"Hey," Luc said.

"I'm not ready,"

"What?"

Alison laughed, not surprised.

"Come with me?" Fiona asked him as she stepped toward the door. "Pizza? A walk? I haven't seen you in so long."

Luc looked at Alison filling the syringe. He looked back at Fiona. "Wait," he said. "You could just snort it."

"No," she said. "Maybe I'm just scared I'll like it too much." She tried to laugh.

"I'll be right here with you."

Luc was begging. She could see it in his face and his hands and she knew if she said no it would be an ending for them.

More than Billy, more than her not telling him about Doug, more even than giving up dance, her "no" would catapult her away. He was her reason for living, but she couldn't.

"You're afraid of everything." The corners of his mouth turned down in disgust. He squinted his eyes as he looked up at her. "Everything I do frightens you."

Alison began to laugh. Fiona went to the apartment door. "Come with me," she said again.

"Later, 'Gator."

She left. She stumbled down the stairs, pushed through the big door and out onto the crowded street. The people flowed around her. She stepped into the current and let herself be carried along, a bit of flotsam destined to sink.

39.

How does it happen? How does time pass? We don't do anything, and yet time keeps moving forward. What if we stayed still, lay in bed and never got up? Or if we stood in front of a mirror twenty-four hours a day for ten years without sleeping or closing our eyes, would we see the change, the laugh lines and frown furrows begin? Maybe not. But if we turned our back to the mirror for one instant—say the lights went out or we had to answer the door—when we came back, no matter how briefly we'd been gone, we would be shocked at how old we had become.

Luc slept on his side beside me. I wrapped a curl of his hair around my finger. His mouth hung open and I saw the fillings in his teeth, the many trips to the dentist. The hair around his face was more gray than brown. Even in the gentle late afternoon light I could see his pores and wrinkles. He had one leg out over the sheet and his ass exposed. A man's ass, hairy and slack. Thirty years ago I had loved the hollows on the sides of his young cheeks, indentations as if Zeus had picked him up between thumb and forefinger and left his mark before he was born. Luc would light his first cigarette of the morning and I would watch the sun and shadow sculpt him. He was a living work of art—as exquisite as marble, but light and quick, impossible to pin down. This ass in the bed beside me was not immortal. This Luc would annoy me with his habits: picking his teeth, cutting his toenails, snoring. I would beg him to stop smoking and he would lie to me and sneak them when I wasn't home. I would be jealous of every young, lithe New Age masseuse or yoga instructor in his clinic. I'd pick his clothes up off the floor and do his laundry and complain and the romance would falter. But we would always have those ten months in 1979 when we were together and as young as we ever were and I would think of that time and I would love him. I would always love him.

I wanted to take a picture of him, even though it would be impossible to explain to Harry. Then I remembered: I was leaving Harry. He would never see this picture. I had a momentary pang thinking Harry wouldn't know anything about me from here on. I wouldn't know anything about him, if he got the hemp journal job, if he took Jack out to dinner, if our dog died or our house fell down or if he started dating that librarian. It would be none of my business. I squeezed my nose, blinked my eyes.

I tiptoed across the room to my purse and turned on my phone. The afternoon sun fell across Luc's lower leg, his calf muscle shadowed and defined, his bare foot exactly as I remembered. My phone vibrated. I had four phone messages plus a text. Unbelievable, Harry couldn't leave me alone for one day. I clicked on the text. It was from Jack and I smiled until I read his message, "Dad 911." My hands were shaking as I dialed my inbox. Every message was from Jack.

"Mom? Something's happened to Dad. Call me right away."

"Mom. Mom. Call me."

"Shit. Sorry. I don't know what to do."

And then a hang up, Jack too panicked to leave a message.

I didn't want to talk to Jack naked. I threw on my clothes as I dialed his cell phone.

"Oh my god." He began to cry. "Mommy."

Dead. That was my first thought. I had imagined earlier how easy it would be if Harry was dead. Oh no, no, no. "It's okay, Sprout. I'm on my way." I tried to keep the terror out of my voice. "I'm packing as we speak." I was. Luc was stirring in the bed, looking at me through half-opened eyes. "What happened?" I asked Jack. "Take a deep breath, and tell me what happened." Car crash, bus accident, an explosion.

"He…he went nuts, completely nuts. Hung a sign up at some insurance company."

"A sign?"

"A great big sign, a banner, I don't know. He had a chain around his leg. Kept shouting about breast cancer. Crazy stuff. They arrested him. It was on the news."

Oh Harry. Poor, angry, frustrated Harry. I was so glad he was alive I actually almost laughed. He had lost his mind, but he was alive. Alive and fighting for me. Still fighting for me.

"Where is he? What did they do to him?"

"I have a number. He's in jail. Or someplace. I don't know, Mom."

"I'll call them. I'm getting on the next plane. I'll be there tonight. You stay put. Hold down the fort." An expression he had loved as a child, getting his fortress of couch cushions and blankets ready.

"Okay."

"I'll call you as soon as I know anything else." I took a deep breath. "I'm so sorry I'm not there."

"Dad's the one who went nuts. Not you."

Really? I wanted to say.

In twenty minutes I was standing at my rental car ready to

drive back to the airport. I had a ticket on the seven o'clock flight to LA. I'd spoken to the police. Harry was spending the night under psychiatric observation. He hadn't hurt or even threatened anyone, just hung up his sign and refused to leave.

Luc handed me a small manila envelope. "Pictures," he said. "A trip down memory lane."

"Thanks."

"I'd like to meet Harry," he said. "You know I have a soft spot for crazy people."

"That's probably not going to happen."

"I know."

I waited for him to tell me to deal with Harry and Jack and then come to Florida. He didn't.

"Write to me," I said. "Will you?"

"Of course. Yes. We'll figure something out." He gave me his best Luc grin. "How about once a year in Newport?"

My most beautiful Luc. The man of my dreams. The love of my life. Once a year? "I can do that."

"See you next fall."

We hugged.

"Don't cut your hair," he said. "Please."

I watched him walk down the cobblestones back to the hotel. He still had that fluid swagger, a dancer's walk.

"Don't leave me," I whispered. It was what he had said to me. I waited for him to turn around and come back. "Don't leave me." I held my breath. If he turned around I would run to him. I would let Harry fend for himself. I would leave Harry and Jack and the dog. Please, Luc. He stopped. I rose onto my tiptoes. I almost called his name. He looked out at the sea. In the fading light, I saw that jaw, that neck, the head full of curls I would love forever. The man attached wasn't the boy I remembered, but it was possible the boy I remembered had never existed.

He turned back, away from me, and kept walking. He was so confident I was watching him that he lifted one hand in a backwards wave. I had seen that wave before, another good-bye he said without turning around. The long arm and elegant hand in my memory were like a knife in my gut.

In Lola's apartment, Fiona packed her clothes into the same canvas duffle bag she had taken on the boat. It still smelled of salt water, diesel fuel, and vomit. When she got back to school she would throw it away. For now it was the only bag she had. That and a small cardboard box. Not much to show for her life in New York City.

She heard Luc giggling, high and screechy, in the hallway outside the apartment. He was out there with his sister. "Luc?" she called.

He came in, gray and slouchy as an old pair of sweatpants. His eyes like slits. "What?"

Lola came in behind him and went to the kitchen sink for a glass of water.

"You sure I can take this book to read on the train? I'll send it back."

"What book?" He had already forgotten the discussion they'd had that morning. She held up the book. He nodded, dismissing it, and the motion almost knocked him over. Her dancer. Her perfect specimen.

"Drink this." Lola tried to give him the water.

He shook his head.

"Come on. You're dehydrated."

"I feel great." Luc sat down on the couch. It had been their bed.

Just look at me, Fiona wished. Just look. His eyes closed

and his head slumped forward. She refused to cry. Her hair, her skin, even her knees were screaming at her not to go. Her body wanted Luc, to curl up beside him and stay there until they were back to the way they used to be. Her mind was dragging her away, but her legs and arms were fighting it, holding on to the other side. She wasn't sure she could walk out the door.

"Luc," she said again.

Lola crossed her arms. "What time is your train?"

"I can go tomorrow."

"You've been saying that for a week. If you're going…" Lola threw up her hands—a gesture Luc had made a thousand times.

"Look at him." She pleaded with Lola.

"You're not helping. Go or stay. Choose."

"Choose," Luc said from the couch. "Choosey mothers choose Jif."

"Luc!" Lola yelled and banged the coffee table. "Cut it out!"

"What?" He looked up.

"Walk your girlfriend to the train."

"He doesn't have to." Fiona didn't think he could. "I'm fine."

Luc managed to stand. "Okay."

"You're not up to it."

"I'm up and at 'em. You know I am. I'm sad you're leaving. That's all. I will miss you."

But when she put her arms around him he didn't hug her back. She looked over at Lola's disapproving face. Up at Luc's absent one. Don't go, her heart cried, don't leave him. It was threatening to stop. It was slowing down in her chest, hurting, punishing her. Don't go, it said, you will be forever sorry. Luc swayed on his feet and sat down hard on the coffee table. Fiona knew if she left she would be killing another man.

"Come with me," she said. "Just for one semester."

He shrugged, turned his back. "I graduated."

"We can come back for the summer."

"I'm staying here," he said, but he wasn't really there at all. "New York is my town. Go. I want you to go."

She was afraid she would fall over if she heard him tell her to leave one more time.

"3:30," she said to Lola. "My train—this train—leaves at 3:30."

"Better go."

Fiona gave her a little smile, the briefest of hugs. "Bye. Thanks for everything."

The apartment door closing behind her was the saddest sound she had ever heard.

Luc walked her down the block, but stopped at the stairs to the subway. She knew he couldn't make it down all those steps. He hadn't carried anything. She held her box and her bag. It was impossible to hug him. She was crying and she couldn't wipe her runny nose.

"This is temporary." He put his hands on her shoulders and for a moment he was Luc again. He smiled as if about to make a joke. Instead he said, "I won't—I mean, I can stop anytime." He meant the smack was temporary, not their separation.

"I'll stay. I can help you. I can."

His eyes narrowed and his words were clipped. "It's not so easy for me."

It hadn't been easy for her either, to watch him disappear into another world without her. She wanted to go with him, but not really. Luc had yelled at her, scaredy-cat, scaredy-cat. He was right she was afraid, but not for herself. She stopped going to Alison's with him, didn't want to watch them shoot up and then crumple on the couch. Instead she sat in the Metropolitan Museum for six hours one day and seven the next and eight the day after that. Day after day, she stayed until the guards sent her home. Night after night, she had waited for him. He stopped coming home. He forgot to call. He didn't go to dance class and when he showed up at the apartment, he was scratching and jittery or loose and lethargic. He told her to go back to school with a sneer. He commanded her to leave.

At the entrance to the subway he said it again. "You won't stay and get high with me, so fucking go."

"What about dance?" She was desperate. "You have to dance."

"For chrissakes, dance is everywhere. Look up, you see dance. Look down, there are your feet. I'm dancing right now. My soul is dancing and my heart is dancing."

She shifted the box and bag. "Maybe you should stay away from Alison."

"You won't be here."

"I'll call you when I get there. I'll call you."

"Sure. Okay." He looked up at the sky. "Don't forget me."

"I love you. More than anything in the world. More than life itself."

"Okay. Okey-dokey." He turned and walked away. "Love ya!" he called.

He didn't look back, but raised his hand over his shoulder, one arm up in a backwards wave.

That is how I had always remembered it. For thirty years I had remembered him walking away and seen only what I had done to him, that I had left him to die. Both then and now, he didn't turn around. Both thirty years ago and that night in Newport he walked away without looking back. Then, I had been sure it was all my fault. This time I realized what I should have then: I couldn't save him. I couldn't give him the life I wanted him to have—so I saved myself.

I cried most of the way to the airport, but I didn't get lost. The drive was easy. Even in the dark I knew my way home.

40.

I sat on a cold plastic chair in an ugly, industrial green room, waiting for Harry to be released. Jack had picked me up at the airport; I'd dropped him at his place and driven straight to the hospital. I'd spent the night in the rundown waiting room. I was dirty and tired, but glad Harry would be allowed to come home with me. The insurance company did not want to press charges—he had never made it further than the lobby. He'd painted "murderers" in dripping red paint on a six-foot banner. He had chained himself to a chair and refused to leave until the CEO met with him. It was just a protest, an unhappy, aggravated man demanding his wife with cancer get the treatment she needed. I wondered if they would cancel our insurance or pay for Harry's upcoming visits with a psychiatrist. Maybe they thought he was still a reporter for the *LA Times*.

As the rising sun came through the barred windows, I took out the envelope Luc had given me. I expected pictures of dance, Lola, his kids, I didn't know what. I hadn't wanted to look on the plane. I felt bad enough, guilty enough. Harry was in the loony bin because of me. If I'd been home, I could have stopped him. I should have been home. I thought I would look at whatever was in the envelope and then throw it away before Harry saw me. But I pulled out a stack of photos taken on the boat. I didn't remember Luc taking any pictures.

The first was of Luc and me on deck before we set sail, clean, happy, standing tall. Luc is laughing and I am smiling. Then there was a photo of the handsome, bearded Captain Joren, his arm around Nathan, who is wearing, of course, his ubiquitous fisherman's sweater still somewhat clean. Nathan's long hair blows across his face, his eyes are open and calm—no sign of the turbulence to come.

And then there were four pictures of me, of who I was then, of Luc's girlfriend, Io. In the first two, Newport is behind me. I am sitting alone behind the helm. In the next, I look up into the rigging. I am posing for the camera and I look like I'm trying too hard. The next photo was after the Coast Guard ship got us back to land. I look thin and tired and banged up and heartbroken and I am standing next to a yellow taxi cab.

Who is that girl? In every photo there is the same hopeful, slightly worried expression on her face. The smile tremulous, her eyebrows wrinkled together. In the last one, she sits beside Doug. He smiles dreamily at her, but she looks only at the man taking the picture. I love you, her eyes say desperately. Love me.

I know her. The skin so young and flawless, the eyes so bright. I hated her then. For thirty years I loathed her and felt guilty about the things she did. But thirty years is long enough. It is time for her to recognize her mistakes and be done with guilt. It doesn't help. It won't fix anything. I look at these photos and now I love her, her paleness, her messy hair, fleshy thighs and all. She is not a monster. She is not dumb, thoughtless, or bad. She is just a girl. I wish I could put my arms around her, comfort her and tell her it will be all right. It hurts me to see how much she needs someone to reassure her. So much time she has wasted and will waste worrying, trying to please, being afraid.

I hear the voice in her head. It is the same voice that speaks in mine. It is my voice. Survive, it says. What else can you do? Survive.

Listen, I want to tell her. Listen.

LIFE # 8

I climbed carefully onto the railing of our front porch. I perched, hanging on to a post with my good hand, and began taking down the Christmas lights with the other. It was easy, the nails had been there for years and this was always my job. But the string of lights got hooked on a bent nail at the corner and I had to shake it to get it free. I wiggled it and finally I yanked and the cord came loose and I lost my balance. I slipped. I teetered. The hard, packed dirt of our yard was far below, and if I had fallen I would have died, but I caught myself just in time, pulling at my still tender stitches and biting my cheeks from the pain.

I took a deep breath. Harry and Jack were inside watching football. I could hear them laughing. Neither cared much about the game, but they didn't argue about it. Harry was taking a break from CNN. His therapist thought it for the best. I knew my husband and son would help me if I asked. I knew they would yell at me for doing it by myself. I'd had a mastectomy three weeks before and it hadn't been as bad as I anticipated. Chemotherapy had begun and it was as awful as everybody said, but Harry was wonderful. He might be—no, definitely was—crazy, but he was a kind and capable caregiver.

I looked out at my small yard, my lazy dog lying in the dirt, my world. The wind had picked up and the sky was the color of lead. I heard the waves against the side and the sails flapping. The boat was rocking, but I was not going down.

In the kitchen, Harry and I did the dishes side by side. "Harry," I said. "Would you still love me if I only had one breast?"

"One breast is plenty," he said.

"What if I had a big, puckered scar and dents and bumps across half my chest?"

"You know I think scars are cool."

"Would you still love me if I didn't have any hair? It was my very best feature."

"No, it wasn't. Your best feature is you." He wrapped his arms around my bald head and ran his hand back and forth, back and forth. "Rubbing your head is good luck. I know it."

We hugged, we pressed against each other. A perfect fit. My head just above his shoulder, his broad chest a cheerful rest stop for my journey. He smelled of minty deodorant and soap. He held me close.

"I have a question for you," he said.

I hummed that I was listening.

"Would you still love me if I went completely bonkers? If I lost my mind someplace far away and couldn't find it no matter how hard I tried?"

"Yes," I said. "I will help you search. No matter where you go, I'll go with you."

This is my last remaining life.

Acknowledgments

First and foremost, I'd like to thank the United States Coast Guard for all they do, and specifically, the late Captain John E. Williams and the entire crew of the Coast Guard Cutter Active of 1979 for saving my life. Very special thanks to the boat coxswain, Bob Bragdon, for sharing his memories of our rescue and admitting he was as scared as I was. Thanks to the Jentel Artist Residency Program for giving me the most beautiful place to work in quiet and with fabulous colleagues. Great big thanks to David Feinman for his expert sailing advice and teaching me the difference between a rope and a line. My heartfelt thanks to Dr. Stephen Quentzel for his insights on addiction and mental health. I'd truly be lost at sea without Heather Dundas, Donna Rifkind, Ellen Slezak, and Diane Arieff, Seth Greenland, Denise Hamilton, Sally Harrison-Pepper, Dinah Lenney, Kerry Madden, and Lienna Silver; thank you for reading and re-reading. Thank you to my thoughtful and tireless editors, Elizabeth Clementson and Robert Lasner, and my stalwart agent, Terra Chalberg. Most of all, I want to thank my family and especially my husband, Tod Mesirow, who keeps my feet on solid ground.

LARKSPUR HOUSE

Dear Friend,

You ~~HAVE TO COME HELP US~~ are cordially invited to a house ~~THAT WANTS TO SCARE YOU~~ unlike any you've ever entered——one that understands your wishes and dreams, and wants to ~~KEEP YOU FOREVER~~ help make them come true.

Few have been called ~~AND EVEN FEWER ESCAPE,~~ but if you're reading this, you're one of the Special ones. Come. Let's play.

Most sincerely,

~~Larkspur~~ *SHADOW HOUSE*

Enter Shadow House . . . if you dare.

1. Get the FREE Shadow House app for your phone or tablet.
2. Each image in the book reveals a ghost story in the app.
3. Step into ghost stories, where the choices you make determine your fate.

 For tablet or phone.

scholastic.com/shadowhouse

SHADOW HOUSE

The Gathering

SHADOW HOUSE

The Gathering

DAN POBLOCKI

SCHOLASTIC INC.

Library of Congress Control Number Available

ISBN 978-1-338-09127-4

10 9 8 7 6 5 4 3 2 1   16 17 18 19

Library edition, September 2016

Printed in China 62

Scholastic US: 557 Broadway • New York, NY 10012
Scholastic Canada: 604 King Street West • Toronto, ON M5V 1E1
Scholastic New Zealand Limited: Private Bag 94407 • Greenmount, Manukau 2141
Scholastic UK Ltd.: Euston House • 24 Eversholt Street • London NW1 1DB

For Bruce

CHAPTER 1

WHENEVER POPPY CALDWELL glanced in a mirror, she saw another girl standing behind her.

There were plenty of other girls at Thursday's Hope, the group home where Poppy had lived since age six. But the Girl wasn't like the other girls.

Poppy was pretty sure she was dead.

In the mirror, the Girl always appeared smiling, hazel eyes glinting with playful kindness, long dark hair slanting sharply across her forehead. She always wore the same white pinafore over a dark dress, with large pockets that gaped near her hips and seemed filled with mystery.

Poppy knew that seeing the Girl was odd. Was she a ghost? An angel? Once, Poppy had worked up the courage to ask her bunkmate Ashley if it was normal for girls to appear behind you in mirrors—girls who couldn't speak, girls who weren't actually in the room with you when you turned around. Ashley had laughed so hard, Poppy had forced herself to giggle too, pretending it was all a joke.

She thought she'd be able to keep her secret. But Ashley didn't like keeping secrets.

Tales of Poppy's visions spread through the dormitory like smoke, and Poppy acquired an unfortunate nickname: *Crazy Poppy*. For a while, she tried to argue, hoping that she could convince the others that the Girl was real. It only made the teasing worse.

Poppy started to believe that she actually *was* crazy.

But whenever things got really bad, when the other girls of Thursday's Hope badgered her ruthlessly, the Girl was Poppy's special comfort—a friend who made her less lonely, less afraid. Sometimes when a mirror caught her eye, Poppy would find the Girl peering back at her, and the Girl would remove an item from one of the giant pockets of her smock and then hold it up as if to make Poppy smile.

The next morning, Poppy would discover the item tucked under her pillow.

The first time, it had been a thin wire twisted into the shape of a finch. Then came pressed flowers, out-of-print comic strips snipped from yellowed newspapers, a paintbrush with dried green paint at its tip.

Old things.

Surprising things.

Strange things.

At first, Poppy couldn't believe it was happening. But the objects were there—she could hold them in her hand, and that meant they were real. Unexplainable, but real.

Poppy treasured these items, tucking them inside a book she'd hollowed out to keep them secret. But Ashley took particular pleasure in raiding Poppy's belongings, passing the Girl's treasures to the others, who would tear and sometimes destroy them. On those nights, Poppy had nightmares of terrible fires, and watched, screaming, as her bunkmates burned around her. The worst part was that in those dreams, Poppy was always the one to light the flames.

In real life, Poppy didn't know how to fight back . . . until the day Ashley got her hands on a delicate charcoal sketch of five kids in masks and uniforms, all lined up against a stone wall. Poppy had hidden the sketch in a separate place, between the pages of a book she loved, a book she knew Ashley would never, ever read. But Ashley was a better snoop than Poppy had imagined. Poppy found her standing beside their bunks, the drawing held roughly in her hands.

"Is this from your *friend*?" Ashley asked with a thin, flat smile. She tensed her hand threateningly on the sketch.

Something inside Poppy broke. Before she could stop herself, she reached for Ashley's favorite possession, an ornate mirror on their shared nightstand, and swung it. There was a smash. A scream. Ashley clutched her hand into a fist—but the sketch had already slipped away from her. Miraculously, it landed unharmed on Poppy's bed.

Poppy just watched as Ashley howled for help.

Poppy had never been sent to Ms. Tate's office before. Its cold, metal cabinets and big oak desk had always intimidated Poppy when she walked past it. Now she was seated in front of the desk, in the chair for troublemakers. The secretary told her in no uncertain terms to not touch a thing and to wait there until Ms. Tate had checked on Ashley.

Poppy knew she should listen. She was in enough trouble already. But her stomach was churning with so much anger that it burned her usual meekness away. For once, she didn't hesitate to take the chance she'd always dreamed about. As soon as the office door closed behind her, Poppy was out of her chair and searching the cabinets for her own file. If she was already in big trouble, why not get in a little more?

The room smelled too sweet, as if there was bubble gum stuck underneath every piece of furniture. Sunlight streamed in through the tall window, illuminating a dust-mote storm that swirled around Poppy as she searched. The filing cabinet stood against the far wall. Poppy found the correct drawer, removed her folder, and placed it on Ms. Tate's desk.

Pawing through the material, a veil of disappointment fell on Poppy. There were report cards and medical records, pictures she'd painted when she was much younger, but not a single thing from before she'd arrived at the group home. She'd wanted to find out about her parents, but as far as the file was concerned, her parents had never existed. Poppy had come from nowhere.

This was highly unusual.

And then it got more unusual.

Near the back of the folder, Poppy found a sealed envelope with her name on it. She turned it over again and again, almost dizzy with excitement.

In the upper-left corner, written in pen by a delicate hand, were the words *Larkspur House, Hardscrabble Road, Greencliffe, NY.* The postmark was smudged, so Poppy couldn't read the date it had been sent.

A letter? The anger flooded her again. Why had Ms. Tate never given it to her?

Poppy slid her fingernail carefully under the flap. Inside rested a slip of salmon-colored stationery with intricate floral designs lining every edge. It was one of the most beautiful objects she had ever seen. There was a small photograph of a luscious country mansion tucked in the envelope too. Placing that aside, she began to read.

My Dearest Niece,

Oh what a relief to have finally found you! You have no idea what the family has been through, though I'm sure it is nothing compared to the life you've been forced to lead. Poor thing!

You may call me Great-Aunt Delphinia. I live on a grand estate in the Hudson Valley with more room than I know what to do with. It would be such an honor if you would consider coming to stay with me. I will provide the best schooling, cuisine, and clothing—all the comforts that any girl could ever wish for— though I'm sure you understand that those things would be worthless without the loving household that will form the foundation of your new life here at Larkspur. The photograph of the grounds should provide an idea of what you are in for!

I would come down to Thursday's Hope to collect you if it weren't for my health. But please do let me know that you've received this letter, and I shall arrange for your immediate travel from the city. We've so much to discuss!

Yours truly and with love,
Delphinia Larkspur

Poppy closed her eyes as chills brushed her skin, and her eyes flooded with tears. This was better than any treasure the Girl had ever given her. It was like something out of a fairy tale, and not something that could happen to a girl like her. Family! A happy ending!

Somewhere in the office behind her, the floor creaked. Poppy whipped around to find the director standing just inside the doorway.

"And just what do you think you're doing, Miss Caldwell?" Ms. Tate glanced at the folder lying open on her desk as well as the envelope in Poppy's hands.

"I want to ask you about my file," said Poppy, trying to hide the trembling in her voice.

"That file is not meant to be seen by you," Ms. Tate chided in her best *rules-are-rules* voice.

Poppy's face burned. "I found this." She held up the envelope. "A letter. Addressed to me." She made herself look Ms. Tate in the eyes. "Why would you hide it from me?"

Ms. Tate's expression shifted from anger to confusion. "I would never! Let me see that."

Poppy handed it over reluctantly. She watched as Ms. Tate scanned the writing. "Poppy, I've never seen this before. I swear."

"I have a family!" Poppy said.

"Let's not jump to conclusions."

"My great-aunt Delphinia knows all about me." Poppy's voice was small but insistent.

Ms. Tate sighed, looking like she'd seen this sort of thing before. "The return address is vague. There's no phone number. No email. How do you expect me to even get in touch with her?"

I don't, Poppy thought. *I'll figure it out myself.*

At the look on Poppy's face, Ms. Tate rounded the desk and sat down in front of her computer. Poppy watched, barely daring to breathe, as the director searched the Internet for evidence of this Larkspur House. "I'm not getting much. Just a dozen or so real estate listings from all around the country. And I can't find a thing about a Delphinia Larkspur."

Poppy's chest collapsed in on her. "So that's it?"

"I know the girls have not been kind to you lately." Ms. Tate leaned back in her chair and gave Poppy an apologetic look.

9

"I think you're going to have to accept that this was a joke. And in the meantime, you still have your actions to account for. What you did to Ashley is inexcusable." Poppy was still very much in trouble.

Later that night, when Poppy approached the mirror over the sink in the bathroom, the Girl was not there.

This had never happened before.

Only after Poppy had slipped beneath her sheets, watching the reflected glow of car headlights drift across the ceiling, listening to the wheezing of Ashley on the lower bunk, did she make the connection: *Maybe now that I have the possibility of Larkspur House and Great-Aunt Delphinia, I don't need the Girl anymore.*

Poppy couldn't have been more wrong.

CHAPTER 2

MARCUS GELLER HEARD music that no one else seemed to notice, music emanating from inside a nearby room that only he was aware of.

There was no way to fight this music. No way to ignore it.

So whenever he could, Marcus tried to play along.

Marcus had just sat down on the stool in the corner of the dining room, hugging the cello between his knees and raising the bow, when his mother called out to him. "Marcus! Would you come up here, please?" Her voice sounded thin and far away, and he knew that she'd parked herself at her computer in her bedroom upstairs, her usual spot for hiding from the real world.

Marcus felt a knobby object rise up his esophagus. He hadn't even begun practicing yet today, and already his mom was preparing to stop him. He squeezed his hands into fists and then released them slowly before answering, "Can you give me a minute!" Then he drew the bow across the strings, filling the room with a deep, resonant hum that drowned out all of his worries, as well as his mother's reply.

Practicing at home had always been difficult—finding privacy when you have three older siblings living under the same roof is akin to discovering a unicorn sleeping under your bed—but recently, the problem had been even more complicated.

Marcus's music seemed to be affecting his mother in an unusual way.

His mother's younger brother, Shane, had also played the cello. According to everyone in the family, he'd been really, really good at it. He'd had a bright future as a musician—

But then something horrible had happened.

Marcus didn't know the details of Shane's death. Nobody talked about that part of the story.

All he knew was that Shane had been twelve years old when he died.

The same age as Marcus was now.

Maybe it was because of the age thing. Or maybe it was because Marcus was getting good at the cello. Whatever the case, it was freaking his mother out—and she was taking it out on him.

Which wasn't fair.

It wasn't like Marcus could stop playing. If he did, he'd be overwhelmed by all the music that no one else seemed to hear.

To Marcus, the sounds of the strings and the brass and the reeds were so bright and vibrant, the rhythms so wild and wicked, he couldn't believe that he was alone in his experience of it. And as a young child, he'd spoken incessantly about it, humming the melodies aloud so people would believe him.

Eventually his parents took him to see a doctor who suggested medication to stop the "hallucinations." Afterward, Marcus realized that maybe the music should become a secret instead. He didn't want it to end, even if it *was* all in his head.

This was around the time he'd finally begun to pick up whatever instrument was available from the music classroom at school and from his uncle's old collection at home to try to mimic the gorgeous melodies constantly floating around him.

It was a perfect transition: Stop talking about the music and start making it. This change alleviated his parents' fear, but it also invited attention from teachers and other adults who were fascinated by Marcus's sudden talent.

Though Marcus liked this attention, he wasn't sure he deserved it. Part of him felt like a fake; it wasn't as though he was inventing the compositions himself.

They were coming to him from somewhere beyond this world.

"Marcus."

He jerked the bow away from the strings and then opened his eyes. His mother was standing in the dining room doorway clutching a piece of paper. Marcus hadn't realized how lost he'd gotten in the music, nor how peaceful the afternoon had become. "Sorry, Mom," he said. "I was distracted."

To his surprise, she smiled. "It's okay." She held out the piece of paper to him. "I just got this message. Figured it was easier to print it out and bring it down to you."

"What is it?"

"Read it and find out."

Dear Mrs. Geller,

My name is L. Delphinium, and I am the director of the Larkspur Academy for the Performing Arts in New York State. I work with several professional scouts around the world, and when one of them attended your son's recent recital at the Oberlin campus in Ohio, she was overcome by the power of his performance. We would love it if Marcus came to study with us.

14

At Larkspur, Marcus will have access to the most accomplished visiting faculty from New York City's best companies. We have attached a file that includes our brochure with additional information about our music program and what we stand for.

We realize it is a little late in the season for an invitation such as this; however, it is our guiding principle that we seek out the most promising young talent, and we would be remiss if we did not at least try. With a student like Marcus, we would be willing to cover all tuition, board, and any travel expenses. It would cost you nothing.

Please let us know at your earliest convenience.

Best regards,
L. Delphinium
Director, Larkspur Academy

"Is this a joke?" Marcus asked.

"I can't imagine so."

"It's insane! There was a scout at the Oberlin recital?"

"You're a talented kid, Marcus," she said. "Don't act so surprised."

"And you wouldn't mind if I went?"

"I'd be *delighted* if you went." She folded her arms and grinned. She looked a little *too* delighted.

Before he could answer, a blast of noise resounded in Marcus's ears, a cacophony filled with instruments, too many to name. This wasn't like any music he'd ever heard before—it was more like a scream. Marcus flinched, and then, glancing at his mother, tried to disguise his shock as wide-eyed excitement.

She didn't hear it at all.

CHAPTER 3

IN THE DREAM that haunted her, Azumi Endo walked barefoot through the forest behind her aunt's home in Yamanashi Prefecture. The volcanic rock that had long ago spewed from the top of Mount Fuji made the ground there uneven and tricky beneath twisted tree roots and thick underbrush. Ignoring the clearly marked paths that crisscrossed the wilderness, Azumi often tripped, dropping to her knees, dirtying her nightgown before rising and continuing on. She knew that if she stopped even for a moment she might feel a hand on her shoulder, and if she turned around . . . well, she didn't want to imagine what she'd find looming behind her.

Tonight, she'd pushed farther than she ever had before, to a ravine where a drop-off sliced through the terrain. In the shadows and fog, she couldn't make out the bottom. One step forward and she would dive into a pit of sharp branches—a deadly trap rigged to ensnare her. She'd been following one of the long ribbons that had been tied to a trunk near the park's entrance, leading into the heart of the woods.

That was where the bodies were hidden.

In the dream, her skin was covered in a cool sheen of sweat, and her mind whirled, making her second-guess what direction to take. She couldn't lower herself down. The drop was too dangerous. Besides, it didn't seem likely that Moriko was there. Wouldn't she have answered Azumi's call? Azumi suddenly couldn't remember if she'd even been shouting out to Moriko, but she knew that she must have been. Wasn't that why she was there?

She was going to find her sister. She had to.

Now . . .

It was during moments like this—when Azumi began to question how she came to be alone in the middle of the forest at all—that she understood she was dreaming again. The shadow world of these woods was all in her mind. Or at least most of it was. There was another part of the dreaming, another part she never remembered until it was too late.

Because whenever Azumi dreamed of the forest, she also walked in her sleep.

Azumi opened her eyes to find herself surrounded by darkness, standing in the middle of the woods behind her family's house outside of Seattle for the third time that month.

An ocean now separated her from the haunted forest in Japan, but her mind insisted on closing that distance, putting her right back in the place where she'd lost her sister.

The mossy ground of Washington State was cold and wet against the soles of her feet, the summer air cool and humid. She could barely see in the darkness, uncertain whether the ravine had only been part of her dream, or if she was really a few steps from disaster.

Not now, not again, she thought, crouching down to protect herself against the night. *Mother and Father will be terrified.* How could she put them through this after what had happened to Moriko, after what Azumi herself had done?

She had lost her sister.

She couldn't lose herself.

The morning after Azumi's latest nightmare, an idea came to her about how she could protect both her parents and herself. She had to accept that if she were to stay home, her dreaming would bring her deeper into danger, closer to a place from which she too would not return.

On her computer, she searched for boarding schools on the East Coast of the US, as far from the Pacific Ocean as she could get.

Strangely, only a single website popped up.

The Larkspur School.

She tried the search again. And then again. She turned the computer off and then on—but the result was always the same.

Larkspur.

It must be some sort of sign, Azumi thought. *Maybe this is supposed to be* the one.

She glanced over the school's mission statement. *The Larkspur School has stood for over a century as a symbol of academic, artistic, and social excellence. Our pastoral campus is ideal for scholars who wish to shine . . .*

Azumi didn't need to read any more. This place sounded perfect.

CHAPTER 4

ONE OF THE producers barged into the sunny room where Dash and Dylan Wright had been waiting for the day to begin. "We're going to need you downstairs in fifteen," said the bouncy brunette, whose name neither boy could remember. "Just a heads up. 'Kay?"

They'd been trying to stem the boredom of their final production schedule by flipping through different game apps on their phones.

The Wright twins had been professional actors since the age of five, so they were used to all sorts of people coming and going into their lives, and dressing rooms, on a daily basis.

"Downstairs?" asked Dylan with a smirk. "For what? Are we shooting the next scene?" The producer raised an eyebrow and continued to look at Dash, as if only his reply mattered. Dylan waved at her, trying to get her attention. "Uh, hello? Am I invisible or something?"

"We're looking forward to it," said Dash apologetically. "Thanks." The producer blinked and then stomped off as if she couldn't wait to be far away from them both. Dash turned toward his brother with a glare. "*Am I invisible or something?*" he echoed, daggers in his eyes.

Dylan frowned. "What was I supposed to say? She completely ignored me."

Dash sighed and then shrugged. "I guess everyone's tired of your tricks."

"They're not tricks," said Dylan. "They're jokes!"

"Jokes don't usually end with people losing money. When you steal from people, they tend to dislike you."

"I made less money off them than you'd think." Dylan crossed him arms and set his jaw. "But who cares? After today, they won't have to put up with me any longer. I'm so ready to get out of this place."

The twins were nearly indistinguishable from each other. Both had the same dark skin, the same crooked, dimpled grin, the same bright black eyes, the same short curly hair.

They had been on the popular sitcom *Dad's So Clueless* since the age of five. The show was about a large family whose father was a hapless private investigator. For seven years, they'd shared the character of the youngest brother, a cutie-pie with a lisp whose name was Scooter but who was often called *Scoots Ba-Dooter*—a sickeningly sweet running gag that the twins eventually grew to despise, especially when people called them the name in real life.

Recently, the sitcom's head writer had decided to write Scoots off the show, sending the character to a boarding school in France. Today was the boys' last day of filming.

When they'd first received the news, Dash and Dylan were crushed. Dash had been particularly inconsolable, so much so that his parents had threatened to bring him to the emergency room unless he calmed himself down. He didn't tell anyone that he felt guilty for not trying harder to stop Dylan from playing his tricks . . . his "jokes." Maybe there was something he could have done that would have allowed them to continue working.

Dylan assured him that something better would come along. But the assurance didn't help.

Dash had recently begun to experience moments of extreme anxiety. For the past few weeks, he'd been having vivid nightmares about Dylan. In the nightmares, Dylan was in some sort of danger, and it was Dash's responsibility to save him. Dash would wake in the dark, racing down the hallway between their bedrooms to make sure Dylan was all right. Usually, he'd discover Dylan lying in his own bed, snoring softly, completely oblivious to his brother's worry.

Then, two nights ago, Dash had discovered his brother's bed empty—the sheets pulled back in a rumpled mess. Dash ran outside, into the night, turning down unfamiliar alleys and deserted back roads, until he found himself at a fenced-in, abandoned construction site about three miles from home. There, Dash had scrambled around the wide, pockmarked lot, screaming for his brother, expecting to find his broken body beneath a pile of rubble or trapped inside a Dumpster. But when his father showed up with the police they insisted that Dylan was at home, safe and sound.

Later, when Dash discovered Dylan lying in bed, his heart turned over with relief. He couldn't believe it. He'd been certain that Dylan had been out there, needing rescue.

Afterward, the boys had sat up in Dylan's room late into the night as Dash explained what he'd experienced. Dylan had teased Dash, telling him he needed to pull it together, or their parents were going to send him away to a boarding school in France, never to be seen again.

Dash had felt better, ready to fall back asleep, and Dylan offered to let him stay in his room. When Dylan had gotten up to turn off the light, Dash had caught a glimpse of his brother's bare feet.

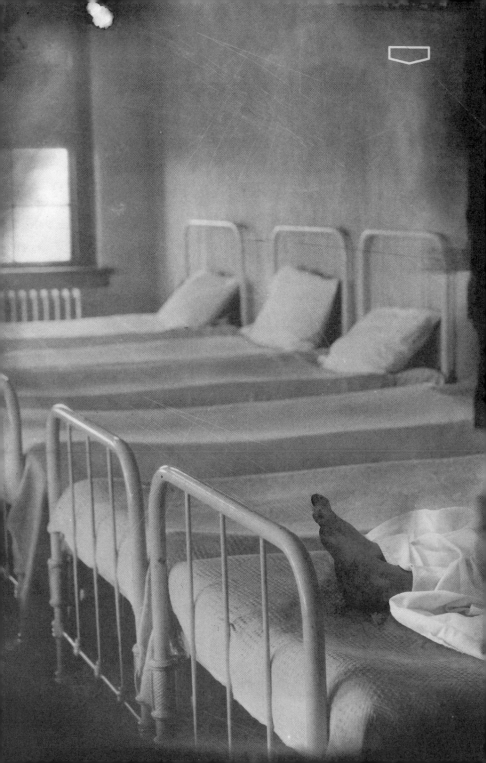

Seconds later, in the new darkness, Dash had been too scared to say he'd seen a flash of Dylan in a strange bed, his soles black and bloody.

"Hey," said Dylan from the corner of the sunny room. "Did you read the email we just got?"

Dash shook his head. He'd been lost inside a game on his phone ever since the brown-haired woman had come to call them for the production meeting.

"Well, pull it up! This sounds like it might be really cool."

Dash saw a text from an unknown number as he unlocked his phone and swiped to the email app. The email's sender was Larkspur Productions, LLC. The subject read: *URGENT—NEW PROJECT FOR YOU.* Dash felt his stomach jolt.

Dylan! Dash!

What's up? Hope you boys are doing well. We're so glad to hear that the troubles with *Dad's So Clueless* haven't squashed your ambitions. As huge fans of Scooter, we knew we had to reach out to you regarding the amazing project we're putting together. We have a script that we'd love you to check out, ASAP.

We've read that you're both fans of horror films. Have
we got something scary for you: a haunted house,
several psychotic villains, and a plot filled with twists
you'll never imagine! We believe that you two will be
perfect for the lead roles: twin brothers who are the
heroes of the story.

If you'd like to hear more, please let us know and we'll
shoot the script right on over to you.

All the best,
Del Larkspur
President, Larkspur Productions, LLC

"Weird," Dylan said. "Right?"

Dash flinched. He hadn't noticed his brother had scrambled across the room to kneel on the floor by his chair. "Weird how?"

"Well, I mean, we'd both have to be our own person this time. We've only ever shared a role before."

"Did you think we'd be doing that for the rest of our lives?"

"No, but . . . you know, the producers always sort of thought your version of Scooter was better than mine."

"That's not even close to being true." Dash tried to keep his expression even. He knew his brother was right. He also believed it was one of the reasons Dylan had so often lashed out at the production crew. "On *this* show, we act exactly the same. Always."

Dylan rolled his eyes. "So . . . you'd consider saying yes?"

Dash was quiet for a moment, thinking about his terrible dreams. "I'm not sure about being in a *horror* movie."

Just then, both of their phones dinged. Another email had come through. Once again, the sender was Larkspur Productions, LLC. Wide-eyed, the boys stared at each other before opening the message.

Dash read it aloud. "Don't worry. The script isn't *too* scary." He glanced up at his brother, and then looked around the room, as if a hidden camera were pointed at them. He scoffed, then said, "Are they listening to us?"

"Oh yeah, totally," Dylan answered. "They're just *so* determined to get us there. Come on, Dash. The guy probably just had an afterthought. Stop being such a wuss."

"*You're* a wuss!" After a moment, Dash grinned. "It does feel good to be wanted again."

Dylan slapped his brother's knee. "We're going to be movie stars!"

"Okay then, who should write back?" asked Dash. "You or me?"

CHAPTER 5

POPPY HAD BEEN hiking up the hill from the Greencliffe train station for nearly fifteen minutes when she realized that someone was following her. Though leafy branches swayed and creaked high over her head and endless birdsong chimed from every direction, Poppy heard the sound of footsteps crunching gravel in the distance. She stopped and turned around. Behind her was a clear view of the path she'd walked minutes earlier— the curving country road, the towering greenery, and way in the distance, the glistening waters that transformed the Hudson River into a wide, jewel-encrusted ribbon.

When Poppy noticed the silhouette of a person at the bottom of the hill, she froze. She couldn't discern too many details, except that he looked small, maybe even smaller than she was.

He was dressed in a black jacket and khaki pants, and he was carrying a large object on his back—Poppy couldn't make it out.

Though the late August air was warm and the sun shone brightly, she felt a chill come upon her. She hitched her ratty pink messenger bag higher on her shoulder and continued walking up the hill, faster now, even though she wasn't sure she was even heading in the right direction.

In her bag, she carried her few possessions: a toothbrush, a face towel, a few pairs of socks and underwear, and her hollowed-out paperback copy of *The Lion, the Witch and the Wardrobe*, which was filled with several small trinkets that the Girl had left under her pillow. As heartbreaking as it had been, she'd had to leave her collection of books behind at Thursday's Hope. In the letter, Great-Aunt Delphinia had promised that once Poppy made it to Larkspur, she'd have everything in the world she'd ever want or need. New home, new school, new family. Before Poppy had managed to scrounge up the train fare to make the journey to Greencliffe, she wondered if this would include some friends too.

On the morning after she'd found the envelope in the filing cabinet, as Poppy brushed the tangles from her hair, the Girl finally appeared in the bathroom mirror again. But she no longer looked like the Girl who Poppy had grown up with. Her face was a strange blur, as if she were rapidly, unconsciously shaking her skull in all directions. Poppy felt as if she could hear the Girl screaming, after all this time finally trying to speak.

It was a message, Poppy understood. But what did it mean?

Before she'd had a chance to think, the mirror had turned black, as if the room on the other side—the reflected one in which the Girl was standing—had filled with thick, churning smoke. Poppy gasped.

A moment later, the mirror had cleared.

The Girl was gone again, taking the darkness with her.

Whenever the Girl had appeared since then, her face remained obscured by that disturbing and violent shaking.

It was such a disconcerting sight that Poppy began to avoid mirrors altogether.

When she heard footsteps coming up quickly on the road behind her, Poppy's instinct told her to run. But as soon as she took the first step, she stumbled on her shoelace and began to fall. She rolled onto the asphalt, twisting into a tumble, and then spun around to face the person who'd been chasing her, hands raised in protection.

To her surprise, no one was there. The trees swayed above her, light from the sky winking from between wide, green leaves.

Far away, around a bend in the road, she thought she could make out the sound of her fellow walker dragging his heels.

So who had she just heard? Had the person dashed away into the woods? Maybe he was watching from somewhere off the road, between the trees.

Crazy Poppy, she heard in her head—the voices of the girls from Thursday's Hope taunting her still. *Crazy Poppy. Craaaazy Poppyyyy.*

To gain her bearings, she stood and took in her surroundings. In the dense brush a few feet away, a tall stone wall was camouflaged by twisted red vines and thin saplings, running alongside the road's shoulder. Was this the boundary of Great-Aunt Delphinia's estate?

A dozen yards ahead, Poppy saw a wide gravel path branching off the main road into the woods. Where the path intersected the wall, a space in the stonework opened up like a missing tooth in a wide, dead grin. Two pillars climbed up from the forest floor to form an entryway. An ornamental iron railing connected the two pillars, its rusted curlicues broken and twisted as if someone with abnormal strength had wrenched it apart. Below, where one would expect to find a pair of decorative gates, the space was empty, the woods beyond forming a tunnel that darkened as it went deeper.

The sight made her mouth dry. Poppy stepped forward, then stopped at the edge of the driveway. That was when she noticed words engraved on stones in the center of each pillar: *Larkspur*.

This *was* the place. Her new home.

With tall grass and weeds growing in sporadic patches at her feet, the driveway looked like it hadn't been crossed in decades. Confusion rattled her brain.

Crazy Poppy . . .

Poppy squeezed her eyes shut. *Stop it!*

Maybe there was another gate farther up the road—one that Great-Aunt Delphinia used more frequently.

These thoughts flew away when Poppy noticed something else carved into the pillars, directly beneath the name of the estate—a familiar symbol, a picture that Poppy could have drawn from memory. The outline of a bird. The image was the same as the twisted wire sculpture that the Girl had removed from the pocket of her pinafore all those years ago, the first present that Poppy had found under her pillow the next morning.

Something crunched the gravel directly behind her.

Wide-eyed, Poppy stiffened. She glanced over her shoulder to find the road deserted. Footsteps moved all around her. "Hello?" she whispered. There was no one there. No one that Poppy could see.

Poppy knew of another way, one that she was terrified to try. But she had to find out . . .

Trembling, she removed her clamshell compact from her satchel and flipped it open. As she brought up the mirror to eye level, she was certain of who would be there.

But this time when she peered into the glass, she jolted.

In the mirror, the Girl was standing several steps behind her. Now, however, the Girl's whole body was shaking. She jerked with lightning-quick spasms, flickering like an image in a sped-up film.

Before Poppy could respond, the Girl bolted forward.

Coldness encircled her as the Girl's arms twisted around Poppy's torso and squeezed. Poppy felt herself yanked backward into the road, away from Larkspur's gate. As she collapsed to the ground, she released a scream of such terror it sent all the songbirds careening nervously from the safety of the high branches, screeching like echoes of her own voice up into the air. They dissipated as Poppy lost her breath, and the sky beyond turned dark.

CHAPTER 6

A SHRIEK RANG out from around the bend in the road ahead, and Marcus Geller nearly dropped his cello. Seconds later, the sound came to an abrupt end, and he grew even more nervous. Could the cry have come from the girl he'd seen leaving the train station before him? Was she hurt?

Marcus laid his things on the side of the road, and took off in a sprint.

As he rounded the bend, Marcus saw the girl from the train station lying in the middle of the road, not moving. "Hey!" he yelled as he ran the last couple of dozen yards. "Are you okay?" Kneeling beside her, he realized that he had no idea what to do. She was on her back, her arms splayed out, her knees bent, her head turned away from him. "Please be alive," he whispered, holding his hand in front of her nose. Warm breath tickled his skin, and he released a sigh.

He knew he had to get her out of the road—at any moment, a car could come speeding around the corner. He took her hand, figuring it might at least get her attention.

The girl's eyelids fluttered and then opened. When she saw him leaning over her, a look of confusion quickly transformed into terror. Eyes like mirrors, she opened her mouth and screamed again, and she and Marcus scrambled away from each other, crouching in the road as if about to spar.

After a moment, Marcus remembered that he'd been the one who'd approached her. He took a slow breath and then held out his hands to show her he meant no harm. "It's okay," he said. "I was trying to help."

As he rose to his feet, the girl reached for the pink bag that was lying on the nearby shoulder of the road and pulled it close to her, as if he might try to steal it. Then she did the same thing to a small black makeup compact, clutching it in one fist.

A second later, she whipped her arm back and then threw the compact across the road as hard as she could.

It skipped like a stone upon water before disappearing into the dense scrub. With a sigh of relief, she wiped her nose with the back of her wrist, glanced up at Marcus, and shook her head.

Marcus felt like he'd just met a girl who'd been raised by wolves.

"I'm Marcus," he said purposefully, as if she might not understand him. "I was down the street when I heard you scream. You were just lying here." The girl blinked and then glanced around. She looked like she expected to see someone else there with them, maybe hiding in the brush. "I'm sorry," he went on when he realized she didn't plan on answering him. "I didn't mean to scare you."

"You're not the one who scared me," said the girl, continuing to examine the trees.

Marcus's skin tingled. His mother had told him he might meet different sorts of people at Larkspur, but this girl was just plain weird. Then again, many musical prodigies were, so he knew he shouldn't be surprised. He wanted to ask her, *If I'm not the one who scared you, then who is?* Instead he said, "Let's get out of the road. Maybe you can tell me what happened."

She finally met his gaze and gave him a look that said she had *no idea* what had happened. But she stood and brushed herself off, and headed toward a stony path that veered from the pavement and edged into the woods. Marcus noticed the wall and the gate standing several yards back, as well as the word *Larkspur*, which was engraved in each stone pillar.

"Oh," he said, startled. "We're here. We've made it."

The girl scowled at him. "What do you mean?" she asked.

"To Larkspur," he said, blushing. "I'm sorry—isn't this where you were headed too?"

"Yes," she responded unsurely.

Marcus spent a moment observing the decay of the entry and the dark tunnel of trees beyond the wall. A soft and melancholy piano melody drifted to him on the wind from somewhere close by. It was the same tune he'd heard the musician behind the wall playing on the day he'd gotten his invitation to Larkspur. The girl didn't notice the music. But then, he didn't imagine that she would. No one ever did. "This isn't really what I expected," he said. "What about you?"

"What do you mean?"

"Is it what you expected?"

The girl looked confused. "I-I don't know," she stammered. "What's your name again?"

"Marcus Geller," he said slowly. She must have hit her head when she'd fallen. Hard.

"And why did you come to Larkspur House?"

"Well, I was invited. Weren't you?" She didn't answer. His nerves kept him talking. "I'm cello mostly, but I like to experiment with other instruments too. Piano. Flute. Harmonica! Harmonica is so much fun." He reached into his back pocket and pulled out the small steel instrument he'd stowed there before leaving Ohio. He held it to his lips and then performed a brief, jazzy riff. "What do you play?" he asked.

"Play?"

"Yeah, what instrument?"

"I don't play an instrument."

"A singer, then. Sweet! You look like you have a nice voice."

The girl's cheeks turned the same pink shade as her bag. "I do?" Her voice was suddenly very soft.

"Totally. I can tell these things. Listen, I dropped all my stuff when I heard . . . well, never mind. Would you mind waiting for me? When I get back, we can walk to the house together." *And then you can tell me what you were doing lying in the road.* "It's got to be just up that path, don't you think?" The girl glanced over her shoulder and into the woods. Then, with her lips pressed together, she turned back and nodded. "You going to be all right alone?" Marcus asked. She straightened her shoulders and tucked her hair behind her ears.

He interpreted that as a *yes*.

After he'd taken several steps down the road toward his bags, he heard a muffled voice come from behind him. Glancing back, he saw the girl watching him. She'd said something that he'd missed.

"Poppy," the girl repeated. "My name is Poppy Caldwell."

The piano melody echoed out again, but it had changed, becoming more upbeat—not quite happy, but certainly not as sad. He instantly thought of it as "Larkspur's Theme," a song that belonged to this place. When he and Poppy reached the house, he'd have to find a piano and play it so she could hear it too.

"Nice to meet you, Poppy Caldwell," Marcus said with a smile.

"And thanks," she managed. "For helping me get up."

He gave her a quick salute and surprised a laugh from her. Okay, so maybe she wasn't completely weird after all.

Marcus had never been away from home for more than a weekend, and here he was, by himself in upstate New York getting ready to spend the year on a full scholarship at the prestigious Larkspur Academy for the Performing Arts. He was about to eat, breathe, and live music with a whole bunch of other talented kids who thought just like him, with no interference from his mom or his brothers and sister. He couldn't believe it.

Maybe, Marcus thought as he came upon his bag and large black case on the side of the road, *there will be people at the academy who experience the world in the same way I do. Maybe I'll meet others who geek out about Chet Baker, Dave Brubeck, and Nina Simone as much as me.*

He found Poppy standing right where he'd left her: at the gravel path that led to the shadowy gap in the stone wall. She looked worried.

"Ready?" he asked. Poppy nodded. Together they stepped forward. "So," Marcus ventured, "do you want to tell me what happened?"

Poppy bit at her lip for a few seconds. Then she said, "Could you tell me more about your invitation to Larkspur?"

"I'm pretty sure it's the same one you got."

"That's the thing," she said as they crossed under the twisted iron railing and past the pillars into the shadowy tunnel of trees, "I'm pretty sure it's not."

CHAPTER 7

AFTER THE DRIVER her parents had hired left her at Larkspur's gate, Azumi dragged her luggage deep into the woods and up the slow ascent, memories of her dark dreams scratching icy branches along her spine.

The previous summer, Azumi and her sister, Moriko, had visited their auntie Wakame at her home just northwest of Mount Fuji on the island of Honshu. Auntie Wakame had forbidden the girls from entering the nearby forest on their own, since it was so common for even frequent visitors to become lost there. With its thick canopy of trees that hid the sun and the iron-filled volcanic rock that messed with compass needles, the national park was known as one of the most haunted spots in all of Japan.

Azumi had promised herself she'd never go back to Yamanashi Prefecture again. But the farther she strolled up

Larkspur's driveway, the distance between the present and the past became shorter and shorter. Everywhere she looked, she recognized parts of the forest where Moriko had disappeared—lichen-covered tree trunks, dappled shadows dancing on the leafy ground, dew clinging to low-hanging, delicate mosses.

Then, with a blink, she was there. Back in Japan. Remembering that horrible day.

"Come on, Azumi," said Moriko, stepping off the clearly marked path. "Don't be such a scaredy-cat."

"I'm *not* a scaredy-cat." Azumi looked around in disgust. "I just think that Auntie Wakame might have a point. Anyone could be hiding in there."

"You can hide too. And while you're hiding, *I* can look for more treasure."

"Treasure? You really think the garbage that the tourists leave behind is worth digging through?"

"Of course! How else do you think an explorer ever finds anything of value?"

"That's deep, Moriko, Treasure Hunter." Azumi scanned the nylon ribbons that crossed the demarcated trails and veered off into the forbidden parts of the woods, disappearing into the shadows. The ribbons came in all different colors, each of them bright so they could be easily spotted by a ranger or a visitor to the park. "Why are all these ribbons here?"

Moriko looked over at her. "People drive out from Tokyo. Sad people. They come here to . . . say good-bye to the world. They tie these ribbons at the edge of the forest so that someone can find them after they're gone. Some say it's *their* ghosts that haunt these woods."

"Like in Auntie's yūrei tales?"

Moriko made her eyes wide, her blue hair changing shades in the dimming light. "Exactly!"

Azumi shook her head, trying to look exhausted or annoyed—anything but the terror she felt bubbling in her gut. "No thanks. I'm not ruining my new sneakers. You go on. Have fun. You always do."

"Azumi!" Moriko called out. "I'm kidding! Don't be like that!"

But Azumi walked away. She hurried along the lonely trails back to their aunt's cottage as the sun began to set.

Her sister did not return to Auntie Wakame's that night.

Their parents traveled immediately from Washington. The search for Moriko was long and exhaustive. No one turned up a single shred of evidence. Not the Ministry of the Environment, not the local police and detectives, not the family.

And Azumi never saw her sister again.

The dreams started shortly after Azumi returned to the United States. It was as if the trees behind her own home had

44

become spirits of the bodies that littered the Japanese forest, calling to her, the hush of a breeze meeting the branches outside her bedroom window like whispers in her head. *Here. Here we are. Come and get us, child. Come and help us find our way home.*

Larkspur's driveway made a sharp turn, and a giant meadow domed by a gleaming blue sky opened up before Azumi. All at once the forest and its shadows were gone.

Perched on the crest of the slope, nearly two hundred yards farther up the path, was the grand structure that she'd first seen online a month ago.

The Larkspur School.

It looked quite different in real life. So much bigger. She took in its steeply pitched roofline and many gabled windows, its ivy-encrusted stone porches, the glinting windows that shone like ice against the dark stone walls, the turrets that lifted up like dark mounds of whipped dessert from the ends of what looked like passageways, and the soaring tower that appeared to spike straight through its massive granite heart.

When Azumi reached the center of the porch, she knocked on the French doors, but no one answered. She opened one of the doors and peered at the shadows just inside. She heard nothing—no footsteps, no talking, not even the tick of a clock.

"Hello?" she called out. "I'm Azumi Endo, and I'm here for school!" But no one answered. "Excuse me! Is anyone here?!"

Azumi tossed her suitcase just inside the door and then sat on the wide stone porch she'd seen from the path. Someone would come by eventually. Until then, she'd take pictures on her phone to send to her parents.

Moriko and Azumi had always been opposites. Several years older than Azumi, Moriko had pierced her nose and dyed her hair and listened religiously to their parents' old punk-rock albums. Moriko's classmates had looked up to her as if she were a superstar, a trendsetter, a kind soul, and a creative spirit. The memorial in the high school yearbook had taken up two pages.

Azumi kept her own hair long and straight and black as night, as it was meant to be. Admiring a clean look, she didn't put up posters on her walls. She always took off her shoes at the front door, just as her baaba had taught her. Azumi didn't have a clue what her own memorial might look like if her friends were to make one, but she would have liked it to contain her seventh grade yearbook photo, the serious one in which she looked like a lawyer or a judge, her mouth downturned slightly and her eyebrow raised in a way that said, *Don't even think about it.*

When Azumi turned thirteen, she realized that she could never be as carefree as Moriko had been. But she could become a diligent daughter and please her parents in all the ways Moriko had refused to: with awesome grades, and the most goals during soccer matches, and *classy* friends who were as determined to succeed as she was. This was why her sleepwalking had been such a nightmare over the past year. She was losing control. Just like she'd lost Moriko. It made her want to scream.

On her phone's screen, Azumi noticed a figure moving near the line of trees, several hundred feet from where she'd exited the woods. Lowering the phone, however, she discovered nothing there but the breeze moving the dense, leafy growth, which caught the sun occasionally, making it *seem* as though someone had been watching her.

She lifted the phone's camera back up to take the picture anyway. When a black patch appeared in the same spot on the screen, Azumi inhaled a sharp little breath and looked closer. The patch wavered before the tree line, as if an impenetrable shadow were being cast on that spot from about six or seven feet above the ground.

A human-shaped shadow.

She took a picture, then zoomed in.

Long, thin arms, sticklike legs, and a head that appeared way too large to be carried on such a gaunt frame.

And eyes. Two sparks of gold, watching her.

The image shuddered, and the screen went black.

In her peripheral vision, Azumi noticed movement by the tree line. She stood, ready to bolt away. But then two kids emerged from the mouth of the woods. A boy and a girl. They were carrying luggage.

Raising her hand over her head, Azumi waved emphatically to the two travelers. They paused on the path and waved back slowly. She had just lowered her hand, not wanting to look overeager, when she noticed that, off the path to their left, standing in the meadow where she'd first noticed its presence, the dark shadow had reappeared.

Slowly, it turned its head toward the boy and girl.

Watching them.

About to pounce.

As Azumi opened her mouth to shout out a warning, the shadow lunged.

"Hey!" she cried. "Over here!"

Don't be such a scaredy-cat.

. . . Shut up, Moriko!

The boy and the girl stopped on the path, staring at her in confusion. Azumi waved them forward, swinging both arms up and back over her head. The dark thing was closing in on them, and they had no idea.

"Hurry!" *Closer. Closer.* "Run!"

Something seemed to click for the pair, and they took off across the grass, sprinting toward the porch. The shadow creature loomed large, gaining ground.

"Don't turn around!"

They weren't going to make it.

Azumi dashed down the porch steps.

In the meadow, the shadow's golden eyes seemed to flicker with delight that Azumi was approaching.

She concentrated on the boy and the girl, who were now only a couple of dozen feet away. "Toss your bag to me!" she shouted to the boy as he came up beside her. She grunted as she caught his luggage, but she managed to hold it tight. He wore another case strapped to his shoulders, something that looked like an enormous backpack.

Azumi turned toward the house.

A rushing, sucking sound came quickly behind them as they raced up the steps to the porch. Azumi didn't look back, not even when she swung open the glass door and pushed the others into the dark entry. Slamming the door shut behind them, she scrambled to find a lock or a latch to hold it closed.

She expected the shadow to barrel into the door at any moment.

But instead . . . nothing.

Through the window, she could see that the meadow and the porch were as empty as they'd been when she'd first arrived. No shadow. No flickering golden eyes. She tried to swallow a deep breath but released an embarrassing squeak instead.

"What's going on?" asked the boy.

Azumi turned, breathless. "I-I'm sorry. I was certain I saw . . ." She glanced over her shoulder again just to be sure. She felt her shoulders tense. "Something was chasing you."

"An animal?" asked the girl, staring wide-eyed out at the morning.

"Well, yeah, it was an animal. A *big* animal. It looked . . . angry." Azumi shook her head. "I can't believe you didn't see it. It was literally about to bite your heads off."

The boy stood by the window, wearing a slight grin, as if he didn't believe her. "It must be hiding now."

"*Obviously*," said Azumi. "I mean, it didn't just disappear!"

"I guess we should thank you," said the girl. "For saving us?"

"If you're going to laugh at me, then next time, you can just *save yourselves*." The boy and the girl looked like she'd just slapped them. Azumi shook her head, embarrassed that she'd allowed herself to say such a thing. "Anyway, my name is Azumi. Azumi Endo."

"I'm Poppy. And this is—"

"Marcus." The boy brushed his red curls away from his forehead and then saluted. He adjusted the straps of the thing he carried on his back, and Azumi realized from the shape of it that it must be a cello.

"Do you know where we can find the others?" asked Azumi.

"The others?" Marcus echoed.

"The other students. The faculty. Anyone." Azumi watched as Marcus glanced at Poppy, as if they knew something that she did not. "What is it? Did I say something funny again?"

"I don't have a clue where anyone is," he said, ignoring her question, the odd expression dropping from his face. "But it's probably a good idea if we take a look around. Right, Poppy?"

Poppy stood there, hugging her rib cage. "I guess so."

"Okay then," said Azumi, picking up her bag. "Good." She peered once more through the windows out at the sunny meadow. Even though she couldn't see it anymore, she was sure the shadow was still out there somewhere—hiding, watching, waiting.

CHAPTER 8

DASH AND DYLAN had insisted that the driver of their limo pull all the way onto the Larkspur property, claiming that they'd pay for any damage that the creeping foliage inflicted on the car.

As the car drove off and left them alone, the boys found a pair of wide wooden doors. They knocked and knocked, but no one answered. Pressing their ears to the glass, the boys listened for a response. Inside, they could hear the echoes of their pounding.

They texted Del to see where he was. But the messages failed to send. *No service.*

"What are we going to do now?" asked Dash. Dylan answered by stepping forward and pressing the latch on the door handle. The doors swung inward with a resounding groan. "Oh yeah." Dash forced a chuckle. "I didn't think of that."

"Good thing I'm here, little brother."

"You know I hate it when you call me that. Being born five minutes after you doesn't make me 'littler' than you."

"You're so right," said Dylan. "*I know* you hate it." He smiled that smile that always made Dash nervous, the one that Dash could never pull off, not even when he practiced in a mirror. The smile that said, *Don't be a wuss.* They weren't perfectly identical after all, Dash knew, especially when it came to their personalities.

With his stomach churning, Dash followed Dylan into the mansion. Inside, his gaze flitted around the cathedral-size room. He took in the details—the wide oak banisters that bordered the central stairway, the wood pillars that rose to the pointed, arched ceiling, the high stained-glass windows that allowed shocking streaks of red and blue and gold light to filter across the intricate, circular parquet floor.

The boys placed their bags in its center.

A harsh tone bounced around the room, ringing in Dash's ears, making him feel dizzy and disoriented. He blinked and saw Dylan standing a few feet away, struggling with his phone.

"Stupid thing," Dylan said.

"What's wrong?"

"Someone keeps calling me, but every time I pick up, the phone goes dead."

"What's the number?"

"It says *unknown*."

"Service here bites."

"But what if Del is trying to get in touch with us? To tell us where to go?"

"Why don't we try to find him?"

Dylan smiled. "Do you want to head upstairs or should I?"

"We should stick together, don't you think?" Dash asked, trying to sound unafraid.

He peered at the grand staircase and froze.

A boy was standing at the bottom, staring at them. He was dressed in dark shorts and a white button-down shirt. But that wasn't what caught Dash's attention. The boy was wearing a mask. A white rabbit with shadowy cutout eyes and a big, pink grin for a mouth.

Dash had a bad feeling—it made him want to turn around and walk away.

When Dylan saw the boy, he called out, "Hey, yo! What's up?"

The boy in the rabbit mask didn't answer. He only continued to stare. "We're looking for Del," Dash added. "Any clue where we can find him?"

The boy in the mask took off, disappearing up the worn marble stairs.

"Hey!" Dylan shouted, hurrying after him. "Wait!"

Dash followed closely, not wanting to be left alone. But when they'd made it halfway to the first landing, Dylan jerked to a stop as if someone had yanked on his spine. Dash reached up to catch his brother before he toppled, but Dylan crashed into him, knocking him off-balance.

Limbs tangled together, they tumbled down the steps all the way to the bottom.

Something like a memory flashed through Dylan's mind. He flinched, cringing at the white-hot blast that burned inside his skull. His entire body prickled with electricity.

The world around him disappeared. He was back in the dressing room on the set of *Dad's So Clueless*. Dash was racing toward him from out of a mass of shadows, his arms outstretched, his face contorted, screaming in anger or pain. A booming sound rattled his eardrums, followed quickly by something that sounded a bit more human—a mewling, crying whisper.

The back of Dylan's skull felt like it had exploded. Little glittering lights swam around what was left of his blurred vision. Then, as the brunt of the sensation began to fade, Dylan understood that the whine was coming from his own throat.

"Dylan? Dylan, are you all right?"

Dylan realized he was lying down, the wooden floor of the foyer cold beneath him. Dash's face hovered over him, eyes wide, looking paralyzed with worry. For some reason, this annoyed Dylan. "Why are you looking at me like that?"

Glancing over his brother's shoulder, he noticed the staircase rising steeply. "I must have tripped."

"You *didn't* trip, Dylan. Something happened to you. It was like a seizure. You knocked us both down the stairs."

"Don't be ridiculous. I don't have seizures."

Dash leaned away, sitting back on his heels. "Fine. Whatever. You're perfectly healthy." He sighed, frustrated. "But you hit your head pretty hard on the way down. It echoed."

Dylan sat up, rubbing the back of his skull. His heart was beating too fast, and he worried that whatever had just happened might happen again. But he couldn't let his brother know. For the past few weeks, Dash had been super worried about him. "Well, I'm okay now." This had happened at least twice before, each time accompanied by a horrifying vision of Dash running toward him, reaching out to either claw or catch him. "Jeez, Dash, sometimes you're worse than Mom and Dad."

"Do you think you can stand up? Maybe we should walk back to town and call for help."

"No way."

Dash rolled his eyes "But, Dylan, you're not—"

"If we find that kid, the one in the mask, maybe he'll help us."

Dash shivered. "I didn't get that sense from him, Dylan. He was full-on creepy."

Footsteps echoed through the cavernous chamber. Dylan turned to see who it was.

Emerging from the shadows was a girl with long black hair that draped far below her shoulder blades. She was dressed in a fitted denim jacket and a long black dress. Another girl with messy dirty-blond hair walked beside the first, wearing a faded purple T-shirt and jeans, clutching a bright-pink messenger bag. Behind them was a boy, who appeared to be carrying a tall backpack of some sort. He wore a black sports jacket and khaki pants. His dark red hair lifted from his scalp in wide curls.

Is this the rest of the film's cast?

Dylan struggled to his feet. He stepped forward, holding out his hand. If he was going to succeed on this set, he knew he had to make the best impression before his brother could beat him to it.

"Hey," he said, laying on the California cool-kid charm that his agents had drilled into him long ago. "How's it going? Dylan Wright." He glanced over at Dash, who looked at him in surprise. "And this is my brother—"

"Dylan, sit down!" Dash commanded harshly. "You might have a concussion!"

A flash of anger jolted down Dylan's spine and rippled in the pit of his stomach. Keeping his face even, he chuckled nervously as the group stared at the twins. "I'm sorry," he said. "My brother can be a little dramatic. Have any of you seen Del?"

CHAPTER 9

POPPY COULDN'T BELIEVE her eyes. Standing before her was one of her favorite television characters: Scooter Underwood from *Dad's So Clueless*. And seated beside him was another version. Two Scoots Ba-Dooters were staring at her as if she might present them with a key to the house.

This must be in my head, she thought. Blood pounded in her ears, and she heard the girls from Thursday's Hope chanting again. *Crazy. Poppy. Crazy. Poppy.*

But now Marcus was making introductions. "Hi, I'm Marcus. This is Poppy and Azumi." Azumi waved as Poppy remained frozen, unsure of herself. "Are you students here too?"

The seated boy finally stood and brushed himself off. "I'm Dash. Dylan's brother. And, um, no, we're not *students here*."

Marcus frowned and shook his head slightly.

"You guys are actors," said Azumi. "I've seen you on television."

Actors, thought Poppy. Not the real Scoots, but the boys who played him. Twins.

"Yeah," said Dylan. "Aren't you guys actors too?"

"No," said Marcus cautiously. "I'm here on a music scholarship. Azumi's here for academics. And Poppy . . . Well, Poppy's story is kind of complicated."

Poppy couldn't keep herself from blushing. *Complicated* was an understatement. She hunched her shoulders, though she knew she was only making herself look more foolish, like an ostrich hiding its head in the sand.

"Dylan," said Dash, placing his hand on his brother's shoulder, "I really wish you'd sit down." He turned to the trio. "He just fell down the stairs."

"Do you always let your brother talk to you like he's your dad?" Azumi asked Dylan, hands on her hips.

Dash flinched. "I was only trying to—"

"We *both* fell down the stairs," Dylan growled before looking at the group again with a forced smile. "But we're both perfect now. Promise. So . . . if you're not in the cast, you must be on the crew."

"The crew?" asked Azumi.

"Why are you here?" A hint of frustration slipped into Dylan's otherwise smooth voice.

"Marcus already told you," said Azumi. "This is our school."

"Why are *you* here?" Marcus retorted.

Dash spoke up. "Del Larkspur is filming a new horror movie. We're playing the leads."

"Del Larkspur?" Poppy squeaked. "Did you say *Del Larkspur*?"

Dylan sighed. "Finally, we're getting somewhere. You know Del?"

Poppy's voice was so soft Dylan had to strain to hear it. "Well . . . no. My great-aunt invited me to live with her. But her name is *Delphinia* Larkspur."

"Could they be the same person?" asked Dash. "We thought Del was a guy, but maybe Del is actually Delphinia."

Poppy's spine tingled and her fingers felt numb. None of this seemed right. "In her letter, my great-aunt didn't say anything about making a movie." She thought back to watching *Dad's So Clueless* in the common room at Thursday's Hope with the other girls, remembering the warm feeling it gave her to see a funny family portrayed on the small screen. To see parents get mad at their nutty kids but then forgive them at the end of every episode because they just loved them so much.

"Hold up," said Dylan, shaking his head, squinting. "What letter?"

Azumi exhaled sharply as she shuffled through her shoulder bag and removed the printout she'd already showed Poppy and Marcus. Marcus followed suit, taking out the email his mother had received from the music school. They handed the pages to the twins. Poppy scrambled to show them her own handwritten letter. The boys scanned everything quickly, and then Dylan pulled his phone from his pocket, opening the message from Larkspur Productions, LLC. After a few seconds, the group looked up at one another, and then glanced around the chamber as if someone were watching them.

"This is weird," said Dash. "Look at the names: *L. Delphinium* wrote to Marcus's mom. *Del Larkspur* and *Delphinia Larkspur* wrote to us and to . . ." He glanced at Poppy, self-conscious. "I'm sorry, what's your name again?"

"Poppy," she said, her voice cracking. She crossed her arms, feeling suddenly cold.

"Right." Dash handed back the invitations, emails, and brochures. "The details don't really add up. I mean, it feels like someone is messing with us."

"Not necessarily," said Marcus, looking around the room. "This house seems big enough for all of it. A school, a filming location, a home."

Azumi spoke up. "Still, it's strange. Earlier, Marcus found Poppy lying in the road in front of the main gate."

"What were you doing in the road?" asked Dylan.

Poppy's eyes went wide. "I'm not really sure. I guess I fainted or something." The twins were looking at her like she was a total freak. Her group-home defenses immediately kicked in. "Speaking of strange, Azumi saw some sort of creature out in the meadow by the woods. She thought it was chasing me and Marcus. But when we all reached the house, the meadow was empty."

"I never said it was a *creature*." Azumi's face lit up, red. "I said it was an animal. A big animal. And I have a picture." She dug in her pocket for her phone and swiped it open. But after a few seconds, she furrowed her eyebrows. "It was right here. A black smudge. It had golden, glowing eyes. It looked like . . . I don't know what." She handed her phone around. When Poppy got it, the image on the screen was of the sunny meadow, clear of any blotches or unusual shadows.

"*We* saw a boy at the top of the stairs," said Dash. "He was wearing a rabbit mask."

"Weird," said Marcus. "It would be really nice if we could find an *adult*."

"Like my great-aunt," said Poppy.

"Like a teacher," said Azumi.

66

"Like someone on the crew," said Dylan.

Dash stepped away from the group and peered up the staircase. "Hello?" he called out, the echo of his voice fluttering around the upper rafters like bats trapped inside the house. "Is anybody here?" The group waited in silence, but no one answered.

CHAPTER 10

AZUMI AND MARCUS placed their luggage in the center of the grand room, beside the twins' stuff. Poppy held on to her bag.

"The boy in the mask ran up the stairs," said Dylan. "Maybe we should go check up there."

Not listening, Azumi disappeared with Marcus through one of the doorways off the foyer. A moment later, she called out, "Whoa. You guys have to see this!"

Poppy paused in the doorway, looking back at the twins. "Coming?" she asked, her voice quavering and small. The boys reluctantly followed.

Marcus stood just inside the entry of a long room.

The space looked like it had been set up for an extravagant

party. Red and white paper streamers hung from high places, drooping down from the corners of bookshelves that were stocked with old board games and puzzles, running up toward the tall windows that lined one long wall, and continuing in daisy chains all the way to the entry. Loose balloons meandered across a thick Persian rug, pushed by what must have been a draft that Marcus couldn't feel. They looked like scurrying animals sniffing around for scraps of birthday cake. The couches and chairs arranged to face the center of the chamber were worn, as if they had been sitting there for a century, getting good use from the children who must have played here.

It's a music school, Marcus thought, eyeing the four other kids. *It has to be.* He drummed his fingers on his stomach and closed his eyes for a moment, itching to get his hands on an instrument. How strange would he look if he grabbed his cello and got down to it right here? The familiar tune continued to play in Marcus's head, the melody still as sweet as blueberry pie. But it was getting louder and louder, and Marcus had to bite at his lip to keep from shouting out to the Musician that he'd heard enough.

Someone squeezed his waist and shouted, "Boo!"

Marcus nearly screamed as Dylan jumped out from behind him.

Dylan burst out laughing, as Dash came up and punched his

arm. "Starting early?" Dash asked, his eyes slivered. He tossed an apologetic look at Marcus, but Marcus couldn't bring himself to smile. Everyone else was staring at him like he was some sort of nutjob. It made him think about how his brothers and sister had looked at him when they learned that the doctors had suggested medication to correct his "hallucinations."

"Dude, I'm sorry," said Dylan, wiping away the last of his laughter. "You looked so intense. Like you were arguing with yourself. I just had to do something about it. You okay?"

"I-I'm fine." Marcus nodded. "Thanks for your *concern* though."

The others strolled before the shelves, examining the trove of games. "Do you guys think the decorations are for us?" he asked. *It's a nice gesture*, Marcus thought. Though it would have been nicer if someone had been here to greet them . . . *and* if someone had answered him.

A strange-looking sphere made out of gray wire sat on a table in front of the windows. On one side of the contraption, there was a handle, bent like an S, as if it were meant to be turned like a crank. Inside the sphere were dozens of little red balls. Curious, Marcus made his way to the table. His grandmother had once taken him to bingo night in the basement of St. Luke's back in Ohio. The person calling the game had used a globe like this to call the numbers. Marcus touched the handle and then gave the sphere a spin. The balls inside rattled and one slid out into a small chute, hitting the table with a satisfying plink.

Marcus picked up the ball and turned it over. There was no number on it, only the letter *L* marked in white. *Weird*, he thought. *Bingo doesn't work like that.* He gave the sphere another turn. Out popped the letter *E*, then *T*. Marcus stopped cranking the handle, but little balls continued to roll out, each one stopping with the letter facing toward him. *L, E,* and *T* were followed by *S, P, L.*

LETSPL

Two more balls rolled free.

LETSPLAY

LETS PLAY.

Something cold shivered inside Marcus. "Um, guys?" he called, suddenly wishing he were fifteen feet closer to the rest of the group.

Azumi was standing on her toes, reaching for a large paper parcel that was high up on one of the shelves. "What's that?" Poppy asked. As Azumi grabbed for the sack, it tumbled off the shelf, and its contents spilled onto the floor. The girls yelped and leapt back.

Marcus only had a brief glimpse of what was in the bag. It looked like small human bodies.

CHAPTER 11

AZUMI DIDN'T KNOW why she had been so drawn to the large paper bag on the shelf above her, but now that the parcel was lying torn at her feet, she felt sick.

There were five dolls splayed on the floor in front of her. They were made out of stiff papier-mâché, nothing a child would play with. Their features, including the clothes, had been painted on with vibrant, glossy acrylics.

The two dolls on the far left were painted light brown and were dressed in shorts, graphic T-shirts, and sandals. Beside them lay a girl with pale skin and splotchy freckles. Dark gold paper hair lay across her shoulders, where a pink satchel had been painted directly onto her body. Next was a boy with red hair. The details of his curls were shaded expertly, giving the illusion that you could pull on a strand and it would spring back to the paper skull with a *boing!* He wore a black sports jacket, khaki pants, and a convincingly dirty pair of white Converse All Stars. Finally, on the far right, was a girl with long dark hair. Her denim jacket was painted to appear buttoned tight, and her black dress stopped just above thin ankles.

"It's us," said Marcus quietly.

"They're even wearing our clothes," said Poppy, reaching out toward the one that looked like her, stopping just before she touched it.

"How?" asked Dash.

"Someone painted them on," said Marcus.

"I can see that," said Dash. "But handmade stuff like this takes time. The prop people on our set out in Hollywood would've needed at least a day to prep for something like this. This paint is dry."

"How did whoever made these know what we'd be wearing today?" asked Poppy.

"Look . . ." Azumi reached forward and touched a piece of twine that was looped around the neck of her papier-mâché counterpart. The other figurines were the same. They were all wearing nooses. Azumi grasped the string attached to the one that looked like her and lifted the thing from the floor. The Azumi doll turned around and around, peering at all of them, as still as a corpse and with eyes just as lifeless. Azumi was tempted to toss it violently away, but she was overcome with a feeling that something very bad might happen if she did.

"It's a piñata," said Marcus. "Like, for a party. Someone forgot to hang them up." He searched the ceiling for hooks. "And aren't piñatas filled with things? Candy and toys and stuff like that?"

Dash picked up the one that looked like him and shook it. Azumi heard something shift inside, like sand sliding through an hourglass.

"I've never played with a piñata before," said Azumi.

"You don't play with them," said Poppy. "You break them."

"I don't want to break anything," said Dash, turning to Dylan. "I just want to get out of here."

To everyone's surprise, Poppy grabbed the doll that resembled her and twisted its arm. Its elbow snapped, and its wrist and hand dangled loosely. Marcus gasped, as if she'd done the same to him.

"What are you doing?" asked Dylan.

"I wanted to see what was in it." Poppy glanced apologetically at the rest of the group. She turned the figure and joggled it. *Swiff. Swiff. Swiff.* The group watched as a gritty gray material poured from the hole in the figurine's arm and wafted slightly around them like smoke. Most of it formed a small mound on the rug by Poppy's sneakers.

Waving the cloud away and covering her mouth and nose with her T-shirt, Poppy placed the figurine on the sofa and then leaned down and pinched a bit of the pile between her thumb and forefinger. It turned her fingertips a dark gray. "Ashes," she said.

"We all fall down," Marcus whispered with an awkward smile. No one laughed.

"What a sick joke," said Azumi.

Just then, Dylan's pocket buzzed and a muffled chime sounded. Everyone stepped away from him, as if a bomb were about to detonate.

CHAPTER 12

PULLING OUT HIS phone, Dylan was surprised to see words glowing on the screen. *You have a new voice mail!* He showed the group.

"Weird," Dash said. "The phone didn't even ring."

"But see!" said Dylan. "They're looking for us. There's just been a mix-up or something." He put the phone on speaker, pressed play, and held up the device so everyone could hear.

At first he heard only static. Then a muffled voice spoke, low and gravelly like a whisper from a person who was very ill. ". . . pleased to see you . . ." Dylan thought he could make out some background noise. ". . . games begin . . . ," the voice went on. "The library."

The message ended with a series of clicking noises and what sounded like growling, followed by silence. Dylan hit the button to call back and let Del know that they were on their way, but there was still no cell service.

"That didn't sound like your great-aunt," Azumi whispered to Poppy.

Poppy blushed. "Maybe she has a deep voice?" The others were quiet for a moment.

Dylan shrugged. "Did you check *your* phone? Maybe you got a message too."

"I don't have a phone," said Poppy. Her face went scarlet. "I mean, I lost it on the way here."

"Uh-huh," said Dylan. Dash glared at him.

A hush filled the room. The dolls stared up at everyone from the floor.

"Well, let's find this library," said Dylan. "Sounds like that's where Del will be."

"Anyone have a map of this place?" Marcus chuckled.

"Yeah," said Dylan. "I picked one up at the visitor's desk on the way in." Dash nudged his brother's shoulder, warning him to bring it down a notch. Dash was always doing that, checking him. Dylan felt a flare of resentment, and he jerked himself away from his brother. "If we split up I bet we'll find it pretty quickly."

"Quick?" said Azumi. "What'll be quick about it? This place is a palace."

Dylan smiled at her, but his resentment grew. "Yeah, I can see that. We'll meet back here in like twenty minutes."

Dash spoke up. "I don't know, Dylan. How's your head feeling?"

"How many times do I have to say *I'm fine* before you get it?" Dylan snapped.

"I just thought maybe you and me could head outside and try to get some reception—"

"Stop! Seriously, chill out. Del said he'll meet us in the library."

Dash flinched. "I'm sorry. It's just—"

Azumi stepped between them. "*I* didn't hear anyone say anything about meeting anyone anywhere."

Dylan frowned. "Me and Poppy will try upstairs where we saw that kid earlier. He was probably heading to the set."

"Uh . . . okay?" said Poppy.

"And who knows, maybe phone service is better the higher up we go. I might even be able to call Del back."

"Azumi and I can search together," said Marcus. "We're both looking for the school people anyway. We'll check out the rest of the ground floor." Azumi nodded in agreement, as if happy to be away from Dylan.

"What about me?" asked Dash.

Dylan smirked. "You stay by the stairs in the foyer, in case someone comes by. That way, you don't have to worry about wandering around a big creepy house."

"But—"

Dylan held up a hand. "Someone should stay with our stuff anyway. It might as well be you."

Dash clenched his jaw. "Fine," he growled. "But if you feel weird, or dizzy, or *anything*, come right back to me. Okay?"

"Whatever you say, little brother." Dylan was already heading out of the room.

CHAPTER 13

"HELLO?" POPPY CALLED out, her small voice sounding surprisingly loud in the second floor's snaking hallway. "Anyone there?" Together, she and Dylan tried the knob on every door they passed. Some were locked, but the ones that were open didn't seem to be remarkable, except they looked old—sitting rooms, reading rooms, parlors, closets—and otherwise empty.

"I really like your show," she said as they turned another corner, the daylight fading behind them. "Scoots is kind of my favorite."

"Gosh, I hate that name." Dylan sniffed, keeping his eyes forward. "I'm actually glad to be done with it."

Poppy blushed, afraid that she'd offended him. "Oh, no! It didn't get canceled, did it?"

"Me and Dash quit. Filmed our last episode just a few days ago. It wasn't working out anymore."

"I think I remember reading about you guys on some blog recently." She tried to remember the article. "Maybe it was about this movie?"

One room was filled with filing cabinets and a couple of desks. It reminded Poppy of Ms. Tate's office at Thursday's Hope. She noticed a charcoal sketch hanging on the wall. Something about it was familiar, but she was so overwhelmed to be standing next to *the* Scooter Underwood, she couldn't remember what.

"Nothing in there," said Dylan. He paused. "Leaving the show wasn't that big of a deal, actually. It was time for a change. That's why me and Dash are here. On to bigger and better things."

"Right." Poppy listened as their footsteps creaked on the wooden floor, sending tiny shrieks out into the passages. "But I mean, you're going to miss it, right? Being in a family like that—"

"That wasn't our family," Dylan interrupted, turning toward her. "They were just a bunch of actors, working for a paycheck. And most of them were jerks anyway. They barely ever blinked at me and Dash."

"Then you did a really good job of making it seem like you all were close," she said, choosing her words carefully. "I . . . I've never had a family. So watching your show sort of made me feel like I was part of it. When you guys laughed, I laughed with you."

Dylan stared at her for a moment. "Wow. That's . . . That's really just . . . *Wow.*"

Poppy felt her cheeks burn. "All I mean is, it was just, like, fun. You know? Funny."

"Yeah, real funny. So what kind of a person doesn't have a family?" he asked as he continued down the shadowed hall.

"What *kind* of a person?" Poppy echoed, her stomach squirming. She asked herself that all the time. What was it about her that made her unwanted? "Lots of people don't have families. Not traditional families anyway. Not like the ones you see on television. I lived in a group home with a bunch of other girls. Some of them were orphans. Others had parents who weren't able to care for them. My mom . . . Well, she kind of took off when I was little. That's how I ended up at Thursday's Hope."

"Jeez, that's harsh," said Dylan. He wasn't even looking at her. "So it must have been really exciting when you heard from your great-aunt."

"Yeah. Of course. Like a dream come true. And now we're going to find her."

Poppy paused, and decided to return to safer topics. "It must be so cool to work with your twin," she offered.

Dylan scoffed. "Dash can be a real pain sometimes."

There was something about his dimples that was really starting to annoy Poppy. "Do you have any clue how lucky you are to have a brother?"

"Yeah, but Dash is just . . ." Dylan stopped and looked at her. "You have no idea how weird he is."

"He really seems to care about you."

"People really care about *him*, that's for sure." Dylan started off down the hall again.

"What do you mean?"

"I mean . . . people are always saying, 'Oh, Dylan, why can't you be more responsible? Why can't you be more like Dash?' But they don't know him! They don't know how far he's willing to take things, how nasty he can really be. *I'm* not the bad twin." Dylan's voice had risen, and he dragged in a shuddering breath, as if surprised at his own outburst. He pressed his fingers against his temples. "I just think people will be really surprised when it comes to the two of us," he finished quietly.

Poppy stopped walking.

"What?" asked Dylan.

"That's an awful thing to say about your brother."

Dylan folded his arms. "I'm sorry. I should have realized you were another Dash fangirl."

Poppy shook her head. "You're not who I thought you were. You seem so *nice* on TV, so I guess you're a way better actor than anyone thought. I feel bad for your brother." She felt herself trembling. "I feel bad for *you*."

She had a small flash of satisfaction as Dylan's jaw dropped.

"I'm going to go back," Poppy said. "I want to check out that office again."

"I'll come with you."

"No, I can do it myself. *You* can leave me alone."

Dylan shrugged and stomped away.

Poppy almost called him back, but she clamped her mouth shut. She was used to doing things on her own, anyway. Still, the hall felt very empty without Dylan there. Something strange was happening here at Larkspur. Something she couldn't put into words.

She turned around and made her way to the office once again.

Poppy approached the small frame hanging on the wall by the door. Upon closer inspection, she could see that the image inside the frame was a sketch of five children. Three boys and two girls. Each face was grim, eyes hollow and empty-looking.

The children were wearing stiff dark flannel and starchy white cotton uniforms, the boys in shorts and the girls in skirts. It looked as though they had all attended the same private school fifty or sixty years prior.

Maybe Marcus and Azumi are right! Poppy thought. The style of the drawing was also familiar to her, and she suddenly remembered why. The Girl in the mirrors had given her a similar drawing—the one that Ashley had threatened to crush. Only in that other drawing, the children had been wearing masks.

The longer Poppy stared at the picture on the wall, the more suffocated she felt by her own skin. Here was proof that her oldest friend, the phantom Girl who'd attacked her earlier that morning, the Girl in the mirrors, was connected to Larkspur House.

"Delphinia, where are you?" Poppy whispered.

CHAPTER 14

DYLAN FUMED AS he continued his search for the library and Del. He couldn't believe the nerve of that girl, Poppy. The way she'd spoken to him about his brother, as if watching them on television meant she knew the *real* them. *I'm glad she wanted us to split up*, he told himself. *She doesn't know anything. She doesn't know that I'm*—The thought stopped cold, as if a door had slammed on it.

The hallway twisted deeper into the house, farther away from the daylight. When Dylan came around a sharp bend, the darkness almost seemed to reach for him. Scrambling for his phone, he held it up and switched on the flashlight. The pale beam shone only a few feet ahead, as if the shadows were denser here. As if they were alive. He scanned the walls for a light switch, but there was nothing except for iridescent-blue-patterned wallpaper, edging off into blackness.

As Dylan checked his phone for service again, he heard something moving in the distance. It sounded like the clink of metal against metal. "Del?" he called. "That you?"

A dim figure appeared from the well of shadows, walking slowly toward him. Dylan squinted. Was its face strangely shaped, or was it a trick created by the dark?

The light of his phone caught the figure, and Dylan saw it was another kid wearing a mask. A boy with the face of a bear. Black eyeholes watched him, as if there were nothing behind the mask but an unending void.

Dylan's skin prickled in the sudden chill that surrounded him. The boy wore metal cuffs around his ankles, joined by a short length of rusted chain.

A sharp pain blasted the back of Dylan's skull, and his eyes watered. His vision blurred, his body tingled as it had during the flash on the staircase, and once again, the world around him seemed to fade into something from a distant memory.

He was shoved back to the dressing room again, on the set of the show. And it was dark, darker than the shadows of Larkspur. His head felt like it had been sliced open with a blunt blade, and when he touched his scalp, a warm and sticky liquid pulsed over his fingers. He tried to yell out, but his lips wouldn't work. He realized then that he was soaking wet, and it wasn't only the blood. He stepped forward, searching for a lamp that was just out of reach. And then Dash rushed at him, coming from the dark side of the room, his face a mask of fear more terrifying than any bear or rabbit could ever be.

And then Dylan's vision cleared. The pain was gone and he was back in the hallway at Larkspur House. He slumped and then used the closest wall to catch himself. The boy in the bear mask watched.

"H-help me." The words had spilled from Dylan's mouth before he could stop them. The bear boy stepped back, cringing away from him.

Dylan shook his head, trying to clear the strange weakness away. If this kid was part of the horror film's cast, Dylan couldn't have him spreading rumors to everyone else before they even met him. Dylan stumbled toward the boy to catch him. "Hold on a second." He took a breath. "I'm fine. I'm looking for Del."

But the boy turned and ran. So Dylan lurched after him. The hallway went on and on, impossibly long. Dylan's phone light caught the slightest glimpse of the boy's chains as they rattled and shook. "Wait up!" Dylan called. "I need to talk to you!"

Ahead, the figure darted to the right. Dylan raced to the spot where the hallway turned. He could make out a thin staircase rising up into the darkness. At the top of the stairs a door swung shut, the click of the handle echoing toward him like a period at the end of a very long sentence.

Dylan took the steps two by two. When he reached a landing, he grasped the doorknob and pulled. The door gave a couple of inches, but then something pulled back from the other side. "Hey," Dylan said, yanking on the door with all of his weight, "I didn't mean to scare you. I just want to—"

The door released, and Dylan fell backward with such force, he slid on his back a few inches along the runner, stopping just on the edge of the steps. His phone had fallen facedown somewhere nearby, and the landing was nearly pitch black.

Something stepped from the doorway.

Clink. Clink. Clink.

The metal cuffs rattled softly. Hushed breath sounded right above Dylan's face.

Huhh. Huhh. Huhh.

Dylan was suddenly too frightened to move. The boy came closer, the wooden floor creaking underneath Dylan's spine.

Dylan closed his eyes, hoping to make himself invisible. There was no way this boy was part of the film production. So why was he here at Larkspur? And why was he wearing a mask?

The breathing came closer still, inches now from Dylan's nose.

Reflexively, Dylan swung his arms up to push the boy away. But his hands didn't meet a body. Instead, they passed through air—very cold air. Dylan sat up, flattening himself against the wall as the sound of chains scrambled away, and the nearby door slammed shut again with a wild *wham!*

Dylan frantically patted along the floor until he found his phone and then shone the light toward the end of the landing.

The door was gone.

Dylan blinked. *The door was gone.*

Where the frame and the dark wood and the metal knob had been, there was only a wall covered in that Gothic blue-patterned wallpaper.

This must be a trick, he thought. The whole thing had to have been a trick. Dylan had played enough of them on other people to know when he was being messed with.

Dizzy, Dylan struggled to stand. For a moment, his scalp stung, and he worried that the horrible vision in his dressing room was about to return again. But he focused on the wall and the feeling went away.

His hands shook as he approached the spot where the door had been. His phone light fluttered. If this was a trick, he wondered, then why was his heart kicking out of his chest?

Dylan made himself touch the wall where the door had been. Then he knocked. It was solid. Glancing around, he searched for a seam or a crack, anything to indicate some sort of purposeful illusion, like something out of a magician's stage show. But there was nothing.

He turned and leaned against the wall, shining his light back down the small staircase. Maybe the boy had slipped away. Maybe he was waiting for him down there, just around the corner. Maybe—

The wall seemed to give under his weight, to soften like a pillow, calling him to sleep, luring his body down for a night of dreaming. Dylan leapt away and stared at the wall. To his horror, he could see his own silhouette pressed into the wallpaper, as if it were a wax mold instead of a wall. The shape almost looked like a shadow of himself—or maybe the boy in the mask— yearning for Dylan to return, as if it were hungry for another, longer embrace.

Dylan turned and raced down the steps, refusing to look back even as the sound of a clicking latch and the squeal of hinges reverberated past him into the dark hallway and the unseen spaces beyond.

CHAPTER 15

"WHAT WOULD A private school need with all this old stuff?" asked Azumi as they strolled past yet another elegant sitting room. "And where are the classrooms?" She and Marcus had seen countless fireplaces, each made out of a different material—stone, marble, brick. Their mantelpieces held hurricane lamps with bulbous glass sconces, frames filled with antique photographs, and little porcelain animals. Paintings hung on the walls—portrait after portrait of important-looking figures in elegant costumes, as well as several ethereal landscapes of the Hudson River valley. But they hadn't seen anything that looked like a school.

"Maybe it's all to impress visitors," Marcus suggested. "Like for when parents come to see what they're spending their money on." He was keeping quiet about his scholarship. He had never seen a house that looked this luxurious before, not even at the Oberlin campus where he'd performed, and he couldn't believe he was going to get to stay here. He held his hands tightly to keep from drumming the Musician's rhythm. Thankfully, Azumi didn't seem to notice.

"This is more like it," said Azumi, stepping through a doorway into an immense kitchen with numerous cupboards and cabinets. An island in its center looked like an enormous carving block that had been stained dark over the years. "Looks big enough to feed several classrooms of kids."

Marcus opened one of the cabinets. "Yes!" He pulled out a few metal trays. "Check it out." He showed Azumi the Larkspur insignia engraved in the center of each—the same little bird that had been carved into the pillars by the gate. "We're not crazy. This is definitely a school."

"But where is everybody?" asked Azumi, tugging at a drawer crammed with beat-up silverware.

Marcus opened a door beside an industrial-size refrigerator. "Hey! There's good stuff in here. Hungry?"

Azumi cracked a smile. "A little bit, actually."

"We're in luck, then." Marcus stepped aside. Through the doorway, a huge pantry was stocked with boxes of cookies and crackers, cans of tuna and tins of sardines, jars of pickles and preserves. Marcus tore open a bag of potato chips. "Tastes pretty fresh."

Azumi slid her finger under the flap of a box of chocolate wafers. Nibbling one of the cookies, she closed her eyes and sighed. "These are amazing. The only thing that might make them better is a cup of my baaba's sencha tea."

"Your *baaba*?"

"My grandmother. She lived with us for years before she died."

Marcus spoke quickly to cover the awkward pause. "We should bring some of this for when we meet up with the others again."

Azumi nodded. Together, they helped themselves, leaning against the shelves, filling their empty stomachs. After such a weird morning, it felt nice to do something as normal as a snack break.

"Where are you from again?" Marcus asked.

"Outside of Seattle," said Azumi after swallowing a graham cracker.

"So, why are you here?" Marcus asked.

Azumi squinted at him. "I already told you. For school."

"I mean, it's so far away from home."

"We're not that close to Ohio either." Azumi opened another door off the pantry, revealing several rows of long dining tables.

High windows near the ceiling allowed daylight to spill inside. "Look. This must be the dining hall."

Marcus was still looking at her. "I came here for music though. I just thought maybe you'd want to be closer to your family. There have got to be good schools on the West Coast. No?"

Azumi passed quickly through the room to an open door on the other side. "My family's a little strange right now."

"Strange how?" Marcus watched Azumi's face turn red and he felt bad for asking. He hurried after her.

Now they were in a laundry. There was a washer and dryer against the far wall, big enough to climb inside. Uniforms hung from silver racks all around the edges of the room—more evidence that they were on the right track. The insignia they'd found marked on the kitchen trays was also embroidered on a bunch of gray sweater-vests. "I'm sorry," he said. "That was really personal."

"It's okay," Azumi said, but she didn't look at him. "We lost my big sister last year."

"Oh my gosh. That's horrible." Marcus didn't know what to say. He reached out as if to hug her, then awkwardly dropped his hands. "What happened?" he asked.

"I really don't like to talk about it." Azumi shook her hair off her shoulders. "But . . . *whatever*. If we're going to be together at

Larkspur, you're going to find out eventually. My sister was being an idiot. She went off into the woods behind my aunt's house in Japan. And she disappeared. I had to come back to the States all by myself." She spoke flatly, as if she were talking about what she had for dinner last night.

"That's horrible!" Marcus said. Azumi was looking at him steadily, but he could feel the tension inside her. He felt that if he touched her, she might actually pop like a balloon. Better to change the subject? "My mom doesn't like it when I practice cello or piano," he said. The familiar tune drifted through his mind again. "She doesn't say so, but I know it bugs her. So I get mad at her sometimes. And my brothers and sister are always around, making noise, interrupting me. They hate when I put on Phillip Glass or my jazz albums. They only like 'songs with words.' Sometimes, I wish they'd *just disappear* too."

Azumi's mouth dropped open. For a moment, Marcus regretted his words. But then she released a loud laugh that reverberated around the laundry room. After a moment, she pulled herself together. "That's probably the worst thing anyone has ever said to me," she told him.

"I didn't mean . . . It came out all wrong."

"You don't really know how to talk to people, do you?"

Marcus crossed his arms, tapping his fingers on his biceps. He struggled to steady his nervous breath. "I never thought about it before. But yeah. I guess *music* is how I talk. It's how I think. Kids at my old school called me a nerd a lot."

"That's not necessarily something to be ashamed of," said Azumi. Marcus sighed in relief. "C'mon. Let's keep looking around before it gets too late. Someone's got to be around here somewhere."

Across the hallway, they discovered the biggest jaw-dropper of all—a ballroom so immense, the white ceiling overhead almost looked like the sky. A line of glass doors stretched across the far wall, covered by gauzy curtains that allowed light to filter in. "I'm pretty sure my entire house would fit in here," said Marcus.

"Mine too," said Azumi. "This is really beyond huge."

"But look!" Marcus pointed toward a far corner. A large black piano stood, its cover open wide, as if it had been waiting for him. His heart gave a great leap and he ran to it, settling himself on the bench and lifting the fallboard. He dragged his fingers silently across the keys and closed his eyes. He pressed down and a chord sang out, ringing through the chamber like church bells. Finally, he was able to release the tune that had haunted him all morning.

Azumi couldn't believe what she was hearing. Standing in the doorway of this new room, she watched Marcus move his fingers across the piano's gleaming keyboard. A beautifully complicated melody filled the space and spilled out into the hallway behind her.

Marcus had been transported to another realm. It looked like the jitters she'd seen on him had evaporated away. Gone were his shaky hands and drumming fingers. Gone were the grimaces that made him look like he was trying to block out imaginary voices in his head. He was amazing. And if he was a nerd, Azumi knew he was the best kind of nerd. The music washed over her skin like warm water, rinsing away all the bad feelings that had accumulated since her arrival at Larkspur that morning. She could have stood there and listened to him forever.

And she might have done just that if she hadn't suddenly heard a voice calling her name from somewhere down the hallway just outside the door.

"*Azuuuumi.*"

It was long and drawn out, as if coming from very far away. Azumi's body tensed. She moved away from the ballroom and stared into the murky distance of the corridor. Then she looked back at Marcus. He was so wrapped up in his melodies that he didn't even lift his head.

"Poppy?" Azumi called back. "Is that you?" But she knew that it wasn't. It was the voice she heard in her dreams, the one that had drawn her outside to the forest behind her house. It was Moriko's voice.

Azumi shut her eyes tight, hoping that when she opened them she'd be lying in her bed back home, this entire trip a dream. She wouldn't even mind if she were to open her eyes and discover herself to have been sleepwalking again, standing in the woods in the night. But when Azumi's eyes finally fluttered open, she was only deeper down the corridor, farther from Marcus's comforting melody.

Tied to a doorknob was a fluorescent-pink nylon ribbon. Just like the one Moriko had followed into the woods. Just like the one Azumi had turned away from on the last day she'd seen her sister, fearing what they'd find at the end of it. It was stretched taut and disappeared into the shadows, as if someone hidden in the distance was pulling on it.

The voice came again. *"Azumi."*

"Moriko?" Azumi called back. She couldn't help herself. She knew it was impossible that Moriko would be here, but with her heart in her throat, she stepped forward, reached out, and then clasped the pink nylon ribbon. With a determined shake of her head, she tried to brush away the fear, and allowed the ribbon to lead her farther down the hallway and into the shadows.

CHAPTER 16

UPSTAIRS, POPPY WAS in the office space.

Several landscapes hung beside the sketch of the five uni-formed children. One tall frame that stood between the door and a red-curtained window had been draped in a thin black sheet, hiding whatever image was underneath. As curious as Poppy was about the house and her family's connection to it, something deep in her brain told her to steer clear of that one.

Desks and filing cabinets filled the room. Papers and folders were stacked on various surfaces, begging to be examined. Poppy imagined herself as a detective in one of her favorite books—Harriet the Spy or Turtle from *The Westing Game*—being clever and picking up details that even adults might miss. Maybe some of Great-Aunt Delphinia's papers were here. Poppy knew she'd have to be careful not to mix anything up in case her great-aunt walked in on her.

The top page of the first pile was an itemized invoice from a grocery store in Greencliffe to be paid by *The Larkspur Home for Children*.

Larkspur had once been a group home, just like Thursday's Hope? Was it still? Great-Aunt Delphinia hadn't mentioned anything about that. Poppy swallowed. This was not a good sign.

From nearby, there came the sound of someone sighing.

"Delphinia?" Poppy asked, holding her voice steady. No one responded.

The invoice was dated from the late 1940s. Poppy flipped through a few more pages. Apparently, Larkspur hadn't just been a home, but an orphanage. She fought against tears. Was she just going to be another foster kid to Great-Aunt Delphinia? She glanced over her shoulder at the sketch by the door. Were the kids in the drawing like her—stuck in the system, waiting for a reprieve?

Then, Poppy noticed a name at the bottom of the page in her hand that sent a thrill of excitement through her. It was a signature, belonging to the orphanage's director—a man named Cyrus Caldwell. *Another Caldwell, just like me!* She couldn't wait to ask Great-Aunt Delphinia about the family tree.

Feeling almost giddy, Poppy continued combing through the stacks of paper. Most were filled with bookkeeping documents, numbers, and data about income and costs, and almost all of them had been signed by Cyrus Caldwell.

She opened a drawer in the filing cabinets and found old files about the orphans who had lived at Larkspur. There were small pictures of the children attached to the folders. Caldwell's name was all over these too.

I wonder how he's related, Poppy thought. The papers had been signed a long time ago. Could the director still be here somewhere? Either way, there were definitely relatives of hers around. Poppy almost slumped with relief. She'd started to think she might have to go back to Thursday's Hope.

Poppy continued her search through the filing cabinet, hoping to learn more about the director or her great-aunt, then turned to the desks by a long row of squat windows at the far end of the room. A single desk there was markedly different from the others. More organized. A couple of folders thick with papers rested on a green blotter. The top one had a tab that someone had written *SPECIALS* on in bright red pencil, so the word practically leapt off the manila paper.

"*Specials?*" Poppy wondered aloud, "What are *Specials*?"

Before she had time to look closer, she heard a voice murmuring somewhere nearby. Poppy glanced up from the folder, trying to pinpoint where it was coming from. It sounded like a young girl.

Turning from the desk, she realized that the room was L-shaped, and there was a section she'd overlooked before. The voice was coming from around the corner.

"Hello?" Poppy called. She closed the *SPECIALS* folder and slipped it into her bag.

As she walked toward the voice, she could make out some of the girl's whispered words: "*. . . the bread crumbs through the forest . . .*" When Poppy was very young, the story of Hansel and Gretel had given her nightmares. It had never been the witch in the candy house who had frightened her, but instead the parents who'd heartlessly sent their children into the woods to die.

Holding her breath, Poppy peered around the bend. The midday sun shone brightly onto a single high-backed chair that faced the windows. The chair was so tall, she couldn't see the girl who was sitting there.

"Gretel didn't waste a moment," the voice continued. Poppy's shyness suddenly returned. She locked her knees and pressed her bag to her side. "She pushed the old witch into the oven, slammed the door shut, and then turned the latch, locking her in. A howl filled the cottage with a rage nearly hot enough to melt the candy walls! 'Tell me, missus,' said Gretel, smiling, 'is the oven hot enough to cook meat now?' Then she turned toward the cage made of bones where her brother had crouched, watching her with both wonder and terror."

The room fell silent, and Poppy's skin prickled. "Hello?" she called again.

The person in the high-backed chair shifted, the chair swiveled around slowly, and Poppy found herself staring into the blank eyes of a girl in a light-gray cat mask. She flinched with surprise. On the mask, the cat's eyebrows were lifted high, as if Poppy shouldn't have dared interrupt the fairy tale.

Poppy tried again. "Um, do you live here? Can you help me find Delphinia?"

Poppy trembled. She recognized the cat from the charcoal sketch that Ashley had almost destroyed. The girl in the chair also wore the familiar dark skirt, white blouse, and gray sweater. Long brown hair fell from the top of her head, a few stray strands caught in the edges of the mask's eyeholes.

But this couldn't be the *same* girl from the drawing, could it? And why wasn't she saying a word?

On the floor by the wall sat the girl's audience—a group of dolls propped up against the baseboard. All of them were damaged in some way. Disfigured. Some of them were burnt, their faces mottled and blackened. Others were missing limbs and blank-eyed. One of the larger ones was slumped over

with a smashed head, a gaping hole in its fragile porcelain skull.

The girl in the cat mask followed Poppy's gaze down to the pile of dolls for a moment before whipping her head back toward Poppy.

"I'm sorry," said Poppy, horrified that some of her revulsion might have shown on her face. She knew better than most what strange things could become treasures. "I—"

But then the girl stood and Poppy retreated into silence. The girl bent down, gathered up her dolls, then stepped toward Poppy, her eyeholes black and empty. "*You came*," said the girl, her muffled voice the perfect combination of Gretel and the witch. "*You actually came.*"

"Wait! Are you the one who invited me?" Poppy asked, her voice barely a whisper, her heart pounding.

The girl emitted a low laugh that went on for a long time. Then, suddenly, she shrieked. The noise was so unexpected that it startled Poppy into a strangled scream too. The girl kicked the high-backed chair away with startling force. It fell to the floor with a hard whack. Then she stepped toward Poppy again.

Poppy backed around the corner. She was enveloped by a strong smell of smoke, and for a moment she imagined that it had followed her out of the girl's story, as if heat from the witch's oven had become magically real. But then hot air breezed against her back. A moment later, bright, flickering flame burst to light behind her.

Poppy screamed in earnest now. The office was ablaze.

CHAPTER 17

ALL OF THE desks and cabinets, the folders and files that Poppy had just searched, erupted into flame. The fire climbed the walls, turning the wallpaper black and the paintings crisp and crackling. In the furious heat, the black cloth that had covered the tallest frame rose up in a hot gust and then slid to the floor, where the fire devoured it, revealing an enormous mirror. Poppy briefly thought of the Girl right before the mirror's glass fractured with a *crack* as loud as a gunshot, creating a spiderweb of breaks that stretched across its tarnished surface.

For a moment, Poppy knew she had to be imagining everything. *There* is *no fire*, she thought. *There* is *no cat girl. This is all in your head. You really* are *crazy. They're going to lock you in a dark room forever and ever. No friends. No family. No mirrors or books. Just you and your stupid, crazy brain.*

Then something grabbed hold of her hair and yanked. Poppy fell backward with a scream and landed on the floor. The cat-faced girl stared down at her. Above the crackling of the flames, it sounded as if she was laughing.

This was real.

Poppy scrambled away and leapt to her feet.

The blaze was closing in on the two of them. "What are you DOING?!" Poppy yelled at the cat-faced girl. Poppy ran across the room, leaping over small licks of flame. But when she yanked on the knob, the door wouldn't budge.

"NO!" she screamed. "Help!"

Smoke obscured the room behind her, shrouding the cat-faced girl in swirling gray. Fire swelled into the room and the heat grew stronger.

Poppy struggled to inhale, but the heat seared her throat and she choked. Out of nowhere, Ms. Tate blinked into her head, standing before the girls in the common area at Thursday's Hope, instructing them on what to do in case of a fire. *Get low to the ground to avoid the smoke.* Poppy dropped to her knees, covering her mouth. *Know your closest exits.*

Exits. Poppy forced herself to think.

There was a window next to the broken mirror! The red velvet curtain was roaring with flames, but the glass was clear.

Poppy grabbed the metal chair at the desk. It was hot to the touch, but she gritted her teeth against the pain. She raised it above her head and threw it as hard as she could at the window. A perfect shot. But to her horror, the chair simply bounced away.

"Dylan!" she screamed, coughing, sweat running down her face and neck, drenching her T-shirt. "Marcus! Azumi! Help me!" The fire was so loud now, the blood pounding so hard in her eardrums, that even if any of them answered, she wouldn't hear them.

The smoke across the room seemed to part like a veil. A figure stepped into the flames—the girl in the cat mask. Poppy froze, unsure again if her eyes were playing tricks. The fire seemed to dance *around* the cat girl. The girl walked slowly forward, clutching her collection of monstrous dolls and staring at Poppy with malice.

"You don't scare me!" Poppy shouted. She hated that her voice sounded so trembling and weak.

The girl tilted her head as if to ask, *Don't I?* She glided slowly through the growing flames toward the spot where Poppy crouched.

You came. You actually came.

The wallpaper beneath the sketch of the masked five was bubbling. Smoke and steam billowed out from the seams, and

Poppy gagged at the fumes. The fire was inside the wall now. Soon, it would rush to the upper and lower floors. Poppy knew the entire structure could collapse.

Know your closest exits.

A fierce anger filled her, the same anger that had made her search for her file in Ms. Tate's office. *If there's no way out, make one.*

Poppy stared into the shattered mirror. Her reflection was a fractured, frightening mess, but it wasn't her reflection she was looking for. "You were trying to warn me not to come here," she yelled to the Girl, *her* Girl, Poppy's voice barely audible over the roar of the fire. "I'm sorry I didn't listen. But please, *please*, if you can hear me, help me!"

The cat girl was now only a few steps away. She held out her dolls, as if to taunt Poppy with what was about to happen.

If there's no way out, make one.

A slight flicker moved inside the broken mirror.

The Girl! She'd come!

The mirror fractured again. A horizontal line broke through the web pattern over Poppy's reflection. Then two more cracks formed on either side of Poppy's face. Turning around, Poppy saw the fissures cracking through the wall she was huddled against. The cracks in the mirror were duplicating themselves on the wall behind her.

The girl in the cat mask howled as Poppy slammed her weight against the wall. When Poppy drew back and hit it with her shoulder again, the wall swung open like a gate.

A moment later, Poppy had collapsed out into the hallway. Inside the burning room, the mirror exploded, shards of broken glass hurtling into the fire. The passage through the wall disappeared with a blink, and Poppy found herself staring at an unblemished hallway.

Poppy leaned back, gasping for breath. She closed her eyes, then opened them and looked again. Nothing. And no burns on her, no hint of smoke.

Craazzy Poppy.

Slamming her palms against the wall behind her, Poppy shoved the taunting voices away. But that only left her with her own voice ringing in her head, and she didn't know if she liked that any better.

This is all a lie. The letter. The invitation. Great-Aunt Delphinia.

Something had wanted Poppy to come to Larkspur, but it hadn't been some long-lost family member. This place wasn't going to be her home. No one here was going to accept her, love her, adopt her.

She fought against the rising flood of tears, her eyes red and prickling. Poppy felt like one of the dolls that the girl in the cat mask had been telling a story to, the one that had been gutted, its stuffing removed. She struggled to stay on her feet and angrily wiped her face clean.

Then Poppy heard the sound of footsteps racing toward her.

CHAPTER 18

POPPY FACED THE footsteps, swinging her satchel from her shoulder and holding it hard in her hands like a weapon—until she saw the face of the person rushing toward her. She was so relieved, she nearly dropped her bag.

"Dylan!" she cried out.

"Nope," said the boy. "But close." His eyes were wide, and his chest was heaving.

"Dash? What are you doing up here?"

"Where's my brother?" Dash looked almost as scared as she felt.

"We decided to split up." She glanced over her shoulder toward the office door. "We need to find the others and then get out of here."

"You saw something too?"

Nodding, Poppy fought tears.

This is all a lie.

"I was waiting in the foyer," said Dash, "just like Dylan told me to. But I heard a noise. When I turned, I saw that kid in the rabbit mask watching me from the top of the stairs. He ran off, so I followed him up here—"

"I don't know what's going on." Poppy couldn't hold back. "I was in an office. There was a fire. A girl in a cat mask attacked me. I thought she was going to kill me. I ran, but the door was locked. And the window wouldn't break. But the wall . . . The fire went out, which makes no sense . . . And . . . And we have to go." She shifted past him, waving for him to follow. "We have to find the others *AND GO.*"

"Not that way," he said.

"What do you mean?" She heard her voice rising. "The stairs are just down the hall."

Dash turned his head to show her the nasty welt on his cheek. Poppy hissed in shock and sympathy. "The kid I followed attacked me too. I managed to pull off his mask." Dash trembled and briefly closed his eyes. "There was black goo spilling out of his mouth and down his neck. He was soaked with it." He swallowed. "I don't want—I don't think we should go back that way."

Poppy met his eyes gravely. "The stairs are back that way. I haven't seen another way out."

Dash peered past her into the darkness stretching down the hallway behind her. "Fine. But if we come across another one of those kids wearing masks, I hope you know how to fight."

"I'm learning," said Poppy, leading the way, relieved to finally put some distance between herself and that office.

Moments later, not far down the hall, they came upon the rabbit mask lying on the floor, lit by sunlight from an open doorway.

It wasn't anything elaborate, just a thin sheet of plastic that had been pressed by a mold at a factory somewhere. But the eyes were wide and dark, their edges marked with deep laugh lines. In the pale light from the nearby doorway, they looked hollow, black. The mouth was stretched in a wide and grotesque smile, with a tiny slit cut in the plastic so its wearer could breathe. There were dried black flecks spattered around this small hole.

"You sure you want to touch that?" Poppy asked as Dash reached for it.

Dash glanced at her. "We can't just leave it here. The others won't believe my story." Poppy understood what he'd meant: *Dylan* won't believe my story. Dash turned the mask over. The bottom half was dripping with black goo.

Poppy gasped and covered her mouth. "Ugh. Nasty!"

"Never mind," Dash said, and dropped it, wiping his hands on his shorts.

Poppy noticed red markings on the inside of the mask, higher up, closer to the rabbit's left ear. Block letters in red marker spelled out *ALOYSIUS*. "What's this?" she asked, pointing.

"I don't know and I don't want to," Dash said. "I just want to get out of here."

They continued on toward the staircase. "Dylan?" Dash called out. His voice echoed back at him, but no one answered.

As they went around the next corner, Poppy yelped. Just ahead, lying on the floor in a sunbeam, was the same rabbit mask, still looking up with its blank eyeholes. "What's going on?" she asked. *Craazzy Poppy.* "Dash, you see that too, right?"

"I don't understand," said Dash slowly. He looked close to tears. "Dylan!" He called out again. He gathered himself together and quietly said, as if to himself, "It's got to be one of Dylan's tricks. He's messing with us."

"After everything we've just seen, you think *your brother* is responsible for this?"

"I don't know what to think!" Dash yelled. "I don't even know which direction to take."

"Let's just keep going?" said Poppy, but her feet felt unsteady.

They walked on for a few minutes—far longer than it should have taken to find the staircase—and suddenly they were back in the same spot. Panic gripped Poppy's lungs, and she felt like she couldn't breathe. Dash rushed up and stomped on the rabbit mask until the plastic was smashed flat.

The hallway shuddered and groaned. Dash grabbed Poppy's hands and brought her low to the floor, as if they were bracing for an earthquake.

"It's not happy you did that," Poppy whispered.

"What's not happy?"

Poppy didn't want to say it out loud. "I don't know . . . The house?"

Inches away, the flattened rabbit mask popped back into shape.

Poppy and Dash leapt to their feet and bolted around the corner and past the rabbit mask. There, they found a new hallway, one they hadn't seen before. They ran and ran, looking for new doorways, new rooms, new details they hadn't yet encountered—anything to get them out of this strange loop.

Poppy yanked Dash to a halt. "You hear that?" she asked, her chest heaving.

"Music!"

"Someone's playing a piano."

"Let's follow it."

"But what if it's—"

"Just go!"

Poppy and Dash raced around a bend, and the landing at the top of the stairs finally appeared. "Yes!" she shouted, feeling like she'd just won a marathon.

Dash bolted past her, down the steps toward the foyer. "Hurry!" he shouted. Poppy didn't need him to tell her twice.

When the two of them finally made it to the bottom of the stairs, a voice called out from up above, "Dash! Wait!" Turning, they found Dylan standing on the landing, wide-eyed and unsteady. He looked like he was about to faint.

"Oh my goodness," said Poppy, shaking her head, confused. "I totally forgot Dylan was there too!"

"Help me!" said Dash. Together, Poppy and Dash raced back up the stairs toward his brother.

CHAPTER 19

MARCUS WAS LOST in an ocean of sound. The piano melody swelled as he danced his fingers across the keys and pressed his feet against the pedals. Marcus could hear the Musician's tune a millisecond before he brought it to life. It felt as if they were playing a duet. The ballroom where he sat was a hazy memory. His head was filled with pictures of home, of kind friends and family, of the scent of Duke's wet fur after a walk in the rain, of the sound of the calliope during the county fairs on Labor Day weekends, of his mother and his siblings sitting in the darkness of the auditoriums' first rows—memories that were now so entangled with the Musician's tunes that Marcus couldn't distinguish one sense from the other.

That serenity was shattered when a group burst through the ballroom doorway, shouting for his attention. Marcus lifted his hands from the keys and opened his eyes, feeling as if he'd been bumped out of a dream.

Poppy and Dash were struggling to carry Dylan between them. His arms were stretched between their shoulders, his feet practically dragging.

Marcus stood up, shocked, pushing the bench back with a squeal that mixed with the reverberation left over from his shattered melody. "What's wrong with him?"

"We don't know!" said Dash, his eyes huge with worry. "He practically fainted on the stairs again. This is all my fault!"

Dylan fell to his knees, holding his head. As the last of the echo seeped into the woodwork and faded away, he finally looked up. "I'm sorry," he said, with no trace of his former cockiness. "I don't know what happened to me."

"I told you to come find me if you felt strange!" Dash said, crouching beside him.

Dylan winced. "I didn't feel strange until I found you, so please . . . stop shouting at me."

"Where were you guys?" Marcus asked.

"Upstairs," said Poppy. "The music led us down to you."

"There are other people here," said Dylan. "Kids wearing masks. I think they're messing with us. Playing tricks." He glanced at Dash.

"You saw another one too?" asked Dash. Dylan nodded, swallowing hard, as if he were fighting nausea. Dash's mouth flattened. "The rabbit-faced boy we saw earlier attacked me. And Poppy said a cat girl came after her. We need to get out of here."

Poppy jumped in, "Upstairs, I found an old office filled with files. I think this building was an orphanage once. All the paperwork, for decades, was signed by its director. He has the same last name as me—Caldwell!"

"One more reason to just run," said Dash, edging toward the row of windows on the other side of the room. "Come on!"

"That is weird," said Marcus, crossing his arms. Kind of unbelievably weird. He wished they would leave him alone so he could sit down again at the piano and play. He wanted that warm feeling back, the pleasant memories, the safety of it all. "Maybe everyone should just calm down and talk this out. It sounds very confusing."

"But that wasn't even the weirdest part!" said Dash. "There was a fire, and Poppy got locked in the room, and then—"

"Wait," said Dylan. "There's a fire upstairs?"

"Not anymore," said Poppy. "It went out."

Marcus raised an eyebrow.

"And then," Dash went on, "when we were trying to find our way back to the foyer, the hallways kept moving."

"The hallways—" Marcus crossed his arms. "I'm sorry. That's not possible."

Dash looked at Poppy. "Am I lying?"

Poppy shook her head, blushing. She followed Dash to the line of windows.

"Do you think all of this could be part of the horror movie?" Dylan asked. His voice was low and strained.

"No!" said Dash. "And you don't either! There's something seriously wrong with this place." Dash made a beeline toward the French doors. "I am seriously creeped out. It's time to leave. I don't care *what* we all came here for."

"Agreed." Poppy exhaled on a shaky breath. "There's nothing here for any of us. My great-aunt. Marcus's school. The film shoot. It's all just . . ." She hesitated, glancing around the ballroom. "Where is Azumi?"

Marcus looked behind him. "She was just here. Wasn't she?"

"Not when we came in," Dash said. "When did you last see her?"

"I'm not sure." Marcus walked to the doorway and peered into the hall, glancing in both directions. "I was caught up playing the piano. I thought she was listening to me."

"How could you let her out of your sight?" Dylan demanded. "Were you really that wrapped up in playing a stupid piano?"

"She's a big girl!" said Marcus. "She can do what she wants!"

Poppy sighed. "Not in *this* house, she can't. Here, we're like mice in a maze."

"It's not my fault she's gone!"

Dash grabbed the handles of the French doors. "You guys can hang around waiting for Azumi, but I'm out." But when he pulled down on the handles, they wouldn't budge. He struggled for a few moments before backing away, looking for a latch or a lock that he could release.

"What about Del?" asked Dylan, coming up behind Dash.

"Didn't you hear Poppy?" Dash shouted, moving toward the piano. "She said Del doesn't exist! And I believe she's right." He dragged the piano bench several feet back toward the door.

Poppy's eyes were wide and scared. "I tried to smash a window upstairs with a chair, but it wouldn't break," she whispered.

Dash tossed it at the glass anyway. It bounced off, clattering to the floor with a raucous echo. Marcus ran back into the room, shocked.

"See?" said Poppy.

"I can't believe this." Dash tried to toss the bench several more times, but the door remained intact.

"But the email," said Dylan quietly. "The voice mail. We *heard* his voice." Nobody paid him any attention, even as he stomped his foot. "Am I invisible?"

"We came in through the front door," said Marcus. He tried forcing himself to remain calm, but the fright of the others was slowly infecting him. "We could leave that way too."

"I don't think it'll be any different," said Poppy. She seemed to be fighting against tears again.

"How would we even find our way back there?" asked Dash.

Marcus shrugged. "By going to look for it."

"You didn't see what we saw upstairs," said Dash. "The hallways were moving! The whole house keeps changing shape." The group stared at Dash for a moment. "If it doesn't want us to leave, I don't think we can."

"What do you mean *if it doesn't want us to leave*?" said Dylan. "How can a house not want us to leave?"

"We have to find Azumi before we do anything else," said Poppy, heading toward the hallway. "Right? I mean, maybe she'll already have found a way out."

"Let's try for the front door," said Marcus evenly. "Maybe we'll run into Azumi. We can figure out what to do from there."

"I already know what we can do from there," said Dash, making his way back across the room in a huff. "We can go." He took his brother's arm and disappeared into the hallway.

CHAPTER 20

MARCUS SHOOK HIS head at Poppy and followed the twins. "Me and Azumi found a whole bunch of stuff that made it pretty clear this place is a *school*. A boarding school, like with uniforms and a big kitchen with silverware and food trays and . . . and a pantry with enough food to feed an entire—"

"Orphanage?" Poppy interrupted, her voice growing higher. "That doesn't sound so different from a boarding school. I mean, right? That was what I found upstairs. Files and files and files." Poppy blinked and gathered herself. Ahead, Dash and Dylan were rushing side by side down the hallway. The light at the end of the hallway looked familiar. Hopefully it was coming from the grand foyer. "Please tell me we're all thinking the same thing," she said quietly. "I don't want to feel like the one weirdo here."

"And what should we all be thinking?" asked Dylan over his shoulder.

"That Larkspur is haunted," said Poppy. "The girl that I saw *walked through fire*. How is that possible? And she spoke to me. She said, 'You came. You actually came,' as if she'd been expecting me! What if these kids in masks are making us see, feel, and hear things that aren't real? Or that *were* real once . . . I don't know! I have no clue how hauntings work."

All three boys stopped and stared at her, not moving, as if too frightened to agree.

Marcus touched her elbow, and Poppy flinched. "I think maybe you should find a place to sit," he said.

Poppy shook him off. "No! I've seen things before. Really strange things. And I'm beginning to wonder if those things have to do with why I'm here."

"What kind of things?" asked Dylan.

Poppy closed her eyes briefly and shook her head. "I always thought of her as if she were a friend. My only friend."

"Her *who*?" Marcus asked. Was it Poppy's imagination, or had Marcus gone pale?

"Promise you won't laugh."

"We promise," said Dash.

Poppy took a minute. She'd kept the secret clenched inside herself for so long that it was almost an effort to let it out. "A

Girl. She stands behind me whenever I look in a mirror." Poppy locked eyes with Dash. He *had* to believe her. "My whole life I've seen her. My mother . . . she left me when I was five. I grew up in a group home. So this Girl was special to me." Dash raised an eyebrow and glanced at his brother, who looked away. Poppy swallowed her nerves. "The Girl was always smiling. Always warm. Until I found my great-aunt's letter. Then she changed. In fact, when I reached Larkspur's gate, I'm pretty sure she's what grabbed me and threw me to the ground. That's where you found me, Marcus."

Marcus wouldn't look at her.

"I thought she'd turned on me," Poppy went on. "Jealous or something. But she wasn't trying to hurt me. She was trying to stop me from coming here."

Dylan looked revolted. "That's as creepy as . . . I don't even know what."

"But you believe me?"

Marcus wouldn't meet Poppy's eyes. His own Musician had gone silent for the moment, but Marcus remembered the therapist and the threat of medication. He remembered how he'd forced himself to keep the Musician a secret so that he could keep the music in his life. Marcus balled his fists. Poppy had said she didn't want to be the weirdo here; well, neither did he.

"Not really," he heard himself say. Poppy looked at him with wide, shocked eyes.

It suddenly struck Marcus that what everyone was suggesting—to leave this place, to give up on everything each of them had hoped to find here—would bring him back to Ohio, to his ordinary life where his siblings and classmates just didn't understand jazz or classical music, to his mother, who hated listening to him practice because of her memories of her dead brother. He hadn't realized until this moment how much he *needed* to stay at Larkspur, to believe that this was the music school he was always meant to attend. His Musician's tune had proven this, hadn't it? He'd never felt more truly at home as he had playing the melody on the ballroom piano.

The twins glanced at each other, unsure what to say.

Marcus went on. "Have you ever seen a doctor about these visions?"

Poppy scowled. "The Girl's not a *vision*. She's . . . It's hard to explain."

"I mean, it sounds pretty simple to me," said Marcus, hating himself. "People sometimes hallucinate."

"Was Dylan hallucinating?" Poppy asked. Her face was flaming. "Was Dash?" She turned toward the foyer and continued walking. The boys followed.

"I don't know!" Marcus shouted. "But they're not the ones who've seen imaginary girls standing behind them in mirrors their whole lives."

"I told you, she's *not* imaginary," Poppy yelled.

"Here we are!" Dash cried out as they made their way into the foyer. "The main entrance!" He raced to the solid double doors, grappling with the handles. But just like in the ballroom, the doors would not give.

"But this is how we came in," said Dylan, moving toward the tall, thin window beside the door, peering out of it. "How are they locked *now*?" He smacked the pane hard with his knuckles. There was a loud thud, and Dylan groaned. The glass did not shatter.

"This way," said Dash. The group rushed to follow him into the game room. He went for the closest window lock, but the lever wouldn't turn. None of them would.

"This is so messed up," said Dylan, grabbing the wire bingo globe off the nearby table, the plastic letters rattling inside it. It was heavy; it took two hands to arc it back behind his head and then whip it at the closest window. The globe hit it with enough force to snap a couple of wires, but the glass didn't break. The little red balls inside spilled onto the floor, rolling in all directions, looking like beads of blood. "I don't understand," said

Dylan. He moved from window to window, pounding on the glass.

"What about the door's hinges?" Poppy asked. "Can we take it apart that way?"

Dash ran back to the entry. "There are no hinges!" he called out.

"How can a door not have hinges?" asked Marcus.

"They're gone." Dash returned to the game room and threw his hands into the air. "How can *any* of this be happening?"

Poppy grabbed the back of one of the game room couches. "Maybe if we use the furniture to make some sort of battering ram . . . ?"

"A battering ram?" said Marcus, shaking his head. "This isn't a video game, Poppy."

"It was just a thought . . ."

"I don't think *anything* we do will get these doors or windows open," said Dash, his voice strained and trembling. "Poppy was right. It's this place, or those kids, or something. They wanted us here. And now they won't let us go."

A wave of cold fear grabbed at the four kids, and for a moment all they could do was stand there, shuddering, frozen in place.

CHAPTER 21

AZUMI HAD BEEN following the pink nylon ribbon down the dark and twisted corridor for so long, she almost expected to arrive back at the starting point. But she kept going and going, wandering around corners, stumbling up and down steps, without even crossing the path she'd already walked.

How big is this place? Azumi wondered.

The ribbon was starting to feel like a safety line back to the way out.

The hallway stretched about a hundred yards farther before coming to another T-shaped crossing. With her phone's flashlight, Azumi could see the nylon ribbon veer around the corner to the right. She listened to her breath, counting in her head with every exhalation so that she had something to focus on other than the growing strangeness of the situation.

Azumi didn't see the backpack on the floor until her sneaker caught on the strap, and she tripped, letting go of the ribbon and landing sprawled on the floor.

Her hand trembled as she reached for the backpack. Its blue canvas was faded, as if it had been bleached by the elements. Its front pockets had been worn through and the sides were ragged, as if torn open by hungry animals. Inside, Azumi could see what she knew were stacks of notebooks, once waterlogged but now dry. She knew that if she were to reach in, pull out one of the books, and open it to any page, she'd see ink that had bled into gray splotches, words that had been leeched away by water.

Azumi kicked the bag away hard, and it arced away from her and hit a distant wall with a satisfying smack.

This backpack had been one of the first objects that she and Moriko had stumbled upon in the forest behind Auntie Wakame's house in Yamanashi Prefecture. And here it was, waiting in Larkspur for Azumi to find it again.

Something shifted down the hallway. There was a scuffling of feet.

"Who's there?" Azumi demanded. "What is going on here?" She grabbed her phone and shone the light into the shadows. A few more objects were scattered throughout the hall in the darkness ahead of her, but from where she sat, Azumi couldn't make out what they were.

She stood slowly, waiting for the scuffling sound to come again, but the hallway was quiet. Following the ribbon, she made her way to the next object. It was a wrinkled photograph, its subjects staring up at Azumi. She knew this one too. It was a snapshot of a father standing with his daughter on the corner of a busy street, her arms slung around his neck, both of them smiling for the camera. Azumi knew it was taken in Tokyo. She also knew that if she were to flip over the photograph, she'd find kanji written on the back in ballpoint pen: *Good-bye, my lovely girl. Forgive me.* Azumi's Japanese wasn't nearly as good as her parents wanted it to be, but she'd studied this photograph before too—in the forest on the day Moriko went missing. With every discovery, she felt herself growing giddy, as if she might lose control and start laughing again, like she had done with Marcus in the laundry. She pulled her jacket tight across her middle and forced the feeling away, determined to keep hold of herself.

Azumi remembered the time last year when Moriko had tried to pierce her belly button with a sewing needle. Azumi had run to tell her parents what her sister was about to do. They'd laughed, and Azumi had fumed. "It's going to get infected!" she'd insisted.

"So then let it get infected," her father had said. "Your sister will learn, won't she?"

Let it get infected. That was the thought that had gone through Azumi's head when she headed back to Auntie Wakame's cottage on that last afternoon. Those were the words she thought of as the sun had set and she'd held her tongue about leaving Moriko alone on the path at the edge of the woods, holding on to that stupid pink ribbon. *Your sister will learn, won't she?*

Azumi had no idea at the time how that infection would spread—how it would sneak into her brain like a worm, turn her into a mindless zombie, and walk her unknowingly into the darkness of her dreams.

Coming to the end of the hallway, Azumi ran around the corner, following the ribbon. There was light up ahead coming from a doorway on the right. Pieces of paper were strewn like bread crumbs all the way into the distance. Azumi ventured on, bending down to examine these pages. Picking up several of them, she noticed that the same words were written in pencil at the top of each: *Dear Sister*—

Someone was toying with her. With all of them. The creepy papier-mâché figurines that looked like the group of kids she'd met that day and now the ribbons and things from the woods here in the house . . .

She picked up another page. This one was different. The words *Dear Azumi* were followed by a series of thick black lines, Magic Marker inked over the rest of the message. Azumi looked closer. Holding the flashlight in just the right position, she was able to make out indentations in the paper, more of the message that someone had tried to erase.

Dear Azumi,
I miss you so much. If only we could see each
other face to face...

A spark of anger lit in her stomach, and she had to stop herself from crumpling the page. Someone had mimicked Moriko's writing perfectly. Who would make fun of her sister like this? She hadn't told anyone about Moriko besides Marcus. Was this the type of joke that he'd try, to get back at her for whatever dumb thing she might have said earlier to offend him?

A muffled cough echoed from up ahead. A figure was standing in the pale light filtering through a doorway, holding the end of the pink ribbon. Azumi squinted. "Hello?"

The figure didn't answer her. Didn't move. Trying to keep herself from trembling, Azumi approached steadily. "Did you write this?" Azumi found herself fighting tears. "Answer me!" She didn't know what emotion she was feeling. They were all so mixed up.

She thought of the day weeks prior when she'd searched online for East Coast schools and how only one entry kept

Dear Sister,

I miss you so much. If only we could see each other face to face, I know I would finally find the comfort I've needed this past year. I know you would explain everything to me, tell me why you haven't come to find me...

I can't remember what happened anymore... One minute you were right beside me, and the next second I couldn't see you. Did the Director talk to you, too?

Why haven't I heard from you?? Have you gotten my letters? Have I even sent them, or is this just a cruel trick of my imagination, telling me that I've been waiting **and waiting** to hear from you when you have no idea where I am?

coming up. *Larkspur*. Was this person responsible for that too? It didn't seem possible. Not physically, nor emotionally— she'd never imagined that someone could be so cruel.

She was about to tear the papers to pieces, but the figure stepped into the faint beam of her flashlight and Azumi's breath was swept from her lungs.

"Moriko?" Azumi wheezed. Her face was on fire. Her skin tingled, and then the hallway tilted, or maybe it only seemed so.

The figure stepped back into the shadows, the details of her appearance melting away. She dropped the end of the ribbon and then disappeared through the doorway on her right.

"Moriko, wait!" Azumi called out. She raced after her sister.

CHAPTER 22

"HEY, OVER HERE," Dash called from up ahead. He and Dylan were standing in front of a large wooden door on the right side of the corridor. "Maybe this one leads to an exit!" The top of the door rose high over their heads, crowned in a sunburst-shaped arc. Marcus and Poppy approached the twins, and the door, cautiously. Dylan was already pulling at the doorknob.

"I don't think so," said Marcus. "Look."

Dylan hadn't noticed the dozen or more rusty nails that had been hammered along the outer edge of the door, piercing the frame around it. Frustrated, Dash pushed his brother's hands away from the knob. "It looks like someone wants to keep people out of there."

"Either that," said Poppy, "or they want to keep someone inside."

Dash closed his eyes, and Poppy realized that she should try harder to not frighten her new friends. Friends? Was that what they'd become? Despite the animosity she'd already felt building between herself and both Dylan and Marcus, she had to admit that Dash was feeling like a friend. "I'm sorry, Dash," she said. It was hard for her to say. The girls at Thursday's Hope hardly ever apologized unless Ms. Tate threatened them with punishment.

"Listen," Dylan whispered. He brought his ear close to the door but didn't touch it. The others decided they could hear just fine from where they stood. A slight scratching sound was coming from within, like long fingernails dragging along the wood. Dylan glanced at the others. "Do you think it's Azumi?" None of them wanted to call out or make their presence known.

"What if it is?" Poppy asked. "We'd need a hammer to pry those nails away."

"We could go look for one," said Marcus, but nobody appeared willing to head back into the dark passage behind them.

The doorknob rattled violently, and everyone jumped back. There was a sudden pounding, and the door itself jounced and trembled. It bulged outward and the nails in the door frame strained.

Dash whimpered. They were all too frightened to move. Too scared to speak. But Dash knew they were all thinking the same thing he was: *One of the masked kids is in there, and he or she is trying to get to us.*

Then, as suddenly as the pounding started, it stopped—the scratching too. The hallway was filled with a quiet that seemed to ring in their eardrums like a long and steady hum. No one dared to breathe. Which was strange because, all of a sudden, the echo of a stifled inhalation interrupted the silence like a knife.

"Marcus," Dylan whispered, his eyes round with terror. "Someone is standing behind you."

CHAPTER 23

EVERYONE TURNED TO LOOK.

Down the wide hallway, several yards past the door with the nails, a boy was staring back at them. Or at least he appeared to be staring—it was difficult to tell because of his mask. This one was shaped like a dog's head, its lips drawn all the way back to the boy's ears. He had shaggy blondish hair and was dressed similarly to the others they had seen that day: stiff flannel pants, a white shirt, and a gray sweater.

"Who are you?" Marcus yelled. "What do you want?"

The boy in the dog mask stepped closer to Marcus, nodding, as if taunting him. He was clutching a broken violin, holding the jagged body of the instrument in one hand. The neck dangled by the strings, swaying against the boy's leg like a metronome.

"He's just trying to scare us," said Dylan, stepping toward the boy. Dash reached out to pull him back, but Dylan shook off his grip. "Not a good idea, kid. Back up!"

"Dylan, shut your mouth," Dash pleaded through clenched teeth.

"Marcus," Poppy whispered. "You're too close!"

The boy in the mask slowly turned his head as if to acknowledge everyone's presence. Then, all at once, he swung the body of the violin forward. It smacked Marcus in the face so hard that he fell to the floor. Before anyone else could move, the masked boy hurled himself forward and pounced on Marcus, straddling his chest and stretching the strings of the broken violin across his neck to cut off his breath. Marcus's eyes went wide and he let out a strangled scream.

"Stop that!" Dash shouted. "Get off him!" He bolted forward, barreling into the attacker's side. The boy in the dog mask barely flinched, and Dash fell to the floor.

"Whoa," said Dylan. "You are *so* done." He charged, but he was too slow. With a slight feint, the boy twisted his body out of the way. He lifted his knee like a piston and brought it down on Dash's neck, pinning him beside Marcus. Dylan was too shocked to move.

"Dylan!" Dash wheezed.

"Leave them alone," shouted Poppy, throwing off her shock and flying into the fray. She yanked at the strings that were cutting into Marcus's throat. Dylan tried to kick out the boy's knee, but the boy swiveled out of the way.

"Dylan, watch it!" yelled Poppy.

The boy hissed at Dylan, flinching as Dylan swung his fist toward his head. Poppy shoved hard at the masked boy's shoulder, and Dash managed to twist his torso and then scramble out from under him.

Marcus reached up from where he was flailing on the floor. "Get . . . off . . . of us!" he gurgled, attempting to clutch at the boy's clothing to drag him off-balance.

Dylan came forward again, fists raised. He reached out and tried to grab the boy's sweater, but his hand seemed to slip right through it. The boy looked up, and the dog mask seemed to change, the eyes growing wider, the upper lip curling back in a snarl, revealing yellow plastic teeth. He bolted to his feet and then cringed, as if he were startled by Dylan's attempt to touch him.

There was a great booming sound followed by a resounding crack. The building shook, and from somewhere far away came a noise like a roar. The boy scuttled from the group, rolling toward the door with the nails, dragging his broken violin across the rug, cowering. Marcus sat up, gasping and choking.

The four kids retreated to the center of the hallway. They watched the boy in horror, their muscles coiled like springs. But the boy was fixated on the wall behind them. Turning, they discovered a wide, jagged opening staring back. It hadn't been there moments earlier. The booming sound, the cracking noise, the roar . . . The house had changed shape around them again.

At the far end of this dark and dusty passageway, a light blinked on. A small chandelier globe in the ceiling of a brass elevator cage.

The boy in the dog mask groaned and shifted against the far wall. He clutched his broken violin close to his chest and was watching them intently now, as if he'd forgotten the fear that had distracted him from his anger. Deep in his esophagus, his voice rattled wordlessly: *Ehrrrrr.*

Dash jumped to his feet, clutching at his throat. "We need . . ." He struggled to catch his breath. "We need to get away from here." He pulled at Marcus's shirt collar and yanked at Poppy's shoulder. They kept their eyes on the boy as they backed through the new opening in the wall. Moving swiftly into the dank space, the group put about a dozen feet between themselves and their attacker. "Come on."

The boy in the mask rose to his feet, his knees slightly bent as though he were about to pounce again.

147

"This way," Marcus whispered, turning to face the dim light in the elevator car. His vocal cords were raw.

"Everyone run!" said Dash. "Now!"

Dash and Poppy raced ahead of Marcus and Dylan. Dylan supported Marcus with his shoulder and helped him down the new corridor.

"Thank you," said Marcus.

"Just move!" said Dylan.

Marcus could hear the dog boy catching up quickly, but he kept the elevator's glow in the center of his vision. If there were walls around him, they were made of shadow. The house seemed to shiver, the floor rattling, the ceiling creaking, as if the passage were stretching longer and longer behind him. He hoped that whatever was happening would buy them a few extra seconds to get farther ahead of the kid in the dog mask.

Something flew from the darkness to the left of the elevator and collided with the group. Dash and Marcus shouted in surprise as Poppy and Dylan were spun around to face the direction from which they'd just come. Dazed, Marcus noticed that the boy in the dog mask was only several yards away, limping toward them determinedly.

"Poppy!" said an excited, high-pitched voice. "Oh my goodness!"

The *thing* that had barreled into them was Azumi. The glow from the elevator's lamp lit her panicked expression.

"Please help me!" Azumi glanced over her shoulder, looking back from where she'd come. "There's this crazy girl chasing me—"

"In here!" said Poppy, sliding the cage door open with a crash before stepping inside. "Quickly." The others followed. The space, which had seemed tight at first, expanded to fit everyone. The others huddled by the rear wall as Poppy shoved the handle. Accordion-like springs squealed their resistance, and the cage door closed.

A body smashed into the car from outside, rattling the brass gates. The old, cracking plastic of the dog mask pressed through the diamond-shaped holes in the cage. The boy reached inside, swinging his hands like claws in an arcade game, hoping to catch a prize.

Poppy knew it was only a matter of time before the boy grabbed the latch and swung the door open. Her mouth was dry. Her head felt like it was screwed on loosely. She understood she had to focus or she'd collapse. Staying to the side of the car, she looked for a panel of buttons that would send the elevator up or down. But there *were* no buttons. Instead, there was a circular apparatus marked with the word *OTIS* across the front, a small black knob sticking out of its top. "I don't know what to do," she whispered to herself. *"I don't know what to do!"*

"Get back or you're going to lose an arm when this thing moves," Dylan shouted, taunting the boy. Dash clung to his shoulder, shaking.

Azumi shouldered past them, pushing at the attacker's hands while dodging his violent swings. "Azumi, what are you doing?" Poppy asked. "Be careful!"

Marcus stayed pressed against the wall, rubbing his neck, wiping at his eyes, and clearing his throat. "Poppy! Make this thing move!"

"Okay, okay!" Poppy grabbed the black knob, sliding it to the right. To Poppy's surprise, the car lurched, its gears squealing sharply, and then the elevator began to rise.

The dog boy yanked his arms out of the cage and howled—a monstrous, inhuman sound coming from behind his mask—before disappearing into the shadows.

CHAPTER 24

WHEN THE FIRST floor was no longer in sight, Poppy swung the black knob back to the middle, and the car came to a screeching halt. They'd stopped between floors. For some reason, the walls of the elevator shaft weren't visible. Absolute darkness surrounded them, as if they were a vessel lost in outer space. The kids stumbled breathlessly into the center of the elevator, as if a hand might slip inside again and grab hold of them. Somehow, the car seemed even larger than it had been only seconds earlier.

At least they were away from danger. And even if they weren't, the new quiet felt like a balm for their bruises. They spent the next few seconds just breathing, checking their injuries. Each of them felt lucky to be alive.

Dylan was shattered. He was certain that if he hadn't mouthed off to the boy in the dog mask, none of his new friends would have been hurt. Even after all the conversations, after all the stories that the others had shared, he'd still half expected Del Larkspur to walk out from behind some curtain and tell them that it had all been a game. There would be cameras and lights and food and a comfortable place to read the rest of the film script, because that was how jobs always worked. People took care of you. *No one is coming*, he realized. *It's just you and Dash.* They'd been tricked.

He'd tried to push down the sense of terror he'd felt all day, starting with the white-hot panic after the strange flash on the stairs, and then again in the hallway with the boy in the bear mask. His mind whirled. If he was being honest, he'd had flashes of that same terror for weeks now, though he couldn't remember when it started, or why. Had it been in a dream? When he thought about the recent past, he couldn't place events into a simple time line. There were so many missing pieces, so many gaps. Deep down, he knew that Dash and his nightmares were spot on. It had taken something like this trip to open Dylan's eyes.

"Dylan, are you all right?" Dash put a hand on his brother's shoulder. "I'm so sorry."

Dylan felt so foolish he could only turn his head and try to hide his tears.

"Marcus, your neck," said Azumi, "let me take a look at it." Marcus shifted and everybody winced. There were several long ridges where the violin strings had bit into Marcus's skin. One of the marks was raw, oozing blood.

"I might have a Band-Aid," said Poppy, digging through her satchel. She pulled out a paperback—*The Lion, the Witch and the Wardrobe*—and flipped through a few pages, revealing several items that were placed inside. And just like that, she handed Marcus a Band-Aid. "You never know," she added. Her eyes lit up. "Oh, and this might help too." She reached again into her bag and grabbed something near the bottom. Opening her hand, she showed him a wrapped cherry cough drop.

"Thanks," Marcus whispered.

"Can I have one?" asked Dash, his own voice sounding raw. "That dog kid got me good too." Poppy nodded, and reached into her bag again. She frowned, pulled out the folder labeled *SPECIALS*, and laid it on the floor in the middle of the kids before reaching into her bag again for Dash's cough drop.

"Are *you* all right?" Dylan asked Azumi, who'd been watching them all with concern. "That girl who was chasing you—"

"She didn't hurt me," said Azumi. The others waited for her to go on. "I heard a voice calling to me, so I went to check it out. I got lost. Then . . . I thought I saw my sister—"

Marcus interrupted. "But isn't your sister—"

"Gone," said Azumi. "Yes, just like I told you, Marcus. I went after her anyway. When I got close, I saw that it wasn't Moriko. It was a girl wearing a chimpanzee mask. She growled at me!" Azumi flicked her long hair behind her shoulders, as if trying to compose herself. "She came at me, so I ran." She squinted at the file Poppy had placed on the floor before glancing at the group again. After a moment, she added, "So what do we do now?"

CHAPTER 25

DASH BENT DOWN and touched the folder. "What is this, Poppy?"

Poppy shook her head. "I grabbed it from the office before it . . . well, before it burned. I forgot I had it in my bag."

"*Specials?*" Dylan knelt beside his brother and flipped open the cover. "Whoa."

Inside, bundles of pages were divided into five groups, a large rubber band holding each group together.

Her heart skipping like mad, Poppy knelt by the twins. She spread the five bundles of paper out across the elevator's rug. A small black-and-white photograph was glued to the upper left side of each: portraits like mug shots of three boys and two girls. Poppy gasped. "I've seen these kids before," she said. "They were in the charcoal sketch I saw by the office door." She shot a self-conscious glance at Marcus. "Weeks ago, my Girl in the mirrors also gave me a sketch with them in it. They were standing in front of a stone wall, like the one near Larkspur's gate, wearing masks. Exactly like the masks we've seen in this house. I knew the Girl's drawing was a message when I first saw it, but I had no idea what it meant."

"This is too much." Azumi stood up and went over to the OTIS device. She placed her hand on the knob and said, "Up or down?"

The others stared at her, shocked.

Poppy shifted toward her. "I don't think we should be going anywhere right now."

"Marcus and Dash are hurt," said Azumi. "Shouldn't we, like, find a way out?"

"What do you think we've been trying to do?" asked Poppy. "For right now, we're safer in here than we were out there."

"We don't even know what *out there* is," said Azumi. She furrowed her brow and squeezed the knob tighter. Finally, she released an exaggerated sigh and joined the group again. "Fine."

Everyone focused on the folder again.

"So these have to be the kids who've been chasing us," said Dash. "Right?"

Poppy read the names in the files aloud. "Matilda Ribaldi, Randolph Hanson, Esme Alonso, Irving Wells, and Aloysius Mears."

"Aloysius! Poppy, that's the name we saw on the rabbit mask!"

"None of them look particularly *special*," said Dylan. "In fact, they all look pretty worn out."

He was right. Their eyes lacked the kind of spark or energy you usually saw in kids. Poppy had noticed the same in the sketch she'd found earlier hanging in the office. She'd noticed it in some of the kids at Thursday's Hope, especially when they first came in. And though something twisted inside her to admit it, she worried that she saw some of that same blankness in herself.

In the file photos, dark hollows marked the children's eyes, their mouths were downturned, and their postures were stiff, as if they were tensing against something awful to come. *It's like they're facing a firing squad*, she thought, then pushed the morbid thought away.

She removed the rubber band from the stack that belonged to the girl named Matilda and began sifting through it, reading bits and pieces of her life. "It says, 'Matilda is fond of story time, books, dolls, and singing nursery rhymes to herself. She is often shy and has to be coaxed to participate in any other group activities.'"

"We should read through the rest of these," said Dylan.

"There's no time!" said Azumi.

Dash scoffed. "We have nothing *but* time."

"Dylan's right," said Marcus. "If we can learn a little more about this house and the people who live—or lived—here, maybe we can figure a way out of this place."

"There are dozens of pages," said Azumi. "How are we supposed to get through all of this?"

Something echoed off in the distance—the sound of some small object hitting the ground from a great height. Everyone held their breath, waiting to hear another noise. But none came.

Poppy released a slow breath. "We have to try," she said, and then divided the stack and handed everyone a piece. "Five of them. Five of us. We work better when we work together."

CHAPTER 26

WHILE THE GROUP read, that same noise pinged out from the darkness every few minutes. It startled them each time. Thankfully, it didn't sound like it was getting any closer.

"Can I see your pages?" Dylan asked Dash, and he passed them over. After a moment, Dylan said, "Someone blacked out a whole bunch of the personal history sections in both the Irving and Aloysius files." The others nodded, showing him their files too. The papers were covered in thick markings.

"Maybe it was that Caldwell guy," said Dash. "The orphanage director." He glanced at his brother. Poppy noticed he was always looking over at Dylan, checking in with him. She envied such a close connection.

"That's what I'm hoping to find out," Poppy said.

Dash went on, scanning the sheets. "For some reason, the director didn't want anyone to know where the kids came from, or who they were before they got here."

"But there is a little bit about their personalities," said Marcus. "I think this whole folder was a small part of something larger. Look, there are notes throughout this one that show Cyrus must have kept more information about these kids . . ." As Marcus read more, his eyes grew wide. "And what he did to them," he added.

"What do you mean?" asked Poppy. "What did he do to them?"

"This kid, Randolph, was a musician." Marcus looked up at the others. "Just like me," he said slowly, pausing as if to absorb what that meant. "It says that Cyrus refused to let Randolph play his instruments. The boy in the dog mask attacked me with a broken violin. I think *he* was Randolph."

"Oh my goodness," said Poppy, holding her hand to her mouth as she read. "The director made Matilda destroy all of her dolls. They must have been the same dolls she tried to show me in the burning office."

Dash held up his pages. "Aloysius was mute. He had a sweet tooth. The director wrote that he contaminated Aloysius's favorite candies with a dye that stained his mouth and made him ill."

Dash looked sick himself. "I guess that was the black gunk I found inside the rabbit mask."

"'Irving loves being social and playing games,'" read Dylan. He cringed as he scanned what was on his page. "The director forced Irving to wear cuffs and chains around his ankles to stop him. Just like the kid I saw in the bear mask."

"What about your folder, Azumi?" asked Marcus. "What did you find?"

Azumi's face was frozen. When she spoke, her voice was tight and measured. "Esme missed her older sister," she said. Her eyes glinted with a flash of something dangerous, and for a moment, Poppy felt frightened to sit beside her. "Mr. Caldwell would not allow her to send letters. To respond at all. Even though she begged and begged and begged him. Esme was so angry, she wished she could . . ." Azumi glanced up, her vision clearing. "She must have been the one I saw in the ape mask."

After Poppy had heard all of this, she was nauseated. She couldn't imagine that this man—who shared her own last name—might possibly be related to her. The monster. "There's one thing no one's brought up yet," she said. The others watched her expectantly. "These pages were signed decades ago. If the kids who we encountered today are the same ones from this folder . . . well . . . you all know what that means, right?"

"You said earlier that you thought the house was haunted," Dylan answered slowly. "I guess we've found our ghosts."

"I don't understand," said Marcus. "How could someone be so horrible to a bunch of kids?"

"Because people can be horrible," said Poppy, her face like stone. "They don't need reasons."

"No wonder they're all so angry," said Dylan. "They've been hurt."

"*Hurt* is not the word I'd use," said Poppy. "It's way worse than that."

"Sorry if I don't have too much sympathy for them at this point," said Dash, and Azumi nodded emphatically. "Especially if they're the ones who brought us here."

"*Someone* contacted us," said Dylan.

"Can ghosts use the Internet?" asked Dash. "Can they mail letters?"

Dylan shrugged, looking off into the darkness surrounding them. "I don't know. It was just a thought."

"Let's say Dash is right," said Marcus. Dylan nudged his brother's shoulder playfully, and Dash managed a brief smile. Marcus cleared his throat and went on. "Let's say these orphans—"

"The Specials," said Dash.

"Right," said Marcus. "The Specials. Let's say they're the ones who wanted us to come to Larkspur." He paused, seeming lost in thought. "Why us? What's so special about us?"

"Well, Dash and me are kind of famous," said Dylan.

"Does that really make you special though?" asked Azumi, raising an eyebrow.

"Some people think so," Dash said.

"I'm still confused about the animal masks," said Poppy.

"The director wrote something about that too." Azumi sorted through Esme's file again. "Here it is." She read, "'The masks remove the children's identities. Whenever they glance in the mirror, they shall see nothing of their past. And whatever future they try to imagine shall be devoid of malignant expectation. These children will be my empty vessels. And I shall fill them with wonder.'" Azumi's laugh was dry as dust. "*Wonder*," she spat, as if rejecting the word. "Mr. Caldwell had a pretty warped sense of it."

Poppy had been quiet, but she had been thinking hard. She frowned, turning the idea over again and again in her head. When she finally spoke, she wasn't loud, but what she said made the group sit up and listen. "What I think is more important is the connection that *we* have with the Specials."

"What do you mean?" asked Dylan.

"Five of them, five of us, right?" said Poppy. "There's Matilda and me. She loved her storybooks. And my books are my favorite treasure. Esme Alonso, the girl in the ape mask, was trying to reach out to her sister. And . . . and Azumi's sister went missing. That's another connection." Azumi squeezed her eyes shut in rejection. Poppy moved on. "Then there's you, Marcus, and Randolph Hanson. Both musicians. Both prodigies."

"What about *us*?" asked Dylan. "Am I supposed to be like the kid named Irving? The chained-up bear? What are you implying?"

"You *are* pretty charismatic," said Dash with a grin, peering over at Irving's paperwork. "'Social, and friendly, and at times persuasive.'"

Poppy held back surprised laughter while Dylan glared at her. He turned to his brother with a smirk. "If that's the case, then *you're* the mute one."

Dash didn't take the bait. "Well, I don't talk that much, it's true."

Azumi's mouth was a flat line. "So we *are* like the Specials," she said.

"But what do they want with us?" asked Dash.

"Maybe they want us to take their places," said Dylan. "Maybe, like, if they trap us here, they can go free."

"We already *are* trapped," said Azumi. "And they haven't gone anywhere." She crossed her arms. "Maybe they want us dead."

Dash went gray and jumped to his feet. "DON'T SAY STUFF LIKE THAT!"

"Hey!" Dylan knocked his brother with his elbow, tossing a look that said *Chill*. Dash was still ashen, but he sat back down.

"We're lucky to have this folder," Dylan said. "Thanks, Poppy." He shuffled through the pages lying between them. Poppy blushed, squeezing her hands in her lap. "I don't think they expected us to get ahold of it," he added.

"Or maybe they did," said Azumi. "And it's filled with a bunch of lies." Everyone stared at her for a few seconds. "What? Did I say something funny?"

"There's something else we're missing," said Poppy, trying to sound upbeat. "Something that's not in this file. We haven't talked about how *we* are connected. The five of *us*."

"Sounds like you have another idea," said Marcus.

"Poppy's had a lot of good ideas, actually," said Dash. "If we stick with her, we might actually get out of this awful place."

Poppy felt herself flush red. She glanced around the group and realized that everyone was paying attention to her, as if she'd suddenly become their leader. This had never happened before, not in school, not at the group home, not anywhere.

"Spit it out, Poppy," said Azumi. "We don't have all day."

That same pinging sound echoed out from the darkness again. No one gave it a thought, until a few seconds later, when it was followed by another noise. A scraping, like something being dragged across the floor. And very, very close.

CHAPTER 27

EVERYONE LEAPT TO their feet and huddled in the center of the rug, crushing some of the file pages beneath them. They peered out anxiously through the bars of the cage, searching the ocean of black for movement.

"Someone's coming," whispered Azumi. "I *told* you."

The overhead lamp dimmed slightly. "No, no, no!" Poppy whimpered, and Dylan shushed her. She covered her mouth with a shaking hand.

There was movement in the distance, four figures emerging from the murk, closing in on them from every side of the elevator. The cage had never been a refuge. Instead, like a phosphorescent glow in the deepest depths, its lamp had created a lure. And now the predators had arrived. The scraping sounds got louder from all directions, as the figures marched slowly toward the elevator, a bull's-eye with an ever-shrinking circumference.

"Is it them?" asked Dash. "Is it the Specials?"

Marcus leaned forward and squinted, trying to make out the figures in the gloom. He snapped back into the middle of the huddle, as if for protection. "No," he said. "It's something else." The elevator lamp cast light only about a dozen feet from where they stood. And as the shapes came closer, their details were finally apparent.

"It's us," whispered Poppy, an echo of what Marcus had said in the game room hours earlier.

Approaching the cage were four papier-mâché figures like the ones that Azumi had pulled down from the mantel in the game room. But these dolls were as tall as the kids themselves. With their joints locked in place, the figures moved stiffly, swinging their weight from side to side, each of them dragging one foot and then the other in a syncopated rhythm.

There were the two identical figures painted light brown, dressed in shorts, graphic T-shirts, and sandals. Brothers. Around the corner from them, a girl painted pale pink hitched and swayed. Splotchy freckles covered her cheeks, and across her torso was the strap of a pink satchel. Adjacent to her was the boy with red hair. Around each of their necks hung thick white cords dragging along the floor behind them. Nooses.

The figures moved slowly, purposefully, sure of themselves, as if they knew they had all the time in the world.

"What do we do?" asked Dash in a strangled whisper

Dylan broke toward the OTIS device in the corner. "Up or down?" he asked.

"Up!" yelled Azumi.

"Down!" screamed Poppy at the same time.

Dylan tried to push the knob left, but the little sphere came off in his hand. The elevator didn't move. Panicked, Dash grasped at the end of the rod, but he only ended up cutting the tips of his fingers. The figures were within several feet. Poppy yanked the twins back into the center of the car, away from the walls of the cage.

Dash's whisper was practically inaudible now, as if he was mute with fear. "What do we do?" he repeated.

"Stay calm," said Poppy, thinking furiously. "I mean, these things are made out of paper. *Empty vessels*. Right? What could they possibly do to us?" But she had spoken too soon. The Poppy figure's right arm was severed below the elbow. Her words from the game room came back to haunt her. *You don't play with them. You break them.* From the hole in the plaster dangled an ashen arm, its fingers wiggling slightly.

As if reading Poppy's mind, Azumi said, "Those things aren't empty."

CHAPTER 28

MARCUS TURNED FROM the horror of the Poppy figure to end up face-to-face with his own, staring in at him from the other side of the brass bars. He steadied his feet, trying to find the lowest point of balance. Adrenaline spiked through him. He was going to have to fight.

The elevator was surrounded now, the figures pressed tight against the cage. The thing inside the Poppy figure raised its hand from the broken sleeve with a stifled groan and grabbed one of the bars.

The other figures began to groan too, twisting their limbs to crack out of the plaster, turning necks, bending elbows. Chunks of papier-mâché crumbled and fell to the floor.

The puppeteers were revealed. The Specials.

It was as Poppy had guessed. Matilda had come for Poppy, Randolph for Marcus, Irving for Dylan, and Aloysius and his black gash of a mouth had come for Dash. The cat, the dog, the bear, and the rabbit. Their eyes were empty pits.

For a few seconds, the masked orphans, the Specials, watched the group in stillness and silence. Dust coated their clothes and skin, clouds of it settling onto the black floor beneath them. Then, all at once, they attacked.

The bars of the cage clanged as the Specials threw themselves at them, screaming and shrieking. They yanked at the metal, banging their heads, whipping their arms and legs in a frenzy of movement.

Azumi, Poppy, Marcus, Dash, and Dylan clung to one another, some of them whimpering, some too stunned to make a sound. The metal around them began to squeal and cry as the brass bars bent under the pressure of the attack, making space for the Specials to reach farther inside. Clawlike fingers swiped at the group. Poppy screamed as Matilda got close enough to pull out a hank of her hair.

"They're going to tear us to pieces!" shouted Azumi. The others cringed in fear.

"That's not going to happen!" Poppy yelled. "We have to fight them! NOW!" And the kids inside the elevator broke apart.

Poppy and the twins flung themselves at their orphans, while Marcus spun away from the bars as the dog boy caught his jacket, and Azumi slipped quietly toward the elevator door.

"*You came*," said Matilda's muffled voice as she swiped at Poppy's face. "*You actually came.*"

With the flat of her palm, Poppy smacked Matilda away from the wall of the cage. "I don't know you!" she shouted. Matilda laughed and swiped for Poppy again.

Aloysius and Irving tore at the twins' T-shirts, twisting the hems in their clenched fists.

Dash shoved himself into Aloysius's arm, pinning it against a bar. Irving released Dylan and grabbed for Dash, but Dash ducked away.

Out of reach of the orphans, Dash noticed Dylan's whole body stiffening. *He's going to have another attack!*

"DYLAN!" he yelled. He released Aloysius and jumped back, yanking his brother into the center of the cage.

Dylan snapped out of it. "What do you think you're doing?" he snarled.

Aloysius lunged, his hand coming perilously close to Dylan's face. Dash kicked out at him and then at Irving, who hissed and roared like the bear whose head he was wearing.

Marcus was struggling to rip his jacket away from Randolph's clutching fingers when he saw Azumi at the cage door, pulling frantically at the latch. "Azumi!" he shouted, yanking himself fiercely away from the dog boy. He flew across the cage, knocking her away. "What are you doing?!" he said. "You could let them in!"

Azumi blinked, as if coming out of a trance. She nodded. "We need to run."

"Run where?" he asked. "They're too fast. They'll catch us."

A noise above startled them. Randolph had leapt up above them, climbing up the bars of the elevator cage to the top. Marcus cowered in the center of the cage, covering his head and ducking to avoid Randolph's reach. Azumi jumped up and swiped at the boy, smacking his hand away. Randolph yowled, and Azumi shrieked, "Leave us alone, you nasty thing!"

Grabbing Poppy's bag, Matilda released a muted chuckle. She pulled herself violently backward, slamming Poppy's body into the cage. Poppy grunted and then straightened her shoulders to keep from tumbling out into the shadows. Clasping the bars, she struggled to stay upright.

All around her, the others were shouting, and Poppy wished she could help them. Everything was happening so fast. If it lasted much longer, the orphans would be inside the cage and Azumi's prediction would come true—the Specials would tear the group apart, as easily as Poppy had torn the arm off the papier-mâché doll. *There's got to be a way to escape this*, she thought, her brain spinning. *If we all huddle in the center of the cage . . . If we take them one at a time . . .*

But then Matilda got Poppy's hair in her hands again and jerked as hard as she could. Poppy screamed, feeling pinpricks of pain as follicles were torn from her scalp. Without thinking, Poppy reached through the bars and grabbed hold of the cat mask. She whipped herself backward, the mask still in her hands.

Matilda yelped and stumbled, holding her hands in front of her face. Poppy flung the mask to the floor of the elevator, steadying herself for the next round. But to Poppy's surprise, Matilda lowered her hands, revealing a shocked and horrified expression. Her icy eyes were frightened, her pale skin covered in patchy blotches of plaster.

The battle was still raging around them, but a stillness descended upon the two girls, something that Poppy was certain only they could feel. They stared into each other's eyes. Matilda's were blue and glistening. Seeing past the mask for the first time, Poppy felt a shock. There was a real girl inside, not just a monster. All of these orphans were *real kids*. Dead kids, probably, but real kids nonetheless. Poppy sensed a kind of desperation emanating from the girl, as if she expected that this respite would not last long.

It was then that Poppy realized the fighting had stopped. Turning, she noticed both groups were staring at her—the orphans and her friends.

The other three Specials, the ones still wearing masks, stepped away from the cage and toward Matilda.

"No!" said Matilda. The desperation on her face made Poppy sick. "Leave me alone. Leave me alone!" The three leapt upon Matilda, dragging her to the ground as she flailed and screamed, then huddled over her in a mass. *It looks like wolves feeding*, thought Poppy. She wanted to squeeze through the bars and help the poor girl, but she knew she couldn't take the time.

"Let's go!" said Poppy. She pushed through the group toward the elevator door. Unhooking the latch, she dragged the heavy accordion springs back slowly, slightly, opening a small gap. One by one, they all slipped out into the mysterious darkness that surrounded the cage.

They ran blindly for a while until Marcus stopped them. "Hold on. Where are we?"

"Yeah," said Azumi. "Poppy, which way should we go?"

Looking over her shoulder, Poppy could see the Specials rising from their spot on the floor. From their center, Matilda pushed her way out. She was wearing the cat mask once again. Poppy blinked. The mask that Poppy had torn from her face was still lying on the rug inside the elevator car. Where had this new mask come from?

A disturbing idea slithered into Poppy's skull: The mask had *grown* back.

Matilda darted forward. The others followed, backlit now by the elevator's lamp, making them into featureless hunters.

"It doesn't matter which way," said Poppy, grabbing Azumi by the hand. "Just run!"

CHAPTER 29

THEY SPRINTED THROUGH what seemed like endless dark.

They'd left the glow of the elevator's lamp, and Dash and Dylan were using their phones' flashlights to reveal the next few feet of floor, which sloped upward at a steep angle. As far as everyone could see, there were no walls, no furniture, nothing around them. It was as though the house had not yet dreamed up features for wherever they were headed.

Finally, Poppy stumbled over the edge of a rug and nearly shrieked with joy at seeing something familiar. With every step, more details of the house appeared around her, lit by the ghostly glow of the group's flashlights. There was a baseboard. The ceiling. An overturned wicker chair. A toy fire truck. Ahead, at the end of what was now a hallway, a closed door was rimmed with a halo of light.

Leaping to the front of the group, Poppy cried, "In here!" She swung the door inward, catching a glimpse of the space while everyone piled past her into the room. Then she shoved the door closed, turning the bolt to lock it.

Footfalls continued to ring out from the other side of the door, closer now, closer, followed by the moans and groans, screeches and rattling of the Specials, who were approaching faster than wildfire.

Stepping back to catch her breath, Poppy scanned the room. *Think, Poppy!* Thick curtains were drawn shut over several windows. Amber light emanated from two small crystal chandeliers that hung from the arched ceiling on opposite ends of the space—one in front of a wall of books, the other before a fireplace. In the corner were half a dozen musical instruments propped up on black metal stands. There were heavy chairs and tables just like she'd seen throughout the rest of the house scattered around the room.

If we can't find a way out of the house yet, we need to make a safe place inside it, she thought.

"We need to build a barricade," Poppy announced. She felt like Meg Murry from *A Wrinkle in Time*, saving her brother, Charles Wallace. "Bring anything heavy. And hurry!"

Marcus spun in place, carefully scanning what was available.

The twins practically attacked a substantial leather chair, dragging it to the door.

"Marcus!" Poppy called out as she made her way to a weighty desk. "Help me with this." She and Marcus shoved it up against the door. Azumi carried several piles of books as the twins went back for a small table made of dense wood. "Hand those to me," said Poppy, and then dropped the heavy books inside the desk drawers.

The twins' table wobbled as they lifted it atop the desk. Marcus grabbed a leg to keep it steady. "I've got it." Twisting it, the boys pushed it underneath the lip of the door frame.

"Give it a shove," said Dash.

Boom! Boom! Boom! The Specials had arrived. They began to pound on the door from the outside as the group stacked up everything in the room against it.

"Put that there," said Poppy as Azumi came lugging over a wide ceramic container with a potted palm sprouting from its center. The girls sat the plant on the leather chair's seat.

The pounding at the door grew stronger. The barricade shivered.

Azumi and Dylan stared at the barricade as if they could will it to hold. Marcus wandered into the corner of the room, examining the musical instruments Poppy had seen when she'd entered the space.

Poppy looked around again, wondering if there were any other doors that needed to be reinforced, checking all sides of the room, remembering what Dash had said earlier. *Poppy's had a lot of good ideas.* She blushed again. And that's when she noticed it—a large painting in a gilt frame. Almost four feet tall, it hung over the marble fireplace at the far end of the room, near the spot where the heavy desk had been. Poppy blinked, certain that her eyes were deceiving her, that her exhausted brain was playing tricks on her.

It was a portrait of a girl dressed in old-fashioned clothes and a flower pendant hanging from her neck. The painting's details were remarkably lifelike. But it wasn't the clothing or the skill of the artist that had captured Poppy's attention—it was the girl herself. Wide golden eyes. Pale skin that made the girl's brown hair, which was pulled behind her ears, even darker by contrast.

No longer trapped in a mirror, the Girl was staring at Poppy once more.

This was *her* Girl.

She seemed to watch as Poppy approached.

A small brass plaque had been screwed into the metal at the bottom of the frame. Engraved there was a name: *Consolida*

Caldwell—Beloved Daughter and Sister. When Poppy read it, she released a yelp that sounded around the room.

A hand grasped her shoulder, and Poppy jumped. Turning, she found Dash standing behind her. "What is it?" he whispered.

She pointed at the plaque at the bottom of the frame. "This is the Girl. My *Girl*. From the mirrors."

"She has your name too?"

Poppy nodded.

Dash stepped closer to the fireplace mantel. "The painting is signed by someone named Frederick Caldwell. Who's he?"

"Her father? Her brother? I don't—" *Boom! Boom! Boom!* The pounding at the door rose in volume and strength, shaking the room.

Dash stared at Poppy in desperation, as if her answer would save them from all the trouble they were in. But she didn't have any ideas.

"I don't know!" Poppy cried. "All I know is that if we don't find somewhere safe to hide, and soon, I might actually lose it." Her bottom lip began to tremble, and she bit down on it until it hurt.

CHAPTER 30

SOMETHING ABOUT THE instruments in the corner had mesmerized Marcus, and it wasn't just the idea that he'd finally located an actual "music room" in this mad place. Somewhere far away, the Musician's melody, "Larkspur's Theme," began to echo again.

Boom! Boom! Boom! The furniture at the door shivered slightly. Marcus knew he needed to do something to help everyone here. And quickly.

The last time he'd felt safe had been in the ballroom while playing the piano. The music had provided that serenity. It had protected him, a barrier to keep bad things away.

Marcus couldn't decide what instrument to pick up first. There was a delicate violin, an antique cello, a guitar, a harp, an oboe. And finally, sitting against the wall of bookshelves was a baby grand piano, the twin of the one he'd played downstairs. Its lid was raised, its strings gleaming in the light that fell from the chandeliers.

The tune in his head grew louder, as if the Musician were begging Marcus to let it out. The ivory pieces almost grinned at him as he sat down at the bench. Then, inhaling sharply, Marcus began to play.

The banging at the door faded to a rattle. Poppy, Dash, and Dylan turned to look at him, while Azumi continued to hold herself against the barricade, as if it would break without her help.

Finally, Marcus had an audience. And he found that he liked it.

"Marcus," said Dash, "whatever you're doing, it's working."

"It's the same song you were playing when we found you in the ballroom downstairs," said Poppy quietly. "It's like a . . . a spell." Marcus closed his eyes, remembering how he'd sneered at Poppy when she'd mentioned the girl she'd seen in her mirrors. Was the Musician's tune really so different from Poppy's visions? Of course it wasn't. And now Marcus couldn't look at Poppy without wishing he could take everything back.

As the music echoed off the walls and high ceiling, Marcus found himself surrounded by memories again. Visions of happy family dinners. His oldest brother Isaac's tearful apologies for messing with his instruments. Finding time alone in the house after school to rehearse without worrying about his mother's response. He felt safe. He felt like he was home. And he knew the others could feel it too.

CHAPTER 31

BLOOD WAS RUSHING through Dash's head. The room seemed to throb with the rhythm of his heartbeat, like an echo of the banging that had disappeared from behind the door, and his skin felt like it was on fire. Poppy stood with Azumi at the other end of the barricade, transfixed by Marcus's melody, oblivious to Dash's sudden affliction. Something was wrong— *more wrong* even than being trapped in this insane building.

Dylan was right beside him, staring into nothing, but Dash suddenly felt like they were miles apart from each other. He blinked, and the past rushed at him. A memory as vivid as a dream.

The dressing room is dark. Dylan is at the door, soaking wet, reaching for the lamp. Everything is about to change, and it's going to be my fault.

I'm so sorry, Dylan. I'm so, so sorry.

Dash shook the images away. Coming back into himself, he took his brother's elbow. But Dylan didn't seem to notice. After a moment, Dash shook his brother's arm. Still nothing. "Dylan?" he asked. "Are you okay?" When Dylan still didn't answer, Dash turned him like a rag doll so they were face-to-face.

But Dylan wasn't there. His eyes were blank, his jaw slack. And then Dash knew—whatever Marcus's music was doing to this room, whatever protection the tune was offering, whatever it was that had driven away the Specials, was affecting Dylan too. But how? Why?

"Dylan! Dylan, can you hear me?"

Dylan's eyes focused slightly, zeroing in on Dash's face. Then tears welled up on his lower lids.

"What's wrong?" asked Dash. "What is it?"

Dylan opened his mouth as if to say something. "You . . . you . . ." Saliva clicked in the back of his throat. "You . . . were . . . there . . ."

Dylan's mouth went wide in a silent scream.

Opening his eyes, Marcus blinked away tears and looked down at his hands, still moving across the keys, hammers hitting the strings that vibrated the air around him. Sounds of a scuffle came from the doorway, but he knew he had to focus on the music.

To his surprise, Marcus heard another instrument chime in—the high hum of a violin beginning to accompany the piano. At first Marcus thought it was only in his head, but then he glanced across the room; the violin was hovering in the air, its bow slowly sliding across the strings. Marcus nearly fell off the bench, but he steadied himself, not daring to pause, hoping that his momentary break in concentration wouldn't end whatever enchantment seemed to have blessed this space. The atmosphere around the violin shimmered, as if someone invisible to ordinary human perception was standing there playing it. The violin's high voice swooped and swirled, not *matching* the tune of the piano but adding something to it that made the melody even more hypnotic and lovely. Soon, it was joined by several other instruments. Marcus watched in awe as the guitar leaned forward and began to play by itself, followed by the cello and the flute.

The music swelled as a boy materialized, the conductor of this magical orchestration. He glanced at Marcus and then turned back to the instruments. He lifted his hands and the instruments almost seemed to nod at him. Marcus recognized the boy's red curls, his deep brown eyes. It was his uncle, Shane.

It was the Musician. Of course. He felt a surge of love for this person, whom he'd never met and yet had always known. They didn't need to speak. This music was their conversation. It always had been.

"Marcus!" Poppy called out from across the room. Was she kneeling on the floor beside Azumi? "*Who is that?*"

"Don't worry," said Marcus, raising his voice over the music. "He's a friend."

CHAPTER 32

THOUGH POPPY WAS worried about Azumi, who was looking blankly on the floor at her knees, she couldn't peel her gaze away from the strange figure that had appeared by the piano—a redheaded boy who looked, if not exactly like Marcus, then at least like a close relation. Where had he come from?

Poppy shook her head. She felt the same sense she'd gotten whenever she'd seen the Girl in the mirror. Marcus looked happy to be playing with him, as if he'd known this boy for a long, long time.

He'd called her crazy.

Crazy!

He must have known she was telling the truth about the Girl. He'd *known*, but he'd still made her feel . . . wrong. Wrong about herself. Wrong about her own story.

A flash of rage rushed over Poppy's skin, a hot wave that pushed away the chill of fear in the house. She wanted to rush across the room and knock Marcus from the bench, throttle him. But before she could even move, she heard a deep rumble of laughter. She looked around for a moment before realizing that the laughter had come from inside her head.

Poppy knew: Something very bad was about to happen.

CHAPTER 33

THERE WAS A loud crack, and the piano trembled. Marcus nearly jumped out of his skin. He forced himself to continue playing, but several of the piano keys went mute. Peering into the body of the instrument, he could see snapped strings, their hammers hitting only air.

His uncle's tune was suddenly missing part of its register, and to Marcus, it was as jarring as if he'd just witnessed someone lose a limb.

One by one, the silver keys of the flute snapped away from the body, clattering to the floor until it could only yelp out a flat whistle.

Shane vanished, and Marcus screamed. "No!"

There was another shocking *SPROING* as eight more of

the piano's strings broke, silencing another octave, weakening the strength of the melody.

From a few feet away, there came a shattering smash. The string section of the concerto was eradicated. The violin and the guitar lay on the floor in wooden slivers, as if they'd exploded.

A wave of nausea swelled from Marcus's stomach and knocked at the top of his head. That feeling of safety that had come from his uncle's music was quickly disappearing. Something in the house, in the room, was determined to send the music away, to stop the good memories, to *frighten* him. He closed his eyes, trying to picture his uncle's face again, but all he could see now was black.

Across from the piano, the shimmering spots that had surrounded the instruments were disappearing, replaced now by the oddly visible notion of stillness and quiet.

The only instrument that continued to accompany him was the cello—its melody began to stretch and strain, losing pitch, as though someone were wrenching the tuning brackets this way and that. Then, with a finality that was almost painful, the last strings on the piano and cello snapped. All that was left of the music now was a distorted echo.

Movement by the portrait of Poppy's girl caught his eye. Dirt and dust fell from the chimney.

Poppy and Dash were staring at the instruments from the barricade by the door. Azumi was lying on the floor, lifting her head as if coming back to consciousness. And Dylan stood wide-eyed, frozen, as if in shock.

Then two figures dropped from the chimney. Dust dissipated as the figures slowly stood up, revealing their masks. The music had stopped, and the dog and the cat had found their way in.

CHAPTER 34

"WHERE AM I?" Azumi asked, color returning to her cheeks.

"You fainted," said Poppy. "You'll be okay. We just have to move away from here. Like, now."

"What's going on?" Azumi turned to see Matilda and Randolph stepping slowly away from the fireplace, toward the group.

Dash helped her to her feet. The trio gathered around Dylan and then backed away from the intruders, staying along the wall for safety.

Poppy's mind rushed through the events of the past hour. Back at the elevator, Matilda had been lucid for a moment, as if she'd regained her sense of self. *Maybe*, Poppy thought, *if I talk to her now, she'll answer me.*

"Matilda—" she began, but the girl in the cat mask threw back her head and shrieked, as if hearing that name pierced her like an ice pick through the forehead.

The group hurried away from the two orphans, quickly meeting Marcus at the wall of bookshelves at the opposite end of the room.

Poppy squeezed her eyes shut, trying to reason out what exactly had happened in the elevator. *You came*, Matilda had said. *You actually came.* There was a tussle and then . . . Poppy had yanked off the stupid cat mask.

That was it. The mask! The orphanage director had written it himself in the *SPECIALS* file: *The masks remove the children's identities.* What if they only needed to recognize one another, to share their true selves? To forge a connection, like Poppy had done with her Girl whenever she'd looked in mirrors?

Poppy blinked.

The Specials were now only a few strides from the group. Randolph, the dog, the music prodigy, carried his smashed violin. He dragged its battered body along the ground behind him, where it bounced and skittered, its strings squealing as they twisted and rubbed against one another. Matilda, the cat, held one of her ruined dolls by its matted hair, as if she intended to bludgeon someone with it.

The pounding noise at the barricaded door started up again. Now that the house, or *something*, had stopped Marcus's music from playing, the other orphans had returned.

"We have to take off their masks!" yelled Poppy.

Dylan pressed his head firmly against the stacks of shelves behind him, gasping for breath.

The two Specials lunged forward.

CHAPTER 35

THE GIRL IN the cat mask came at Dash, scratching at his arms, his neck, his torso. He howled at her cold, sharp touch, trying to bat her away, but she was too strong. "Help!" he called out to Dylan, but Dylan was still weak from whatever had happened to him by the doorway.

A trilling of notes sounded nearby, shocking everyone out of the struggle.

Turning, Dash saw that Marcus was beside him, blowing into a harmonica—*Where did Marcus get a harmonica?*—performing the same tune that he and the ghostly young conductor had played several minutes ago.

The orphans began backing away from the group. They held their hands to their ears, as if this new noise was painful to them.

This song filled Dash with a sense of warmth and calm, but Dylan was squirming, as if in discomfort. Azumi sat hunched over him. Was she trying to help him somehow? "Dylan, what's wrong?" Dash screamed.

"Now!" said Poppy at the same time. "Grab them!" She leapt toward the masked pair.

Poppy flailed with Matilda, their arms locked around each other's necks. "Dash! Please! Help me!" Poppy's fingers strained toward the edge of the cat mask. Randolph sprang toward them.

Adrenaline flashed through Dash's system. He leapt to his feet, taking the dog boy by surprise. "Got you!" he yelled, and ripped off the mask.

Everything stopped. Slowed. Even the dust went still. It was as if the entire house was listening to the drawl of Marcus's harmonica. Matilda and Randolph's masks were on the ground, torn.

Matilda and Randolph straightened, their jaws slack in disbelief. Their eyes were wide with hope and fear, glistening with what Dash could only think of as *life*.

Holding his breath, he brought his attention back to Dylan, who'd gone blank again. There was something he knew he needed to do.

You . . . were . . . there . . .

Dash reached out to wipe away his brother's tears, but Dylan released an unearthly howl, and Dash was shocked into stillness. Then the room went dark.

CHAPTER 36

FLASH.

You . . . were . . . there . . .

Dash is hiding in Dylan's dressing room on the set of *Dad's So Clueless*. It's dark. The lamp on the table beside Dylan's favorite chair sparked when Dash tried to turn it on, so he left it alone. The only light is coming from a crack in the door where Dash has left it slightly ajar. Dash has placed a bucket of water on top of the door—a trick—to get back at Dylan for all the cruel tricks he's played on the cast and the crew of the show over the years. When Dylan opens the door, the water will spill down, soaking him, shocking him, making him scream. Dash will jump out and laugh, and yeah, Dylan will be mad, but he deserves it. Maybe after this, Dylan will learn his lesson, and Dash will stop getting blamed for his brother's mischief.

Footsteps approach, and Dash covers his mouth to hold back a snicker. The door opens and the bucket tips. Water splashes. Dylan shouts: *What the . . . ?* But then the bucket falls. It hits Dylan's skull with a solid *THUNK*.

That wasn't supposed to happen.

Oww, says Dylan, stumbling into the dark room. He clutches his head as he staggers toward the lamp—the same lamp that sparked when Dash had tried to turn it on minutes earlier.

Dash sees what is about to happen. He leaps out from his hiding place, screaming for his brother to *Stop! Wait! Don't move!*

But Dylan is confused. He's dripping wet with water and blood. He touches the lamp's switch.

White light fills the room—flashes like paparazzi taking pictures at a Hollywood premiere. Dash screams as Dylan's body stiffens, and an electric buzzing blasts the room.

Flash.

You . . . were . . . there . . .

At the emergency room, his parents give Dash the bad news. "It was an accident," they say. "It wasn't your fault."

But Dash refuses to listen. How can Dylan be *dead* when they're still giggling in the backseat on the way home from the hospital? When they're already home, playing hide-and-seek together? When they're whispering secrets to each other late into the night?

Dash thinks it's a cruel way to punish him for what he

did—his parents trying to make Dash believe that he electro-cuted his own brother. He already feels terrible about the trick.

But maybe Dash deserves it. A little bit. At least when Dylan played his tricks, no one ever got seriously hurt.

Flash.

You . . . are . . . here . . .

But I am not.

"We're going to need you downstairs in fifteen," says the bouncy brunette, whose name neither boy can remember. "Just a heads up. 'Kay?"

She isn't a producer, Dash realizes. In her white coat, he can see that she's a nurse. Or a doctor. And she's not just playing one on TV.

"Downstairs?" asks Dylan with a smirk. "For what? Are we shooting the next scene?" The producer raises an eyebrow and continues to look at Dash, as if only his reply matters. Dylan waves at her, trying to get her attention. "Uh, hello? Am I invisible or something?"

Or something.

"She completely ignored me," says Dylan.

But of course she did, Dash understands now. Everyone does. Dylan is not the patient. Dash is. This is not the set of *Dad's So Clueless.* It is a hospital. A real hospital where they are struggling to make Dash see the truth.

The truth.

He remembers now. His parents admitted him after they found him wandering far from home one night, when he was insisting that Dylan was out there and needed his help. But that had been *after* Dylan's funeral. A funeral that, to Dash, is still only a vague recollection.

The doctors insist on keeping an eye on him. Dash has been seeing things. Seeing his deceased brother. He's been carrying a guilt so powerful, Dash thinks now, that it has managed to raise the dead.

There are emails and texts and cards from the cast and the crew, but no one is allowed to visit. Dash is a special case. He needs special care. He knows he won't be returning to the set again.

Did they write Scooter off the show? Was it Dylan's fault for always being so difficult? Or was it what Dash had done?

Nothing makes sense anymore.

Nothing, that is, until the email from Larkspur Productions, LLC, arrives. The email from Del.

Dylan! Dash! . . . What's up?

Dash yanked himself away from Dylan, as if a static shock had jerked him awake after a long, long night of dreaming.

CHAPTER 37

DYLAN TURNED AWAY, unable to look at his twin any longer.

"How long have you known?" asked Dash, still hearing music in the background. It sounded like a faint memory.

"Just now," said Dylan, his voice tired. "Before, I had glimpses. But now, with this music, and the house, and . . . I've seen everything." Dash tried to take Dylan's hand, but Dylan flinched away from him.

The girl, Matilda, was staring into Dylan's eyes. Her gaze was piercing, almost painful. She knew too. She knew everything.

Poppy faced the twins, confused. "How long have you known what?" she asked.

Dylan ignored her, looking into Matilda's sad blue eyes

instead. "I can't say," he said. Dash hung his head, breathless. "I don't know how. I don't . . ."

Matilda nodded, cradling the doll in her arms. "You will," she said. Her voice was singsong, almost motherly, as if the girl had long practiced this character with her dolls. "You'll do it together."

Suddenly Matilda's face crumpled as if she'd been stabbed in the stomach. She bent over, moaning. "He won't let us go." Matilda glanced up, her gaze settling on each of them. "And he won't let you go either." Her voice started to fade.

"Who won't let you go?" said Poppy. "Do you mean Cyrus? Cyrus Caldwell? The man who hurt you?"

But Matilda covered her face with her hands, too pained to answer.

Marcus was still playing his harmonica, and Randolph stepped toward him. Marcus backed away, but Randolph dropped the broken violin on the ground. He listened to Marcus's song, breathing it deeply as if it were oxygen.

Marcus stopped. The silence was so jarring that everyone jumped. "They took away your music," he said to Randolph. "Here. This is yours now." He wiped the instrument off on his shirt and then held it out to the boy. Randolph's eyes lit up, like a kid at a birthday party. "Go on. Take it. Play."

Randolph grasped the harmonica, holding it up to the light, looking as though he'd never seen one before. He placed it against his lips and blew tentatively. Within seconds, he was mimicking Marcus's tune. The notes danced around the room, surrounding them with the sensation of shelter from a storm.

Something strange was happening to Randolph. As he played, his joy coursing through the air, his body began to change. To lose color.

Randolph was fading, Marcus realized. He could look right through him, at Dylan's astonished expression.

Then the boy who'd attacked them simply went away, taking the happy tune with him.

"Randy?" Matilda asked. Now she sounded like the little girl that she was—or that she once had been. She tilted her chin as if sensing something the rest of them could not. Then she flinched, grasping her stomach again, and doubled over. She dropped her ruined doll, and it hit the floor with a soft *thud*. Poppy hurried over but Matilda stepped back, not wanting to be touched.

"What happened?" Dash asked.

"Marcus gave him back what Cyrus took away from him," said Dylan, his voice flat. "His music."

"We can help you too!" Poppy said to Matilda.

"Yes," said Azumi, breathless. "What is it that *you* need?"

"No . . . time," the girl whispered. Already, her face was shifting, beginning to resemble the mask that Poppy had ripped away from her only minutes earlier. Matilda ran across the music room and tore into the barricade.

"Wait!" Poppy took several hesitant steps after her. "They might still be out there."

But Matilda wasn't listening. As soon as she'd cleared enough room, she slipped out into the hallway and was gone.

For several seconds, the group waited in horrified silence for the masked orphans to come piling through the doorway. But soon, they realized that the Specials had vanished, leaving Poppy, Marcus, Dylan, Dash, and Azumi alone with one another.

"Is it safe?" asked Azumi, finally rising to her feet.

Marcus continued to look at the gap in the doorway. "For now, maybe. I hope."

"Do you think if we do the same for the others," said Poppy, "if we help Esme, and Irving, and Aloysius, and Matilda . . . if we give them what the director took from them . . . do you think they'll be free, like Randolph?"

"Maybe," said Dash. Eyes closed, he added, as if desperate, "Maybe once we do that, the house will release us too."

Just then, Dylan shouted, unable to control himself. He fell to his knees and screamed out what sounded like the last of the life that was still inside him.

CHAPTER 38

DYLAN HAULED HIMSELF to his feet and streaked toward the door!

"Dylan, stop!" Dash cried out after him. "Wait!" But he stayed where he stood, as if frightened to actually approach.

At the door, Dylan turned. "No! I don't want your help. Your *help* is what got me into this mess in the first place." His expression twisted, as if he were fighting to keep an angry beast pinned down somewhere deep inside himself. "I guess we do actually get to play our own roles from now on, little brother."

Dash's face crumpled. "You can't leave."·

Dylan sneered, heaving breath. "Apparently, none of us can! And maybe some of us *don't deserve to.* So what difference does it make?" He swiveled his shoulders and, like a sigh, slipped out into the hallway and disappeared into the darkness.

Dash stared at the others, stunned. "You can't leave *me*," he whispered, as if to himself. "That's what I meant."

"You asked him *how long he's known*," said Poppy. "What did you mean?"

"There was an accident." Dash looked up. He chewed his bottom lip for a few seconds. "On the set of our show. Dylan . . . He . . . He was killed. It was my fault. I was trying to teach him a lesson."

Azumi stared. "What are you talking about? He was just here."

Marcus shoved his hands in his pockets. "No! You're saying . . . What are you saying?"

"He's saying that his brother is a ghost," Poppy answered carefully. "A spirit. Whatever you want to call it. *Him*. I'm sorry, Dash."

"A ghost?" Two blooms of color appeared on Marcus's parchment-white cheeks. "Dylan?"

"Yeah," said Poppy. "Kinda like that boy who appeared next to your piano. The one who looked just like you." She glared at him. "After everything that just happened, you're really going to question this?"

Marcus shuddered. "Today it's like I've been going crazy, but I know I'm not crazy. What I've seen is real."

"Interesting," said Poppy. "*How do you think that feels?*"

"*Crazy*," Dash whispered. "I remember now. I was in a

212

hospital. I kept talking to everyone about Dylan like he was alive. No one believed that he was right there beside me. No one could hear him or see him like I could. It was like I thought they were all teasing us by ignoring him. When we got that email from Del, we snuck out together. Went home. Found Dylan's secret piggy bank. I knew he'd been stealing from the cast and crew for years. But I had no idea how much he'd collected. We took a cab to the airport and bought two tickets. Nobody said a word to me about the empty seat, the one I'd paid for. They must have thought I was . . . Well . . . I don't know what they thought. But in this house, things were different. You could see him too."

"I remember now," said Poppy, her jaw dropping. "I'd read about the accident online. I'd heard one of you was hurt. But I didn't realize—"

"You guys must think I'm so stupid," said Dash, wiping furiously at the tears streaming down his face.

"No one thinks you're stupid," said Azumi. "Our minds can be the worst kind of tricksters. Especially when bad things happen. And bad things *do* happen. They'll keep happening too. As long as we're here." She looked back at the busted piano. "When Marcus's music was playing, all I could think of was my sister."

The four who were left in the music room didn't know what else to say or do. Marcus tried to squeeze Dash's shoulder, but Dash only shook him off. Poppy and Azumi found themselves holding hands. It took several long seconds for Poppy to gather herself. She went over to the door and closed it again, then shoved some of the furniture back into place.

"So when we were downstairs, you lied," Poppy said to Marcus in a low voice. "When I told you my story about the Girl in the mirrors"—she glanced at the portrait hanging over the fireplace—"you said that I was *crazy*. But you had experienced the same thing. Why would you do that?"

"You're right," Marcus answered softly. "He . . . the Musician's always been with me. I think he's my uncle. I should have told you, but I was scared. I'm sorry."

Poppy's eyes flashed. She exhaled and regrouped, her mind churning. After a few seconds, she added, "At least we know now what we all have in common."

"And what's that?" asked Azumi.

"We've all been haunted," said Poppy. "In our own way. Maybe that's the real reason we're here. Maybe that's how this place, or the spirits inside it, were able to find us."

"To lure us," Marcus added.

Azumi nodded. "To trap us."

"Or at least to try," said Poppy. "We know now that we're different. But I think whatever lives here underestimates us."

"Maybe not," said Dash. "Maybe the evil inside this place knows exactly what it's doing."

Quiet filled the room for a moment, like a held breath.

"We'll go find your brother when you're ready, Dash," Poppy said. "And then we're getting out of here. Now that we have a better idea of how. We're getting out of here together." A flicker of motion captured her attention, as if the portrait of the Girl had caught fire, but looking once more at the painting over the fireplace, nothing had changed. Or had it? Poppy noticed Consolida Caldwell—beloved daughter and sister—smiling at her. Had the Girl been smiling before?

When Poppy turned back to the group, Marcus and Azumi stared at her as if they expected her to spout out all the answers they needed to hear. Dash hung his head, tears dripping silently from the tip of his nose.

Poppy didn't have any answers. She knew that none of them did. What they did have was one another. And maybe that was enough to keep them going, to keep them strong, until they could find their way out of this nightmare. Poppy wanted to believe that more than anything. She really did.

Making her way to the other three, Poppy held out her arms and gathered everyone together. And for the first time in a long time, she felt safe.

From all corners of the room, there came a series of creaks and cracking sounds, as if the house were settling into the earth, satisfied.

ART CREDITS

ENDPAPERS
Photos ©: 2 wallpaper and throughout: clearviewstock/Shutterstock, Inc.; 2–3: hole: CG Textures; string: Scholastic Inc.; 2–3 hand: Alex Malikov/Shutterstock, Inc.; 3 girl: Larry Ronstat for Scholastic Inc.; 4: paper: Scholastic Inc.; fire: CG Textures; 5 sticker: Scholastic Inc.; 6–7: mansion: Dariush M/Shutterstock, Inc.; fog: Maxim van Asseldonk/Shutterstock, Inc.; clouds: Aon_Skynotlimit/Shutterstock, Inc.; composite: Shane Rebenschied

INTERIOR
Photos ©: 4: Illustration by Ben Perini for Scholastic Inc. based on masks by CSA Plastock/Getty Images; 25: main: Lewis W. Hines/Library of Congress; feet and sheet: Keirsten Geise for Scholastic Inc.; 46–47: mansion: Dariush M/Shutterstock, Inc.; fog: Maxim van Asseldonk/Shutterstock, Inc.; clouds: Aon_Skynotlimit/Shutterstock, Inc.; moon: Mykola Mazuryk/Shutterstock, Inc.; composite: Shane Rebenschied for Scholastic Inc.; 57: rabbit mask: CSA Plastock/Getty Images; boy: Fancy/Media Bakery; staircase: Anna Bogush/Shutterstock, Inc.; lollipop: Hayati Kayhan/Shutterstock, Inc.; 72: background: Ppictures/Shutterstock, Inc.; bingo machine: Jonathan Kitchen/Getty Images; bingo balls: GeoffBlack/Getty Images; 106: standing doll: ejay111/Getty Images; clear-eyed doll: Prachaya Roekdeethaweesab/Shutterstock, Inc.; burnt head: AAR Studio/Shutterstock, Inc.; torso doll: mofles/Getty Images; clothed doll: Perfect Lazybones/Shutterstock, Inc.; wall and floor: Lora liu/Shutterstock, Inc.; 138: paper: Scholastic Inc.; floor: CG Textures; 145: hallway: Peter Dedeurwaerder/Shutterstock, Inc.; violin: AtomStudios/Getty Images; pants: michaeljung/Shutterstock, Inc.; boy: Keirsten Geise for Scholastic Inc.; dog mask: CSA Plastock/Getty Images; 158: girl photo: Larry Ronstat; pen: Scholastic Inc.; paper/folders/rubberband/scratches: Scholastic Inc.; scissors: Photodisc; wood texture: CG Textures; 171 background: phoelix/Shutterstock, Inc.; gate: Songpan Janthong/Shutterstock, Inc.; left arm: Khakimullin Aleksandr/Shutterstock, Inc.; doll top: Faded Beauty/Shutterstock, Inc.; doll bottom: Jeff Wilber/Shutterstock, Inc.; wig: exopixel/Shutterstock, Inc.; 190: room: Library of Congress; cello: DK Arts/Shutterstock, Inc.; 216 girl: robangel69/Fotolia; frame: Chatchawan/Shutterstock, Inc.; mantle: Zick Svift/Shutterstock, Inc.; wallpaper: Larysa Kryvoviaz/Shutterstock, Inc.

About the Author

Dan Poblocki is the author of several books for young readers, including *The House on Stone's Throw Island*, *The Book of Bad Things*, *The Nightmarys*, *The Stone Child*, and the Mysterious Four series. His recent novels, *The Ghost of Graylock* and *The Haunting of Gabriel Ashe*, were both Junior Library Guild selections and made the American Library Association's Best Fiction for Young Adults list in 2013 and 2014. Dan lives in Brooklyn, in an apartment with walls that happily do not move around while he's writing. Visit him online at www.danpoblocki.com.